The Old Town

MJ Judge

For my husband, Gary. My best friend.

Chapter 1

"You can't be serious! *Jindabyne?* It's a country town! What's going on? I thought you were better. That you got the all-clear from the cancer!" Her boss gaped at her.

Chief Inspector Durant's hawk eyes were the stuff of legend. Even the toughest of her colleagues cowered when those laser beams turned in their direction. Today, those eyes were aimed at her, and they felt like they were boring holes in her face.

A nerve twitched at the corner of Anna's eye as she held his gaze. His reaction was no more than she had expected. She was, after all, one of his best performers. Her case closure rate was the highest in the team. Of course he would be crying foul at her desire to leave. He was losing one of his strongest team leaders and his stats would reflect that in the coming months. But even as she thought it, she felt guilty. She was being unfair. Though he was a tough boss, he had been flexible and protective of her during her treatment over the last eleven months.

She lifted a hand to scoop her hair behind her ear and stopped short. Her long auburn hair was no more ... her hair now little more than a fuzzy dark red halo covering her pale scalp. Her hand dropped to her lap.

Her chin lifted slightly. "I *am* better, Chief ... no, it's not that," she lied. "But it has been a challenging year"—her mouth twitched at the gross understate-ment—"and I feel I need a change of scenery. Somewhere I can ... *recoup* and get my mojo back."

"If you go ahead with this transfer, Anna, you'll have effectively stalled your career. Do you understand that?" He jabbed a finger into his desk. "Besides which, you're going to be bored out of your brain. You need to be challenged! And that's aside from the fact that you'll be completely *wasted* down there!"

She looked at him steadily. "It may be a bit quieter than Sydney, Chief, but I *really* think that's what I need right now."

The Chief looked at her—more carefully than he had in months. He was suddenly struck by the dark blue shadows that underlined her eyes, her skin, so pale it seemed almost translucent, and how skeletally thin she was. He sat back, shocked. How had she deteriorated so much and he hadn't noticed! He looked out of the window at the Sydney skyline to give himself a moment. He knew, without a doubt, that she was lying about being better. He coughed, cleared his throat noisily, and turned back.

"What about any ongoing treatment? Surely being here in Sydney is better than being stuck out in the middle of nowhere."

"They have an oncology outpatient unit in Cooma which is only three quarters of an hour drive from Jindy, and then, if I need more than they can provide, Canberra is only two hours away. Jindy is where I grew up, and my sister still lives there, so I'll have plenty of support." Anna gave him a small smile.

"All you'll be doing is giving rich skiers *bloody* speeding tickets!" he growled under his breath, knowing he was fighting a losing battle.

Anna swallowed, feeling the mood shift.

He shook his head slowly. "You've made up your mind?"

"Yes, Chief."

"I think you're making a huge mistake, Farrow."

Her eyes lit up. "But you'll approve the transfer?"

He made an inarticulate noise of frustration but nodded.

"*Thank you—*"

"No! Don't thank me." He scowled. "Like I said, I think you're making a big mistake. Let's agree that you're on loan for ... one year. Any longer than that and you can kiss your career goodbye. You'll be forgotten and pigeon-holed. You just keep that in mind! We'll review after twelve months. I think you'll be more than ready to return by then." *If you're still with us,* he added silently. He glanced away and roughly cleared his throat again.

"Thanks, Chief. I appreciate it."

"No one else will," he responded sourly. "Okay, let's talk about how we can transition you out of here."

They spent the next hour working through the logistics of passing over Anna's case load to others in the team. Fortunately, as her illness and treatment had taken a toll, her normal case volume had reduced and there was considerably less to worry about than there would have been a year ago.

Later that afternoon, Anna walked slowly through Hyde Park. It was her escape, and fortunately only a few blocks from the pressure-cooker of work. When she needed time to think—when her brain felt overloaded to breaking point—*this* was where she came. It was the oldest park in Australia and something of that longevity, of times past and the thousands of people who had walked its paths, put her problems into perspective.

Having grown up in the Snowy Mountains, she missed the crisp fresh air and alpine bushland of her childhood, but the park provided her with the sense of space and openness she craved. She smiled, remembering the first time she had come here, thrilled to have found this small oasis in the middle of the concrete jungle that enabled her to breathe and recharge, however briefly. She had found it not long after she had been posted to the Sydney City Unit.

Anna shook her head, thinking of her younger self: so independent, ambitious, and fiercely determined to shed any hint of her parochial and rather *alternative* upbringing. She felt, walking into the department that first morning, that she had made it. But she had found since then that making it was not the final destination, it was no more than another step on a far longer journey. Over the years she found herself challenged in so many ways—mentally, professionally and emotionally—but she had stepped up each and every time, dug deep, and emerged the victor when many of her colleagues had succumbed to the pressure and fell by the wayside.

For her, it was all about the next case, the next task. The constant opportunities to test her skill, her knowledge, and her nerve. She thrived on it. She loved it. And now this—the ultimate challenge. And one her knowledge, skill, and nerve would not be what carried her through. She was in the hands of others' expertise and experience and only that, and a good dose of luck, might see her survive ... *if* all the stars aligned. Of all the indignities, trauma, and pain that she had experienced in the eleven months since her cancer diagnosis, it was the lack of control over her own destiny that had been the most bitter pill to swallow. She had been called 'control-freak' so many times now that she no longer saw it as disparagement, but embraced it, and wore it like a hero's mantle.

Perhaps life resented my cast-iron control and is giving me some payback?! But even as she thought it, her eyes rolled. *All the treatment has seriously affected my brain if I'm thinking that!*

Walking slowly, Anna breathed in the spicy scent of mown grass and enjoyed the hint of autumn in the air. Her footsteps took her to the Anzac Memorial. It sat at the southern edge of the park: tall, stately, and imposing. She had found herself here many times over the last months.

As always, she gravitated to the Hall of Service where she learned the stories of those who had sacrificed their lives for their country and the communities that they came from. They were so young some of them. Their lives snuffed out before they could make their mark as an adult. And for some reason, strangely, this always made her feel calmer. She supposed it was because it made her feel as if she was not alone in being cheated out of life, hers by cancer, theirs by a bomb or a bullet. It made her aware that not only was life not fair, it was completely unbiased. There was simply no point in asking: *why me?* Look at the evidence—hundreds of young men and women dead—and why them and not others? Wallowing in anger at what life had thrown you was simply wasted time.

The memorial worked its usual magic, and she walked away feeling calmer and accepting that death was nothing to fear. When the time came, she would be in very good company.

Chapter 2

Anna glanced over at her son, Riley, sprawled out in the passenger seat of the car. His head was turned away, his fair hair ruffling in the breeze from the open window. She knew he must be upset at leaving Sydney but, being the sensible fourteen-year-old he was, had not voiced a single protest in the weeks since she had told him of her decision. On the surface, he seemed to have accepted their move with equanimity, but she suspected he was harbouring some deep-seated anxiety.

She sighed, hating to cause him more pain. *Had he not had enough to deal with?*

A father who had moved to Queensland, abandoning them both before Riley was even born. Who occasionally deigned to drop unannounced into his son's life, sprinkling fairy dust and presents around, and then disappearing for another few years without a word. And now, a sick mum to deal with on top of the usual adolescent turmoil. She wondered whether she should have organised a counsellor for him. But then an image of her sister, Dee, came to mind, and she knew he was shortly going to have the best counsellor on the planet at his beck and call.

Anna glanced over at him again and smiled. It seemed only yesterday that he was in a booster seat in the back. Now he was taller than she was and almost as skinny since he'd shot up another six inches, seemingly overnight! He was all ankles and elbows now. Mostly, he looked like her—green eyes, long lashes, fair skin—though his hair was blonde like his dad's and not her dark red. He was the best thing in her life, and she loved him fiercely.

It had been quite a juggling act being a single mum and a rising star in the New South Wales Police Force, but she felt she had navigated that precipice *reasonably* well. She had made it to most of his important school and sporting events and was at home *most* mornings to see him off to school … and was there *most* evenings for dinner. But she knew she was lucky. Riley was an even-tempered, sensible kid, who accepted the constraints of her job and rolled with the punches. It had always been just the two of them—ignoring the rare and slightly disruptive visitations by his father—and they had always been close. At least that was, until she got sick.

Cancer. It was such a hateful word. Not only did it destroy the life of the person who had it, but its destructive influence also affected everyone they were close to, like ink spilt on paper. From the moment Anna had read up on Inflammatory Breast Cancer and realised her chances of survival were limited, she shut down and pushed everyone away, including Riley. Away from the knowledge that her life now hung in the balance and that death knocked on her door. She corralled her fear and pushed it down hard in an attempt to see her way forward. She knew he felt the wall she had put up between them, but what was her alternative? Explain to a fourteen-year-old that his mum was most likely going to die soon? How could she dump that on him?

"What did your dad say when you told him the news of our move?" Riley had rung his father the previous night to let him know.

Riley shrugged. "I don't think he even heard me, he was too full of his own news," he said to the window, his tone flat and uninterested.

Anna glanced over with a frown. "What do you mean? What news?"

He looked over at her. "Serena is pregnant," he said, with a hint of a sneer.

Oh, for Christ sake! Are you kidding me?! Anna fumed silently. *Could the stupid bastard not put his son's needs first, just once?*

She took a deep breath and tried to put irritation aside. To say she was shocked was an understatement. David had never shown the slightest interest in being a dad. He had basically shot through not long after she told him she was pregnant. He treated Riley like a long-lost mate on the rare occasions that he saw him. She didn't think another venture into fatherhood was even on his radar. But Serena, his girlfriend, who was ten years his junior, must have had other ideas. *God help her!*

"*Ri-ght!* So ... how do you feel about that?"

Riley shrugged again. He was starting to do that a lot lately, and she blamed herself. He was building his own wall.

"Well, more family is always a good thing," Anna said eventually. "You'll have a half-sibling in the world you can show the ropes to at some stage. God knows, with a dad like yours, it's going to need a big brother to lean on."

Riley nodded absently and turned to look out the window again.

Anna looked at him worriedly. *Should I have made the move sooner? But how would that have been possible? First the chemo, then the double mastectomy, and then radiation. It was just one thing after another.* She'd hardly had time to think, let alone wrap her head around it. It took all her physical and emotional strength to get through each day let alone plan ahead.

The miles flew by with only the radio to break the silence between them. An hour passed and neither of them had spoken, when Riley took a deep breath and, turning towards her said, "Why didn't you get rid of me?"

Anna's head jerked back, and she clutched the steering wheel in a white-knuckled grip. "*What?*" she said, though she'd heard it clearly. She just needed a few more seconds to gather her scattered wits.

"Why didn't you get rid of me before I was born?" Riley repeated sullenly.

"You mean get an abortion?"

He nodded. "You didn't want kids," he said, stating it like it was an undeniable fact.

Anna was utterly floored. "Why would you assume that, Riles? I've never said that!"

"No. But it's pretty obvious. You never got married. You never had more kids. You love your job and you're good at it."

Anna glanced over at him. He was looking at her intently, with those green eyes so like her own. She swallowed and turned her focus back to the road. The silence lengthened. Riley turned and looked back out the window.

"When I found out I was pregnant," Anna started in a low tone, several minutes later, keeping her eyes fixed on the road, "it was a shock, I admit. Your dad and I had been going out for a couple of months but we both knew it was just casual. We were too different and probably that's why we were together for that short time. He was irresponsible, outgoing, carefree—everything I wasn't—everything I'm not. On the day that I found out I was pregnant—I found out at the doctor, by the way—I thought I was sick, so the news came as a complete bolt from the blue. Afterwards, I walked around for hours in the park."

She stopped and glanced over at him again; he was staring at her, his face pale. It seemed to have that strange combination of hope and fear etched on it that children get sometimes when they want something very badly but are equally sure it won't happen.

She swallowed. "All my thoughts were of how I was going to manage. Being a single mum. I knew your dad wouldn't stick around. And quite frankly, I didn't want him to. It was really frightening, Riles. I was daunted by the prospect of going it alone. I knew your Aunty Dee would do what she could, but she was a five-hour drive away. Your grandparents were already gone by then. But ... I never once ... contemplated ... getting rid of you. Not once! *Ever!*"

"Really?" Riley's voice was high with emotion. The sound tore at her heart.

"Really. It's hard to explain ... but as soon as I found out ... it was like you were real. A person already. Someone I was waiting for."

Riley wiped his nose on his sleeve, something she would normally chide him about, but this time she let it slide. She might have to do it too shortly!

"The day you were born was the best day of my life, Riles. Never, *ever* doubt that." She sniffed. Damn it, she *was* crying!

She put her hand out and Riley grabbed it and held on.

"Hungry?" she asked a few minutes later when she had her composure back.

"Always!"

"Okay, let's stop for lunch. I need to pee."

They renewed the drive after lunch. Riley seemed more himself than he had in some time, and Anna wondered how long that question had been burning inside of him.

"I'm not sure how long we'll stay with your Aunty Dee before we start to look for a place of our own," Anna said conversationally.

"I don't mind. We can stay forever; Aunty Dee's a great cook!"

"Oww!" Anna grabbed her chest as if shot through. "That's a low blow. C'mon! I'm not *that* bad of a cook. Look at you—fourteen and already taller than me—how the hell did you think you got so big? On food *I made,* buster!"

Riley grinned.

She was pleased they were joking around. There hadn't been much laughter between them in the last few months. She knew he was worried about her, and of course, now she had uprooted him from his home and friends, and at fourteen that was a *big* deal. But she had metastatic breast cancer, she wasn't going to get better. With treatment she may, with luck, have several more good years, but would never be cured. It was all about keeping it at bay now. And if luck wasn't on her side ... well then, she needed to make sure Riley was with someone who would love and care for him, and that was Dee. *God knows it wouldn't be his dad,* she thought bitterly. Even if the Chief thought she was making a mistake by moving to Jindy, she wasn't. That decision had been easy. Dee was her safety net.

Chapter 3

ANNA SLOWLY PULLED OFF onto Milo's Flat Road and they bumped their way down the rough dirt track the last half kilometre to Five Gates Farm.

Five Gates Farm. Where she had grown up. Snuggled into the side of Barker's Ridge on the south-western edge of the Kosciuszko National Park. It was a place of remarkable beauty and sometimes vicious weather ... but it was home.

As they pulled up in a swirl of dust in front of the house, Anna felt the tension drain away. She'd made it. She hadn't realised how much she was counting on Dee until that moment. She felt slightly guilty for disrupting Dee's life, but the relief was just *too* overwhelming to dwell on for long.

Dee's dogs, Spook and Longey, rounded the corner of the house barking like the hounds of hell and then stood whining impatiently at Riley's door. Tails wagging furiously.

"C'mon Mum." Riley stepped out eagerly. The dogs went wild, jumping and licking his face. He dropped to one knee and lapped it up.

Anna sat, soaking in the view. The house looked the same. It was an old weatherboard, circa 1950s, that her parents had bought in the late seventies. They had died in a car accident when Anna was twenty-four and Dee, twenty-two. Anna, already launched on her career in the police force, was happy for Dee to stay and make it her own. The house and farm were Dee's idea of heaven, *she* was truly their parent's daughter. Anna, on the other hand, was the cuckoo in the nest.

Her mum and dad had been hippies through and through, though ten years too late to really be called that. They preferred the term alternate life-stylers. They grew their own food, wove their own cloth, and had a very relaxed attitude toward parenthood. It had been a mostly idyllic, if rather chaotic, childhood. While most of their ilk had followed the sun north to Byron Bay and Mullumbimby, her parents had escaped south to the alpine region of Australia, loving the clean, crisp air and wide-open spaces. She had loved them both and missed them sorely but still harboured a good amount of resentment for the names they had bestowed on their children: Annabelina and Daisy-belle!

Anna looked up to see her sister hurrying around the side of the house; her hair pulled back into a ponytail that hung down her back, her long flowing skirt fluttering around her ankles, and a huge grin on her face.

"You're here at last!" Pushing the dogs aside, she reached up to enfold Riley in a big bear hug. Anna saw him flush with embarrassment, but he looked pleased as he hugged her back. She swallowed the lump in her throat. Everything would be alright now.

Anna got out of the car and stood looking at her sister.

Dee pulled out of her embrace with Riley and stood holding him at arm's length. "Good grief! You're all skin and bones! We need to feed you up. You're in the same room as always. Grab your gear and get settled, and we'll have some afternoon tea."

Riley grinned, always keen for food. He picked up two bags from the back seat and, dogs in tow, loped off towards the house.

Dee watched him walk away and then turned to Anna. She gave her a wry smile and they walked together into a long hug.

Dee pulled away, tears in her eyes, and sniffed. "Now you've done it ... made me cry!" She pulled a hanky from her pocket.

"It's *so* good to be here, Dee. Thank you!" Anna whispered back.

"For what?" Dee said, taking a big breath and wiping the tears away. "I haven't done anything yet. And remember, this is your house too. About time you got to use it." She lifted a bag from the back seat.

Anna got the last bag, and they walked inside together. As Dee opened the front door, the waft of freshly baked scones had Anna's mouth watering. With a final one-armed hug, Dee headed off to the kitchen.

Anna sat down on the bed in what had been her childhood bedroom. She had shared it with Dee back then, but now it was just the guest room. Her room. Dee had painted it, but otherwise, it was just the same. Old, scuffed hardwood floors covered in handwoven rugs: care of her mum's nibble fingers. A big multi-paned window looked out on the drive and the fields that bordered it. A mob of kangaroos hopped into view and after a brief look around settled in to feed. Anna's eyes closed, and with a deep sigh, she flopped back on the bed, arms wide.

Though she and Riley had been here many times over the years, this time felt different. Those other visits had been holidays. And whatever the Chief wanted to delude himself with, *she* knew this move was for good. There would be no going back.

She had thought she might feel like she was retreating—running from her life in Sydney—but lying there, fingering the familiar crocheted bedspread, all she felt was relief and a strong sense of home.

Later that night, with Riley settled in front of the television—Dee's own small rebellion against their technology-free upbringing—Anna and her sister wandered outside, ostensibly to check on the goats.

The air was crisp and still. They were both bundled up against the chill, Anna with a thick, woollen beanie over her bare head. A cacophony of bleats and 'mehs' erupted as the tribe rushed over. Dee pulled stalks of spinach and carrots from her coat pockets and pushed them through the high steel fencing of their enclosure. There was a bustle of activity as the goats jockeyed for the treats.

"No more," Dee said loudly, showing empty hands. Used to this as the signal for the end of feeding, they wandered away after a few more hopeful bleats.

Dee stood with her back to the fence, watching Anna who had her hand pushed through the wire, scratching the head of a small kid. Dee choked up suddenly and turned away. *She was so pale and thin!* Dee had felt every vertebra when she hugged her earlier.

Taking a deep breath, she said, "What haven't you told me, Annabelina?"

Anna turned and gave her a glacial stare. "Don't you Annabelina me, Daisy-belle Farrow!" Her face softened to a half-smile, and she shook her head. "God, I loved them … but Mum and Dad had shit taste in baby-names!"

Dee laughed. "Yeah, right up there with Mum's mung bean soup and home-made tofu!"

Anna shuddered theatrically and groaned. "Pah-lease don't remind me; that bloody stuff scarred me for life!"

They both laughed.

Dee waited. A puff of wind blew a wisp of hair across her face.

"You know I have breast cancer," Anna started softly.

"Mmm, I sort of figured that when they removed your boobs," Dee muttered.

Anna hmpf'd. "Well, I've got a bad type," she said eventually.

"There's a good type?"

"No … but there are better ones to have than others. I've got the rare aggressive one."

Dee looked at her anxiously, her heart pounding. "What are you telling me?"

"It's metastatic, Dee. That means it's gone beyond my boobs. I had several other lesions in my chest cavity."

Dee stepped back in horror and tears started in her eyes. Slapping a hand over her mouth to stop the scream she felt rising from coming out, she looked up. The sky was brilliant with a million stars. *How could it look like that? How is it the world hasn't slipped on its axis? How,* the hell, *is my bullet-proof sister telling me this?* She swallowed thickly.

"But ... you didn't even have a lump! You told me. You only found out because that crazy bastard attacked you!"

"Yeah, that's true," Anna said, remembering the doctor explaining that *her* cancer was the exception to the rule. No lumps! Just sheets of cancer cells. She would have preferred a lump.

"This type doesn't form a lump, or it does sometimes under your arms in your lymph nodes. But it causes your boobs to get red and hot and heavy. When the guy punched me in the breast, the pain and swelling didn't go away after a week or so as it should have. That's why I had to have more tests and then the biopsy."

"So did the punch cause it?" Dee whispered.

"No. The doctor told me I probably already had it when the guy hit me. He told me I was 'fortunate that I was assaulted because it meant that my diagnosis came earlier than it would have otherwise' ... pompous so-and-so!" she added under her breath.

"Well ... if they found it early, that's a good thing, isn't it?" Dee said, scrabbling for some good news.

"Like I said, Dee, it's an aggressive form of cancer. It spreads quickly."

"So—?"

"So, it means I'm not going to get better. The prognosis ... the outcome," she added, seeing Dee's frown, "is poor. Less than one in five people make it to five years."

Dee uttered a small, anguished sound, turned on her heel, and walked away into the darkness.

Anna put her fingers through the fence and patted one of the kids. *God, I hate this!*

Ten minutes later, Dee walked back from the dark shadows and gathered Anna into her arms.

Later, as they sat sipping a glass of red wine together in the kitchen, Riley safely asleep, Anna looked at Dee carefully. Her eyes were still a little red, and her natural ebullience much subdued after their earlier conversation.

"Dee, I'm so sorry to lay this all on you," Anna murmured softly.

Dee looked up and gave Anna a half-smile. "What are sisters for?"

"Yeah, well … on that, ah, I have one more favour to ask of you."

"Yes," Dee answered abruptly.

Anna looked at her sideways. "I haven't asked it yet."

Dee shrugged. "I know. It doesn't matter. Whatever it is, the answer is yes. But maybe you should tell me what it is, so I know what I've just agreed to." She grinned, trying to lighten the mood.

Anna smiled too. Then her smile faded. "If something happens to me, I … I need you to look after Riley. I mean, have him live with you permanently." The tension made her throat hurt.

Dee's eyes filled with tears, and she started to speak, stopped, shook her head, and tried again. "You don't have to ask me that, Lina," she whispered, using her childhood nickname for her sister. "I love Riley. Of course he will live with me, and I'll look after him."

Anna nodded and breathed out. Though she knew in her heart Dee would say yes, it made all the difference to hear her say it out loud.

After a few seconds, Dee took a deep breath and wiped a hand under her nose. "But we should make it official Lina, just to make sure there isn't any problem, you know … afterwards."

"That's a good idea. Do you know someone in town who does family law?"

"Well … it just so happens that I do." Dee's tone implying a lot more than her words. "I just happen to be seeing a very nice lawyer—"

"You didn't tell me!" Anna cried.

Dee laughed. "Haven't had the chance yet. His name is Brian. I think you'll like him. He's new in town. Just starting up his legal practice. He owns a couple of acres about five kilometres up the road."

"Oh, that's great. I'm so happy for you. I can't wait to meet him!" A thought suddenly popped into Anna's head.

"I'm sure he'll get it all sorted out," Dee continued.

Anna smiled at her confidence. "Good. And once I get settled in at work, I'll start to look around for somewhere for Riley and me," she added, voicing her thought.

Dee sat back and frowned. "No. You won't!"

"Dee, we can't stay here indefinitely—"

"Yes. You can!" Dee interrupted emphatically. "This is half your house! Mum and Dad left it to *both* of us. About time you used it, don't you think?"

Anna smiled and shook her head. "No! This is *your* house—"

"And I said no! You and Riley will stay here with me. It'll give me a chance to look after *you* finally and besides"—she took a steadying breath—"*if* something happens to you ... just think, Riley will already be here with me. He won't have to relocate again. It will make it a lot easier if this is already his home, won't it?"

Anna frowned. She agreed but was loath to invade Dee's space. "But what about Brian? We'll cramp your style, won't we?"

"We're not going to be running around having sex in every room, you know! Or at least not while you're here." She grinned, but then her smile fell away. "And besides, if Brian can't handle having you guys here—*my family!*—then he's not the man for me!"

The next morning, over breakfast on the back deck, Dee and Anna watched Riley head off to the creek with his fishing rod, the dogs bounding alongside.

"He really loves it here," Anna said, a soft smile pulling up the corners of her mouth.

Dee watched the emotion play across her sister's face and slowly shook her head. "Why are you bothering to go to work, Anna? Stay, rest, and spend the time you have enjoying your life with me and Riley."

Anna shifted uncomfortably. "I can't, Dee. I need to keep busy. You know I've always been this way. I can't change now. I'd go crazy sitting around twiddling my thumbs. Being a detective is who I am."

Dee's lips compressed and she sighed heavily, but she knew it was an argument she wouldn't win. "Does Riley know what you told me last night?"

Anna shook her head. "Not all of it. He knows I have breast cancer, of course, but he doesn't know the rest."

"You have to tell him—"

"No! He's been through enough. He has a lot to deal with at the moment: new school, new friends. Let him get through all of that. Then, when the time's right, and *I* feel he needs to know"—she glared at Dee pointedly—"I'll tell him!"

"Oh-kay," Dee conceded with a roll of her eyes. "On another note," she added, tactfully changing the subject, "I've invited the neighbours over for drinks this afternoon."

"Dee-ee!" Anna moaned.

"Hold on! It's not for you ... it's for Riley. Bob and Belinda have a girl his age, Madison, and they'll be in the same year at school. I thought it would help him to know someone on his first day."

Anna smiled.

Chapter 4

"Hope you have a good day, Riles." Anna gave him a quick peck on the cheek as the school bus came into view along Milo's Flat Road the next morning. She had driven him to the gate.

"It'll be okay, Mum, don't worry. Madison said she'd introduce me around," he said, an eager smile on his face.

Anna smothered a grin. It had been very clear the previous afternoon that Riley had taken quite a shine to their next-door neighbour. She shook her head in wonderment. Her sister was a genius. The instant the vivacious Madison had emerged from the back seat of her parent's car and flicked her long, curly chestnut hair over a shoulder, Riley was entranced. Fortunately, Madison seemed equally impressed with Riley so, at least in the short-term, Anna didn't have to deal with issues of adolescent unrequited love.

He boarded the bus and sat next to Madison, who waved at Anna through the window. She waved back as the bus moved off, continuing its circuitous route along country roads before heading into town and the high school.

After a quick check of her watch, she pulled out after the bus.

"Can I help you?" the sergeant on the front desk asked.

"DI Farrow. I'm meeting with Chief Inspector Harden; has he arrived yet?"

The sergeant's eyebrows rose sharply. He knew they were expecting a new inspector, but she was nothing like what he had in mind.

Anna's gaze turned icy at the prolonged scrutiny, the sergeant coughed and turned away.

"Ah, not yet. I'll buzz you in and get one of the team to give you the tour while you wait," he muttered, picking up the phone handset. A loud tone sounded, and Anna pushed open the heavy door to the sergeant's left. She stepped inside and stood breathing in the aroma of police station: dust, printer ink, body odour, and coffee. She smiled to herself, feeling right at home.

A young woman rushed up. Anna put her age as late twenties, early thirties. She was small and compact with a shoulder-length helmet of glossy, dark hair, brown eyes, and clear olive skin.

"Inspector! Hi, I'm Sergeant Lissoni, Margot Lissoni. We weren't expecting you until later."

"Really?" Anna checked her watch. "It's eight. I thought the Chief was meeting me at eight thirty?"

"Yeah, that's right," Lissoni answered brightly.

"Okay." Anna frowned, slightly confused. "Well, perhaps you can show me around in the meantime."

Lissoni gave her the tour. The station was small by Anna's standards, but no more than she had expected. Lissoni kept up a running commentary and then showed Anna to her office.

"And this is you." Lissoni indicated with a wave of her hand.

Anna stood in the doorway, silent, contemplative.

"Something wrong with it?" Lissoni added anxiously, catching Anna's look.

"It's fine. But I don't like the idea of being in an office apart from the team." Anna tucked that thought away, determined to resolve it at the earliest opportunity.

Lissoni looked surprised. She hadn't expected that. In fact, she had assumed the opposite, that the DI would prefer her own space.

"I might just visit the bathroom and grab a coffee before the Chief arrives," Anna said and walked off.

Lissoni watched her for a few seconds, then slowly walked back to her desk.

"So, what's the goss? What's she like? She looks like a dyke," Sergeant Hausser whispered eagerly, his head popped out around a partition a few metres from Margot's desk.

"Oh, for God's sake, Hausser, keep your prejudices to yourself! You keep it up and I'll dob you into HR myself!"

"Don't get huffy, just making an observation."

"How the hell you ever became a cop, I'll never know. You have the observation skills of a mole! It's bloody obvious she's been sick!" Without having given it any thought, Lissoni knew she was right. The DI did not look well. She looked, in fact, like a strong breeze would blow her over.

"Oh! Right!" Hausser murmured, abruptly disappearing behind his partition as he spotted the new DI emerged from the tea-room with a mug in hand.

Lissoni shook her head. She didn't know what to expect from the new boss. She had a good track record—at least that's what they'd heard on the grapevine; a real highflier—so why the hell was she transferring here?

A short while later, Lissoni escorted the Chief to Anna's office. He closed the door and sat down opposite her. She guessed he was in his late fifties, with the red face of a dedicated drinker. His salt-and-pepper hair was short and neat, and in stark contrast to his thick, wiry eyebrows with hairs pointing every which way, set above sharp blue eyes.

"Farrow"—he nodded with a brief smile—"Jimmy has been singing your praises. You have a lot to live up to."

"Jimmy?" Anna repeated, looking confused. "That's DCI Durant, I presume ... Ah, got it! *Jimmy Durante*, right? The nose certainly fits!" She grinned.

"He said you were quick! He also said you were sick," Harden added bluntly, looking at her speculatively. He was more than a little shocked, despite Durant's warnings. She was painfully thin, and her skin had a slight blueish tinge where the veins ran just underneath. Her hair was no more than a haze of dark red across her skull. She was very striking looking though, especially her bright green eyes, which were now regarding him keenly.

"Did he?"

"Wanna tell me?"

Anna looked away briefly and then turned back. She wondered how he would take it. She knew she had to be honest. It was one thing to hang back on the full extent of her illness to Durant—she had needed him to approve her transfer—but it wouldn't be right not to disclose it to her new boss. He needed to be prepared if her health deteriorated suddenly ... and then there might be ongoing treatment.

"I have breast cancer ... a particularly aggressive form of breast cancer. It progresses rapidly and had already spread before I was diagnosed. It's not curable. I've had extensive treatment over the last ten, eleven months. Chemo"—she flicked a hand to her head—"surgery, and radiation. I'm okay for now. But I will need constant check-ups and possibly further treatment."

She looked at him steadily through this recital, and she could see the dismay growing on his face. But to give him credit, he hadn't looked at her chest when she'd said 'surgery'.

"Well ... *shit!*" he said after a long pause, sitting back in his chair.

"I'm fine to work. In fact, I'm looking forward to it."

Harden swallowed. "Are you *cleared* to work?"

Anna nodded. "Yep. HR have already been on to me. I have my doctor's okay to work." *So long as I can*, she added silently.

He nodded slowly, processing it.

"Okay, then." He sat forward and leant on her desk. "We'll proceed as planned, but only if you keep me up to date on how you're coping." He held up a hand as she went to speak. "I mean it. You and I will keep in close communication. I'm not going to lie to you ... I'm more than a bit shocked and concerned at what you've told me, but I'm also keen to start this detective unit here and we need someone with your level of experience."

Anna let out the breath she had been holding, it was going to be okay.

"I have your word, you'll keep me informed, right?"

She nodded firmly. "Yes, Chief. I will."

"Right. Let's move on then. As mentioned, this is a new unit. All cases in the region have been handled by the Cooma office up until now, but Jindabyne is growing rapidly, and I think having a team here locally will be more efficient."

"Who have I got on the team?"

"Two very junior sergeants. You met one, Lissoni. The other is Jakob Donaldson. They've been working for the last few years in the Cooma office and both have passed their sergeants' exams in the last few months. I'm sorry they're so green, but I can't spare more senior officers. They both live locally, so they were keen for the move. So, a big part of your role here—and Jimmy tells me you're the perfect person for this—is to mentor them. Train 'em up. They need it. To be frank, the DI they've been under at Cooma hasn't pushed them, so you're going to have your work cut out for you."

Anna frowned. That didn't sound promising. "I'm happy to work with them, but I'd like to know what my options are if they aren't coming up to scratch. If there are only the three of us … I really can't afford to have dead weight."

Harden nodded. "Yes, true. Just see how you go. If you really think they won't pan out, then we'll talk about it. You will have access to other officers already posted here in the Jindy office. You can request them off Krejci. He's the other inspector here. I'll introduce you."

They ran through all the open cases in the area, and then the Chief walked her over and they sat and had a discussion with Krejci. He didn't seem very friendly, and Anna wondered if she may have taken the position over one of his friends. She hoped he wasn't going to be one of those petty bastards who'd make her beg any time she needed assistance just to make a point. She gave a mental shrug. She'd handle it.

"How was it?" Dee asked, sliding a cup of tea in front of Anna that afternoon.

"Chief was okay. I think he was a bit worried he'd been handed a lemon at first, but he seemed happy enough by the time he left. I just need to keep him updated on how I am."

"Did you tell him?"

Anna nodded. "Yeah, it's best that he knows, then if ... well ... he'll be prepared."

Dee got up abruptly and crossed to the handrail that ran along the back of the wooden deck where they sat, soaking in the last of the afternoon sunshine. She looked up at the dark mass of Barker's Ridge, tipped in gold with the setting sun.

Anna sensed her anguish. "Not too sure about the two sergeants he's lumbered me with, though," she added loudly.

"Why's that?" Dee turned, ready to accept the blatant attempt to divert her.

"Green doesn't come close." Anna sighed. "The first one—Jakob Donaldson, early thirties, rugby player build—I don't know what to make of him yet. Very close-mouthed. Wary of me, I think. Not sure whether he's always like that or maybe he just doesn't like reporting to a woman."

Dee's eyebrows rose. "Wouldn't think that would be such an issue in this day and age. Maybe just nervous to find himself working for the *sooper*-detective," she said with a laugh and a poor American accent. "What about the other one?"

"Lissoni—"

"Patricia?"

"No, Margot, you know her?" Anna asked.

Dee shook her head. "I know her parents, Neal and Linda. Nice people."

"Well, she seems really ... *young*." Anna frowned, trying to pin down her thoughts. "Bright enough I think, but ... I don't know"—she shrugged—"maybe she's intimidated by me."

Dee laughed. "Sounds about right, one blast of 'The Look' and they'll all be intimidated."

"What are you talking about?"

"The Look—you know—the one that causes frostbite in the unwary and shrivels other transgressors into dust."

Anna looked shocked and amused in equal parts. "You're kidding right?"

Dee turned and yelled inside, "Hey, Riles! Come out here for a sec."

Riley ambled out, scanned the table for food, and looked briefly disappointed.

"Riles, you know the look your mum gets when she's not pleased ... you know ... *The Look?*"

"Oh, yeah." he nodded.

Anna scoffed loudly. "I do not have *a look*."

"Yeah, you do, Mum," Riley responded matter-of-factly. "Death ray eyes, but I'm used to it ... We gonna eat soon?"

"In about fifteen minutes," Dee said with a smile, and Riley walked back inside.

Anna looked gobsmacked.

"Told ya!" Dee grinned.

Chapter 5

THE KAYAKS MOVED STEADILY along in tandem, swirling the mist that rose in wisps off the surface of the lake; far enough apart to manoeuvre but close enough to hail the other should the need arise. In the early morning light, the two men looked slightly bear-like in their life vests over heavy jackets.

The sun burst over the horizon, bathing the lake in golden light. The kayaks trolled slowly. It was more than an hour after sunrise before the zing of fishing line abruptly broke the silence. Stan turned, keen to see the fight.

Al pulled and wound, pulled and wound; the line whizzed and stopped each time the fish ran and changed direction. His boat dragged and spun freely as the battle ensued. The fish suddenly broke the surface in a violent leap, jerking and writhing, trying to shuck the lure. Al let out a whoop. It was a rainbow trout, and a good-sized one to boot.

Several minutes later, Al scooped the exhausted trout into the net, and Stan, still trolling, started to paddle over to admire the catch. He was ten metres away when his own line let out a zing. He turned on the spot and the line went silent.

"You on?" Al called.

Stan pulled up on his rod and yelled, "Nope. Hooked up on something." He shook his head disgustedly. He hoped he wasn't going to lose all his gear, it was his favourite lure!

He pulled hard and the rod bent over with the strain, but the line didn't move. Stan wedged the rod into the rod holder and paddled in the opposite direction, hoping to release the snag. He grabbed the rod again and pulled. It gave slightly and then stopped, still snagged. He paddled further around and pulled again. The line gave suddenly. Stan started to wind, but it was weighty and sluggish; he had something on. He wound steadily. *God, whatever it is it's bloody heavy*, he thought, hoping his line would hold up under the strain.

He peered over the side as the object slowly emerged from the depths, but he couldn't make it out. Grabbing the net, he scooped it underneath. Then, he quickly stuck the rod in the holder, needing both hands to drag it aboard. With a final heave, the net and its contents hit the floor of the kayak at Stan's feet, sending water everywhere. He looked down, then jerked back, yelping in surprise.

"Al! Get over here," he called nervously.

"What is it?" Al paddled alongside. He peered over the edge of Stan's kayak and swore loudly. There, in a puddle of water, next to a black diving boot, were the remains of a human foot.

They looked at each other anxiously. "We need to call the police," Al whispered.

Chapter 6

ANNA STOOD ON THE rocky shore. The lake was deep blue and just starting to shiver as the rising wind scudded across the surface. McEvoy Island—a small, bare outcrop poking its face above the surface of the lake, with just a few hardy, stunted pines breaking its rocky outline—sat a few hundred metres in front of her. She turned slowly. Old Kosciuszko Road ended abruptly behind her. Years before it had continued on to a crossing of the meandering Snowy River. Now, that had disappeared beneath the lake when the new dam flooded the valley more than fifty years ago. The shore on which she stood was denuded of vegetation where the falling waters of recent drought had exposed the rock. Clumps of golden tussock grass started ten metres further up the shore. This jut of bare land was still largely undeveloped. Anna imagined that the huge, million dollar plus homes that dotted the next point around would start to encroach here soon. The expansive lake views and snow-capped mountains in the distance were too much of a draw card for it to remain untouched for long.

With a last look across the lake, Anna turned from the damp smell of the shore and picked her way carefully over the uneven ground to where Lissoni was interviewing one of their fishermen.

Anna smiled at the sight of their witness. She guessed him to be in his late seventies or even early eighties. His face had the drooping jowls of an English bulldog; his skin, weathered and creased from years of outdoor living, and his eyes, a watery pale blue under straggly white eyebrows. He wore a home-knitted beanie of blue and white stripes pulled well down on his forehead.

"Mr Lloyd ... Stan. This is Detective Inspector Farrow," Lissoni said.

Stan peered intently at Anna. "You look like my Elsa," he said abruptly.

Anna's eyebrows rose, and, sensing what was coming, took a deep breath in preparation. "Do I, Mr Lloyd?" She smiled gently.

"She had the cancer," he said with a nod. "She lost *her* hair. She was a redhead, like you. You got the cancer too?"

"Yes, unfortunately I do, Mr Lloyd. I'm very sorry for your loss," Anna murmured, recognising the past tense in his description.

He nodded sadly. "I lost my Elsa eight year ago now. Not a day passes I don't miss her. But won't be long now and I'll join her. I hope it works out better for you."

Anna swallowed. "I hope so, Mr Lloyd. Now I understand it was you that pulled up the foot?"

"Yeah, you could have knocked me down with a feather. Thought it was just a piece of iron or wood, something from the old town, you know? We like fishing right over the top and sometimes you hook up, but it's the best place for trout. They like to hide in all the nooks and crannies down there."

The original town of Jindabyne had been the victim of the rising waters, and a new town was built on higher ground to the south to replace it. So underneath the calm blue waters of the lake lay the remnants of the old buildings, left to disintegrate in the muddy bottom.

"I'm sure it must have been a huge shock for you. You estimate you were ... where?" Anna beckoned to Lissoni who was holding a map.

"Well, we usually fish around the old hotel. Reckon they bite better after a drink!" He chuckled to himself, and Anna smiled.

"Had quite a few drinks in there meself in the early days, before the fire took it in sixty-four."

"You said you were directly off this point, immediately south of Tyrolean and in line with Cub and Lion Islands, correct?" Lissoni prompted, indicating the spot on the map.

"Yeah, that's right," he said, squinting at the map. "The old road ran along here"—he ran a dirty fingernail along the page—"the bridge started … there. And the pub was … just about there."

"And you estimated you were fishing in a depth of approximately twenty-five to thirty metres, Stan." Lissoni smiled at him encouragingly. The old man nodded.

"Approximately how far out from shore were you, do you think?" Anna asked.

Lissoni went to speak, and Anna held up a peremptory hand without even a glance in her direction and the sergeant's mouth snapped shut.

Anna looked expectantly at Stan; if he saw the interplay, he ignored it.

"I reckon we might have been only about seventy or eighty metres offshore now that I think on it," Stan said slowly, staring at the lake. Anna felt Lissoni shift next to her.

"It changes all the time; the water level, I mean. A year or so back, the water was way up there"—he pointed behind him—"and now look at it."

"Yes, it does change a lot, and that would make it hard to judge. But that's all very helpful, Mr Lloyd." Anna smiled. "Thank you very much for staying and answering all of our questions. If Sergeant Lissoni has your contact details, then I think you can head home now. We'll let you know if we need to check anything further with you."

She watched Stan walked over to his mate before turning to Lissoni. "Sergeant, if I ask a question that you have already asked, it's okay; let them answer it again. Stan was alright, he was willing to adjust his answer. I'm assuming he told you something different?"

Lissoni swallowed and looked down. "Yeah, he said they were about hundred metres or so off the shore the first time, but Al was adamant it was only about seventy metres when I interviewed *him,* so their information agrees now."

Anna nodded. "Not everyone will correct themselves like Stan, because most people don't want to look like they aren't sure. In other circumstances, they may not remember their lie and will give us a completely different answer the second time around, which is important. So, *let* them say it again, *don't* spoon-feed them!"

"Yes, Inspector," Lissoni muttered. Though the inspector had spoken quietly and calmly, she felt chastised. But Lissoni could see her point. It made sense and she parked it away for future refence. She didn't know what to make of the inspector. The interview with Stan had been a revelation. Other than the not so surprising news that the inspector had cancer, it was her gentle and friendly approach to the old man that had taken Margot aback. She shook her head wondering how she was going to fare under her management.

Anna turned at the approach of vehicles. A silver Range Rover pulled up next to the police constable on station at the top of the rise. After a brief discussion, the car pulled over to the side, and a man exited. He was of medium height and build, with thinning grey hair and round wire-framed glasses. She assumed he was the pathologist.

She walked up to meet him.

"Morning," he said brightly. "Dr Rodney Marchand."

"Inspector Anna Farrow. Our foot is over there." Anna pointed towards the lake edge.

"Don't get down to Jindy very often," he added conversationally as they walked across together.

"Well, I'm hoping if the police divers find the rest of the body later today, we can save you another trip," she responded, closing in on a white sheet lying a few metres from the water's edge.

The doctor crouched down and pulled back the top sheet to reveal a black wetsuit bootie, and the partially skeletonised foot that had been dumped out in Stan's boat. From the ball of the foot back to the ankle, it was mostly just skeleton, with cartilage and ligament connecting bones, but weirdly, all of the toes were largely intact. The foot had parted company with the rest of the body at the ankle.

"Interesting," Dr Marchand murmured, snapping on some gloves.

"Inspector," a voice said at Anna's elbow. She turned to see Jakob Donaldson at her side.

"I'll be back in a moment, Doc," Anna said over her shoulder, and she and Donaldson walked back towards the vehicles.

"When can we expect the police divers?"

"They said they'd be here in about two hours," Donaldson answered.

"Call them back and give them the estimated location of the find. Lissoni has the map coordinates. Tell them we'll relocate to Tyrolean Village. The closest access is probably off Tulong Close, but depending on their vehicles, they may need to launch near Rainbow Reserve."

Lissoni emerged from her car as they approached. "No abandoned cars have been found at the southern end of the lake in the last three years, Inspector. We had one in Kalkite though—that's at the northern end—about two and a half years ago."

Anna nodded thoughtfully.

"Once we get more of an idea how old this body is, we can narrow down the search. I think we should look for abandoned boats as well. Also, do a search of missing persons, same time period, three years." Lissoni nodded, scribbling the instructions down in her notebook.

"Sergeant"—Anna turned to Donaldson—"find out all scuba organisations who conduct dives in the lake. It's an advanced dive experience so you'll need to conduct a fairly wide search, there will be organisations as far afield as the coast and Sydney who might offer that."

"What? You think they lost a *diver*! I think they might have noticed that!" Donaldson smirked.

Anna turned and looked at him witheringly. He couldn't keep eye contact and dropped his gaze. Several seconds of icy silence followed.

"Get a schedule of all dives that have occurred over this part of the old town," Anna continued. "And then obtain all the photos and video footage they took.

We'll go back three years. Again, we can narrow that down once the doctor gives us more information. Let's get on it."

Anna walked back to where Dr Marchand was picking and peering over the foot.

"What's with the abandoned cars and boats?" Donaldson said sullenly.

"The guy must have gotten here somehow," Margot responded.

"Bit of an ice princess isn't she?" he muttered darkly, watching Anna pick her way tentatively over the uneven ground.

Lissoni shrugged and turned away to start the search on her phone. But she could see what he meant—the DI came across as cold and aloof—but then again, she'd been warm and friendly to Mr Lloyd. Lissoni shook her head. Donaldson's comment was just stupid and bordering on insulting, so he was deserving of the slap-down. And there was no doubt in her mind, that the inspector had delivered a reprimand ... but interestingly, she had not actually *said* anything. Now there was a skill!

"Anything of interest, Dr Marchand?" Anna called as she came up behind him.

"Rodney, please." He stood with a groan. "Bad knees!"

"Please call me Anna."

"Well, Anna, our foot belongs to a white male. My initial guess is perhaps somewhere between mid-twenties and forty. I'll know more when I can do some tests in the lab. I'd estimate his height as one hundred eighty centimetres, give or take five either side. Of course, if we find the rest of him, that will make the whole process much easier."

"Any thoughts on how our fellow might have parted from his foot?"

"It doesn't appear to be an amputation like you might see after a boating accident. At least not from the remains we have. All the bones and tissue are intact other than evidence of predation, probably by eels or yabbies. The ankle seems to have parted from the leg at the cartilage. Like it was pulled apart from the leg bone rather than sheared off."

Anna wrinkled her nose. "God, I hope he was dead when that happened!"

The doctor nodded. "If not, then I'd say that might be the cause of death. He would have bled profusely and died shortly thereafter without immediate medical attention. I'll see if I can determine if it was pre- or post-mortem."

"And now the big question—"

"Time of death," Marchand cut in. "Don't hold me to it, but I'd guess maybe a year or possibly eighteen months, at most."

Anna nodded. So, eighteen months was a reasonable boundary for their searches. That was good, it narrowed down the possibilities. It also meant it was near enough in time that people might remember something useful.

"I'll package up our foot. Now, did I hear the police divers are on their way?"

Anna checked her watch and nodded. "They're roughly two hours away, apparently. We'll head over to Tyrolean Village. It's the closest accessible spot to where the old boys pulled up the foot. Are you able to hang around or do you need to head back?"

"I might go into town and get some lunch and then come back and meet you there. It's not worth me trying to drive back to the lab now, and then possibly having to turn around if they find something. If we do find the body, I'll need to get the van out. I can't transport a full body in the car ... well, I can and I have ... but my wife complains about the smell, so I try not to," Dr Marchand added with a cheeky smile.

Anna laughed. "I'll bet! I think I might object too."

Chapter 7

THE POLICE DIVERS ARRIVED mid-afternoon. After a quick briefing on Stan and Al's approximate position, they zoomed out from the shore in their large black inflatable boat, keen to get as much of the area searched as possible while they still had the light. Anna watched it circle around as they reached their estimated starting point well beyond Stan and Al's guess of seventy metres. The motor stopped, and the boat rocked violently for a moment in the wake. Then four divers sat in a line on the edge of the boat, rolled backwards into the water and disappeared beneath the surface.

Daylight faded to black as they descended. They switched their spotlights on. Tunnels of soft green pierced the gloom filled with millions of tiny specks of silt suspended in the frigid water. They continued down with slow measured sweeps of their fins, the only sound the hiss of air as they breathed.

Senior Sergeant Grant Travers checked the depth; they were approaching thirty metres. He touched his transmitter. "Nearing target depth," he said shortly.

They spread out and slowed their descent. The black arms of a large tree suddenly reached out towards them.

"Eyes on," Travers murmured as the geometric shapes of man-made objects slowly appeared out of the gloom. "Mark your positions."

The divers each inflated a small buoy attached with a long tether to a weight, which they lowered to the bottom. The buoys floated to the surface.

"Look for disturbances. The old guy had quite a struggle to pull the boot up apparently." Transmitter clicks responded, acknowledging his statement.

They hovered with skilled minimalist movements, spotlights carefully scrutinising the surface beneath them. They moved two metres forward with a small flip and checked the area below.

Travers hovered over the ruins of a small building. It looked like an old hut. The roof had collapsed, but several beams of the frame remained upright. He navigated lower, resting a finger on a crossbeam. Silt swirled around his finger. He peered into the rubble, the light picking out an old brick chimney. He worked his way around to it. *No body.* He checked his orientation and moved on, keeping his movements to a minimum.

Fences, gates, concrete blocks, broken walls, and an old cart emerged out of the green gloom as they slowly made their way towards shore.

"Time, guys," Travers said into his transmitter, checking his watch. "Mark your positions."

The divers inflated another marker and then ascended. The boat, watching for the markers, repositioned and was waiting for them.

"Man, that was fantastic! Almost forgot what I was down there for!" Bowyer exclaimed, pulling off his mask. "I'm coming back here for a rec dive!"

Travers smiled. "Beats storm water drains, or shark infested waters, that's for sure."

They downed hot soup from a thermos and muesli bars before descending again.

The afternoon dragged on.

The wind picked up steadily and the lake started to heave with white caps. Clouds scudded rapidly across the sky and threw racing shadows across the water. The inflatable appeared and disappeared from their view as the water began to toss it around like a child's toy. Waves crashed on the shore, sending a thin, wet mist over the waiting group. Anna shivered and huddled into her thick jacket; she also pulled on a beanie and gloves as the temperature dropped. She was very glad it wasn't her in the water.

"Glad it's not me in there," the doctor, standing beside her, echoed her thoughts.

Threads of pink and orange had started to spread across the sky with the setting sun when a triumphant shout was carried to them on the wind.

It was full dark by the time they laid the body out on the shore. The corpse was still kitted out in a full-length wetsuit, the hands clad in wetsuit gloves; the mask, slightly askew, was still on the skull. The body looked slightly flattened, but still chunkier than Anna had expected, except for the leg that was missing the foot. That looked deflated, like the wetsuit leg was empty. The scuba tank, which had been removed before the body was brought to the surface, lay next to him along with a single fin.

"We'll head back down in the morning. Can't see diddly-squat down there now that we've stirred up the silt," Sergeant Travers said, as he and his colleagues, entirely unembarrassed, stripped down at the back of their van.

"I appreciate it." Anna nodded. "Can you describe where the body was? I mean, was it trapped or deliberately secured in some way?"

Travers towelled himself dry as he replied. "I'll send you the photos tomorrow, but luckily, he was lying on top of the remains of an old concrete structure, possibly an old water tank. We might not have found him otherwise; there's a lot of stuff down there. The strap on his tank—the one that attaches to his BCD—"

"His what?"

"Buoyancy compensation device. This thing." He held up the vest he had been wearing. "Basically, an old piece of wire caught under the strap at the back, and he was hooked up like a fish. The only option at that point was to undo the vest, remove it, and then release the hook-up. Unfortunately, most people panic when they find they can't move and hyperventilate. We've checked all his equipment. There's nothing wrong with any of it, except the tank is empty. All connected, no damage. I assume he just panicked and blew through what was left of his air."

Anna winced. She could envisage what had happened ... the lack of oxygen would have caused confusion and lessened his ability to make a clear decision.

There would have been an excruciating, but fortunately rapid, downward spiral to unconsciousness and death.

"Could someone else have hooked him up?"

Travers paused briefly before answering. He shook his head. "No. I don't think someone else could have done that unless he was already unconscious. They would have had to manhandle him quite firmly, and that's hard to do in water. Especially this water, at that depth. Any type of struggle would have stirred up the silt, and I'd think you'd be hard-pressed to work out where the wire was, let alone hook your man on it, if the silt was swirling. And also, he was hooked top to bottom, which implies a forward motion like if you're swimming. If someone else was trying to hook him, they'd have more than likely tried bottom to top, down to up, like you were forcing someone down on to it." As he explained, he hooked his fingers in an upward motion with one hand and jammed the other over the top to ensure she understood.

Anna nodded. "Thanks. I'll let you do your thing tomorrow. I'll stick to the office. Can you give me a call when you're done to give me an update?"

"Sure thing. Oh, and one other thing that might be helpful, is that your guy was in a wetsuit." He gave a firm nod as if this were significant.

Anna raised an inquiring eyebrow.

"The water here is cold, very cold. In winter, you'd only wear a dry-suit, or you'd develop hypothermia in a heartbeat. So, I think your man would have entered the water in the warmer months, say between November and April."

"Excellent, that's good to know." Anna nodded and then turned as headlights appeared behind them. The mortuary van bumped its way down the hill. After checking to make sure they had accommodation organised, she thanked Travers and the others and walked back to Dr Marchand.

"No outward damage to the body that I can make out, Anna." He stood up slowly, massaging a knee. "Other than the missing foot, of course. I don't want to remove the wetsuit here, I'd rather do it at the lab, there's a lot of loose bits rattling around in there." He grinned.

"So, nothing that looks like a head injury? Something that might have rendered him unconscious?"

Marchand shook his head. "Nothing that I can see, *or feel*, at this stage, but when I get the wetsuit off, I'll know a lot more."

"When will you be able to have a detailed look ... tomorrow?" she queried hopefully.

He nodded slowly. "I should be able to take a look tomorrow. How about I give you a call with my preliminary findings tomorrow afternoon?"

"That would be great Rodney, thanks. Any change from your initial thoughts of an age range of mid-twenty to forty and in the water for between twelve and eighteen months?"

Rodney looked speculatively at the corpse and then back at Anna. "No, I think that's about as good as I can get right now. Oh, and the height is one hundred eighty-two centimetres."

"Great thanks, anything else?"

"You might like to take a look at this." He picked up the corpse's arm and pointed to a rather sophisticated dive watch on the body's wrist.

Donaldson whistled from over her shoulder. "*Ver-ry nice!*"

"Sergeant, take some shots of the watch, will you? It might give us a clue to his identity."

Donaldson, who had been chronicling the retrieval process and the remains in film, took some close-up shots of the front and back of the watch. Then Marchand attached a bag over the hand and forearm and secured it with tape.

"Well, that gives us something to work on." Anna nodded to herself.

The next morning, Anna's team sat in her office. She made a mental note to rearrange the place and make it more of a meeting room for case reviews, but for now, they had more important fish to fry.

"So, what do we know?" Anna looked expectantly at Lissoni.

"Boats. We have two canoes and one small sailboat, a Laser 4.7, that were found abandoned on the lake in the last couple of years."

"How big is a Laser? It's quite small, isn't it?"

Margot typed quickly. "According to Wikipedia, *the 4.7 is the smallest of the Lasers, intended to be manned by one person … and … it's got an optimal crew weight of fifty to sixty-six kilograms,*" she quoted.

Anna frowned. "Our guy is one eighty-two tall, he must have weighed at least, seventy-five kilograms, possibly more, and then with dive gear—what's that add?"

Margot typed into her laptop again. "Ah, let's see … yeah, here it is. Dive equipment typically weighs around twenty-two kilograms, not including *buoyancy weights.*"

"That means we're looking at one hundred kilograms minimum, way too heavy for that boat." Anna shook her head. "Not sure how he'd manage getting in and out of a canoe either with all that equipment unless he's Houdini. We can't dismiss it outright, but I don't see any of those options as being reasonable possibilities for our diver," she added thoughtfully. "Now, correct me if I'm wrong—you said we had three missing persons from the local area in the last two years: a girl of seventeen, a man in his sixties, and a man of twenty-six?"

Lissoni nodded. "That's right."

"So based on the doc's prelim findings, only the last man is an option. What description do we have for him?"

"Caucasian, dark brown hair, blue eyes, stocky build, and one seventy-two centimetres tall," Lissoni read out.

"Damn! Not our man; too short." Anna sat pondering for several seconds.

"A guy goes diving in the lake. There are no abandoned boats that he could reasonably have dived from, and no abandoned cars in the area. What can we assume from that?" Anna looked from Lissoni to Donaldson.

"He was driven there by someone else, either in a car or boat," Donaldson shot out.

Anna nodded slowly. "And if that's right, then there is definitely something criminal about it, because they didn't report him missing."

"Could he have swum ... like from one of the houses around the point?" Donaldson went on.

Anna turned to look at him speculatively.

"I mean—"

"Good idea, Sergeant," she said, cutting him off. "It's definitely a possibility. But, then he's either a local—"

"But then it would have been reported, wouldn't it? We'd have a missing persons report," Lissoni interjected.

"—or he was here on holiday," Anna continued. "If he was in holiday accommodation and he was alone, then he'd have left all his gear behind, which someone would have noticed, or ... we come back to some criminal activity where the partner covered it up."

"What if he's *not* local and someone dumped him in the lake after, you know, dressing him up in a wetsuit to look like it was an accident?" Donaldson said eagerly, angling for another 'good idea, Sergeant'.

"I think that's unlikely. Have you ever put on a wetsuit? It's like getting into sausage casing. No way someone could manage to dress an unconscious or dead body in a wetsuit. No ... I think our man got himself dressed. Which you would only do a short while before getting in the water. The question is, did he go in by himself, or with someone else?" She tapped her chin thoughtfully. "Where's the photo of the watch?"

Donaldson got up quickly, walked to his desk, and returned with his laptop. He typed briefly and then swivelled the screen around. Despite being submerged at the bottom of the lake for more than a year, the watch, dotted with small smears of green algae, looked as if it had just been purchased.

"No inscriptions ... *damn*," Anna muttered, enlarging the image that showed the back of the watch. "I'm no expert, but this looks expensive. Sergeant, find out the make and model and let's see if that brings us closer to identifying our man."

Donaldson nodded.

"So, getting back to your thought," Anna continued. "If he *swam* to that spot at the old town, that would most likely have been from the village where we found him, or possibly this side of East Jindabyne, maybe off Sandy Beach."

Silence greeted this statement, and Anna looked up to see two startled faces.

"You guys didn't do your homework. When you get a new boss, it pays to check them out. I grew up here," she said dryly. "You wouldn't want to walk too far with all of that gear, it's pretty heavy. That should narrow down the possibilities."

She turned to Donaldson. "Did you get anything on the scuba organisations who dive the lake yet?"

"Ah-h, no, not yet."

"Okay, split that task between you ... and don't forget about the watch. We'll reconvene in two hours."

"When the hell did she expect me to get that done?" Donaldson complained as soon as he was out of earshot of the inspector.

"I don't know, just get on it." Lissoni shrugged irritably, in no mood for Donaldson's bitching.

Anna sat at her desk, reviewing the images of the submerged old town that Sergeant Travers had sent through. Each image appeared as if it had been taken through the bottom of an old green bottle. Old trees still stood, branches outstretched, next to the collapsed remains of houses. She knew at Kalkite and near Waste Point you could see whole cottages still standing, but here they had fallen into rubble. Heavy beams, blocks of cement, doors, fences, and old window frames—all mingled with the detritus of human habitation: old tins, a jerry can, a broken chair. The murky green water made it hard to make out anything very clearly; she couldn't imagine how the divers had navigated around under there. Visibility would be no more than two or three metres maximum.

Anna picked up her phone and dialled. It was answered immediately.

"Farrow," the Chief said, "heard you have a body."

"Yeah, a scuba diver found on the submerged old town on the East Jindabyne side. Doc thinks it might have been there about a year or maybe eighteen months. Don't know yet what the cause of death is, but it could be accidental according to Travers, the police diver. The body was hooked up on a wire. Trouble is ... why was he there at all? No one has been reported missing, at least locally—"

"What about Webb? Tyler Webb?"

Anna frowned. "Tyler Webb?" The name sounded vaguely familiar, but she couldn't pin it down.

"Wife was found murdered around this time last year; Webb was suspected of killing her, but he disappeared before he could be questioned. There haven't been any sightings of him since."

Anna's mouth compressed into a thin line, her anger rising. "Thanks Chief. I'll look into it."

She rang off and sat for several minutes assimilating the information before searching on her computer. It didn't take long. At that moment, she could well imagine she had 'The Look' that Dee referred to on her face, because she was fuming. She sipped her cooling tea, then got up and walked to the doorway.

"Lissoni," she called, her voice ice-cold. Margot looked up. The DI crooked a finger and then walked back to her desk.

Lissoni shot an anxious glance at Donaldson, who just shrugged and shook his head in response. She stood, and feeling as though she was approaching the headmaster's office at school, walked into the DI's office.

"Shut the door and sit down," Anna said, her tone ominous. "Sergeant, have you heard the name, Tyler Webb?"

"Ah ... yeah, sure. He was ..." Her voice petered out and her face paled. Her breathing increased as the full magnitude of the implications dawned on her.

"I ... I ..." she stuttered as the DI looked at her. She now knew how a bug felt just before it was pinned onto a specimen board.

"Webb absconded after his wife was murdered last year," Anna continued bitingly, "and hasn't been heard from since. That would mean he's … *missing*."

Lissoni swallowed. "I'm sorry, Inspector. I didn't think of … I just checked the Missing Persons Register." She struggled not to squirm under the DI's glacial look.

"Tell Donaldson to continue with the dive organisations and the watch. I want you to pull out everything on the Webb case from last year. We'll meet at three o'clock," Anna snapped.

Lissoni stood, and resisting the urge to apologise again, walked out.

Anna sat for several minutes, flicking through the online case file. Normally, she would have remembered such a graphic case, especially as it had occurred in her state. However, looking at the date she realised that she had been assaulted a few days before, during a drug raid, incurring 'the punch' that had started her breast cancer journey. She'd taken several days off to recover and then was playing catch up on her own cases, without the bandwidth to concern herself with others.

Chapter 8

"There are only two companies who conduct dives in the lake. It's a specialty dive, limited to fully PADI-certified advanced divers. They are sending me all the photo and video footage they have from the old town from the last three years," Donaldson reported after they reconvened at three.

"Good," Anna muttered shortly, "and the watch?"

Donaldson's eyes brightened. "The watch! Well, it's a top-of-the-range Swiss-made dive watch ... an Aquatimer Expedition Jacques-Yves Cousteau. It works down to about three hundred metres and costs about ten grand."

Anna tapped her chin with a forefinger, deep in thought. *That's one very expensive watch.*

"Dr Marchand called," she said, pulling herself out of her reverie and clasping her hands in front of her. "Our body is fairly well preserved, as the cold water slowed down decomposition. So, he's adjusted his estimate. He believes it's been underwater for approximately ten to eighteen months. There doesn't appear to be any injuries that would have rendered him unconscious. The body has suffered some predation from the local aquatic life, which has been confined to the exposed areas of the face and leg. We do have a partial face. The section under the mask was fairly intact, but obviously that's not something we can use for identification since the lower half of the face is largely gone. The doctor estimates our man is in his early thirties, one hundred eighty-two centimetres, medium build, brown hair, blue eyes. This matches the description of Tyler Webb."

Donaldson shot a look at Lissoni. She'd filled him in after her 'talk' with the DI. He felt a bit sorry for her, but his main feeling was one of relief that it hadn't been *him* in the firing line. Lissoni didn't return his look, she just stared down at her notes.

"Do we have any DNA of Tyler Webb?"

"Yes, Inspector," Lissoni answered quietly. "They took samples from the house at the time of the murder. That included Mr and Mrs Webb and their son, Ethan."

"Good. I asked Dr Marchand to cross-check if it was available. But that's going to take a few days."

"Did the doc say how he died?" Donaldson asked.

"Asphyxiation. He ran out of air."

"So, the foot—?"

"Well, it seems our body had a ten centimetre slice through the lower leg of his wetsuit which would have caused a fairly substantial injury. I think we can assume that was accidental. If it was inflicted by someone else ... why the ankle? And why only the one wound? If you meant to kill, then why not finish the job? Travers said that the body was 'hooked up' on a piece of wire and apparently the only way out of that would be to take off the vest and tank, unhook and then put the gear back on. But he didn't do that. So, he's either panicked when he hooked up, and in thrashing around, sliced open his leg. Or he sliced his leg and then managed to hook up. The blood lost from his wound might have contributed to a lack of consciousness, which meant he didn't have the presence of mind to unhook himself. We'll probably never find out what happened there.

"According to Dr Marchand, the blood and open wound would have attracted underwater predators, and they attacked that point, both up the leg and down into the bootie. Eventually, only a thin piece of cartilage linked the foot to the leg, and Mr Lloyd pulled that apart with one good heave on his fishing line."

"So, are we thinking this was just an accident?" Donaldson frowned.

"Divers usually don't dive alone," Lissoni noted quietly.

"Correct!" Anna agreed, glad that Lissoni was offering an opinion and wasn't going to sulk.

"Which means Webb either had a partner who left him there, or he did dive alone—" Lissoni continued.

"And *why* would he do that, is the question," Anna interjected. "It's a challenging dive. Lots of hazards, poor visibility. Why do that on your own? It's extremely risky, as evidenced by what happened to him."

"Maybe it isn't Webb?" Donaldson suggested.

"No," Anna replied bluntly. "Two men of similar age and description, and the date of his disappearance falling neatly into the range for our body? No ... it's Webb."

Lissoni nodded with resignation. Having reviewed the file in detail she agreed with the DI. It was definitely Webb.

"The Webbs lived at Tyrolean Village, right near the lake," she added, knowing it was the clincher.

"Good. We'll proceed as if it's Webb for now, *but,* we will not be announcing it as Webb until we have confirmation of the DNA. However, in saying that, we need to give his next of kin a heads-up. There will be a lot of media speculation. You said he had a son, Sergeant?" She looked expectantly at Margot.

"Yes, Ethan, he's nine, and lives with his grandparents. That's Samantha Webb's folks. They're out near Dalgety."

"Tyler's parents still alive?"

"No. Both dead. Mum when he was a teenager and his dad died about two years before he disappeared."

"Right, so son's guardians it is. You can come with me." Anna nodded to Lissoni. "We'll do that now. This stuff doesn't get better if you leave it. While we're gone"—she turned to Donaldson—"check into the financials of the Webbs and see if you can find the watch purchase, that'll be another point of confirmation. Message me if you find it. Also, review the Webb case file, we'll get into it tomorrow morning."

Anna's phone rang and she answered it. A brief conversation ensued and then she rang off.

"Travers. They found the other fin, but nothing else in the immediate vicinity of where they found the body." She looked thoughtful for a few seconds before standing.

"Okay, let's bite the bullet," she sighed, looking at Lissoni. "We'll both drive. Send me the address, I'll meet you there."

Lissoni's drive was not a comfortable one. She spent the entire journey berating herself. She was angry, extremely annoyed, and humiliated to have been hauled over the coals. But she had to admit, though the DI had made it very clear she wasn't happy, she hadn't belaboured the point. Her previous boss would have railed for a good ten minutes at the top of his voice. But despite that, she felt more criticism from DI Farrow with her frosty silence than she had ever felt from her old boss.

She was so irritated that she had missed Webb. She knew all about the case. It had been a sensation the previous year, and though she hadn't been directly involved in the investigation, she would have had to be living under a rock to have missed it. She thumped the wheel angrily. She was better than this; she needed to focus. Thank God the DI hadn't said anything more at the meeting that afternoon. She had steeled herself for another pointed barb and was thankful it hadn't eventuated.

As she pulled into the driveway, she was still trying to work out whether accompanying the DI on this visit to the Webbs' son and his grandparents was a sign the DI had forgiven her or whether it was intended as punishment.

Chapter 9

After a couple of minutes, the DI pulled in behind her and Lissoni stepped out of her car. She watched the inspector walk towards her. Lissoni had noticed her slightly hesitant gait down at the shoreline but had assumed that the DI was just being careful not to turn an ankle on the rough ground. Looking at her now, it seemed that she walked—not so much slowly, as *deliberately;* each step carefully placed before the next. Lissoni wondered if there was something wrong with her legs. As the DI drew level, she put her musings aside, and they turned and walked to the house together.

It was a sprawling ranch-style home set atop a small rise which gave it 360 degree views over the sweeping champagne-coloured grasslands around it and the rising hills to the west. To the south of the house, several horses grazed in the fading afternoon light. Anna pulled her jacket closed as a gust of wind, carrying the first hint of rain, hit them. Together, they stepped up on to the wide bull-nosed covered verandah.

Lissoni knocked on the front door. It opened to reveal Ethan Webb. He was small, with hair that flopped into his eyes à la a young Justin Bieber, and his teeth looked too big for his mouth as if they had outgrown the rest of him. He looked at them interestedly.

"Hello?"

"Hi there, Ethan, is it?" Lissoni said with a smile.

"Yeah," he answered with a worried frown.

"Are your grandparents at home?"

"Sure. Ah ... wait here. I'll go get them." He closed the door carefully and they could hear him run off.

A few moments later, heavier footsteps approached, and the door swung open again.

Samantha Webb's mother was of medium height with short iron-grey hair. She wore well-worn jeans, fluffy slippers, and an old checked shirt. They had obviously interrupted dinner preparations as she was wiping her hands on a tea towel.

"Can I help you?" she queried in a puzzled tone, her eye wandering over Anna's bare head.

"Detective Inspector Farrow, and this is Sergeant Lissoni, Mrs Carter-Ellis. We'd like to have a brief chat to you if we could," Anna said.

The woman's eyes clouded over, and she looked over her shoulder at Ethan hovering in the hallway behind her.

She swallowed. "Please come in. Ethan, go get your grandad, will you?" She watched as Ethan streaked away.

They proceeded to a small room off the hallway, which seemed to serve as both sitting room and office.

"Please sit down. Is this about Tyler? Have you found him?"

"We think so," Anna said, taking a seat.

Confusion bloomed on the older lady's face.

"We've found a body that matches his description," Anna added.

The old lady gasped and put a hand to her mouth. A few seconds later, her husband appeared in the doorway, with Ethan trailing behind.

"Ethan, we've got some business to discuss with these ladies, how about you go play on your PlayStation? We won't be long, and then we'll have dinner, okay?" his grandmother said, overly brightly.

Ethan's eyes widened and he shot off before she could change her mind. He was not normally allowed to play his game except on the weekends, so this was an unexpected boon not to be ignored.

Mark Carter-Ellis frowned and sat down next to his wife. He was a big man, with a ruddy, weathered face and tortoise-shell framed glasses.

Anna introduced herself and the sergeant again.

"They think they've found Tyler, Mark," Sally whispered.

"Well, I hope you've arrested the bastard," he growled.

"No need," Anna said. "We've pulled a body from the lake that matches your son-in-law's description and his disappearance fits within the timeline of death."

The old man sank back into the lounge. "So, he's ... dead," he muttered in shock.

"We won't have DNA confirmation for several more days yet, but we thought it best to let you know of the very strong possibility that it is him."

Anna waited, she knew these things took some time to sink in.

"You said the timeline of death fits with when he disappeared ... what's that mean?" Mark frowned.

"The body we've found appears to have died between ten and eighteen months ago. Mr Webb disappeared thirteen months ago."

"So, he died maybe ... three months after he killed our Sam. Is that right?" Sally said, sounding doubtful.

"Well, actually, Mrs Carter-Ellis, if it *is* him, then he may have died anywhere between when your daughter was killed, and three months or so, afterwards. We don't have a clearer idea of the date of death than that at this stage."

"Oh, I see," the old lady muttered, still looking confused.

"I don't mean to cause you any more pain but what can you tell me about your son-in-law? His personality, habits, that type of thing—"

"He's a monster, he murdered our little girl," the old man spat in a furious whisper, tears of rage starting in his eyes.

"Mark! Don't!" his wife pleaded, her hand gripping his arm.

He dropped his gaze and swallowed his next words.

His wife turned to the detectives. "We ... didn't like Tyler much," she started hesitantly. "He was ... flashy and insincere. But Sam was infatuated, and she wouldn't hear a bad word about him. She was always headstrong," she added, earning an outraged look from her husband.

"Well, she was, Mark," she responded with irritation. "Anyway, they married. It was a disaster, and they hated each other in the end."

"I see. I believe they worked in real estate together?"

"Yes, that's right. That's how they met. Sam went to work as the receptionist to a local real estate agent in Cooma. Then, she got interested in it and got her licence. After that, she started work back here in Jindy in the same office as Tyler. They eventually bought out the principal and ran the business together."

"I gather the business was going well?" Anna said, thinking of the watch.

"Oh, okay, I think," Sally murmured vaguely.

"Did Tyler and Sam have any other joint interests?"

"Not really. Tyler was always hanging around with his mates. Sam never stopped complaining about it."

"His mates?" Anna cast a glance towards Lissoni and was pleased to see she was taking notes.

"Three idiots that he went to school with. Never grew up, that was his problem. No idea how to be a husband or a father," Mark declared bitterly, his lip curling. "Thought life was just one big party."

"When was the last time you saw Tyler?"

The Carter-Ellis' exchanged a look. "Here. For my birthday," Mark said. "A few days before our Sam was … killed."

Chapter 10

THE BAR WAS HEAVING with bodies. Sleeting rain had driven all the mid-week revellers indoors with the result that it was well past capacity. The atmosphere was steamy, the rain-wet patrons and overheating inside combined to create a sweaty funk. Most of the occupants had stripped down to T-shirts with jackets tied at their waists.

Dean Teasel, beers held high over his head, edged his way to the tiny table that he and his mates occupied near the window.

"Man, it's worse than usual in here," he commented, placing the drinks on the table and taking a seat.

They all took a sip of beer.

"So, you think it's him?" Dean asked, leaning in.

"Of course it's *bloody* him. Who *else* would it be?" Jonathan Russo muttered scornfully.

"Yeah. Must be him," added Mick Bialy quietly. "I mean … *something* had to have happened to him. No way would he have gone this long and not contacted us."

The other two nodded. The three of them had discussed Tyler's disappearance endlessly over the last year. They had accepted that he must be dead. The four of them had been close since kindergarten. There was no way that Tyler would not contact them, he knew he could trust them, whatever he'd done. It had always been that way.

On the face of it they were an unlikely group of mates.

Dean Teasel: accountant, working for a local tax agent, good at school, quiet, anxious, and desperately thankful to be a part of the group.

Michael 'Mick' Bialy: without doubt the leader of their group since they were five years old. Organiser of games, settler of disputes, captain of their activities, and issuer of commands. Mick was the success story having taken over his father's fertiliser business at twenty-five, which was now a thriving concern.

Jonathan Russo: brooding, the muscle of the group, talented with horses, and therefore sought after in some circles, though it was said he was difficult to deal with.

And Tyler Webb: easy going, the extrovert, the party-man, could be relied upon to supply the girls and alcohol when needed. The only one of their number to be married and a father.

They all missed Webby. Though Mick was the glue that held them together, Webby had been the icing on the cake that made it all worthwhile.

"So, he never left Jindy ... he's been here at the bottom of the lake all along," Mick muttered into his beer.

"Do you think it was an accident?" Dean asked tentatively.

"I don't know ... I suppose so." Mick shrugged. "What the hell was he doing in the lake?"

"Scuba diving," Jono responded sullenly.

"*Ya think?*" Mick sneered with impatient sarcasm.

Then after a few seconds of silence, Dean added, "You don't think he, like ... topped himself ... after Sam, do you?"

"Nah! Of course not!" Jono cried, his tone scathingly. "They said he was found in scuba gear. You wouldn't do that if you were just going to kill yourself, and besides, we all know he would have been celebrating to be rid of her."

"Geezus, Jono." Dean rolled his eyes in disgust. He darted a quick look around to see who might be listening, but the crowd nearby was loudly engaged in their own issues and oblivious to their discussion.

"What? Are we going to pretend that it was all sweetness and light between them now? They *hated* each other. *You* know that!"

"But why did he go into the lake afterwards?" Mick asked again to no one in particular. "On his own? Why not get one of us to go with him? He's never been in there on his own before."

"So what are you saying? He killed Sam and then went for a midnight dive? That makes no sense at all," Jono scoffed.

"Well, what's your take then?" Mick turned on him angrily. "He kills Sam, and then we hear nothing—not a peep. Whatever he did, we know he would have contacted us. He knew we'd help him. He had to have gone into the lake soon after he did it. The place was crawling with cops later that night and the next few days."

"You saw him last"— Jono turned to Dean—"he must have said *something!*"

Dean looked aghast. "*No!* He didn't! I'd have told you if he had."

"That was the day before Sam was killed, wasn't it?" Mick added with a frown.

"We've been over this a *thousand* times already! I went by the real estate on Wednesday morning and spoke to Webby about some receipts for the business. He was just the same as usual. And anyway ... Sam was ... k-killed the next night, so anything could have happened between when I spoke to him and then." Dean picked up his glass only to find it empty. "I need another drink," he muttered.

"My shout," Mick said, getting up and walking away.

"He must have said something!" Jono spat out. "You can't tell me he had a whole chatty conversation with you, and the very next day kills Sam and *then* goes for a scuba dive. He must have *said something!*"

"He didn't! I told you! He was the same as usual," Dean declared, his face slick with sweat.

Jono looked at him keenly. He could feel the anxiety coming off him. *He knows something!* They'd always thought Tyler had killed Sam and then took off. But why he hadn't contacted them was a mystery. After weeks of waiting, they had assumed something had gone wrong with his escape plan, and that he must have been dead somewhere. What other explanation was possible for not contacting them? His mates? But now ... he'd been found at the bottom of the lake. How the hell did that fit in? *The last thing anyone would do is go scuba diving after killing someone ...*

They had never been in any doubt that Tyler had killed Sam, though the ruthlessness of it had shocked them. They didn't think he had it in him to be that vicious. But then, he'd never stopped complaining about what a complete bitch she was and how life would be so much better without her. They'd just assumed that he'd finally snapped and gone berserk.

But the scuba diving ... *What did that mean? What the hell was Webby doing?*

Mick returned with the beers and set them down.

"*You* know something," Jono muttered in a low tone, his eyes burning holes in Dean. "What is it?"

"What's going on?" Mick asked, looking between them. Jono looked mean and Dean looked ... *stressed.*

"Nothing! I don't know what you want me to say!" Dean cried.

"Leave it!" Mick flicked an impatient hand at Jono, who looked like he wanted to push it further. Jono picked up his beer and downed half of it in one long swallow before banging the glass down on the tabletop and glaring at Dean.

Several minutes passed without further discussion. Then Mick lifted his glass.

"To Webby," he whispered.

"The spiderman." Jono nodded, lifting his glass.

"Tyler," Dean added quietly, completing the ritual, and they all drank deeply.

Chapter 11

"THANK YOU, HAUSSER." ANNA surveyed her remodelled office early the next morning. She had coerced him into helping her move her desk out and a worktable in.

"Anytime, Inspector," he panted, sitting back down at his desk.

"Inspector! I could have helped you with that," Donaldson murmured half-heartedly, walking up with a frown. He was far from impressed that the inspector would be sitting only two metres away from him rather than in a separate office, preferably with the door shut.

"No problem. Constable Hausser gave me a hand. You could wheel that whiteboard in." She flicked a hand at the board in question, standing in the corner.

With the whiteboard in place, Anna was pleased with their case review slash meeting space. She dropped the rather thin case file on the table and looked up at Donaldson standing in the doorway.

"Let's grab a coffee and hopefully Lissoni will be here shortly, and we can get underway." She walked off towards the lunchroom.

Ten minutes later, coffees in hand and Lissoni having arrived, they sat around the table.

"Have you both reviewed the Webb case file?" She was rewarded with nods.

"I think we'll need to go over a lot of old ground, unfortunately. There's a lot less information in here"—she tapped the file in front of her—"than I would have expected."

Lissoni and Donaldson exchanged a look. Their old boss had been the investigating officer for the Webb murder and neither wished to stab him in the back by agreeing with her.

"Let's start with a timeline." Anna got up and walked to the whiteboard.

"Samantha Webb was found dead at her home on Thursday, 17 March at 11:12 pm. A triple zero emergency call reporting her murder was recorded at 10:44. The voice was muffled and assumed at the time to be Tyler Webb." Anna wrote the time and dates on the board with key information.

"According to the pathologist—who was Dr Marchand, I'm pleased to see—Mrs Webb died at around ten." She scribbled this on the board.

"What's our last confirmed contact with Tyler Webb?" Anna looked at Lissoni.

Lissoni typed quickly on her laptop. "Wednesday morning, at his office. The receptionist said he left at a few minutes before noon."

"So, no phone calls on his mobile ... no credit card activity after then?" Anna queried Donaldson.

He shook his head. "Not according to the reports at the time."

"Let's confirm that," Anna stated briskly.

Anna sat down at the table and flipped through the file quickly, pausing at a page.

"Both Tyler and Samantha's cars were found in the garage. I didn't see anything in here that said whether either of them owned another car." She tapped the page in front of her. "It's strange ... if there is no other car, and no credit card receipts or phone records beyond March 16 ... why did they assume Tyler had left town?" she murmured to herself, still staring at the file.

What the hell?! Donaldson mouthed at Lissoni. She gave a miniscule shrug in reply.

"Let's double check the car situation," Anna said, looking up. "Last confirmed contact for Samantha?"

"She phoned her mother on Thursday morning at 9.05 to ask her to keep Ethan another night," Lissoni replied.

Anna tapped the whiteboard marker on her chin thoughtfully. "Rather fortunate in hindsight, wasn't it? And it's interesting that Ethan was at his grandparents mid-week, particularly since they live well out of town, which meant they had to drive him to and from school." She stood and added to the whiteboard: *Ethan—why at grandparents?*

Anna turned and leant on the back of her chair. "Now, if he walked to the lake ... it's how far?"

"Only about sixty metres or less down the street, Inspector," Lissoni responded.

Anna nodded. "So, we know Webb went into the water sometime between the early afternoon of March 16 and the end of April, based on what Sergeant Travers said about him wearing a wetsuit, which is suitable only in the warmer months."

"But we know he was around on March *17* ... after all, he killed his wife!" Donaldson said sharply.

"Did he?" Anna answered mildly, taking both sergeants aback.

"Of course, he did," Donaldson snapped. *Was she just going to rubbish everything that had been done before just for the hell of it?*

"So, what's the theory then?" Anna looked from one to the other. "Tyler kills Samantha in a domestic violence incident and then disappears, with no car, using no credit cards or his phone. And then, sometime before the end of April, arrives back home to get his scuba gear so he can go for a dive in the lake. I am assuming it is *his* dive gear, that's something we need to check." She added, *Dive gear?* to the whiteboard.

"Well, I don't know about the second half of it ... but I don't see how you can doubt it was Tyler who killed Samantha," Donaldson continued, his mouth set in a thin line.

Anna flipped through the file again, withdrew a photo, and turned it around to face the other two, tapping on it with a fingernail.

"What's wrong with this picture?"

They both peered intently at the image. It wasn't pretty. Samantha Webb's head lolled to one side exposing the gaping bloody mess where her throat had been slashed open. Her left eye was partly closed and swollen, and her lip, puffy and split. She had been beaten before the knife ended her life.

Lissoni sucked in a breath. "Her hands are tied to the chair!"

"Exactly." Anna gave one firm nod. "Very unusual for a DV incident, which are usually done in the heat of the moment. This looks much more like an interrogation, don't you think?"

Donaldson's head reeled back. *Had they missed this before? No, they must have seen it!*

"Is there a history of domestic violence in their relationship?" Anna continued.

"Nothing on record," Lissoni murmured.

Anna nodded. "Not that we can say it *wasn't* Tyler who did it at this stage, but I think we have to question the whole domestic violence theory until we have more information.

"Now a critical piece of evidence in support of the DV theory is apparently a video. I haven't seen it yet. Let's bring that up and have a look." She glanced at Donaldson expectantly.

He looked down at his laptop and brought up the video, he pushed it across the table, and then he and Lissoni walked around to stand behind the inspector.

The image was soundless and grainy but clearly showed the Webbs in their kitchen. That they were having a vicious argument was evident by their aggressive stance, glaring eyes and jabbing fingers. A few minutes in, Tyler stepped back and grabbed a knife from the knife block on the bench. He held it in front of Samantha's face. It was clear he was threatening her. Then Tyler turned, threw the knife in the sink, and stormed off camera.

"What's the origin of this video?" Anna asked, hitting pause.

"Security camera in the ceiling. Apparently, the Webbs liked to keep an eye on the babysitter who looked after Ethan after school," Lissoni said. "There is a camera in the lounge room as well as the one in the kitchen. They're on a timer and record from three to five thirty each weekday afternoon. There was about a month on record, but this was the only one showing the Webbs together."

"When was it taken?"

"Eight days before Samantha Webb was killed," Lissoni answered.

Anna stared at the frozen image. "I'm going to replay it, and this time, I want you to focus on Samantha, not Tyler, when he gets the knife."

"Notice anything?" Anna asked when the video ended.

"She looks like … she's … *grinning*," Lissoni offered hesitantly.

Anna nodded slowly. "Yes, that's what I thought. She doesn't look intimidated. She doesn't step back. She just looks at him and smirks."

Donaldson straightened up and walked around to the other side of the table and sat down with a thump. *Had they got the whole thing wrong? No! It couldn't be. It just wasn't possible.*

"I'd really like to know what was being said … I wonder if we can find someone who can lip-read to give us an idea," Anna pondered aloud.

"My uncle is deaf, he lip-reads," Donaldson muttered a little stiffly. "I can ask him."

"That would be great. Do you think he might be able to take a look this afternoon?"

Donaldson nodded.

"Good thanks. Ask him to please keep it in confidence. Now, I'm going to be out for the rest of the day. Can you follow up on those items we've discussed, and I'd like to have a closer look at the financials. Did you get a chance to pull those together?" she asked, looking at Donaldson with raised eyebrows.

"Ah … no. I just reviewed his credit card information for the watch, but I didn't find it listed," he murmured resentfully. *When the hell was he supposed to do all this stuff she expected?*

"Okay, let's meet again tomorrow morning and review where we are."

Chapter 12

"'Someone who's *not* Tyler Webb'," Dee quoted with a laugh. "I can't believe you said that!"

"Well, how stupid is that reporter? 'If it's not Tyler Webb then who is it?' I mean *really?* What the hell did he expect me to say? The moron!" Anna fumed. She had been ambushed on her way outside to meet Dee. Word had spread quickly about the body in the lake and the rumour mill was grinding furiously. Several reporters had pounced on her as she walked down the steps in front of the police station.

With a heavy sigh, she had stopped to answer their questions. Yes, they had found a body in the lake, which had not yet been identified. Did she think it was Tyler Webb? Mr Webb was a possibility, but until the DNA results were available, they were not able to say definitively that it was him, which led to the rather desperate question from a junior reporter and Anna's scathing reply.

"Well, it was honest at least," Dee chuckled as she accelerated up the rain-soaked highway.

"I just hate interviews. The inane questions. All they want is something sensational for their next news report," Anna growled.

"So, *do* you think it's Tyler Webb?" Dee asked avidly.

Anna sighed. "Yep, I'm pretty sure it is. Though when and why he was in the lake are going to be tough questions to answer."

"How's the junior team going?"

"So-so. I'm not impressed thus far. Donaldson seems fairly closed-minded, unfortunately. He sticks to the party line and doesn't look closely enough at the evidence or challenge first impressions. Lissoni is slightly less blinkered, but she doesn't like to put herself out there; scared of criticism perhaps."

"Well, you are a bit scary, you know." Dee threw a glance at her older sister.

"I don't know why you keep saying that!" Anna exclaimed with mild frustration.

"Well, maybe *intimidating* is a better description. They'll loosen up and settle into the job when they know you better." Dee nodded confidently.

"They're professionals. They need to step up and get the job done, whether they know me or not," Anna replied bluntly. "I could have driven myself you know," she added irritably.

"Of course, you could, but then I would have had to pull every tiny fact out of you bit by bit. This way, I'll get to hear it all firsthand and save us both the angst," Dee said, her tone smug.

She had insisted on accompanying Anna to her appointment with her new oncologist. At first, Anna had flatly refused—preferring to maintain her privacy—but Dee was nothing if not persistent and had not let up. Finally, recognising that it might, in the longer term, be better that Dee understood what was happening with her prognosis and treatment, she conceded the point and agreed to let her come ... though now she was starting to regret it.

"Annabelina Farrow," a voice called down the hallway, and Anna winced.

Dee giggled.

They got up and walked to where the doctor stood in a doorway. Dee let out a barely audible whistle of appreciation and Anna shot her a steely-eyed, 'behave yourself' look.

The doctor was tall and well built, with short dark hair and soft grey eyes. He was what their mother used to call, well put together.

He smiled and beckoned them inside and followed behind.

They all sat.

"Annabel—"

"Just Anna," she cut him off swiftly. "Please," she added, aware that her tone had been quite sharp.

He grinned. "Sure. Anna. I'm Dr Cameron Childs and this is ...?"

"Daisy-belle Farrow, my sister," Anna said through clenched teeth.

"Just call me Dee." She grinned.

"Great names," Dr Childs said, but catching Anna's rather cool look, he coughed and looked down at her notes.

"I've read your history, Anna, and I called Dr Vaswani in Sydney and had a chat as well. Given that it's eight weeks now since your last radiation treatment, we both think you'll need some more scans to assess the situation."

Anna nodded tiredly. *More scans ... I'm going to glow in the dark soon.*

"But first, I'd like to examine you, so if you wouldn't mind stepping behind the screen. You can leave your underpants on," he said, with clinical detachment.

Anna moved behind the screen and started to strip off.

"So, have you been doing this type of doctoring long?" Dee asked brightly.

Dr Childs smiled. "Oh, yes, a few years now."

"What made you get into this type of work? It must be a bit depressing."

Anna rolled her eyes behind the screen.

His eyebrows rose. "Well ... it's a rapidly advancing field of medicine, which I find very interesting and, while it can be challenging, it can also be extremely rewarding."

Anna cleared her throat loudly and Dr Childs stood, grabbed a set of gloves and walked behind the screen, pulling them on. He examined her thoroughly, asking questions and murmuring instructions, which Anna followed robot-like, having been through similar examinations a multitude of times in the last few months. He noted that the scars where both breasts had been removed had healed well.

"How is the neuropathy in your legs and feet?" he said, testing her reflexes.

Anna shrugged. "Not too bad. It hasn't improved, but it hasn't gotten any worse either."

"You can get dressed, Anna," he said, snapping off his gloves and walking out. He sat back down at his desk.

Anna emerged only a minute later still buttoning her shirt. She didn't want to leave Dee with Dr Childs for too long in case she started her inane questions again.

"Once we have the results of the scans and if everything looks okay, I think we could consider planning breast reconstruction."

Anna shook her head. "No, thanks."

Dr Childs frowned. "If you're concerned about the procedure, it's quite straightforward and the results are generally very good these days. Let me show you some before and after shots." He started up from his desk.

"No, don't bother, I'm not interested." Anna shook her head firmly.

The doctor sank back down in his chair and looked at her quizzically.

His first thought was how beautiful she was, and he immediately chastised himself for that very 'un-doctorly' assessment. But it was true. She was far too thin, but that made her cheekbones stand out and her skin was like cream. However, it was her eyes that made her remarkable, a vivid malachite green with a thick fringe of long dark auburn lashes. Even the fact that she had little more than peach fuzz on her head didn't detract from her looks. It looked soft and touchable.

Suddenly realising he had been staring at her, he coughed and shuffled the papers in front of him.

"I don't need boobs to do my job or look after my son," Anna said softly.

He frowned and shot a look at Dee, hoping for some support, but she had her head down, he watched as a tear dripped onto the hand in her lap.

"You're too young not to give it some serious thought," he replied gently.

"I'm not so young, Doc, forty-one is getting on." She smiled wryly.

He gave her an answering smile. "Well, I'm forty-two and I don't think I'm old."

"Forty-two! Well ... you'll know the answer to everything then," Anna said cryptically.

Dee's head shot up.

Dr Childs looked momentarily confused and then barked a laugh as he registered the reference: "*Hitchhikers Guide to the Galaxy?* Well, if I'm supposed to know everything then we're all in trouble." He laughed.

"I just feel it might be a waste of money and I need to consider my son's future," Anna continued after a few seconds, and the mood sobered instantly. "I know the survival rate, at five years, for my type of cancer is around fifteen percent."

Anna registered Dee stiffen at her comment, but she continued to look calmly at the doctor.

He nodded. "The survival rate is closer to nineteen percent now, but you have to remember that you can't ascertain five-year survival until five years have passed ... so that figure is based on patients receiving treatment from five to seven years ago. So much has changed since then." He leant forward. "There are many more treatment options available now and we know so much more than we did back then."

Anna gave a brief half-smile at his obvious enthusiasm. "Well, that's good news. But I think I'll just park the whole new boobs thing for a while," she repeated firmly, though smiling to take any admonishment out of her tone.

"Well, that was a shock," Dee said, as she turned out of the hospital carpark sometime later.

"I told you the survival rate was low, Dee."

"No, not that ... you ... flirting with the dishy Dr Childs!"

"What? I did not flirt with him—" Anna spluttered.

"'Forty-two! Well ... you'll know the answer to everything then'," Dee mimicked in a breathless high-pitched tone. "Puh-lease! Bastardising Hitchhikers like that—what other possible reason could you have?" she added, sounding scandalised.

"I don't sound like that!" Anna said, an outraged look on her face. "Nor was I flirting! I just thought I'd lighten the mood a little."

"Oh yeah, sure." Dee rolled her eyes. "But seriously ... why not go for it? He's single. I checked with the receptionist."

"Dee! You *didn't!*"

"*What?* Why not? He obviously likes you ... though God only knows why! You are *so-o* ugly and crabby."

Anna whacked her sister playfully on the arm.

"He's single, your single ... what's the harm?" Dee persisted.

Anna shook her head. "There's just too much going on, Dee," she muttered.

"There's always stuff going on, Anna. You deserve a little happiness ... and I'd bet the hunky Dr Childs could provide a *lo-ot* of happiness!" she said, her voice full of innuendo.

"You're incorrigible!"

Chapter 13

THE NEXT MORNING, THE team reconvened in the meeting room.

"Any luck with your uncle, Sergeant?" Anna asked, sipping on a takeaway coffee.

"Yes, and no. The image is too grainy to make it all out, and of course, they're moving around, so their lips are not always towards the camera. However, he did get some snippets. It might be better to review in context." He pushed his laptop over in front of Anna and got up to stand behind her. Lissoni leant in over Anna's other shoulder.

Anna pushed play to start the video, and they watched as Samantha Webb walked on screen into the kitchen and opened the fridge. Tyler walked in and slammed the fridge door shut in front of her face.

"'I've had enough!' he says," Sergeant Donaldson read, scanning his notes and watching the video simultaneously, his eyes darting from screen to paper. "... 'I want out!' he says."

Samantha steps back and jabs a finger into Tyler's chest, her face inches from his. "... 'better suck it up' ... 'let you just walk away' ..."

"... 'don't give a fuck what they think'."

"... 'you'd better give a' ... 'get over yourself' ... 'little girlfriend' ..." Samantha appeared to taunt him.

Tyler lunged and grabbed the knife. "'I could kill you right now' ... 'trouble'."

"... 'big man' ... 'nothing' ...'" Donaldson finished as Tyler stormed out of the kitchen. Donaldson and Lissoni sat back down.

"'What they think'?" Anna repeated in a puzzled tone. "Hmm, well, I think it's pretty obvious they hated each other, and he wants out of the relationship. He has a girlfriend … that wasn't in the case file, so I assume that's new information. We need to find out who the girlfriend is, or was," she commented, standing and adding it to the whiteboard.

"So, who is the 'they' and what is preventing them from splitting up?" Anna pondered.

"Do you think he's referring to Samantha's parents?" Lissoni said, sounding doubtful.

"What hold could Sam's parents have over them? And having spoken to them the other day, I'd have guessed they would have been ecstatic if Samantha and Tyler had split up."

"Perhaps Sam and her parents wanted them to stay together for Ethan's sake?" Donaldson ventured.

Anna grimaced. "Does anyone stay together for their kids these days? Aren't we more concerned about what they see and learn from a destructive and malignant relationship than the damage a broken home might cause? And what about that last comment? 'I could kill you right now and something, something trouble' … *Save me* trouble? *Save them* the trouble?"

"Save *them* the trouble goes with 'what *they* think'," Donaldson suggested.

"Yes, it does," Anna muttered as a thought popped into her mind. She mulled it over briefly, tapping the marker thoughtfully against her chin. It had possibilities, but there was nothing to support it at this stage, so she parked it at the back of her mind for now.

"Okay, let's get that written up. But before we look at the financials and the phone records"—she noted the embarrassed grimaces on both their faces and sighed—"I want to listen to the triple zero call from the night Samantha died. After that, I want to take a look at the Webbs' house." She looked over expectantly, and they both jumped up.

A few minutes later, Lissoni sat back at the meeting table and waited for the inspector to finish her call. "I've organised the keys to the house. It's been unoccupied since the murder. Mrs Carter-Ellis said they haven't been in there at all," Lissoni said.

"That's good."

"I've got the triple zero call." Donaldson came in a few minutes later. He sat down at the table and, looking around to see if the other two were ready, pushed play.

"Police emergency—" the operator started.

"Sammie's dead ... she's dead ... dead ..." a muffled voice sobbed. The operator obtained the address in fits and starts and the caller hung up.

"So that was assumed to be Tyler Webb," Anna said to no one in particular. The two sergeants exchanged a glance, having no idea what could be gleaned from that short, somewhat distorted voice recording.

"Okay," she added, getting up. "Let's go have a look at the house."

The Webbs' house sat on the right-hand side of a road that rose sharply from the lakefront, fifty or sixty metres below them. The hill was so steep that each house seemed to overlook the one below. Anna paused and looked out over the lake, today a dark forbidding grey mirroring the sky above. The rain had stopped momentarily, but judging by the thickening purple-grey clouds amassing on the southern horizon, another drenching was not far away.

It was obvious that the architect had made the most of the steep terrain by building the house over multiple levels. The grey render on the brickwork and a dark grey tiled roof gave it a slightly sinister air. Though Anna mused that it was more likely a result of knowing what had occurred inside rather than the rather bleak colour scheme. The small front yard had a few hardy and frost tolerant bushes and a minuscule lawn of dying weeds. It looked neglected and sad next to its neat and tidy neighbours.

Lissoni unlocked the front door and a waft of stale air tinged with decay emerged.

"When they said they hadn't cleaned up, they meant it." She wrinkled her nose and pushed the door open.

The short, marble-floored entrance opened onto a large, open-plan lounge and dining room. Anna's first impression was of overwhelming white. The floors were a very pale wood and the walls and ceiling were painted white. The windows were dressed in white plantation shutters. Two white leather corner lounges formed a u-shape in front of a gigantic TV screen that dominated the far wall. The other walls were dotted with large, bright, and expensive-looking abstract paintings. A huge glass coffee table, in front of the lounges, sat atop an enormous rug of palest grey and white.

The room had that slightly dishevelled appearance of a thorough search, which Anna found reassuring.

They walked through to the kitchen and halted. The smell that had greeted them at the door was much more pronounced here. The thick cloying smell of old blood and decomposition clung to the back of their throats. Lissoni gagged and quickly pulled out a tissue to hold over her nose and mouth.

"What exactly are we looking for?" Donaldson muttered, a disgusted look on his face.

"Anything and everything." Anna looked around keenly. The kitchen, as they had seen on the video, was quite large. The bench tops were littered with a variety of expensive gadgets which appeared to be rarely used given their pristine appearance.

The floor of pale grey tiles was coated in a thick layer of dried brown and rust-coloured blood that had also splattered the cupboards and nearby wall. The impression of multiple footprints could be seen, where the police and pathologist had tracked through the gore to remove Samantha from her home. The chair and restraints that held her had been removed to the evidence locker.

Anna peered up at the ceiling. "Where was that video taken from?"

Donaldson looked up and, with a dip of his head, indicated, "There, near the smoke alarm."

Anna nodded. She looked at it carefully but said nothing.

A doorway to their left led to a laundry and drying room and then down into the garage. A late model four-wheel-drive Lexus and a huge American RAM truck sat there.

Along the far wall was a large floor to ceiling cupboard with sliding doors. Donaldson slid one of the doors open.

"Well, he was definitely into diving," Anna said, fingering two wetsuits and a dry-suit hanging in the left-hand section of the cupboard, which also housed spare tanks, fins, masks, regulators, and other diving paraphernalia.

"Also into golf by the looks of it," Donaldson added, peering into another section of the cupboard.

A third section stored multiple sets of snow skis, two snowboards, and assorted helmets and poles.

Lissoni hit a button, and the rear roller door of the garage opened to reveal a boat on a trailer with two jet-skis, also on trailers, parked next to it. These were all housed under a carport which occupied the lower half of the backyard. The other half of the backyard, which was on a higher level above a retaining wall, was taken up with a large entertaining area. An outdoor kitchen and lounges overlooked a steep gully that ended at the lake edge. Anna walked to the back of the yard and stood admiring the sweeping views over the western part of the lake. She turned slowly, taking it all in before walking back inside.

"Real estate business must be doing very well," she commented.

Lissoni's phone rang as they were entering the media room. After a brief conversation, she ended the call. "Inspector, the lady next door has called the police to let them know 'there are intruders in the Webbs' house'," she quoted, tongue in cheek.

Anna looked amused. "Well, that's good—we have an alert neighbour—well worth a chat. We're nearly finished here, anyway. You go next door and reassure her. I'll be in shortly."

Lissoni nodded and left while Anna and Donaldson walked through to the very impressive media room, complete with blackout curtains, theatre seats, a vast screen, gaming consoles, and a library of gaming options, joysticks, and the like. Donaldson would have liked to linger, but Anna moved them on to the bedrooms upstairs.

The first was a diva's dream. A king-sized bed with rumpled white silk sheets and a white doona-cover with pink and pale green floral edging held centre stage. A multitude of white and pale pink throw pillows were piled haphazardly on a bedside blanket box. To the right of the bed a doorway led to a bathroom. Its gleaming white-on-white tiles and porcelain made both Anna and Donaldson squint. A doorway to the left of the bed led to a walk-in robe. Equal in size to the bedroom itself, it was filled with racks of designer clothes, shoes, handbags and scarves. Many with the original labels still attached.

A corner nook, mirrored on three sides, was clearly where Samantha Tyler examined herself before venturing forth.

"Wow!" Anna exclaimed, shaking her head; even Donaldson appeared impressed.

The other bedroom was the antithesis of the first, with a strong all-male vibe. It was of equal size to the other bedroom, but done in tones of dark blue and pale grey. One half of the walk-in robe was devoted to normal wear and the other to sportswear: ski gear, golf wear, hiking.

A third bedroom, down the hall, was clearly Ethan's as it was decorated in Marvel comic themes, with Spider-man predominating.

Two other bedrooms, with ensuites, occupied the far end of the hall, both of which appeared unused.

They walked back to the front door. Anna turned for a last thoughtful glance. *Money was definitely not an issue for these people, but as the saying goes, money doesn't buy happiness.*

They walked next door and Donaldson knocked briefly. The door opened before he had lowered his hand. A short, rotund woman in her mid-sixties waved them in.

"Your sergeant is in here," she said in a tone that implied they'd lost her.

She led them into a small, overheated sitting room. Lissoni sat on one of the chintz-covered armchairs sipping on a coffee. A plate piled high with biscuits sat in front of her. She looked up guiltily as they entered.

"I'm Inspector Farrow and this is Sergeant Donaldson—"

"Coffee or tea?" the older lady enquired abruptly.

"Eh, coffee for me, thank you Ms—?"

"Everington. Francene Everington. Just call me Fran. So, coffee for you ... and for you?" She looked up at Sergeant Donaldson.

"Coffee, thanks Fran." He smiled, moving over to take a biscuit from the plate in front of Lissoni.

"Right. Sit yourselves down. I'll be back in a jif." She bustled away.

Anna raised an eyebrow at Lissoni who answered with an embarrassed shrug.

Fran Everington was back within a minute with a tray holding two coffees, sugar, a small jug of milk, and more biscuits.

"Thank you, Fran." Anna took a mug from the tray. They tended to their coffees while Fran settled herself in an armchair opposite, her brown eyes snapping with interest behind wire-frame glasses.

"Suppose you want to hear about the Webbs? Everyone does. Told the police the first time. Definitely him that did it. Always fighting and carrying on. Loud enough to wake the dead some nights."

Anna subdued a smile; Fran's staccato way of speaking reminded her of an old sergeant she'd had when she first graduated from the police academy. He was an old curmudgeon, and most of her colleagues were terrified of him, but he'd taken a shine to her, and she'd learned a lot under his tutelage.

"So, you are in no doubt that Tyler killed Samantha, Fran?"

"No. None at all. They were always at each other's throats. Screaming and yelling. The language they used! That poor little boy. Ethan, his name was. How they carried on in front of him … I just don't know … some people!" she sighed disgustedly.

"He's with his grandparents now. A better situation for him, I think," Anna took a sip of her coffee and winced. Dishwater would have been an improvement. She slid it back on to the table. "So, when was the last time you saw either of the Webbs?"

"The day before," Fran said without further thought. "Him, he arrived at lunchtime in that god-awful truck he had. She arrived as usual in the later afternoon."

"And you didn't see either of them the following day?"

"No." Fran shook her head, clearly wishing otherwise.

"And going back to the days before Samantha was killed, do you remember any visitors to their house?"

"Well, I keep myself to myself, you know. Can't stand nosey neighbours." She looked intently at Anna who bit the inside of her cheek to suppress a grin.

"No, of course not, I agree totally, but living in a close neighbourhood, you hear and see things in the usual course of the day, don't you?"

"That's right. The houses are way too close here. Back in the day, the houses were smaller. Now they have these huge houses on the same sized lot. No place for the kids to play and no privacy!"

"Absolutely," Anna agreed. "So, did you happen to notice any visitors in the weeks or days leading up to Samantha's death?"

"Well … I don't like to speak ill of the dead you know—"

"No, but in the circumstances, it may be very important." Anna nodded encouragingly, knowing full well Fran was bursting to tell them.

"*Mrs* Webb did have a male visitor occasionally, when *Mr* Webb was out." Fran nodded and looked at them wide-eyed.

"Really?"

"*He* used to come over once or twice a week. He'd arrive in the evening. Stayed sometimes to the next morning," Fran said, her tone heavy with implication.

"Did you mention this to the police at the time of Mrs Webb's death?" Anna asked, knowing full well that it was not in the case file.

Fran looked briefly uncomfortable and then thrust her chin out stubbornly. "No ... as I said, I didn't like to speak ill of the dead. And besides, there seemed little point in saying anything, since everyone knew who'd killed her," she reasoned, plainly satisfied with her answer.

"I understand," Anna responded mildly, swallowing her irritation. "Do you have an idea of how long this ... friendship was going on for?"

Fran's lips pursed as she considered it. "Oh, well ... better part of a year, I'd say."

"Perhaps you might give us a description of him, Fran. You seem to have seen this fellow on several occasions."

"Can you write that up, please, and get a move on with the financials and phone logs for both Webbs," Anna directed briskly, as the three of them stood on the street outside of the Webbs' house. "I need to be somewhere this afternoon, so I'll see you both bright and early Monday morning, and we'll start to dig a little deeper."

Chapter 14

ANNA WALKED BACK INTO the office later that evening. She was exhausted and that damn MRI had given her a blinding headache, as it always did; it was the incessant pounding that was clear and unrelenting despite the headphones they gave you. But at least it was finally the weekend, and she could get some rest and spend time with Riley. After swiping her card, she walked slowly through the darkened floor, an occasional pool of light spotlighting those on the late shift. Murmuring quiet greetings, she worked her way to the far-right-hand corner.

Lights and the faint burble of voices alerted Anna as she approached her desk.

"—she's just trying to make her mark." She heard Donaldson say and slowed to a stop to listen. "Dragging up all this stuff and acting like she knows what she's doing. Rubbishing everything the last team did and trying to find another explanation just so she can show us country halfwits how big-city girl does it. And we get dumped with all the useless busy work," he muttered bitterly.

"And how come she gets all this time off, I'd like to know," Lissoni added in an indignant whisper. "I wouldn't mind a Friday afternoon off!"

"Not bloody likely under the ice princess," Donaldson sneered.

"More likely to catch frostbite," Lissoni laughed. But the laughter died in her throat as Anna walked into view and stood there looking grimly from one to the other.

Donaldson, who had been leaning on the partition separating his desk from Lissoni's, straightened abruptly, spilling coffee down his shirt.

The tableaux remained frozen for several seconds before Anna broke the silence. "I think we'll continue this conversation in the meeting room," she said quietly, and walked away.

The other two looked aghast, hearing the echo of their damning words. Lissoni stood and, feeling more dread than if they were facing their last moments in front of the guillotine, they followed her slowly into the meeting room.

Anna stood at the window, looking out at the twinkling lights of the town rising up the hill from the lake that was just out of sight. She pressed the heel of her hand to her head, willing the pain away. The sergeants entered and sat down, but she remained standing at the window, she was in no hurry to start the conversation.

After several minutes, she turned and leant back against a filing cabinet. She surveyed them dispassionately. Lissoni was staring at her lap, her face pale and her posture tense. Donaldson was watching her, seemingly defiant, but Anna could see the sheen of sweat on his forehead.

"When I spoke to the Chief on Monday," she began in a low, cool tone, "he told me I was to work with two very new sergeants. I was, to say the least, not impressed that I had no experienced officers on the team. However, we agreed that I would work with you both, and if, after a period of time, I felt that either or both of you did not show an aptitude for the work, or if the team, since it is so small, wasn't gelling, then he and I would reconsider the situation." She paused to let that sink in.

"In light of what I've heard tonight," she continued, watching them squirm, "I realise that *my* opinion is not the only one to be taken into consideration. So ... let's agree on two weeks for us all to decide if this team continues as it is. Next Friday week, we'll have another conversation. But I need to warn you that, at this point in time, neither of you has met my expectations, so I need to see some considerable improvement before I would agree to you remaining on my team. Ideally, I would have worked with you both for some months before making that judgement call. However, I think we can all agree, given the immediate circumstances, that a quick decision may benefit everyone. But you need to understand one thing—on that Friday, if you decide to stay and I'm in agreement that you will—then you will do so without bitching and moaning behind my back; without calling me names, or acting put-upon like two recalcitrant fifteen-year-olds," she finished bitingly. "Questions?"

Donaldson, whose face had gone a dull dark red during her statement, thrust his chin out. "You said we weren't at the level you expect, what do you mean?"

Anna looked at Lissoni. Her head was still bowed down. "Lissoni?"

The sergeant looked up miserably and nodded, understanding the implied question.

"Well then, I'll start with you." Anna pushed off from the filing cabinet, walked to the table and grabbed the back of a chair, facing them.

"You show sparks of aptitude, but you aren't thorough, nor do you take any initiative. You wait for me to tell you exactly what you are to do. As a sergeant in a detective unit, I would expect to see a lot more resourcefulness."

Anna turned to Donaldson.

"You also show some glimmers of potential, Sergeant. However, you have what I'd refer to as a fatal flaw." She paused as his head jerked back in shock. "A detective needs to keep an open mind, which you don't have. A good detective formulates a theory to fit all of the facts, but you want the facts to fit your theory and if they don't, you dismiss them as inconsequential."

Donaldson's lips compressed into a thin line.

Lissoni stirred. "I'm very sorry for what I said, Inspector—it was childish and unforgivable—it's just that you seem so remote and unfriendly. We don't know anything about you."

Anna straightened and walked back to the window. She pinched the top of her nose trying to ease the pain pounding behind her eyes. She desperately wanted to tell them both to grow up. She wasn't there to be their friend; but Dee's face swam before her, and her words echoed in her ear: *'They'll loosen up and settle into the job when they know you better'; 'you can be intimidating'.* She swallowed her anger.

Taking a deep breath, Anna turned to face them. "Fair enough. What is it you want to know about me? What will help you feel more comfortable around me?"

"Are you sick?" Donaldson shot at her.

Anna rolled her eyes. "Sergeant ... of course I'm sick," she said in a frustrated tone. "Aside from how I look, which I would have thought might have given you a clue, I'm sure Lissoni told you of the conversation I had with our fisherman, Stan Lloyd." She took a deep breath and massaged her temples briefly.

"I have breast cancer," she added abruptly.

"Are you going to be okay?" Donaldson asked with a frown.

Anna paused. "Maybe."

Donaldson huffed.

"You think I'm equivocating?" Anna snapped. "How's this? Unlikely ... but I'm hoping to survive. That better?"

He had the grace to look embarrassed.

Anna took another deep breath to calm herself, venting her ire was not going to help the situation. Perhaps, like the Chief, they had a right to know. After all, if they stayed on her team, her health or lack of it, would affect them too.

"It's metastatic, that means there is no cure," she said bluntly. "As to my swanning off from work," she added with an edge that made Lissoni cringe, "I went to see my new oncologist yesterday and had an MRI scan this afternoon. I have several more tests scheduled for next week. Once we have the results of those tests, then I'll know whether I need to have further treatment."

Donaldson's chin lifted. "But why come here to Jindabyne? Surely, the treatment options were better in Sydney. You were a hot-shot up there. Why come here?"

Anna ignored the implied barb in the 'hot-shot' comment. "As I've already told you, Donaldson, I grew up here. My sister lives here. I have a fourteen-year-old son. If something were to happen to me, I need him to be taken care of. My sister has agreed to do that for me. I thought it best to relocate him now before ...”

Donaldson swallowed, wishing he could take the question back ... but then he had really wanted to know. He hadn't even known she had a son. He reran her answers in his head and looked up.

“What should we call you? You call me Donaldson or Sergeant. It's all a bit formal, don't you think?” He recalled the conversation that he and Lissoni had earlier in the week. Every conversation with her sounded stiff and forced. If they were going to get all the issues on the table, then this needed sorting out as well.

Anna sighed. “My team in Sydney referred to me as Anna, Boss, or Inspector, depending on the situation and the audience. 'Ice Princess' is not an option,” she added, looking at him with a raised eyebrows.

He flushed and nodded. “Sorry,” he muttered.

“I might mention that neither of you has suggested I call you anything else either.”

“You can call me Jake ... Boss,” Donaldson answered, taking the bit between his teeth.

“Margot, if you like, though Lissoni is fine, Inspec— Anna,” Lissoni ended awkwardly.

“Well, if you have no more questions ... I think that's enough personal revelations from me for now. I need to head home. You can let me know your decision in two weeks' time. I don't want to waste time if you're not keen to stay. Fair enough?”

Chapter 15

Anna roused slowly on Saturday morning. Her consciousness returned as if it were a feather floating down from on high and gradually coming to rest on the ground. Her limbs felt heavy, and an unusual lethargy seemed to hold her unmoving in her warm cocoon of blankets.

She turned her head slowly on the pillow to access the light stealing in around the curtain. It looked late. But even that thought did not galvanise her to move.

She slid her hands over her chest as she had so many times over the last few months. All she felt were thickened ridges of scar tissue where once her breasts had been. When they'd told her what needed to happen—that she would need to lose both breasts—she had accepted it as a reasonable price to pay if it meant staying alive. She'd accepted the pain and indignities that her treatment had inflicted, stoically. She was a practical person by nature, and to mourn a part of her anatomy that was doing its damnedest to kill her, seemed a wasteful exercise and an indulgence she could ill-afford.

After the surgery, she had forced herself to get used to the 'new' her; had stared at herself in the mirror objectively. Had accepted the change in her looks and, if she were honest, the cost to her femininity, with equanimity. She had even dismissed the offered counselling.

Ever since her diagnosis, her focus had been on two things: survival and Riley, nothing more. The act of juggling the tsunami of treatment that followed her diagnosis, her job, and Riley's care had taken every ounce of her stamina and thought. But now, here, in her childhood home, she could feel the strain of holding it together on her own start to ease for the first time.

The scene from the evening before, with Donaldson and Lissoni, flittered into her mind. Anna sighed. That they didn't like her bothered her not at all. That she had to deal with it the previous night was inconvenient, but she was not sorry it had come to a head. She felt comfortable with her analysis and her handling of the confrontation; she wondered briefly whether one or both of them would step up to the challenge she had laid down. But whatever the outcome, she would work through it. It had always been that way: her ability to sideline her feelings and focus on the task at hand.

David, Riley's father, had accused her of being cold and clinical before he disappeared from their lives. But she knew herself well enough to know that she was not cold. Far from it, in fact. That he could abandon his baby son seemed to *her* the height of cold selfishness. Her laser focus on Riley's wellbeing had been from love. A deep bottomless well of love that had formed at the precise moment that she had heard she was pregnant. And, in that moment, she saw David for what he was, a shallow, selfish, and careless individual. She was not sorry he had departed from her life. She only wished that, on those rare occasions when he parachuted into her son's life, she could protect Riley from the knowledge of his father's thoughtlessness. But unfortunately, that was not possible, she could only love her son all the more as compensation for his father's dearth of feeling.

No, she was not cold, though others had accused her of it many times. Donaldson was not the first to call her 'Ice Princess', though she would never tell him that. She had been called distant, unfeeling, unfriendly, and elitist. But she preferred to think of herself as selective. Aside from her family, which was now whittled down to just Riley and Dee, she had a few very good, and close friends and didn't feel the need to expand that.

Cameron Childs' face suddenly popped into her mind and she shook her head. Damn Dee! Putting that thought in her head. She couldn't deny he was good looking, and of course, she'd picked up that frisson of interest in his glance, but this was hardly the time in her life to start a relationship. Her hands slid across her chest again, particularly given what she looked like now. She swallowed and pushed the whole idea aside along with the blankets, and shivering, headed to the bathroom.

Some minutes later, Anna walked into the kitchen. The smell of newly baked bread and coffee made her mouth water. Dee's culinary skills had definitely improved her appetite. She heard voices and looked out to see Dee teaching Riley to milk a goat. It did not seem to be going well. Dee stood with her hands on her hips, laughing uproariously, while Riley was trying to manoeuvre a goat into position, but the nanny was having none of it. An upturned bucket nearby showed the results of his previous effort.

Anna poured a much-needed coffee and walked outside, then quickly retreated, donned a heavy jacket and beanie, and re-emerged. The day looked bright, and the sun glowed in clear blue skies, but the air was frigid. She'd forgotten just how cold autumn could be here.

She stood leaning on the railing, watching the two of them. Her sister, with her light brown hair tied back, dressed in a heavy patchwork jacket over loose overalls and gumboots, and a broad smile lighting her face. Her son, tall and lanky, with a bony, angular look to his face and hands that boys get when they've grown too fast. His face ruddy in the chill air and his fair hair tucked under a black, woollen cap. He looked happy and carefree as he smiled back at his aunty. It was a look that had become very rare on his face in the last year. Anna swallowed the lump in her throat. He was worth every effort and any sacrifice. She was so thankful he had Dee ... that they *both* had Dee.

After breakfast for Anna and morning tea for Riley and Dee, the three set off to walk down to the creek that formed the far boundary between the property and the national park. They walked along the well-worn trail through a field of thigh-high tussock grass that shimmered and waved in the light breeze. It was a view Anna would never tire of—those silvery beige hummocks undulating as one—it always took her breath away.

They left the tussock grass behind and entered an area of alpine bush-land—thick with billy buttons, silver daisies, wattles, and the short eucalypts, black sallees.

They reached the creek and, in the dappled shade, turned to walk along its edge. The olive-green water was so glassy, each rock on the bottom was clear, even in the deep pools. Dragonflies flashed across the surface, their iridescent yellow spots catching the sunlight. After ten minutes, they reached a beautiful glade with a deep pool where the trout lurked.

Anna shimmied along the trunk of an old tree that had blown down during a storm when she and Dee were kids. Though its root plate had been unearthed, and half of its branches lay in the waters of the creek, it had not died but continued to grow and flower each year in its near horizontal aspect. It had been Anna and Dee's favourite spot as kids; swimming and fishing in the deep pool. Sometimes they would use the old trunk as a ceiling beam, laying other branches against it to form a low hide from which they watched the wombats lumber along the creek edge, and on rare occasions, the platypus swimming upstream of their pool.

It was cold under the trees. The air, so clear and fresh, it was quite heady and smelled faintly of eucalyptus and tea tree. Anna breathed deeply and watched Riley trying his luck with a fishing rod. Dee wandered around behind her, rooting around for mushrooms in the damp undergrowth.

After a few minutes, the birds, startled into silence by their intrusion, started to stir and chirrup and twitter in the trees again. Anna listened to the fluttering and chittering; the mournful cawing of the crows and the distant chuckling from the kookaburras.

She had forgotten how unfettered life was here. She smiled, remembering how she had sometimes resented the lack of structure, or conformity, in her growing up. As a young child, it had not seemed to matter that much, but after she reached high school, the marked difference in her home life to others around her had chafed. She supposed, in hindsight, she was fortunate that her parents had even sent her to school, though of course, whether she attended or not was her own choice. They never made her, or Dee, do anything they didn't want to. Attending school, having a bath, going to bed, doing chores, even eating dinner was left entirely up to them. Her parents would suggest something, and she and Dee would either follow it or not, without repercussion, and only a benevolent smile from their parents. It was not that they didn't care—both she and Dee knew they were very much loved—it was just that they felt that 'children needed space to find themselves without societal restrictions'.

It was only when Dee started to run completely wild that Anna had realised the disastrous consequences of the lack of discipline in their lives. When Dee was twelve, she decided she didn't want to go to school anymore. Anna knew that Dee's differentness had led to ostracism, as it had for herself. The isolation and constant teasing had eventually become intolerable, and she had just stopped going. Dee began staying out late or sleeping in their hide quite often and not bothering to come home. When Anna complained to her parents, they just told her it was a phase Dee was going through and she would find her level soon. But, as the weeks dragged on, Dee just got more feral.

The crunch came when Anna came home from school one day and went in search of her sister, only to find her asleep with her head sticking out of an abandoned wombat hole. She was filthy and stank.

Something snapped in Anna. She dragged Dee all the way home where she bathed her, made her sit at the table and eat, and then put her to bed. Her parents hadn't intervened, since they felt Anna had a destiny to fulfil too; she was entitled to take charge if that was what she wanted. And take charge she did. From that day on, Anna dictated the pattern of their lives, brooking no argument from Dee. She established a strict routine, and they both followed it.

Anna shook her head in remembrance. That wombat hole was probably not far away, she decided to see if she could find it. She edged forward off the tree trunk intending to drop the foot or so to the ground, but her legs gave way as her feet touched grass, and she collapsed in a heap.

Riley threw down his rod and ran over. "Mum! ... Are you okay?"

He helped her up.

"Yes, I'm okay," she muttered irritably, smacking the dirt off her pants more firmly than was warranted. She straightened and saw his lips tighten in doubt.

"I'm fine." She nodded firmly. "It's just that all the treatment has messed up my coordination a bit."

"Is that why you've been walking funny?"

She went to kid him about the implied insult but saw the look of deep worry etched in his eyes and decided this was not the time to make light of the situation.

"Yeah. The doctor said it would probably wear off now that I'm not having chemo." She put out a hand and took his arm. She suddenly noticed how tall he had become, in that in-between world of man and boy. *Wow!* He'd shot up so much that she now needed to look up to meet his eye, but he had not yet filled out with the strength and muscle of a man. Her breath caught in her throat as she looked at him. *Will I see you grow to be a man?*

"Are you ... going to be okay?" Anxiety was coming off him in waves. Anna looked over his shoulder to see Dee standing there, nodding gently at her, tears trickling down her face.

"Sit down with me," Anna murmured softly, as she lowered herself gingerly to the ground. Riley sat down next to her. He pulled his legs up and wrapped his arms around them. Anna recognised the defensive gesture and dreaded the next few minutes. How she wished she could protect him; save him further pain, but life was not fair. She sighed and put her arm around his shoulders, feeling the boniness of his adolescence.

"The answer to your question, Riles, is ... I don't know. I wish I could tell you I'm cured now, but that would be a lie. The cancer is still there ... in me ... the treatment has ... killed off a lot of it; slowed its progress, but it hasn't gone away."

He looked at her, his face full of terror. "Are you going to *die?*"

"I'll do everything in my power not to," she whispered, "but that might not be enough."

Riley dropped his head onto his arms and Anna felt his shoulders heave with a sob. Pulling him close, she laid her chin on his bowed head, feeling tears threaten.

"I'm *so* sorry, Riles. I would give anything to tell you something else," she murmured into his hair.

Dee walked over and sat down next to Riley and wrapped her arms around them both.

Later that evening, Dee and Anna, bundled up against the cold, walked out to visit the goats. Dee pushed carrots through to the many eager mouths and then put up her hands to show them that all her treats had gone.

She rummaged in her pocket and pulled out a small pipe and then a folded paper packet from her other pocket.

"Oh, Dee! For goodness' sake!" Anna muttered.

"What? Like you haven't done this before?" Dee finished packing her pipe, and then looked up. "I seem to remember a time when you couldn't get enough!"

"That was a long time ago." Anna looked sideways at her.

Dee lit the pipe and pulled in the smoke in a long draw. The pungent smell of marijuana filled the air. "Here, have a puff." She held it out.

Anna equivocated. Dee was right, she had enjoyed a puff now and then when she'd been younger.

"Do you good." Dee smiled. "It'll give you the munchies and maybe you'll eat something, you look like a puff of wind would blow you away like tumbleweed."

Anna laughed and took the pipe. She sucked in a quick draw, feeling the smoke fill her lungs.

"You're a bad influence, Daisy-belle Farrow," Anna choked out, giving it back and feeling a wave of pleasant relaxation wash over her.

"Given how much poison your body has been subjected to in the last year, I'd say marijuana is the least of your worries, Annabelina Farrow," Dee declared, taking a last long draw.

Chapter 16

"OKAY, LET'S GET UNDERWAY," Anna called over her shoulder as she walked past her desk and into the meeting room.

Lissoni and Donaldson gathered laptops and notes and followed.

Anna sipped her coffee while they got settled and wondered how they would approach the week following Friday night's *discussion*. She had her own ideas and wondered how right she would prove to be.

As before, Anna sat with her back to the whiteboard, while Lissoni and Donaldson took seats opposite.

"I'd like to get your impressions of the Webbs' house." She looked from one to the other.

Donaldson opened his mouth to answer, but Lissoni cut him off. "Everything about the house indicates that the Webbs had a considerable amount of disposable income."

Anna nodded. "I agree. Did you notice the kitchen? It had every appliance and gadget known to man. I doubt I could name the purpose of even half of them"—her lips quirked upward—"but the majority of them looked unused. The games in the media room ... many still had plastic wrap on them."

"Sort of ... looked like they were trying too hard," Donaldson offered.

"Maybe they were trying to compensate for their unhappiness," Lissoni added. "You know, buying their way out of the pain."

"A strong possibility," Anna agreed. "But it's still a lot of *stuff*. All of which adds up to a *lot* of money." *And just where was it all coming from?*

"Another interesting point of note," she continued, "was the position of the camera in the kitchen. I remember you mentioned earlier, Margot, that the security cameras were there to monitor the babysitter's care of Ethan."

"Yes." Lissoni nodded. "That's what it said in the previous case notes."

"Hmm, well, I'd say it was to make sure that the babysitter didn't make off with anything from the house." Anna grimaced.

Donaldson frowned, doubt written across his face.

Anna caught his look. "The camera only covered the exits: the door to the laundry and the sliding door to the backyard, not the entire kitchen."

Donaldson shut his mouth with a snap. *How the hell had she seen that?!*

"I suppose we were lucky it covered the area near the fridge or we wouldn't have caught that argument between the Webbs. I'd bet the lounge room video was placed to monitor the front entrance," she said, and then sighed. "But in saying that, I don't think it moves our case forward, though it does shed some light on the Webbs as parents. Did you notice there were no children's skis in the garage, and no bike or play equipment in the yard? I hate to say it, but I think Ethan's landed on his feet at his grandparents," she added, shaking her head. *Some people really shouldn't have children.*

"Thoughts on what Fran Everington said?" Anna asked, changing tack.

This time Donaldson beat Lissoni to the punch. "Looks like Samantha had a boyfriend."

Anna nodded thoughtfully. "So, we have both Mr and Mrs Webb with possible romantic relationships, giving us even more reason to question why they did not split up."

She sat pondering that thought for several seconds before standing and walking to the window.

"How did you go with the phone records?" she asked, turning around and leaning on the sill.

"That's me," Donaldson answered immediately, thumbing quickly through the pages of his notebook. "There was no further activity on Tyler Webb's phone *after* Mrs Webb's murder. But the interesting thing is that there were no outgoing calls from his phone after the morning of the sixteenth. That's the day *before* Samantha Webb died."

"And his last call out was to ...?"

"The office. Said he wouldn't be in that afternoon, according to the receptionist for their business who was interviewed at the time. No reason given, apparently."

Anna gave him a thoughtful glance; he seemed to be putting in an effort. *Perhaps there was hope yet.*

"But what's more interesting," he remarked, trying to sound confident though he was well aware that it all contradicted his initial opinion, "are the incoming calls ... all of which went unanswered."

"Oh?"

"Seventeen missed calls from Samantha, starting from 5 pm on the sixteenth and ending at about 9 pm on the seventeenth."

"*Seventeen?*" Anna echoed.

"Yep. And five other incoming calls in the same period," he added. "One from Dean Teasel at around 9:30 pm on the sixteenth, and another four from a Lucy Manning. Two calls at approximately 8 and 10 pm on the sixteenth, and then, at around 11 am and 4 pm on the seventeenth. Lucy made one final call at ten, the morning of the eighteenth. I checked back and there were a lot of calls to and from Lucy over the last twelve months."

"Looks like we might have found our girlfriend. Let's set up an interview with Lucy. See what she has to say for herself," Anna said, a gleam in her eye. She loved the hunt; unpicking the intricate relationship of lies and facts that finally led to the truth.

Anna paced to the opposite wall and back to the window and turned with a finger up. Both sergeants watched her every move.

"So, Tyler comes home around lunchtime on the sixteenth and is not seen or heard from again until Stan raises him from the deep," Anna began. "The previous investigating team didn't find his phone or wallet, did they?" she added abruptly.

Donaldson shook his head. "No, they didn't."

"They searched both the house and office and neither was found," Lissoni added, "which they took to be an indication that Webb had taken off after the murder."

"Hmm, possible, especially now we know he had a girlfriend who might have picked him up," Anna pondered aloud as she sat back down at the table. "But …" she started, and then stopped, thinking it through. *It still left a lot of gaps, but it made sense.*

"What if he came home and went diving that afternoon and never returned?" Stunned silence followed.

Donaldson bit back a snort of disbelief. "Well, that works with the unanswered phone calls," he ventured finally, though doubt hung off every word.

"Are you saying someone killed them *both?*" Lissoni said, incredulous.

"Not necessarily … Tyler obviously intended to go diving, as he was in a wetsuit, so he *intended* to go into the lake. He *may* have been murdered, or his death may be an accident. All I'm saying is, what if he died on the sixteenth and Samantha was murdered on the seventeenth?"

Seeing the look of scepticism plastered on Donaldson's face, she added, "I have to admit, it *is* far-fetched … but let's say for the moment Tyler did go diving on the sixteenth. He comes home, gets changed and …' Anna paused before continuing, "Did either of you notice there was a track from the left-hand corner of the backyard down the gully to the lake edge below?"

Both Donaldson and Lissoni shook their heads. *Damn, she was observant.*

"No?" Anna queried mildly. "It *was* hard to see the gate. It would be a steep climb with a tank and fins, et cetera, but it *would* explain why no one saw him leave the house. So, what I'd like to do … or I should say, what I'd like one of you to do, since my legs are probably not up to it"—she sighed—"is to walk down that path and search the entire area at the bottom."

"You think his phone and wallet might be down there," Lissoni exclaimed.

"Worth checking, I think, even if it just rules it out," Anna said, pleased Lissoni had worked out the implications.

"Now circling back ... who is Dean Teasel? You said that was the other person who called Tyler's phone." Anna looked over to Donaldson.

"Their accountant."

Anna's eyebrows shot up. "And he was calling Tyler at nine thirty at night? Working overtime, was he? He'll be worth having a chat with as well, but let's have a quick review of the financials first."

"That's me," Lissoni said, pulling out a group of three clipped bundles of paper from a folder. "I've made a quick summary." She handed one each to Anna and Donaldson. She had, in fact, worked hours over the weekend pulling it together, knowing the inspector had asked for it at least twice before. She walked them through her calculations over the next several minutes.

"Their business pulled in less than two hundred thousand last year?" Anna frowned. "They don't do holiday rentals?"

"No, just straight sales," Lissoni replied, shaking her head.

"And they paid out over one hundred and forty thousand in credit card debit. Paid the receptionist fifty-five thousand. Then, there are leases on both cars, rental on their business premises, their house mortgage, school fees ... This doesn't add up." Anna tapped a fingernail on the summary in front of her. "Where's the money coming from?"

She got up and walked back to the window and looked out, though she took in nothing of the view.

Finally, she turned, walked back to the table and leant on a chair back. "Margot set up a time to talk to the accountant. There's more here than meets the eye. Jake, can you locate Lucy Manning? I'd like to pay her a visit tomorrow morning. And also, can one of you find out if either of the Webbs have other phones registered in their names, say, in the last three years, and also check whether Ethan has a phone in his name."

"*Ethan?*" Jake queried.

"Yeah, I had a case about a year or so ago where the guy used his child's phone for some rather suspect dealings."

"So, you're thinking they had some criminal connections," Lissoni said.

"Good chance of it judging by what you've dug up ... unless the accountant can pull a rabbit out of his hat.

"And I want to pay Mrs Carter-Ellis another visit ... but this time, preferably *without* her husband. So, let's get out there this afternoon, Margot, about the time *he'll* be off collecting Ethan from school with a bit of luck."

Chapter 17

"Why did you want to speak to Mrs Carter-Ellis without her husband there, Inspec ... er, *Boss*," Lissoni asked as she turned out of the police carpark.

Anna gave her a small smile. "We'll all get used to the names soon. It just struck me that she had a more ... *objective* view of her daughter than her husband. You'll remember she called her headstrong? Whereas *he* seemed to want to put all the blame for the failed relationship at Tyler's feet and his daughter on a pedestal. I may be wrong, but we'll see shortly."

Lissoni nodded, thinking it through. She had heard everything the inspector had at that first interview and had failed to recognise any of that. But now that she'd said it, Margot realised it was true. Samantha's father *was* the more emotional one. She gripped the wheel harder.

Thinking about Friday night's confrontation still made her stomach churn. What in hell had she been thinking, bagging out the inspector like that? Especially when she really hadn't actually believed any of it. That was the most irritating thing of all! She'd just gone along with Donaldson's ragging ... but no, she couldn't place the blame on him. She had to accept responsibility for what *she* had said. And the inspector was dead right; she didn't initiate, she just followed. Followed Donaldson's lead, *like a bloody sheep,* and look where that had got her!

What the hell is wrong with me?

She had spent most of Friday night churning over the inspector's brutal assessment. But she couldn't deny it. In a short five days, during which most of one day the inspector was out of action, the boss had nailed her to a tee! Was this really all she was capable of? She'd gone round and round over the same thought all weekend.

But no. She couldn't, and wouldn't, accept it. She knew there was more to her than what she'd shown so far. She needed to wake up, assert herself, and have her own opinion. Speak up. Look ahead. Look at what needed to be done, instead of waiting to be *told* what to do.

In the early hours of Saturday morning, her goal had crystallised. She wanted to be exactly like the inspector—confident, authoritative, and a bloody good detective. She had her vision, personified.

Lissoni knew she had a long way to go, but she was determined to turn the situation around. And she didn't need until next Friday week to decide.

The front door swung open. "Hello ... er ... please come in." Mrs Carter-Ellis held the door ajar and ushered them to the same sitting room.

"I'm sorry, Mark is out at the moment picking up Ethan from school, so it's just me," she added.

"That's fine, Mrs Carter-Ellis." Anna smiled. "If *you* have no objection."

"No, of course not," she answered, though her tone was slightly anxious. "Is it about Tyler? Is it confirmed ... that the body is him?"

"Not yet. We don't have the DNA results to confirm it definitively. Hopefully, it will only be another day or so. We just had a few background questions for you. You said the other day that neither you, nor your husband, liked Tyler, but Samantha married him nonetheless." Anna nodded encouragingly.

The older lady sighed heavily. "Yes, that's right. At first, we thought he was all right. At least he seemed a marked improvement over her previous boyfriend! Though that wasn't saying much," she added bitterly. "But then, as we got to know Tyler, we realised he was another poor choice for her."

"In what way?"

Sally looked away, considering her words, and then turned back. "My daughter, Samantha, was ... *difficult.* I think it was largely our own fault, we spoiled her. You see, we had trouble conceiving and when we finally had Sam ... *well* ... she was everything to us. Mark particularly indulged her. She could do no wrong in his eyes. When she was small, her tantrums and demands were *endearing* and *showing character*, but as she hit the teenage years, I realised we'd made a rod for our own backs. She would throw a violent tantrum if she didn't get what she wanted ... and she *wanted* a lot! She wouldn't do anything I asked of her and Mark ... well, she had him wrapped around her little finger." She sighed again.

"Samantha had a string of awful boyfriends and became quite wild for a time. There seemed nothing we could do. My hope was that she would find someone who could help her become a responsible adult. Do what we had failed to do, I suppose. But Tyler was just the opposite. A young man who was equally irresponsible. Whose idea of adulthood was to do as he pleased. Even when they had Ethan, they carried on as if nothing had changed. He was foisted on a number of nannies and babysitters, poor little boy! We stepped in as much as possible to try and give him some proper care."

"You had Ethan at your house on the night before Samantha died, I understand."

The older lady nodded; she suddenly looked older. "Oh, yes. We had him most weekends and usually one- or two-nights midweek."

"Why was that? Did they work late?"

Sally shook her head. "Not usually. They were just ... *busy.* Drinks, and dinners, and whatever they felt like," she declared, bitterness edging her tone.

After a brief pause to let that settle, Anna continued, "Mrs Carter-Ellis, there's been an indication that Samantha may have had a boyfriend. Do you know anything about that?"

Sally closed her eyes and shook her head, but seemingly not in negation, since she added, "I thought as much. There were a few times when she rang, and I could hear someone there with her ... and it wasn't Tyler. She was not one to exercise restraint—if she wanted something, she went after it—she never considered the consequences."

"Do you have any idea of who that person might have been? Did you recognise the voice?"

The old lady shook her head. "No. I'm sorry." Her face clouded over, and she frowned. "Are you suggesting it might *not* have been Tyler who killed her?"

"We're exploring all possibilities," Anna commented with deliberate vagueness. "You mentioned that Tyler was a step up over her previous boyfriend. What can you tell me about him?" she added, earning herself a sharp look from Lissoni.

Sally grimaced. "Oh, he was just awful. A thug and a criminal. He threatened Mark one day when Mark told him off for swearing at Sam. He meant it too! His name was Nathan Foley." She shuddered.

"What business was he in?"

"Oh, goodness knows! Something illegal. He would never say, and neither would Sam. But I can tell you he always had loads of money. I'm sure that was part of his appeal for Sam."

"I see, thanks. Now I believe Samantha rang you the morning she died," Anna queried.

"Yes, that's right. We didn't speak long. She just asked me to keep Ethan for another night," Sally said, her voice strained.

"Did Samantha sound any different? Or did you notice anything particular about her during the conversation?"

"Well, actually"—she clenched her hands tightly together—"she sounded stressed. I asked her why she wanted us to have Ethan another night. Not that we didn't want him! It wasn't that at all," she added quickly, as if Anna might get the wrong idea. "We loved having him. It's just … well … I was trying to make a point, I suppose. She always just assumed she would get her own way and sometimes …" She closed her eyes and shook her head.

"I can imagine that might have been tiresome," Anna agreed softly.

"Yes, it was. But I've regretted it so many times since then as she blew up immediately; screamed at me ... accused me of abandoning her when she needed help." The old lady's voice was tight with emotion.

"What do you think she meant by that?"

Sally shook her head, eyes brimming. "She said something like ... Tyler had ... eff'ed off ... excuse me ... and *she* was left to deal with the fallout."

Anna heard a car pull up outside and knew their time was limited.

"And then?"

"I said I was sorry and that, of course, I'd keep Ethan another night. She hung up. That was the last time I spoke to her. I didn't even tell her I loved her!" she whispered.

Anna murmured something inarticulate in sympathy. She had heard that cry from victims' families countless times. That they hadn't got to tell their husband, wife, child, or other family member, just how much they were loved before they died. *Was it so important to say it at that moment? Wasn't it more important that the person knew they were loved? Did they need to hear it that one last time?* She shook her head. Whatever she thought, situations like this affected people deeply; who was she to question it?

The front door opened, and they could hear Ethan's piping voice.

Anna stood up. "Thank you, Sally. We appreciate you being so candid with us. Mr Carter-Ellis," she added with a nod, as he entered the room.

He stopped abruptly, his gaze swung from his wife and then back to Anna. His mouth tightened. "More questions?"

"Just a couple. We're trying to pin down some timeframes," Anna said.

"About when I last spoke to Sam," Sally added quietly.

"Thanks again." Anna gave her a brief smile and with another nod at the old man, they walked out.

Lissoni shot glances at the inspector on the drive back. Anna was staring out of the side window and looked preoccupied. Lissoni hesitated to interrupt her thought process, but finally curiosity, and her new resolve to be assertive, overcame her reservations.

"Boss, can you tell me what the question regarding the old boyfriend was about?"

Anna pulled herself out of her reverie and turned towards Lissoni.

"Well, Mrs Carter-Ellis mentioned him in passing—she didn't need to—and I've found that people only do that when something about it bothers them. It may turn out to be nothing. Only that she disliked him and felt he was a bad influence on her daughter. But even so, it was further illustration of the type of personality Sam was. I have a feeling I wouldn't have liked her much," Anna said drily.

"Me either! She sounded like a complete bitch!"

Chapter 18

"WHAT'S UP? WHAT'S THE emergency?" Mick asked as he sat down and accepted the beer that Dean pushed across the table.

Jono just rolled his eyes and hugged his beer.

"The police called this afternoon, and they want to see me tomorrow," Dean blurted and then looked around to see if anyone had heard. But as usual, the bar was busy with the after-work crowd, and everyone was too intent on their own business to bother taking any notice of them.

"So?" Mick smacked his lips after taking a long swig.

"So? What am I supposed to say?" The stress made Dean's question come out in a near squeak.

Mick looked at Jono, who shrugged in reply, his expression bored and uninterested.

"You were their accountant ... I'd imagine they want to talk to you about their finances." Mick frowned. "What are you afraid of? What's going on?"

Dean swallowed and ran a hand nervously back and forth over his dark hair.

"You were cooking the books, weren't you?" Jono declared suddenly.

Mick looked shocked and turned to Dean. "Is that true?"

Dean's breathing increased, and a slick of sweat shone on his face. He nodded.

Mick sat back abruptly, but Jono lurched forward, grabbed Dean by his shirt front and pulled him half out of his chair.

"You *bastard!* You did that for *them?* How about *me?* How come you didn't do it for me!"

Mick grabbed his arm and shook him loose. "Chill, Jono," he murmured, looking around with a reassuring smile at the other patrons, who had turned to check out the raised voices.

He waited until they all became engrossed in their own business again and then turned and glared at Dean disgustedly. "I'd like to know the answer to that question too," he said in an ominous undertone.

Dean shook his head and rubbed a hand through his hair again. "Look I'm *sorry*! They had more opportunities … with the business and all," he murmured, sounding lame even to his own ears.

Mick stared at him. "What about *my* business?" he bit out in a furious hiss.

Jono leant forward. "You were sniffing around after Sam, weren't you?" he said, perceptive as always.

Dean looked down at the table and then up again; guilt written all over his face.

"Shit!" Mick grunted with disgust. "You *stupid* prick! She talked you into it, didn't she?"

Dean nodded miserably.

"What? You thought if you got her some extra cash, she'd put out for you, did you?" Mick sneered.

"No, no!" Dean cried. "Of course not! She just—"

"That's *exactly* what you thought!" Jono barked a laugh and slapped him on the shoulder in one of his rapid changes of mood. "Ha! You might have got some in the end, too. Sam wasn't choosy," he added cruelly.

Dean flushed hotly but made no comment.

"Well, she's fucked you now, mate." Jono laughed delightedly at his own wit.

"What the hell do I *do?*" Dean asked desperately.

"Well, I'm not sure how Jono and I can help you, Deano." Mick's tone was deceptively quiet.

Dean cringed and shook his head; he looked close to tears.

"You must have thought this might happen eventually," Mick added after several minutes of brooding silence.

Dean nodded. "I just hoped they wouldn't dig too deep. And they didn't after Sam died, but it looks like now they've found Webby they aren't satisfied …"

"Well"—Mick shrugged, and Dean looked up hopefully—"I'd say whatever you need to. Remember, *they're* both dead. They can't deny anything you say, so blame them.

"But for that bit of advice," he added, his eyes narrowed, leaning into Dean's face, "I'm gonna expect some creative accounting from you in the future!"

Dean threw himself on the couch when he arrived home barely a half an hour later. He lay there for a while before sitting up and putting his head in his hands. Not only did he have the police interview tomorrow, and God only knew what he'd say then, but now he'd pissed off Jono and Mick as well.

Not for the first time, Dean wondered how his life might have been different had he picked other friends. But he knew that given the time over again, he'd have chosen the same path. He still remembered his five-year-old self on his first day at school, sick with anxiety and wishing the floor would open up and swallow him. His mum crying and clinging to him at the school gate in front of everyone. Even the memory of it still made him cringe. He hadn't even walked in the schoolroom door, and he was marked as different. All the other parents just gave their offspring a quick hug and a smile before departing, a wet eye, *at most,* amongst their number. A far cry from his mother's almost desperate wailing. His teacher had to come and extract him from his mother's clutches in order to get him into the classroom.

He had suffered through that first week, alone and lonely and hating every minute of it. He watched the other kids gravitate to each other, forming cliques and friendships, and yet he was never able to work out how it was done. Weeks turned into months and still he remained the odd one out. And after that it seemed like a self-fulfilling prophecy—because he had no friends, the others thought him strange, which meant they didn't want to be his friend.

Sometimes, he tried to imagine how life would have been had Tyler not intervened when one of the older kids started to bully him. He never understood why he did. Tyler was not a caring or compassionate soul. In fact, truth be told, he was far from it, being self-absorbed and shallow for the most part, but for some reason on that day, he had stepped in, and Dean's life suddenly changed. He had dragged Dean over to the other two sitting on the far side of the playground.

"What did ya bring *him* over here for?" Jono sneered.

Tyler just shrugged. "He's okay," he'd said and pulled Dean down next to him. After a brief moment of thoughtful consideration, Mick nodded, and that was that. From then on, he was one of the 'four'. The inseparable four. And his life changed. He had friends; he was normal.

Was that why he'd agreed to doctor the books for the Webbs? Risk his career and potentially his freedom? Payback for that simple but life-changing gesture from Tyler. In part perhaps, but he knew, in the end, it had been Sammie. Jono was right there. He always was uncannily perceptive, Jono. Probably because of reading his dad's moods to avoid getting belted.

If Dean had to suffer his mother's separation anxiety and smothering, Jono had a far worse situation. His father was a mean, angry alcoholic. Jono had been only four years old when he was left to the tender mercies of a violent and unstable father, after his mum finally had enough and departed their lives. Other than instilling him with uncanny instincts, it had also made Jono a resentful and bitter man, who approached life with an attitude of hard-done-by belligerence.

Dean sighed. *Sammie.* Wild, wicked, selfish Sammie.

He had been under her thrall from the first moment that he saw her at twenty-one: standing, incandescent with anger, in the doorway at a raucous party at Mick's. Her large, unfettered breasts bouncing under her thin cotton dress as she jabbed a finger viciously in her boyfriend's chest. Her long blonde mass of hair sliding across her shoulders and her eyes blazing. The boyfriend shoved her away and stormed off, and Sammie stumbled back against the wall.

He never remembered crossing the distance to help her, but he remembered the electric jolt he'd felt as he put a hand on her arm. She had shoved *him* away, threw back her hair and tugged down her dress. He just stared at her.

"What's *your* problem?"

"I ... I just wanted to see if you were alright," he stuttered.

She looked him up and down candidly and gave the briefest of nods, as if he'd just barely met her criteria of acceptability.

"How about getting me a drink?" She pouted, suddenly all wide-eyed and inviting smile. He nodded like a marionette and rushed off to get her drink of choice.

He returned just five minutes later to find Tyler leaning against the wall. In front of him was Sammie, all boobs, long, golden hair, and gleaming white teeth, seemingly happy to be bracketed by his rival.

"Thanks, mate," Tyler quipped, taking the drink from Dean's numb fingers and handing it to her with a grin. From that moment, Tyler and Sam had been an item. And from that night, Dean had loved Sammie unequivocally.

What was it about one person that struck a chord deep within you, so deep that common sense and your conscious mind had no control over it? Sammie was not kind or funny or intelligent, not any of the things you would normally associate with the person who was the love of your life.

She was, in fact, so self-absorbed that she saw things only in relation to how they impacted her. Sammie's world revolved entirely around herself. Even the birth of Ethan had not revealed a deeper, less selfish Sammie. Her irritation and annoyance at the constant inconvenience of her baby's existence were the only additional notes to her personality.

But despite seeing all of Sammie's flaws, his love for her had not dimmed one iota.

Where did that wellspring of feeling come from? he wondered. *Was it some chemical attraction, one born in the skin and therefore totally outside intelligent analysis?* He had pondered it so many times and yet was no closer to working it out than he ever was.

Sammie. He sank back into the couch and let the essence of her wash over him. He could still feel her velvet-soft, pale gold skin under his fingertips, smell the scent of her arousal, feel the silk of her hair as it slid across his chest.

Jono was right. She had offered him the taste of her body for dodgy-ing up their accounts. But even Jono had never suspected that he had taken her up on it. For Sam, it was purely quid pro quo at first, and he was only too aware that he was receiving no more than payment in kind. But as her relationship with Tyler deteriorated—as it could only ever have done with two such selfish individuals—her desire to keep him, Dean, on a string, increased. *Was it just to satisfy her sexual desires? A means of getting back at Tyler by sleeping with his friend? Or was it a way for her to feel desirable and needed when her husband treated her as no more than part of the furniture?* Whatever her reason, he hadn't cared, so long as he could be with her.

Sammie. God, he missed her so much!

Chapter 19

"Great thanks, Rodney," Anna said, ending the call early the next morning.

Lissoni looked up from her desk expectantly.

"It's Webb," Anna called over the partition.

Lissoni nodded. Her first inclination was to say, 'That's great news', but other than the fact that it meant they hadn't been wasting their time over the last week, it could hardly be considered good news that their dead body was confirmed as someone's father or friend.

"Morning." Donaldson walked up, his light brown hair slicked back, still wet from his morning shower.

"Morning," Anna and Lissoni answered in unison.

"Let's catch up," Anna added, walking into the meeting room.

"—she sounded like a right piece of work!" Donaldson commented, some minutes later. Lissoni had just finished describing their meeting with Samantha Webb's mother the previous afternoon.

"True." Anna nodded, glancing over at him. "Excellent work on finding the wallet and phone."

He had called to give her the news as Lissoni drove them back to the office.

She saw his chest swell and his naturally dour expression soften and suppressed a smile. *Funny how just a few words of praise could make such a difference!*

"Yeah! It was *right* there," he enthused. "The path looked really steep, but actually it wasn't too bad once you were on it, so I could see how Webb would have used it as easy access to the lake.

"Basically, at the bottom there's a small beach, and on one side, a rocky overhang. A bag with his keys, wallet, and phone was there, as were a pair of shoes. I found an old towel in the scrub behind the beach. Not sure if it was his or not, but it would have made sense to have one if he was coming out of the lake."

"Right so, he definitely *intended* to go into the lake. The question is why?" Anna pondered for a few seconds before turning her attention back to them.

"Perhaps Ms Manning might shed some light on the matter."

They left Jindabyne and skirted around the southern end of the lake, before turning left and following the Alpine Way into the mountains. As Donaldson was driving, Anna took the opportunity to relax and appreciate the scenery. It had been several years since she'd last been into Thredbo, the small alpine village tucked into a steep valley in the middle of the national park.

The day was bright with the crisp, clear air of late autumn. In another four or five weeks, the roads would be jammed with eager skiers and snowboarders keen to make the most of the short Australian ski season. But their journey today was unhindered, with only resort and national park employees on the road, busy with pre-season activities.

Anna eventually pulled her gaze from the deep green of the dense bushland that crowded the winding road and turned to Donaldson.

"What do we know about Ms Manning, Tyler's supposed girlfriend?"

"Well, from what I could find out, she's twenty-two and works as marketing coordinator for the Snowy Ski Resort," Donaldson responded, his eyes glued to the winding road.

"Twenty-two?" Lissoni repeated from the backseat with raised eyebrows.

"Hmm, young," he agreed. "She grew up around here, went to Jindy High and then did a course in marketing at TAFE. She's been working here at the resort for the last couple of years."

Anna nodded, pleased he'd done some homework.

He turned right and wound his way down to the village, pulling into the carpark fronting the river that separated the tiny town and lodgings from the ticketing office and ski slopes. They stepped out of the car and quickly buttoned jackets, and Anna pulled on her woollen beanie.

She took her time on the steep steps that rose from the valley bottom and into the main village square. Donaldson raced ahead, taking the stairs two at a time, but Lissoni slowed to match Anna's pace. She took pains to look nonchalant, as if this were her preferred speed.

Anna blew out a long breath. *The damned neuropathy wasn't improving at all!* This, more than anything, made her feel like she was sick, and she hated it! She gritted her teeth as they approached yet another set of steep stone stairs.

As she reached the top, she took a deep breath and slowly followed Donaldson, who had been waiting impatiently, towards a small office building to the right. With the sergeants leading the way, Anna entered a small, but well-appointed office. The reception desk was unmanned, but the fading tinkling of a bell had announced their arrival. A lady, who looked to be in her late forties, approached with a welcoming smile.

"Good morning. Can I help you?"

The smile slid off her face as Lissoni introduced them. It contracted to a concerned frown when they asked to speak to Lucy Manning.

"Lucy?" she repeated in a horrified tone.

"Is she here?" Lissoni added.

"Oh ... yes, of course." The lady nodded, shooting a glance over her shoulder, but making no effort to move.

"Do you have a meeting room where we might speak to Lucy privately?" Anna asked, swiping off her beanie.

"Yes, yes, I do," the lady replied, completely flustered. "Er-r, do you want to come through and then I'll get Lucy, shall I?"

"Thank you, that would be great." Anna smothered a smile. It was always fascinating, the variety of reactions that she and her colleagues evoked when out and about in the community. Likely, this was the first time this lady had ever had an encounter with the police, other than perhaps the odd parking or speeding fine. She acted as if they had just dropped from the moon or, perhaps more likely, rose from hell.

They followed the woman down the hall and into a small meeting room. She stood wringing her hands in the doorway.

"Thank you, Ms ...?" Anna paused, looking expectant.

"Er—Banks, Helena Banks," she responded.

"Well, Ms Banks, if you wouldn't mind fetching Lucy now, that would be helpful," Anna said.

"Oh, yes ... *right*," she mumbled and rushed away.

"Geezus! Do we really look that frightening?" Lissoni chuckled as she took a seat.

Anna gave a depreciating grin. "*You* don't ..." She ran a hand ruefully across the auburn fuzz that covered her skull.

They settled down and waited in silence. It was several minutes later that the handle turned, and the door opened slowly.

Lucy stood in the doorway, her face pale, and her strawberry blonde hair pulled back into a long ponytail. Her wide hazel eyes held a look of pure terror.

"Lucy." Anna smiled, feeling rather like the wolf in Hansel and Gretel. "Come in and sit down."

Lucy hesitantly approached the table, pulled out a chair, and sat on the very edge of it. She looked ready to bolt.

"Lucy. This is Sergeant Donaldson and Sergeant Lissoni and I'm Inspector Farrow from the NSW police," Anna said, looking at her intently.

Lucy swallowed, started to speak, then stopped and started again. "Wh-hy are you here?"

Anna folded her hands in front of her and leant forward. "I think you know why we're here," she said gently.

Lucy's face crumpled, and tears sprang into her eyes. "It's ... about ... *Tyler*, isn't it?"

Anna nodded.

"Then it's definitely him?" Lucy whispered.

"Yes. The body in the lake *is* Tyler Webb."

Lucy put her hands to her face and cried, broken-hearted.

"Jake, can you see if you can find some water," Anna asked after a minute and, looking back at Lucy, added, "and some tissues."

He nodded abruptly and left, only too glad to have something to do *outside* of the room.

Lissoni stood up and patted Lucy's shoulder sympathetically. Anna checked her phone for messages.

It was a further fifteen minutes before they were all settled around the table again. Only red eyes and the occasional sniff from Lucy remained as evidence of her crying jag.

"Are you going to arrest me?" she said pathetically, looking around at the three of them, her gaze settling finally on Anna.

"That would depend on what you have to say and how cooperative you are, Lucy. Let's begin, shall we?"

Lucy nodded, looking miserable.

"Tell me about your relationship with Tyler," Anna asked. But then seeing the blank look on Lucy's face, added, "Where and when did you meet?"

Lucy swallowed and took a deep breath. "We met when Tyler was showing my parents a house they were thinking of buying. I went with them to check it out. He ... we ... well, we sort of started seeing each other after that."

"When was this?"

"January, two years ago."

"And the relationship continued until—?"

"Until last March when he ... *he ... disappeared,*" she wailed, dissolving into tears again.

Anna looked over to see Donaldson roll his head back, clearly frustrated. She sighed. *Yep ... I know exactly how you feel.*

The sobbing finally eased off, and Lucy sat there hiccupping quietly.

"Are you okay to continue, Lucy?" Anna asked gently, sensing the moment had come.

"Yes, I'm okay," she answered weakly.

"You knew Tyler was married?"

Lucy nodded. "Tyler told me right at the start that he was married. He was very honest about it. His wife was *horrible* to him. There was *nothing* between them anymore."

Except their son, Anna felt like saying.

"We were going to get married. Tyler loved me and I loved him. He wanted to get a divorce. He talked about it all the time, but *she* wouldn't agree and ... then just as he'd finally worked it out ... he ... he—"

"So, when you say, 'he worked it out', what do you mean?" Anna cut in, hoping to head off another meltdown.

Lucy swallowed and straightened up. "Well ... he was always on at her to give him a divorce so we could be together, but she wouldn't agree," she said bitterly. "He begged her, but she wouldn't budge. He said it was because she wanted to make him suffer. And then, about a week before he went missing—" She heaved brokenly.

Anna felt Donaldson tense up beside her, but Lucy weathered the emotional storm this time.

"—he said he had worked out a plan. A way to *make* her agree. It was all going to work out ..." Lucy's voice dropped to a whisper.

"Did he tell you what the plan was?"

Lucy shook her head. "No. He said he couldn't tell me. Only that it was foolproof."

Hmm ... *'the best laid schemes o' mice an' men gang aft agley'*, quoted Anna silently. *How often that proved true! Robert Burns had a clear insight into human nature when he wrote that!*

"And when was this plan to take place?" Anna queried.

"March 16 last year."

Lissoni and Donaldson stirred, their interest piqued.

"When did you last speak to, or hear from, Tyler?"

"He came over on Tuesday night; that was the night before, on the fifteenth. He was really excited. He said the plan couldn't fail. That he'd beat the bitch at her own game. He said it would be all over by the next night. I rang him when I didn't hear from him as planned, but he didn't answer. I rang again later in the evening, but he didn't return my call. I rang a couple of times the next day, but he never rang me back. I called him again the following morning ... Then I saw the news," she added in a whisper. "Samantha had been killed. They said it was Tyler."

"What did *you* think?" Anna asked curiously.

"Well, that was ... *messy*," Jake said heavily.

They sat at a small café off the main square in the village. Anna had suggested having lunch in the village before heading back to interview Dean Teasel. It was an opportunity to see how Donaldson and Lissoni processed the interview with Lucy and also, she was absolutely starving.

After placing their orders, they regrouped at a table near a window, which offered a view of the ski runs opposite. The trails were like a network of wide interwoven roads running down through the olive-green bush.

"She was upset, Jake." Lissoni frowned.

His eyes widened. "He's been gone a *year!*"

"So? She'd just found out he was dead! What did you expect?"

Jake looked at her, dumbfounded. "You didn't think it was all a bit over the top?"

"No! I didn't! … What? You think she was putting it on?" Lissoni cried.

Donaldson shrugged as if it were obvious.

Lissoni turned to the inspector. "You didn't think that was put on, did you, Boss?"

"Well, it's an interesting question," Anna said with a hint of a smile, earning a puzzled look from them both. "Let me ask you a question first, Margot. What was your take on Mrs Carter-Ellis yesterday? Did you think she mourned her daughter?"

Lissoni looked taken aback but then gathered her thoughts. "I suppose I thought she was a bit cold and unfeeling. I mean, she was brutally honest about her daughter, wasn't she? And though at the end she seemed a bit upset when said she hadn't had a chance to tell her daughter she loved her … well, otherwise … she was pretty in control the whole time."

Anna nodded. "Interesting. I had the exact opposite impression of her."

Lissoni flushed.

"No, I'm not saying you're wrong, Margot. Your impression is no more accurate than mine. *I* thought Mrs Carter-Ellis was suffering. That she harboured some deep regrets, and though she was honest about her daughter's character, as you said, she was actually heartbroken to have lost her."

"But—" Lissoni started with a frown. "Then, who's right?"

"Both of us and none of us," Anna replied with a wry grin.

"The way I see it," she continued, "and this comes from years of observing victims, villains and the police; as humans, we have a tendency to prefer, or maybe *attribute* more *value* to those who are *like* us; who act like us, *react* like us and, if you go far enough along that path, who *look* like us.

"So, on the big stuff, differences might lead to racist attitudes; but at the next level down, perhaps it's just being uncomfortable around new immigrants because they speak or act differently to us. But it can influence even the little things as well. Take today, for example. *You* thought Lucy's grief believable and quite as expected." She looked at Margot, who nodded, still thinking she had it wrong somehow.

"For Jake and me, however, we thought her reaction was altogether *too* much, a little ... *overly* dramatic, shall we say."

Jake nodded, a smug look on his face.

"What I *think*," Anna said, choosing her words carefully, "is that we tend to believe those people who react like *we* would. It's something, as investigators, we need to be both aware of and very *wary* of. Just because Lucy's reaction made *me* uncomfortable doesn't mean it wasn't just as you said, Margot, a true representation of her deep and heartfelt grief. Remember the Azaria Chamberlain case back in the early eighties? People felt that Lindy Chamberlain appeared cold-hearted and unfeeling. Therefore, there was a groundswell of negative opinion about her and a general willingness to believe she had killed her baby daughter. But just think, if she *had* done it, don't you think she would have put on more of a performance to cover it up?"

"So, how do you work out who's spinning you a yarn and who's telling you the truth if you can't trust your instincts?" Jake asked, his tone slightly frustrated.

"A very good question," Anna said. "You can bounce it off your colleagues as we're doing now, and if they have a very different idea from yours, then that should temper your opinion. But even if you *all* agree, that might still not be correct. It might be only that you all have similar backgrounds and see things in the same light. For me, the *most* important thing to keep in mind is that someone's *reaction* is just one small part of the whole picture. You need to consider what they say, what words they use, the circumstances, and what other facts you have."

"Keep an open mind then," Donaldson muttered sourly, recalling her words from the Friday night before and knowing she was making a point specifically to him.

Anna's lips twitched upwards. "Yep!"

Chapter 20

"Dean Teasel is in Interview Room 2, Inspector," the desk sergeant called as she walked through the front door.

"He's early." She raised an eyebrow. "Keen, or just nervous, I wonder. Jake, can you get the file and notes from my desk? We'll meet you in there."

He nodded and walked away.

"Mr Teasel, thank you for coming in," Anna said as Lissoni closed the door behind them. "I'm Inspector Farrow and this is Sergeant Lissoni. Sergeant Donaldson will be joining us momentarily."

Teasel lifted a shoulder briefly in acknowledgement. He was jiggling a knee nervously. In fact, he seemed very tense, like a tightly wound spring, which piqued her interest.

She looked him over carefully as she took a seat. He had dark, almost black hair, brushed back from a broad forehead and rather striking light hazel eyes. He was fairly tall and had the build of a marathon runner: lean, almost to the point of emaciation, which made his cheekbones and jawline very prominent. She was reminded of that old actor, Montgomery Clift, who always seemed to play the part of the troubled and sensitive young man in his movies.

The door opened and Jake walked in. After placing the case file in front of her, he sat down.

"Mr Teasel, we asked you to come into today as we have some questions for you regarding the financial affairs of Tyler and Samantha Webb—" Anna started.

"So it's definitely Tyler? The body in the lake?"

"Yes, that's been confirmed now. You were their accountant, I believe."

Dean Teasel licked his lips nervously and cleared his throat. "Yeah, well, sort of ... I gave them a hand occasionally with their tax and stuff."

Anna's eyebrow twitched at the equivocation. Apparently, he was going to try to distance himself from the situation.

"Are you saying you *weren't* responsible for their business accounts?" Anna asked.

"Well ... you know ... I gave them advice, of course," Teasel said, trying, *and failing*, to appear casual. "They were friends of mine ... so I helped them out occasionally, but ... they did a lot of it themselves."

Anna let the silence expand for several seconds, which she finally broke with a quiet, "I see.

"So, in your opinion, was their business doing well?" she continued.

Dean shrugged. "Yeah, well enough ... from what I knew."

"From what we've been able to ascertain, the Webbs spent quite a lot more money than they made from their real estate business. Would you have any thoughts about that?"

Teasel shifted in his seat. "I ... don't know anything about that."

"Would you have any idea where they were getting the extra cash from?" Anna queried.

"No," Teasel said bluntly.

"And you know of no other investments or business they were engaged in other than their real estate company?" Anna persisted, knowing she was beating a dead horse.

"Like I said ... *no!* I only know about their real estate business," he snapped.

"You said you were a friend of theirs?"

"Yeah, so?" Dean scowled.

"I'm sorry for your loss," Anna offered, taking him by surprise.

"Oh yeah, it's been ... *difficult*," he answered, slightly disconcerted.

"How did you know them?"

"Tyler and I went to school together. We've been mates since we were five. We met in kindergarten. We were close," Dean finished, barely audible. Anna didn't doubt it.

Mark Carter-Ellis' words resounded in her ear: *Tyler was always hanging around with his mates ... Three idiots that he went to school with.*

"And his wife? How did you know her? Through Tyler?"

"Sort of. I met her the same night she started going out with Tyler," he replied. Anna thought she detected an element of strain in his voice.

"As you knew them so well, what can you tell me about their relationship?"

Dean looked around the room seeking inspiration, then shrugged. "At first, it was good. They seemed happy together. Bought out the guy they both worked for and ran the business themselves. Things were good for a while, but ... then the cracks started to show."

"In what way?" Anna prompted.

"They spent less time together and Tyler started to bitch about Sammie all the time."

Anna paused, letting that comment hang.

"When Samantha was killed, did you think Tyler was responsible?"

Dean nodded, though she could sense his reluctance. "Yeah. They absolutely hated each other in the end. We assumed he just snapped."

"I find it strange that they didn't consider splitting up if they disliked each other so much."

Teasel shrugged again. "I know Tyler wanted to, but Sam wouldn't agree."

"Have you any thoughts on *why* she wouldn't have agreed?"

Dean examined his fingernails. "She just said it would make it too difficult for them to run the business together if they divorced."

"Were you aware Mr Webb had a girlfriend?" Anna asked.

Dean nodded. "Sure. We all knew about Lucy."

"Including Samantha?"

Dean hesitated and then shrugged once again. "How should I know?"

"Lucy was under the impression that Tyler had a plan to persuade Samantha to give him a divorce," Anna said, watching Teasel intently.

Dean snorted. "I'm sure he told *her* that."

"So, you don't believe it? You don't think Tyler had a plan?"

"No. There was no way Sammie was going to let him off the hook."

"You know that Tyler was found in the lake, but were you aware he was dressed in dive gear?" Anna continued.

Dean nodded.

"We could see by the equipment in the Webbs' house that he was into diving. Did he often dive alone?"

Dean shook his head vehemently. "No, never on his own. We always went together. We learnt to dive together, and we always dived as a group, especially in the lake. It's a dangerous dive. Lots of snags and sometimes really poor visibility. It's not the place to dive solo. I don't know why he would have gone by himself. He *knew* we'd have gone with him if he'd of just asked."

"When was the last time you spoke to Tyler, or Samantha?"

Dean swallowed and a faint sheen of sweat popped out on his forehead.

"Oh, well ... I spoke to Tyler on the morning of March 16. He was at the office and I dropped by to ask him about some rece—" He stopped short and then finished lamely, "Er ... some stuff."

"You made a call to Tyler later that night, didn't you, Mr Teasel?"

He paled and nodded. "He didn't pick up," he muttered.

"And Samantha?"

"What about her?"

"When was the last time you spoke to her?" Anna repeated.

"Oh, ah ... I don't remember; no idea."

Chapter 21

"Thoughts on our friend, Mr Teasel?" Anna began as the three detectives sat in the meeting room sometime later.

"My first impression was that he knew a lot more than he was telling us," Lissoni said.

Anna nodded and looked at Jake.

"He was sweating bullets by the end. I think he knew a lot more about their accounts than he was letting on. But with the other two dead, that's going to be hard to prove."

"He *did* confirm what Lucy Manning said this morning, that Tyler wanted a divorce, and it was Samantha who was holding out," Lissoni added.

Anna stood and walked to the window and looked out for a few seconds. The day had changed, and the sky was now a deep leaden grey. She wondered if they might get a snow shower later on.

"Don't you think it ... *sad* ... that everyone—Sam's parents, his girlfriend, and even his close friends—all thought Tyler killed Samantha?" she said to the window. She had been taken aback at Lucy's tearful confession that that was what she had assumed. That Tyler's plan, whatever that had been, had derailed, and, in anger and frustration, he had lashed out and killed Sam.

"Yeah, there doesn't appear to be anyone in doubt that he was capable of it," Donaldson agreed.

"Given what we heard about Samantha from her mother, I'd say that she and Tyler were a perfect match!" Lissoni said with a roll of her eyes.

"Hmm, I think perhaps you're right. But in this case, I have a feeling they were *too* alike for it to work," Anna sighed. Two selfish, thoughtless individuals. In the beginning she could imagine they had shared some wild indulgent times, but as business and family responsibilities intruded on their lives, the resentment and bitterness would have swelled to the fore. Each would have tried to follow their own self-centred interests, at the cost to the other.

"What was your take on Teasel, Boss?" Donaldson asked.

"Well, like you, I thought he was probably up to his neck in some dodgy accounting. I think we might consider digging a little deeper into that once we have the Webbs' deaths put to bed. But I had a few other takeaways from the discussion. Firstly, I think Teasel was genuinely shocked that Tyler went diving by himself, so we can assume that the circumstances must have been *very* unusual for Tyler to have done so. He and his mates are very close from what the Carter-Ellis' said and also the way in which Teasel kept answering with 'we' ... 'we all knew', 'we assumed'. Therefore, it must have been an extremely secret or sensitive reason that made Tyler go into the lake without inviting at least one of them along to help."

"Maybe there is a third party we haven't identified," Lissoni offered. "Perhaps he didn't go by himself, but it's just that he didn't go with one of his mates."

"You're right, Margot. We have no *proof* he went by himself." Anna nodded. They had pondered this scenario initially, and at this point, there was still nothing to confirm or deny it. She was pleased Lissoni had raised it again.

"But if he went with an unknown third party, then we still have the possibility he was murdered, don't we?" Donaldson said. "After all, if it was *just* a dive, then the partner would have called for help if Tyler had gotten into difficulties or, say, accidentally died."

Anna tapped her chin with a pen thoughtfully. "Yes, an unknown third party is still a possibility that we shouldn't discount."

After several seconds of quiet, Lissoni piped up, "You said there were a *few* takeaways from the discussion, Boss, what else did you think?"

"Well, the next thought I had was that Teasel might be our triple zero caller."

"*Seriously?*" Lissoni cried incredulously.

"*What?*" Donaldson blurted at the same time.

"I may be wrong, of course; we need to dig a little deeper." Anna couldn't help smiling at their flabbergasted faces.

"Do you remember the triple zero call?" she continued. "The person called her *Sammie.* Not Sam ... not Samantha ... *Sammie.* Teasel referred to her as Sammie *twice* during our interview. And he was definitely *very* nervous and vague about when he last saw Samantha, which is unusual. In my experience, most people remember the last time they saw a friend when that person dies unexpectedly. It's like the shock of sudden death plants that last encounter firmly in your brain."

"Yeah, it does," Lissoni agreed, nodding. "I can remember *everything* about a call I had with a friend of mine. It was nothing special or noteworthy at the time, but it ended up being the last conversation I had with her as she was killed in a car accident later that same night."

Anna murmured sympathetically before continuing, "And even if you're a bit fuzzy on when you saw them last, you'd take a stab at it wouldn't you? I mean, why not? If there is nothing hinging on it, most people would hazard a guess and say something like, 'Oh, it would have been the week before' or 'I think it was probably when I called to say ...' But he didn't want to do even *that* much. No. There was definitely something between Teasel and Samantha."

"But if he *was* the caller," Lissoni countered, "is he her killer? After all, the caller knew she was dead. Who else would have known that?"

"It's a good point, Margot. Who indeed? And on its own, that evidence would make you think it might be him. But what about the restraints on Samantha?"

"Kinky sex?" Donaldson said with a roguish grin. Lissoni groaned and shot Jake a disgusted look.

"*Possible,*" Anna said, amused by the exchange between Jake and Lissoni, "but given her blackened eyes and split lip, I'd have to say *very* unlikely.

Sado-masochism may be about restraint and punishment, but generally, you wouldn't want to end up looking black and blue. Too much explanation needed."

"Not to mention the gaping great slash across her throat." Lissoni shot a dark look at Jake. "So, how would he have known she was dead if he wasn't the killer?"

"Maybe he was coming over to ... you know"—Donaldson raised his eyebrows, eyes full of innuendo—"and he found her like that."

Anna nodded. "I'd say that's a strong possibility. Remember the description of Samantha's boyfriend that Fran gave us: tall, skinny, Caucasian, and dark-haired, which fits Teasel, though it probably covers a good proportion of the male population of Jindabyne as well. But I think our next stop will be to confirm that with Fran. Can you take a good image from the video of the interview, Jake, and go and visit Fran to confirm?"

He nodded.

"And though we don't have enough evidence for a warrant on his phone at this time, can you check Sam's phone records for his number? If they were in a relationship, we might see evidence of that in the number of calls between them. See if there are any text messages as well. They'll be more informative, I think, as he can always argue away calls as business related.

"What did you think of Lucy's testimony that Tyler had a plan to force Samantha into a divorce?" Anna continued.

"I think Teasel was right; it was all spin. Tyler was just giving her a line, telling her what she wanted to hear," Jake stated confidently. "I mean, what plan could he have to force Samantha into divorce? If he wanted it so badly, why didn't he just leave her? And anyway, I'm sure you can get a divorce even if your partner won't sign the papers. I can check that, but why stay if you hate it that much? It's all bunkum, so he could spin Lucy along."

"Exactly right!" Anna nodded, pleased he'd seen the issue. *Why were they still together?* Lucy and Dean agree that Tyler wanted a divorce. But they were both *convinced* he wouldn't leave the relationship unless Sam agreed. Which is more than strange when he could have walked away at any time."

"Maybe she was threatening to withhold visitation with Ethan?" Donaldson added.

"No, that's not it." Lissoni shook her head firmly. "Neither of them cared that much for Ethan. At least not enough to put themselves into the situation of a tug-of-war over him. Lucy said it was *Sam* that was the problem. She never mentioned Ethan."

"I agree, Margot," Anna said. "Nothing we've heard indicates that either parent would put Ethan above their own wants and needs. So I don't see him being the roadblock to a divorce."

"Then what possible hold could Sam have over Tyler then?" Donaldson asked in a puzzled tone.

"Somehow, I think when we know that, everything will fall into place," Anna murmured in an aside.

"Also, we didn't ask Mrs Carter-Ellis about a potential divorce either. Margot, give her a call and just get an opinion on why she thinks they didn't just split up."

Lissoni nodded, noting it down.

Anna blew out a long breath. "I have some more scans and tests tomorrow, which means I'll be out of action. Can you get the notes updated and chase up those few action items, please? And ... what else do we have outstanding?"

"No other phones in Sam's or Tyler's name. I'm still checking into a phone in Ethan's name," Donaldson replied. "Oh, and the dive shots and videos of the old town have finally arrived from one of the two organisations I spoke to that conduct dives in the lake. One of them only does the cottages at Kalkite and near Creel Bay, so nothing from them. The other mob did a dive in January last year, over the area in question, and they're the pics we've got."

"Good. Can you forward them to me? I'll have a look tonight. You both might also take a look."

"Are we looking for anything in particular?" Lissoni asked.

"No, I have no idea at this stage. Just flag anything that looks different or odd." Donaldson and Lissoni looked at each other and then turned and nodded. They were starting to trust that these strange requests from the boss would yield results in the end.

"We haven't dug into that old boyfriend of Sam's yet," Lissoni mentioned, quickly reviewing her notes.

"Ah! Mr Foley, now I had him in mind for Sam's extramarital liaison," Anna mused quietly. "But even though I think that role has now fallen to Teasel, I think it's still important we find out about Nathan Foley. But of higher priority is to set up a time for us to speak to the administrator of the Webbs' real estate business. Whoever they were, spent every working day with them. I'm sure they'll have some insights into both the business and their personal relationship.

"Text me with any updates or leave a phone message," Anna added, wrapping up.

Chapter 22

Anna growled and clicked hard on the remote control before throwing it on the coffee table.

"What's wrong, Mum?" Riley asked, standing in the doorway.

Anna took a deep breath. "I'm trying to cast the images from my laptop onto the television screen and the … *bloody* thing will just not work!" she said through gritted teeth.

"What images?" He sat down next to her and placed his half-eaten bowl of apple crumble and ice cream (his second) on the table.

"Is it something really gross?" he added eagerly.

"No, nothing like that." Anna shook her head with a smile and passed him her laptop.

"Which ones?" he queried, looking intently at her laptop screen.

She leant over and pointed, breathing in his just-showered, apple crumble scent. "Just those in that folder."

He clicked on the laptop, the TV remote, and back again. She shook her head at his prowess. *When had he acquired these skills?*

"Got it." Riley nodded with satisfaction as the first green-toned images flashed up on the screen.

"If it's not gross, can I watch?"

"Sure," Anna smiled. "So, what we're looking at is the old town of Jindabyne, or at least a small part of it. These images and videos have been taken near to where the road used to lead across the bridge. You remember?" Riley nodded. His mum and Aunty Dee had both told him stories of the submerged town beneath the lake. His mum's had been factual and informative. His Aunty Dee's on the other hand, had been full of murder, mayhem, and hidden treasures which were heaps more interesting. Not that he'd tell his mum that.

"Is this where the diver guy was found?"

"It's the same area. I'm trying to get an idea of what it looked like before the guy who died went there. Then, I'm going to have a look at the images and videos of when he was found and see if I can spot any changes. I think it's a million to one shot, but ..."

"Worth a look, heh?"

They scrutinised each image, then retraced their steps, looking for landmarks and features for comparison.

"Okay, let's see the other ones."

Anna shook her head. "Don't know about that, Riles ..."

"Aw, c'mon, Mum! Why not? I'm fourteen!" he whined. "I watch Game of Thrones! There's more gore in that than anything I'd see on this!"

"Where the hell have you seen Games of Thrones?!"

"At Madisons," Riley declared impatiently.

Anna rolled her eyes. *Geezus! Well, the horse has already bolted if he's watched episodes of that ... in more ways than one.*

"Okay, you can help me ... but if it makes you uncomfortable at any time—"

"Yeah, yeah, Mum, I'll tell you. Okay?"

Not at all sure she was doing the right thing, Anna loaded the photos and videos from the police dive team.

They looked at each image carefully. Riley, standing up next to the screen, pointed out the landmarks they had already identified.

"What's that?" Anna peered at the screen.

"Where? This bit?" Riley moved forward to pick something out of the fuzzy, obscure images they looked at. Anna nodded.

"No, that's the same concrete thingy we saw a few images back." He shook his head, then sat back down and flicked through the images. "See? It's just a different angle."

After some considerable time analysing the images and videos, Anna sat back, shaking her head. "Well, I can't see anything different. Well I can, but I don't know if it's significant or not. How the hell anyone can make out anything down there, I don't know."

"You don't think that thing we saw next to the house steps was anything?"

"I don't know how you'd work it out, Riles, without going back down there and examining it in detail," Anna sighed. "All the different angles and that dark greenish gloom over everything, it makes it pretty hard to work out. Oh, well … thanks for helping me."

Riley nodded but didn't move.

"Mum," he started tentatively, "Aunty Dee says you're going to see the doctor tomorrow."

"Yeah, that's right. I've got a few more tests to do and then in the afternoon I have an appointment with the oncologist again to see how I'm tracking."

"So, he'll tell you if you're going to be okay?" Riley looked at her, eyes full of anxiety.

Anna took his hand, gently rubbing the bony, man-sized knuckles it now possessed. "You remember I told you they can't fix me, right? Not permanently anyway," she asked and watched her son nod. "So, these tests are about just checking to see how I am right now. If there have been no additional tumour spots or growth where I had cancer, then that will be really good news. If not"—Anna stopped to look away for a moment and then turned back—"well then, I'll have to start some more treatment to knock it on the head again."

Riley looked down at their linked hands. A minute or more passed in silence.

Then he looked up at her. "Are you nervous?"

Anna smiled ruefully. "A little bit. It's like taking an exam and waiting on the results, you know?"

Riley nodded, but it was clear he was battling with something else. Anna waited, giving him time to work through whatever was bothering him.

"Mum, can I ask you a question?" he finally asked.

"Anything, Riles, you know that."

He pulled his hand from hers and hunched forward. Anna hated to see him struggling. She reached out and rubbed his back. She heard a small sniff.

"If something happens ... to ... you," he choked out, "will I have to go stay with Dad?"

Anna sat back as if she'd been shot.

"Oh, Riles ... son." Tears thickened her voice. "No, of course not. I'm so sorry ... I should have explained. That's why we're here with Dee."

Riley's head jerked up, and he turned to her with stark fear in his face.

"No. No!" Anna held up her hands, recognising she'd said the wrong thing. "I just meant that we moved here so that *if* something happened to me, then you would be with Dee." She took a deep breath to calm herself down.

"Riley, look at me." She turned him to face her. "I'm looking into making Dee your guardian if ... well, if I'm not here anymore. That way, *she'll* be the one to look after you. Not your dad. I'm not saying anything is going to happen. I don't know, like I told you. But I wanted to make sure that if it did, then you'd be okay. You like it here, don't you? You'll be happy here with Dee, right?"

Riley's face cracked, and he burst into tears. Anna gathered him to her and hugged him hard.

"Riles?" Anna murmured into his hair, as Riley's sobs finally eased to the occasional sniff. "Are you okay with what I said?"

She felt him nod. "Yeah ... I'll be okay here with Aunty Dee," he said into her shoulder.

"Good." Anna pushed him back so she could look into his face. His eyes were glassy and full of pain. "Now, you and I need to improve our communication from here on. I should have explained about me earlier. I should have known you were old enough to handle it. I'm sorry. I can see by not telling you I've caused you some anxiety … and now this whole idea of living with your dad … eww!” She shuddered theatrically, causing Riley to give her an answering smile. “So, let's make a bargain. If you have any concerns or worries, you promise to tell me, or if not me, then at least your Aunty Dee. And I'll make sure to tell you *everything* that's happening. Deal?”

"Deal!"

Chapter 23

GLASS CLINKED HEAVILY AGAINST glass as Dean unsteadily poured himself another triple shot of rum. In one small part of his brain, he registered that this was maybe not a good move, and he would regret it tomorrow, but he was long past the point of logical restraint. He'd been drinking steadily since arriving home after the police interview.

Every time he closed his eyes, he could see that inspector eyeballing him. Those green eyes boring into him like probes. Like she could see right through him, and he knew she didn't believe even half of what he'd said. He took another gulp and felt the alcohol burn its way down his gullet. The interview kept scrolling through his brain like a movie on auto-replay and each time he cringed at his ineptitude. His evasions seemed more transparent the more they reran in his head.

He punched a cushion violently in frustrated anger and then started at the sound of someone knocking on his front door.

After a brief pause, the knocking started again, louder and longer this time. Dean staggered to his feet, shaking his head to clear it.

He swung the door open, but before he could even focus his bleary gaze, the man pushed Dean aside, and walked in.

Dean stumbled back and hit the wall. "Hey? Who the hell are you?" he slurred, turning to follow his visitor's progress into his lounge room.

The man turned to face him. He stood under the ceiling light and Dean frowned. He looked vaguely familiar, but his alcohol-soaked brain would not offer up any suspects. The guy was tall and heavily built. His most striking feature though, was a large bald head which gleamed greasily, and made his deep-set eyes disappear into dark, sinister pits.

"Don't you remember me, Deano?" The voice was whisper quiet but seemed to cut through the air with its hint of menace.

Dean shivered. The sound of the voice brought the memory he'd been scrambling for to mind with a thud. This was the same guy who had appeared just after Sam was murdered. The memory flooded back abruptly.

"Yeah, I remember," Dean croaked and took some unsteady steps forward to put the lounge between him and his unwelcome visitor.

"I hear your mate finally surfaced," the man sneered.

"Yeah. They just identified him."

"What did you tell the police?"

Dean swallowed, not questioning that the man would know about his police interview. "Not much," he muttered breathlessly. Then, in the lengthening and rather ominous silence that followed, he added, "They just wanted to know about Sam and Tyler's finances and ... and about their relationship."

"And what did you tell them?"

Dean dug his fingers into the top of the lounge suite, trying to sharpen his thinking from the murk of alcohol it was swimming in.

"Nothing much." He could hear the slur in his words and tried to speak more clearly. "I told them I did not know that much about their finances, that they did most of it themselves."

The guy nodded, but even that sent shivers down Dean's spine.

"Did they find anything with the body?"

Dean frowned, struggling to make sense of the question. "Find anything?"

"Yeah." The man took a step towards him. "*Did ... they ... find ... anything ... with ... the body?*" he repeated through clenched teeth.

Dean started back and edged further along the lounge. "N-no!" he stuttered. "Well, they didn't tell *me* if they did. And there's been nothing in the news either. What should they have found?"

Dean paled and wished he'd cut his tongue out before uttering those last words as the man seemed to swell. His eyes glowed like red-hot coals from their dark hollows and his fists clenched. At that, Dean looked down, remembering the bloody bandages he had witnessed at their first meeting. He winced, seeing the missing third and fourth digits on the man's left hand.

"The Webbs took something of mine ... I want it back."

"I ... I don't ... know anything about that," Dean managed to get out around the lump in his throat that threatened to close off his breathing altogether.

The man glared. Waves of imminent violence seemed to pour from him, pounding Dean as if they were physical blows.

The man took another step forward so that only the sofa separated them.

"You'd better tell me if they find it, or you're going to end up like that slut ... only I might just take a bit more time about it."

Dean jerked back as the man moved. But the slam of the front door finally registered in his brain, telling him the threat had passed.

He sank to the floor as all strength left his legs.

Chapter 24

"You did it on purpose!" Dee cried.

"I did not," Anna replied mildly. "The hospital made the appointments, not me. How was I supposed to know it was market day?"

Dee shook her head disgustedly.

"What's up?" Riley walked up in his school uniform.

"Your aunty is complaining because she's not driving me to my appointment today in Canberra. She's got the farmer's market on."

"Your mother," Dee stated with a supercilious air, "organised it on purpose so I couldn't go."

"Did not," Anna murmured, hiding a smile.

"Well, I need to hear *every ... single ...* detail when you return," Dee stated, eyebrows raised. "Including every infinitesimal detail about the hunky Dr Childs."

"And *that's* why your aunty *really* wants to go." Anna turned to Riley, who grinned.

"Well, who can blame me?" Dee asked Riley. "Though I have to admit the gorgeous medico has eyes only for your mum. Which means, I have to live vicariously through her—" She broke off as Anna raised a hand threateningly.

They all laughed.

"Ev-er-y detail!" Dee repeated, pointing a warning finger at Anna.

"Okay! I need to go or I'm going to be late. Good luck with the new cheeses!" Anna flicked a wave out of the window. Her sister was trialling several new flavours of her locally sought after organic goat's cheese at the market.

Dee waved and threw an arm around Riley's shoulders companionably and they walked back inside.

"So-o, that all sounds like good news then?" Anna questioned tentatively, hoping she had understood everything that Dr Childs had just told her.

He grinned and nodded. "Excellent news! A ten out of ten for this review. I'll schedule another round of tests for three months."

Anna let out a long breath. She was so absorbed in the feeling of relief that she almost missed Dr Childs' hesitant invitation.

"Sorry?"

"I said ... would you like to have a drink with me ... er ... to celebrate your good news?" he repeated, his face slightly flushed.

Anna could feel her heart rate increase. She struggled to formulate a suitable and sensitive refusal but then took them both by surprise when the words that emerged were, "Okay, sure."

Cameron grinned, looking like an excited kid and then tried to look cool and urbane but failed miserably.

"There's a place about a five-minute drive away," he said.

"Sounds good, but I'll drive myself, as I need to leave straight after our drink. It's a bit of a long drive home," she replied, wondering how she'd managed to agree to this get together.

"No problem." Cameron nodded, ready to concede anything if it meant she was having a drink with him.

They arranged to meet in fifteen minutes, and Anna walked to her car. She was still questioning her sanity in agreeing to his proposal when she pulled up to the kerb just down the street from the bar.

As she opened the car door she suddenly remembered she hadn't called Dee and knew if she didn't immediately let her know her results, she would never hear the end of it.

"Finally!" Dee answered the phone, sounding exasperated. "What's the news?"

Anna winced, feeling guilty for making Dee wait an extra fifteen minutes. "Ten out of ten. Everything is good, Dee," she declared, a flood of relief washing over her again. It was still difficult to believe. She had steeled herself for bad news, and it was taking time for her good results to sink in.

Dee let out a loud whoop, nearly deafening Anna in the process. There was a brief exchange and another loud whoop from Riley in the background.

"So, big celebration then," Dee exclaimed, the relief palpable in her voice. "When do you think you'll be home? Are you on your way?"

Anna grimaced. She should have anticipated this, instead she had gotten swept up in the whole moment with Cameron.

"Er ..." Anna started and was interrupted by a gasp on the other end of the phone.

"No!" Dee cried. "You aren't? Really?"

"I haven't said—"

"Your mum's having dinner with the hunky doc," Dee said in an audible aside to Riley.

"Just drinks!" Anna called over the top of the conversation occurring at the other end of the line.

"Well, that's a start anyway," Dee replied into the phone.

"Don't make more of it than it is, Dee," Anna said firmly, trying to dampen her own excitement as well as Dee's. "It's just a drink ... to celebrate my good news. Sorry I'm not going to get home at a decent hour to celebrate with you guys. I probably won't be home much before nine-ish."

"Oh, don't worry about Riley and me. We'll be celebrating anyway. You just have a *great* time. And remember"—Dee's tone lowered—"I want ev-er-y detail!"

Anna laughed and, with a final admonishment to drive carefully, Dee ended the call. Anna sat for a few seconds, shaking her head at her sister's enthusiasm. Dee was so her opposite, but despite that or perhaps because of it (opposites attracting?) they had always been close. Dee was outgoing, open and friendly, whereas she had always been private and reserved. She thought briefly of her upcoming drink with Dr Childs. It was so unlike her to have accepted an invitation like that, but she couldn't deny the nervous excitement writhing in her stomach at the thought of it.

"So ... *Hitchhiker's Guide to the Galaxy,* eh? A favourite of yours?" Cameron asked, handing Anna her drink and sitting down opposite. Since the evening was fairly mild, they had opted for a table in the courtyard under an outdoor gas heater that shed a glow of radiant heat over them.

Anna smiled and gave a half-hearted shrug. "You might have gathered from our names that Dee and I were brought up by alternate life-stylers."

"Hippies?"

"Mmm, sort of." Anna nodded. "Well, my parents purchased old books for five dollars a box at the local market—they included everything from geology textbooks, Shakespeare, poetry, Dr Suess, Mills and Boon, real life crime stories. You name it, we read it. So, as a result, I had a rather eclectic exposure to all manner of reading material from a young age."

"Really? Your parents didn't censor anything?"

Anna shook her head. "No, they didn't believe that any book should be restricted from an inquiring mind." And then seeing his surprise, added, "Dee and I got our sex education fairly early on from reading Jackie Collins, though DH Lawrence also contributed there."

"How old were you?" he blurted.

"About eight or nine. Of course, some of it went over our heads but we read it anyway and eventually as we got older it all slotted into place." Anna grinned.

"Sounds like you had a very interesting upbringing."

"It was … *different*." Anna sipped on her spritzer. She hesitated before saying more, but he was looking at her keenly. "As you know, when growing up, it pays to be one of the crowd. To fit in. Be normal. Well, Dee and I weren't normal, and we didn't fit in. We had handwoven satchels for our books instead of backpacks. And second-hand everything; my parents being very keen on the concept of reuse and less waste. So, we rarely had a full school uniform. We didn't have toys like the other kids, we didn't dress like the other kids, and we didn't have television. Looking back, I think this was probably one of the most significant differences, since all the kids talked about shows they had watched and who had done what to whom on some TV program."

"That must have been hard," Cameron murmured as she paused.

Anna fingered the dew on her glass. "I was mostly okay with it. I wasn't bothered too much by being an outsider. I guess that suited my personality to some degree. But it had a much more significant impact on Dee. She's a lot more social than I am. She felt the ostracism keenly. It came to a head when I was around"—she cocked her head to the side—"fourteen or so, and Dee was about twelve. She had just started high school, and it was all too much. You know how teenagers are. She had barely coped through primary school but add in adolescent bitchiness and school became a nightmare for her. Anyway, she stopped attending school and after a few weeks, I decided to take things in hand. I started tutoring other kids for money, and then I bought Dee a proper school uniform and all the kit. I bought her a radio so she could at least hear the latest songs." She shrugged. "It helped. She made some friends, and that made all the difference."

Anna stopped, seeing the incredulous look on Cameron's face.

"But … sorry if I'm being rude … but, why did *you* have to help Dee? Why didn't your parents?"

Anna snorted briefly. "Oh, they tried to help her in their own way. They explained that possessions were not important, and that she would find real friends soon, who wouldn't judge her by what she had or didn't have." She grimaced. "I loved them, but seriously, they lived on another planet."

"So, they let *you* buy her stuff ... how did that fit in to their thinking?" Cameron queried, totally fascinated.

"My mum and dad felt that parents should not put any boundaries around their children; that they should not be influenced to think or act in a particular way. And, if left to discover the path that was right for them, they would find their own destiny. So, when I stepped in to help Dee, they considered that was me finding my own path."

"Wow," Cameron croaked. "So, how did that impact you? That sort of home life?" he asked as if she were an experiment of great interest.

Anna smiled. She supposed she was in a way: a weird social experiment. "I grew up with no rules and now I'm a police officer, a career with more rules and regulations than you can poke a stick at." She grinned. "Overcompensating, do you think?"

Cameron laughed.

"But seriously," she continued, keen to explain, though a part of her registered how unusual that was for her to want to talk about herself, let alone care that someone should understand her. "I can't say that I chose the police, as a career, purely because I was seeking structure or as some form of rejection of my parent's philosophy. I had already imposed a lot of structure on my life, and Dee's, well before then. I think what drew me to the police was the constant challenge of it."

Anna paused and took a sip of her drink. "Enough about me. Tell me about Cameron Childs."

Cameron sat back, nodding slowly. "Not too much to tell. I married very young. We were both twenty. Had two kids: Mathew is now twenty-one and Rachel is nineteen. They're both at uni. My wife, Juliet, and I split up about five years ago now," he said, his voice held a tinge of sadness.

"I'm sorry, that must have been difficult," Anna murmured.

"Yes, and then again, not as much as you might think. You see ... Jules and I were best friends, absolutely inseparable at school. And so, for us, it was a no-brainer to get married. It just seemed the logical next step. We both became doctors. Jules is a psychiatrist. I don't really know at what point I realised how distant we'd grown but"—he shrugged and shook his head—"I didn't do anything about it. And neither did she. Was it because we both realised at some point that we married because we were the best of friends, but not necessarily in love? I don't know. I think our friendship had a lot to do with why we procrastinated for so long about splitting. I'd like to say it was me who took the first step, but in the end it was Jules. She'd found someone else, someone who made her happy, and I didn't begrudge her that happiness. I was actually quite ... *relieved* that she'd taken the initiative. I'm not saying it was easy. It was anything but, to be honest ... but I knew that what I mourned was not Juliet so much as the dream of what I thought our lives would be. I suddenly had to reimagine my future without her."

Anna nodded, feeling his pain.

"Matt took it reasonably well, but Rach ..." He shook his head and sighed. "She blamed her mum since it was Jules who moved on with a boyfriend. No matter how much I protested that it was a joint decision, Rachel just wanted to believe I was being magnanimous, and Juliet was the evil adulteress."

"She would have been about fourteen or fifteen at the time?"

"Yeah." He nodded.

Anna winced. "A difficult time in the best of circumstances."

"Yes, maybe the timing could have been better, but then, when is the best time to split when you have kids involved? Rach is a lot better now. She and Jules can have a conversation without it turning into World War Three."

"That's good." Anna smiled. "What's happened since then ... with you?"

"Not much," he replied. But seeing her raised eyebrows, he grinned and added, "Not that I've been a monk, you understand, I've just not found anyone that really"—he looked at her intensely—"got under my skin." He reached out and took her hand.

Anna flushed and dropped her gaze to their joined hands, mesmerised by Cameron's gently massaging thumb. Her heart raced.

She looked up from their entwined hands and found his eyes, looking at her with such deep empathy and fear that it broke her heart. A thousand thoughts churned and fought for supremacy in her mind, but one eventually emerged from the dross. "Have you honestly thought this through?"

"I've spent a lot of time thinking about it. In fact, I've thought of little else in the last week."

"I'm not a good bet," she murmured, eyes brimming with unshed tears.

God! I could drown in those deep green pools. He swallowed. "No matter how much my mind throws up arguments against it—you hardly know her, she's sick, she's your patient—my heart just tells my head to go to hell," he said, willing her to understand.

A tear escaped and rolled down Anna's cheek, and she brushed it away. She looked down at his large hand surrounding her own; hers looked so frail and small by comparison. She gave an infinitesimal nod.

Looking up, she took a deep breath and smiled, and Cameron's heart soared.

"Well, you should know what you're getting into"—she grinned—"in some circles, I'm known as the 'Ice Princess'. And Dee and Riley, my son, tell me that I have a look that causes the unlucky recipient to freeze on the spot, or in some cases, disintegrate into dust."

Cameron laughed, his head thrown back, his eyes crinkled up, and his white teeth shining in the light from the overhead heater. Anna felt her own laughter bubble up. She couldn't remember having ever felt so ... *joyful*.

Once they had settled down again, they sat staring at each other. "Tell me about Riley," Cameron asked.

In what felt only a few moments later but was nearer to an hour, Anna glanced at her watch.

"Oh wow, I need to head home. I'm going to be so late."

"I'll walk you to your car," Cam said, holding her hand tight.

They strolled down the street, and Anna clicked the unlock to her car and turned slowly towards him. He let go of her hand and ran it up her arm and cupped her cheek. She unconsciously leaned into it. His lips met hers and she could feel a flood of warmth ignite her from the toes up. The kiss deepened, and she slid her arms around his back, feeling the strong muscles along his spine as she pressed closer.

Breathlessly, they pulled apart, and Cameron stroked her cheek.

"Anna?" he whispered.

"Mmm?" she answered, lost in his warm grey eyes.

"You need to find another oncologist."

She looked momentarily startled and then laughed.

Chapter 25

"Here, get that into you," growled Mick, shoving a beer in front of Dean, whose head lolled on his forearms across the table.

"Erg ... don't think I can, mate," Dean groaned thickly. He was pale and sweating profusely.

"Hair of the dog. Drink up!"

"What's up with you?" Jono slid into his usual seat and looked over at Dean. "You look like Webby would have when they brought him up from the deep," he added spitefully.

"Massive hangover," Mick said succinctly.

"Interview with the coppers that bad, was it?" Jono asked with some enjoyment at the thought.

"Bad enough," Dean muttered, taking a tentative sip of beer. He knew that Mick and Jono were still dark on him. He expected to be paying for his favours to the Webbs for some time to come. But there was no question in his mind of avoiding them; they were his mates. Regardless of the criticism, insults, and lack of compassion they threw at him, it was to them he would turn every time.

They sat in the easy silence of old friends for the next half hour. Dean slowly sipped his beer and kept it down, in stark contrast to everything else he'd tried that day which had made a sudden and unpleasant reappearance. Jono left to get refills and as the alcohol finally made its way to his suffering brain cells, Dean started to feel marginally better, though his mind still churned with thoughts of his late-night visitor.

"You remember that guy that came to visit me a couple of days after Sam was killed?" Dean asked in a low tone, hugging his beer.

Mick and Jono exchanged a glance and then turned back to Dean.

"Who?" Mick frowned.

"The *guy!* You remember. I told *you!* He came over … must have been the Saturday after. He was going on and on about finding Tyler."

"Oh, yeah, I remember." Mick smirked. "One of Sam's boyfriends, wasn't he? Had the hots for her and was all steamed up about seeking revenge on Webby."

"Yeah, so"—Dean swallowed, trying to collect his alcohol-tortured thoughts—"he turned up again last night."

"What? At your place?"

"Yeah, must have been after eleven. Barged his way in. Big, scary dude." Dean shivered.

"What did he want? Webby's dead. That's what he was after, wasn't it? He's not going to get any deader," Jono muttered bluntly.

"I don't think that's what it was."

"You don't think what was? You're bloody not making any sense, Deano. Spit it out," Jono demanded impatiently.

Dean took a long draught of beer and waited for the alcohol to hit.

"I don't think he wanted to kill Tyler for murdering Sam after all. That's what it sounded like at the time. He kept saying, 'I'll kill the fucking bastard', 'When I find him I'm gonna make him pay'. He said he was Sam's old boyfriend, so I assumed he was … you know … seeking revenge or something. But *I* didn't know where Tyler was, and I told him that. He got really aggressive and—seriously, the guy looked like he was off his head. He had this bloody bandaged hand and was waving it around … I told him I hadn't heard from Webby, and he said that if I ever heard from Tyler, I had to tell him, or he'd make me pay."

"Yeah, I remember now," Mick nodded with an intent frown. "So, what happened this time that makes you think that wasn't what he was on about?"

Dean swallowed, the terror of the moment swelling up and making him feel faint. He breathed deeply and took another gulp of beer.

Mick looked sideways at Jono, who looked equally concerned, without a hint of his usual indifference.

"Like I said, he turned up again last night," Dean whispered. "He knew about my interview with the police. He said, 'Did the police find anything with the body?'"

Mick jerked back. "With Webby's body, you mean?"

Dean nodded. "He said 'the Webbs took something of mine … I want it back'," he added, breathing hard with remembered panic.

"*Gee-zus!*" Jono let out in a long sigh.

"He said, 'You'd better tell me if they find it, or you're going to end up like that slut!' And, he told me … 'he'd take his time over it'." Dean's throat was so tight he could barely get the words out.

Jono sat back in his chair, his mouth hanging open. "*Shit!*"

"*He* killed Samantha," Mick murmured, his face suddenly pale.

The three sat in stunned silence as the loud bustle of the bar flowed over them, unnoticed.

"Who *is* this guy?" Mick asked finally. "What's his name?"

"I don't know, he never said," Dean muttered, feeling infinitesimally better for having shared his story.

"What … so," Jono started, then paused, trying to gather his scattered wits. "So, he offs Sam and then he's after Tyler. So, what the hell happened to Tyler then?"

"And what did Tyler and Sam take?" Mick's gaze narrowed as it fell on Dean.

"You got an idea about that, Deano?" he added softly, though his tone was grim.

Dean looked like he was going to be sick. He shook his head, like he was trying to escape his own thoughts.

Jono shot a hand across the table and grabbed Dean's arm. His fingers dug into the muscle.

"Okay! *OKAY!* Let go!" Dean cried, shaking Jono off.

He leant forward. "I think they were ... dealing *drugs*," Dean said hoarsely, looking around nervously.

Mick sucked in a loud breath. "What makes you think that?"

"I don't know for sure," Dean whined. "I ... well ... it was just something Sam said once."

"Which was?"

"She was *high*. And she told me I should take something ... 'to loosen up'. She said, 'You can have as much as you like', that I could 'have a bath in it' if I wanted to. She knew 'where the *ice* tree grew.'"

"*Fuck me!*" Jono whispered to himself. "That's where all the dough came from!"

Mick's anger faded as he sat back, thinking it through. "Dean, your shout!" he said with an edge after several minutes.

Dean nodded wretchedly and headed to the bar.

Jono leant forward. "Do you think that's what Tyler was doing? Hiding the drugs?"

Mick nodded. "Yeah, why else go diving in the lake on his own? He was hiding the *bloody* drugs. Doing the dirty on the supplier by the sounds of it."

"But why? He must have known they'd come after him. Geezus! Look what they did to Sam!"

Mick nodded, but his thoughts were running along a different line. "The drugs must still be down there," he murmured, in almost an aside.

Jono shot him a look as Dean arrived back with the drinks.

"The police didn't mention anything about drugs or maybe finding something with the body, did they?" Mick asked Dean keenly.

"No! That's what the guy asked me," Dean answered, bewildered.

"There's been nothing on the news." Jono's voice was high with excitement.

"So, they have to be still down there," Mick said again, his eyes gleaming.

"What's down where?" Dean said in a vague, puzzled tone, the beers catching up with him.

"The drugs, you idiot!" Mick hissed, furious that Dean had kept so much secret from them.

"In the lake," Jono added helpfully.

Dean's face paled further, and he looked from Mick to Jono and back.

"What—" he started to say, but he was cut off abruptly by Mick.

"We can go get them."

Chapter 26

Thursday dawned and on the drive into work, Anna still felt torn.

She had arrived home the night before in time to wish Riley goodnight, his shy smile and big hug telling her that he was happy for her.

As she walked into the kitchen, Dee looked up expectantly and waved a bottle of red.

Anna nodded and sat opposite her, accepting the proffered glass of wine.

Dee jumped up and pulled out a plate of lasagne she'd kept warm in the oven and put it down in front of Anna.

"You look different," Dee declared, pulling off her oven mitts and sitting down again, her eyes sparkling with excitement.

Anna felt different and was not surprised that the glow of happiness showed on her face, nor that her perceptive sister had picked up on it.

"Tell me," Dee added simply.

Anna took a mouthful of lasagne and washed it down with a slug of wine, suddenly stalling for time.

"Well," she began, feeling like an awkward teenager instead of a mature forty-one-year-old. "We met at a bar about a five-minute's drive from the hospital and sat outside under one of those gas heaters. He got me a drink, and we chatted. He's divorced about five years now and has two kids—twenty-one and nineteen."

Dee gave a low whistle. "Goodness, he started early!"

Anna nodded. "He said he hadn't met anyone after the divorce that he was interested in ... until now." A flush of blood suffused her face, and she knew she would be irritatingly bright pink.

Dee grinned.

"He held my hand," Anna said, and then the memory of the next part of their conversation dampened her joy. "I asked him if he had thought it through, but he said his head had come up with all the negative arguments, but his heart wouldn't let me go. I *am* worried though, Dee. I'm not sure he has considered it enough," she added doubtfully.

"What's to consider? He should be thrilled to have someone like you!" Dee replied hotly.

Anna waved a fork at her sister, dismissing her sisterly loyalty. "You know why ... I'm sick, Dee. My chances of survival are low. He'd be taking a risk falling for me."

"Sounds like the good doctor has *already* fallen for you," Dee countered smartly, "and, besides, is he more important or special than Riley and me?"

"No! *Of course not!*"

"Well, then it's all okay," Dee said with an easy shrug. But seeing Anna's frown added, "Look, he knows more than anyone what the risks are, Lina—way more than any of us—after all, it's his job, right? And knowing all of that, he's still willing to accept it. You can't protect people, sweety. If something happens to you, then Riley, the doc, and I will all be devastated. You can't change that. Isn't it better for him to have some months or years of you than nothing at all? I'd take that and so would Riley. Don't rate Cameron any less."

Dee's words echoed in Anna's mind, bolstering her confidence each time the doubts crept in, and creep in, they did.

Part of the problem was she hadn't felt like this about anyone in well ... ever, that it was almost as if the foreignness of it was somehow suspicious; something to be wary of, like a possible virus-laden email attachment.

How has he gotten in under my defences so quickly? She hadn't earned the rather derogatory nickname of 'Ice Princess' for nothing. Aside from the rather formal manner with which she approached her job, she had also earned it as a result of some ill-advised invitations from work colleagues, thinking to mix the personal and the professional.

She had never felt the absence of a partner in her life; never pined for a soulmate or a lover. Her few relationships had been enjoyable but short-lived; ending generally at the point when her partner wished to move on 'to the next level' and move in with her. She didn't feel the lack, between her job and Riley, she had always felt satisfied with her life. But now, for once, she understood the draw that motivated others to seek out a life partner.

Having mulled it over on the drive, Anna arrived at the office, no better informed than she had been the night before, but still with a ball of happiness sitting in her stomach. She could feel the smile on her face as she exited the car and quickly rearranged it into its usual focused intensity.

The wind pulled at her jacket, and she looked out over the lake, its dark blue surface ruffled with white caps. Taking a last deep breath of crisp fresh air, she headed inside.

"Morning, Boss," Lissoni called as soon as she spotted Anna approaching.

Jake's head popped up over the partition and Anna could sense an underlying atmosphere of excitement.

"Morning," she answered warily. "What's up?"

"Nathan Foley. Sam's ex-boyfriend, *quite* an interesting character." Jake's voice was loaded with inference.

Anna's eyebrows shot up. "Really? Let's take a seat and you can fill me in." She led the way to the meeting room.

"So, as Mrs Carter-Ellis mentioned, Nathan Foley *was* into 'something illegal' as she put it," Lissoni began eagerly. "We dug into him yesterday but didn't find much locally. Then, Jake suggested we broaden the search and bingo! He has a laundry list of charges against him in Victoria. It came through this morning. We haven't been through it all yet, but one thing stands out—he is heavily into drug trafficking."

Anna sat back, a small grin on her face, her eyes lit up. She got up abruptly and walked to her spot by the window. Looking out, she was blind to the view, her mind spinning at high speed. She turned and saw Lissoni and Donaldson watching her attentively.

"Well, that fits rather nicely with the large amount of disposable income the Webbs had."

"So, you think they were in league with Foley?" Jake queried.

Anna nodded slowly. "I think that explains rather a lot. The money, the execution style of death for Sam, and most of all, the reason Sam and Tyler didn't get divorced."

"You think Sam—" Margot started.

"Didn't trust Tyler. She wanted him under her thumb, where she could keep an eye on him." Anna snapped her fingers. "And I think it makes a hell of a lot of sense out of that video of the two of them arguing. Jake, what did your uncle say?"

Jake typed rapidly into his laptop. "Er ... so ... Tyler starts off saying 'I've had enough!' then 'I want out!' Then Sam says, 'Better suck it up' and 'Let you just walk away'."

"So we know Tyler wanted out of the marriage," Lissoni cut in, "but by the sounds of that, he wanted out of the business too, and she's giving him a reality check."

"They always forget in the rush to acquire easy money, that the piper must get paid," Anna said in a quiet aside. "You don't get to just walk away. Sam had that right." She nodded at Jake to continue.

"Right, then Tyler says ... 'don't give a fuck what they think', and then Sam says, 'You'd better give a' ... fuck, I presume," Jake ad-libbed. "She continues with 'get over yourself', then something about his 'little girlfriend'. That's when he grabs the knife and says, 'I could kill you right now ... something ... trouble'."

"I remember you saying, at the time, Jake, that 'Save them the trouble' goes with 'What they think'." Anna nodded, noting in the periphery of her vision that he was smiling.

"That all makes a lot of sense now that we have the drugs as the centrepiece. I wonder if our greasy little Mr Teasel knew about it."

"Oh, and I checked with Fran, the Webbs' neighbour, about Teasel. I took her a photo of him from the video feed of our interview, and she identified him straight off," Jake said excitedly.

"And there is a bucket load of text messages and calls between Teasel and Sam over the previous year, as well," Lissoni added, eyes gleaming.

"Anything incriminating?" Anna asked, eyebrows raised.

"Not from her," Margot answered. "In fact, if you didn't see *his* text messages, you'd never know they were involved. But our Mr Teasel was obviously *very* smitten with Sam."

"Excellent. Let's pull together some juicy ones and we'll get him in for another chat," declared Anna with relish. She hadn't taken to Teasel; he'd struck her as a rather spineless individual.

"Now, what time was our meeting with the office administrator for the Webbs' business?"

Margot checked her watch. "She said she'd be here at about ten."

"Right then, we have a bit more time. So, let's circle back to Foley. Any luck with the phone in Ethan's name, Jake?"

"Yeah! Ethan Webb does have a phone in his name." He grinned.

"And I presume there are no calls on it after Sam's death and the only other calls on it are to a burner phone, am I right?"

Donaldson looked startled. "Spot on! So—" he paused, thinking quickly, "the burner phone belongs to ... *Foley*. That was how the Webbs got in contact with him."

Anna nodded, watching him work it out.

"And ... since there are *no* calls on it *after* Sam died, he must have known she was dead," Jake continued.

Anna gave him a half-smile. "And that means he might be our killer."

"But why kill her?" Margot asked.

"*That* is the question," Anna agreed. She looked at her watch.

"In the time we have left, let's get started digging up as much on Foley as we can. I'm going to call a friend of mine in the Federal Police and see if he's on their radar."

"Drakos," an abrupt voice answered as the call connected.

"Nickolas Drakos," Anna drawled, "who would ever have thought they would make you a Super!"

"Anna?" came the surprised reply.

Anna laughed. A rich throaty chuckle that had both sergeants looking up in surprise.

"Right the first time! How are you, Nicko?"

"Oh, be still my beating heart," he replied. "If it isn't Annabelina Farrow, love of my life!"

"Ugh! I knew I should never have told you my real name, Nicko. Let this be a lesson to all about the ill effects of too much alcohol." Anna grinned. She and Nick went way back, so far back in fact, that Nick was the first of a long line of rejections that Anna had accumulated over the years. What made Nick stand out was his cheerful acceptance of her refusal and the way in which he had never let his attraction for her get in the way of their friendship.

"How is Sandra? And the girls?" she asked, getting the pleasantries out of the way.

"Sandra's great. Working for DOCS now ... a tough gig, but she's finding it rewarding. The girls are growing like weeds; Harriet is six now and Lilly three. How's Riley?"

"Good, thanks Nicko. Listen, I'll ring and organise a time to come visit. I've moved to Jindabyne, so I'm a lot closer to Canberra now," she added quickly.

She heard the sudden intake of breath and headed it off, "Yeah, long story. I'll tell you all about it when I see you. But for now, I really need to pick your brain."

"Sure, anything," Nicko answered, suddenly all business. That was one of the things she liked about Nick. He was friendly and happy-go-lucky but could switch to professional focus in a heartbeat. He had a very similar work ethic to her own, which had made working with him in the days before his switch to the Federal police so rewarding, and which had cemented their friendship of nearly twenty years.

"What can you tell me about Nathan Foley?"

Chapter 27

"THANK YOU FOR COMING in, Ms Palmer."

"That's okay," Palmer answered brightly with a cheerful shrug. "The boss gave me the day off."

Anna estimated she was in her late forties with long dark hair that was pulled up into a knot on the top of her head. Long streamers of lank hair hung loose around her face. Not a look Anna thought suited anyone, least of all Lyndal Palmer, whose face was rather long and horsey to begin with.

"We're interested in your thoughts of the Webbs; their business and their relationship," Anna stated, being deliberately vague.

"Oh, well, the first thing you have to know is that they *really* hated each other," Palmer declared, eyes gleaming avidly.

Anna nodded. "We *have* heard that from a few people."

"They could barely be in the same room as each other without slinging insults towards the end."

"And what did *you* think of them? I mean, you knew them both so well. I'd be *very* interested in your opinion." Anna leant forward.

Lyndal Palmer flushed slightly and nodded. "I *did* know them well. I worked for them for nearly ten years after all. Even before Ethan was born. I worked for old Mr Bennett before he sold the business to them."

"So, tell me about Samantha Webb," Anna encouraged.

Lyndal's lips compressed into a thin line and her nostrils flared; Anna had a good idea of what was coming.

"She was a rude, lazy, slut," Lyndal snapped.

Don't hold back, Jake thought, smothering a grin.

"*Really?*" Anna said, eyes wide.

"Oh, yeah. When it happened people were all like, 'Oh, my God! How awful, a young woman killed', but *seriously?* It was no surprise to me that she got herself killed. The way she treated people. Me included." She sniffed and then, realising what she had implied, quickly added, "She was up to no good, that one. I could tell. My bet is one of her boyfriends did it."

Anna tilted her head. "Nearly everyone we've spoken to has said they thought it was Tyler who killed her. That was definitely the consensus at the time of her death."

Lyndal shook her head throughout Anna's statement. "No. No, it wasn't Tyler. There is no way it was him. He was nice! I know it was all over the papers at the time that he did it, but I never believed it."

"Why didn't you think Tyler could have done it?"

"Well, like I said, he was a nice man. He just wanted to get away from her. But he wouldn't have killed her, he just didn't have it in him. He was a gentle person."

Anna nodded slowly letting that comment hang for several seconds.

"We've had some indications that one or both of the Webbs had ... shall we say ... *partners* outside of their marriage. Did you get an idea about that?"

Lyndal nodded emphatically. "Yes! What you heard was right. Tyler had a girlfriend. A lovely young lady called Lucy. She called quite often. Tyler took me into his confidence and asked me to help keep it from Samantha," she said, oozing smugness.

"It's such a shame they couldn't be together. He was very much in love with her," Lyndal sighed.

Wow! thought Anna, *Tyler really knew how to work an audience.* She suspected Lyndal was half in love with Tyler herself. Helping him against the evil Sam must have made her feel part of his inner circle. *Now there was a talent!*

"And what about Samantha? Did you know if *she* had a boyfriend?"

Lyndal's sniffed and folded her arms. "Well ... how long is your piece of paper? Mrs Webb had a *lo-ong* list of boyfriends."

Anna nodded, looking suitably surprised. "Really? And how did you become aware of it?"

"Oh, the calls that came through! You can't imagine how many there were, and they definitely weren't work related! And those friends of Tyler's ... like dogs after a bitch in heat," she sneered, rolling her eyes. "I wanted to tell him, Tyler that is, but honestly, I don't think he would have cared in the end who she slept with. All he wanted was to get away from her."

"You said *friends* of Tyler—who were they?"

Lyndal suddenly looked a little wary. "Oh, well, those guys Tyler grew up with. They were always around; always together."

"I suppose Dean Teasel was one?" Anna said, offering Lyndal some bait.

"Absolutely. He did all the accounts for the business. He was always coming around. *Especially* when Tyler was out ... *if* you catch my drift!"

"So, Mr Teasel did all the accounts, did he? Tyler and Samantha didn't do much there?"

"God, no! Without Dean, the whole business would have folded. Neither Tyler nor Samantha had any idea of running a business, at least from the financial side. If left to them, they wouldn't have paid a single bill, let alone my salary!"

Anna could feel Margot twitching next to her, keen to pursue that line of inquiry, but Anna circled back.

"Who are the other 'friends' of Tyler's you mentioned?"

Lyndal scowled. "Mick Bialy and Jonathan Russo."

"You didn't like them?" Anna asked, picking up on the look.

"Mick was okay, he was polite, at least. Russo, on the other hand, is a real bastard ... rude and obnoxious!"

"Let's go back to the day before Samantha died," Anna continued. "What do you remember of that day?"

Lyndal shifted in her seat; Anna suspected she was thoroughly enjoying herself.

"Well, Sam had her usual *morning off* 'inspecting properties'," she said scathingly, air-quoting with her fingers. "Tyler came in early—"

"Sorry," Anna interrupted the flow. "Can you tell me more about Sam's '*inspections*'? You sound like you didn't believe that was what she was actually doing."

Palmer leant forward. "There is no way she was out doing inspections. For a start, no matter how many times I asked her, she didn't provide an address for the property she was inspecting—"

"And she would normally have provided that?"

"*Absolutely!* I usually booked them in with the client and there would always be a follow-up—calls or additional meetings to book in, or contracts to be prepared, or advertising and media—but not with these ones. No client, no address, no follow-up ... *inspections* my arse!" Her lips compressed tightly.

Anna's heart rate escalated a notch. "How often were these 'inspections' of Sam's?"

"I used to call them Sam's Specials," Lyndal scoffed. "They were about every three or four weeks."

"And did Tyler know about them?"

"Yeah, but he just turned a blind eye. I tried to get it out of him where she was going, but he just shrugged and shook his head. I don't think he really cared," she sighed.

"So, I gather from what you've said that you did a lot of the scheduling of appointments for the Webbs?"

Lyndal nodded. "Most of it. Occasionally they'd add something in themselves, but usually they just asked me to."

"I suppose Sam scheduled in her specials herself?"

"At first she did, but in the last few months, she just got me to slot them in for her ... *lazy bitch*," Lyndal added in a furious undertone.

Anna turned to Margot. "Sergeant, do you know if the initial investigating team took a copy of the Webbs' computer system?"

Lissoni frowned. "I don't know. I can check—"

"They did," Lyndal cut in. "And I've got a copy as well. I backed it all up before we closed down the office."

Anna's face split into a wide smile.

"You're very organised, Lyndal. I wonder, could we impose on you again to run us through your scheduling system and show us some of 'Sam's Specials'?"

"Gotta love a disgruntled employee," announced Jake facetiously as they reconvened in their team meeting room a short time later.

Anna's lips twitched in amusement. "Yes, our Ms Palmer was quite helpful. Though her opinion of the saintly Mr Webb is somewhat off the mark."

"Yeah, he played her like a fiddle!"

"So, are we thinking that Sam's Specials are her meetings with Foley?" Margot said.

"It seems likely." Anna drummed her fingers on the table.

"Okay," she added, getting up and walking to the whiteboard. "After what I heard from the AFP, Foley is definitely a person of interest in our case now. He's been on their radar for some time, though gone to ground in the last year, which fits in with Sam's death. So, if we assume that Foley was using Sam and Tyler to distribute drugs—and we assume the Sam's Specials are the meetings to pick up from Foley—where was she meeting him and what did they do after they got the drugs?" She scribbled both questions on the board.

"If Lyndal comes through tomorrow, we'll have the dates of the pick-ups," Jake said, "but as to finding out where—"

"GPS!" Lissoni cried suddenly. "That Lexus would have GPS tracking, wouldn't it? It might have location history."

Anna looked at her, a satisfied smile on her face. "Excellent suggestion, Margot!"

"Battery's probably dead on both cars if they've been sitting there all year," Jake muttered.

"Maybe," Anna added, "but let's get it checked out. You might have to ring Lexus. And check out her phone as well, she may have synched the mapping."

They nodded.

"How does Tyler's death fit in? Are we thinking Foley was involved?" Jake asked after several seconds of thoughtful silence.

Anna shook her head. "I don't know ... nothing so far has offered a clue there." She paused as something tickled the back of her brain. *Nothing so far* ... but perhaps there was something ... she shook her head as the thought continued to elude her. She pushed it aside, she'd ponder it later.

"Getting back to the drugs. They had to be going somewhere, so we need to get an opinion on the drug scene in the area. I'll take that. You two continue with the car's locations ... Oh, and run a pic of Foley past Fran, our eagle-eyed neighbour, see if she recognises him. He's fairly distinctive, I'm sure she'll remember if she's seen him. And can one of you organise access to the backup of that scheduling system before tomorrow when Ms Palmer arrives? We might need an official copy when the time comes. Then get everything you can on Foley as well," Anna directed, thinking quickly. "Oh, and find out who their cleaner was. Probably a dead end, but we should close off that point."

"Cleaner?" Jake repeated faintly, daunted by the list of follow-up tasks Anna had fired off.

Anna looked amused. "It was a huge house. Mostly white. Very clean. And we know that Sam and Tyler were self-centred narcissists who I doubt lifted a finger if they could help it. Yes, Jake, they would have had a cleaner."

He nodded in agreement. It was obvious now that she'd said it. A wave of doubt washed over him. He knew that thought would never have entered his mind.

"Any questions?"

Margot hesitated for a brief moment before asking, "Yeah, I have one. Why didn't you push for more details on Dean Teasel and the accounting situation? Lyndal seemed to know quite a bit about it."

"It's a good question. My thought was that we can always question Lyndal at a later date, and I'm sure if we get a forensic accountant to scour through their accounts and tax records it will be quite obvious that Teasel is completely entrenched in the Webbs' dodgy financial situation. But, at this point, we have two dead people, and they must be our focus, however unsavoury or unlikeable they were."

Chapter 28

Jake frowned and tapped a pen rapidly against the desk. He'd scoured the case file for any mention of the Webbs' scheduling system but hadn't found it. He blew out a long breath, he'd have to run through it all again. The digital evidence was categorised with the location and description of each file. The list was short—*very* short—and nothing included a reference to a scheduling system. He opened and checked each file just in case it had been mislabelled. *Nothing.* He pushed his chair back, put his hands behind his head, and stared at the screen.

Several minutes later, he scooted his chair forward and typed furiously. *That was it! They must have copied it onto an external hard drive, so it was* physical *evidence.* He smiled, pleased he'd thought of it. But his smile gradually faded until eventually, he grimaced.

Bloody hell! Where the fuck was it?

He sighed heavily. There was nothing for it; he'd have to take a run up to Cooma and check in person. He drummed his fingers on the table for a minute before a slow smile grew on his face. Why didn't he think of it before? One of his good mates, Mitchell Dickinson, had been on the team that had investigated Samantha Webb's murder. He'd know right off the bat where it was. *Probably was the one who had misfiled it, the stupid bastard!*

He picked up his phone. "Hey, Mitch, how's it hangin'?"

"Jake! Great mate. How's the Ice Princess? Managed to thaw her out yet?" He sniggered.

Donaldson cringed. He'd drowned his fury in beers at the pub last week-end after the encounter with the inspector and said a lot more than he wished he had.

He forced a laugh. "She's okay," he murmured.

"What? You were the one that said she was the devil incarnate and in dire need of a good ro—"

"Yeah, well, I think that was mostly the beers talking," Jake butt in quickly before he had to endure anymore of his own stupid comments repeated back to him.

"Anyway," he continued, before Mitch could say anything, "I need to find some files from the Samantha Webb case. I can't see them anywhere on the record, but we've been told that the scheduling system and other work applications and files for the Webbs' real estate business were taken at the time of the initial investigation, but buggered if I can find them."

"Oh, yeah, I remember. There was something about that. Let me just check with Rich. Hold on." The phone went quiet.

A few minutes later, there was a rustle and then, "Mate, you there?"

"Yeah, Mitch, still here," Donaldson answered.

"Nah, the files weren't saved."

"Whaddyamean they weren't saved?" Jake replied with mounting dread.

"Well, according to Rich, they didn't bother to add them to the file since they weren't relevant to the case."

"Who said they weren't relevant?"

"Franklin. What's the big deal, anyway? The bitch getting you to jump through hoops, is she?" Mitch sneered mockingly.

"Never mind. I'll talk to you later," Jake mumbled and ended the call. *What the hell?* He was beginning to realise just how right the inspector was when she'd inferred that the initial investigation was a bit 'light-on'. Light-on didn't even come close. They hadn't identified Tyler had a girlfriend; nor that Samantha had a boyfriend; no one had questioned the manner of Sam's death; they hadn't even interviewed Dean Teasel. The whole drug link hadn't been found, and now, they hadn't even saved evidence they'd seized!

"Shit! Shit! Shit!" Jake thumped his desk in frustration.

"What the hell's the matter, Jake?" Margot burst out. She was busy and didn't need the distraction of his ranting.

"The real estate system ... it wasn't saved," he said, glad that the inspector was nowhere within earshot.

Margot's head shot up over the partition separating them. "Wasn't saved?! Why the hell not?" she hissed.

"Not considered relevant. The stupid bastards had their heads up their arse. So sure it was Tyler that killed Sam, they couldn't even be bothered saving the evidence they'd taken."

Margot's head reeled back. Then she looked at Jake, shaking her head. "Well, you'd better hope that Lyndal still has her copy," she declared bluntly, and then sunk back down to her seat.

Jake swore and thumped the desk again, took a deep breath and picked up his phone to call Ms Palmer.

Anna ended the call and sat for several minutes contemplating the information she had received. The Chief had put her on to an Inspector Samuel Monroe of the Queanbeyan office Drug Squad. Despite a rather cool initial reception, he had been quite helpful once she had explained her theory. There was no doubt in her mind now that Foley and the Webbs had been running drugs. Monroe had confirmed there had been a steady supply of crystal meth, aka 'ice', coming into the region for approximately two years. This had stopped abruptly about twelve months ago, but they'd never been able to identify the source. They had ended the conversation with his offer of resources should she need them and her commitment to keep him in the loop.

"Inspector?" a voice said next to her, and she started, so engrossed with her thoughts she hadn't heard his approach.

"Yes, Jake?"

"I'm heading out to the Webbs' to check out whether there's any location history for the cars. I've arranged for a tech guy to meet me there."

Anna noticed his rather subdued tone and wondered at the cause of it.

"Good. Can you cover off Fran Everington and whether she's seen Foley hanging about at the same time?"

"Yep, I've already rung her to see if she'd be home. I'll drop by afterwards."

"Okay, good. Let me know if she does." She watched him walk away. He seemed depressed. She sighed. *I hope this isn't going to turn into another drama.*

Anna glanced over at Jake, wondering how much longer it was going to take. He was working with Lyndal Palmer to load the Webbs' business files from an external hard drive onto his laptop. They'd been at it for the better part of an hour since they'd also had to download and install the software to run the database. She was still fuming that the files had not been saved by the previous investigating team. Jake, red-faced and mortified, had told her earlier, but at least he'd had the sense to make sure Palmer had *her* backup and brought it with her.

After another fifteen minutes, Jake quietly confirmed they were ready to go. Palmer, with a very self-satisfied look as the saviour of the day, walked them through the scheduling system, pointing out the 'Sam's Specials'.

"Lyndal, what does this number and symbol mean?" Anna pointed to the screen, at the icon that appeared against several of the Sam's Special appointments.

"Oh, that just means that the appointment has been rescheduled, and the number of times it was rescheduled."

"So, this appointment in August was rescheduled *three* times?" Anna tapped the screen.

"Yes, that's right. She must have been having a tough time agreeing on a date with her ... *friend*," Lyndal muttered snidely.

"And yet, these later ones in January and February have no reschedules. Sergeant, note down the reschedules as well." Anna nodded to Jake.

"Is there a way of seeing the previous appointment dates on these reschedules?"

Lyndal frowned. "Ahh, yeah, I think there is ... just give me a minute." She typed rapidly on the keyboard. "Here it is," she added several seconds later.

"Let's write those down as well, Sergeant."

They wrapped up not long afterwards, Anna thanking Lyndal for her assistance in getting them out of a tight spot.

"No worries. Happy to help. Lucky mine wasn't corrupt like yours was. I was a bit worried when your sergeant said his copy was unusable since they were backed up at around the same time."

Anna smiled and nodded as Lyndal took her leave and then turned to Jake with a cocked eyebrow. *"Corrupt?"*

Jake swallowed. "I didn't want to tell her we hadn't saved it," he admitted grimly.

Anna grunted in exasperation.

"So, we have location history for Sam's Lexus, but not for Tyler's truck, correct?" She looked pointedly at Jake, who nodded. "Let's have a look at what we have then and see where that gets us."

"Corryong," Jake said a few minutes later.

"Just over the state border." Anna nodded. "Makes sense. Foley brings the drugs up from Melbourne to Corryong. Samantha drives over the mountains and picks them up. It's about a four-hour round trip?"

"Closer to five from where they live," Jake corrected, checking the trip data.

"That's the entire Sam's Special appointment slot. And it doesn't look like she stopped anywhere in between. Office to Corryong to Tyrolean each time." Anna stood and walked to the window. Grey cloud stretched horizon to horizon, and as she watched, spots of rain spattered the window.

She turned slowly back around. "The reschedules ... they were all in winter, weren't they?"

Jake looked taken aback, but on checking his notes, he looked up in surprise. "Yeah, they were. Mostly June to August, one in September in the first year." His eyes rolled as the significance dawned. "The road was closed across the mountains."

"Hmm, tricky in winter, not surprising they rescheduled so many times," she said, her mind already moving on. "Damn! I think we might need Lyndal again ... unless you can access that database, Jake?"

"Yeah, I think I can." He bent to type.

Anna turned to Margot. "Anything on the cleaner?"

"Nothing useful, Boss," Margot replied. "She came twice a week in the early mornings. She said Mrs Webb was always there while she worked. On the odd occasion, Tyler was there, but she said she never spoke with him. She saw Ethan most times and said he was a nice little boy. I got the strong impression that she disliked Samantha. No great surprise there. She didn't see anyone else."

"So, Samantha could be bothered to be home for the cleaner, but not for her son." Anna shook her head. *Some people really shouldn't have children.*

"Right. Good to go." Jake looked up from the screen.

"On the days that Sam was picking up from Foley, what was Tyler doing in the afternoons?"

As Jake looked it up, Margot said, "You think Sam picked up and Tyler dropped off?"

Anna nodded slowly. "Tyler was definitely involved. Based on that conversation he and Sam had in the kitchen, he had a role to play."

"Looking at the schedule, Tyler's got an unnamed appointment each afternoon after a Sam's Special," Jake said, looking up. "So, looks like you're right, Tyler *was* dropping off."

"What's the time slot?"

"Two hours."

"Hmm, that would take him to Cooma and back, but not much further ... certainly not to Canberra or Queanbeyan." Anna walked back to the table and leant on a chair back.

"Did Fran Everington recognise Foley?"

Jake shook his head. "Nope, said she'd never seen him before."

"Pity. That would have been the clincher. Anyway, I'll update the Chief." Anna pulled out her phone, then stopped and turned back to Jake. "Actually, what I'd like you to do on Monday, Jake, is drive to Corryong and check the pubs, hotels, caravan parks, et cetera, and see if anyone recognises Foley. If we can place him there on the days Samantha went, then we'll have a lot more ammunition. At this point, all we have against him is that he was Sam's old boyfriend, and a known drug pedlar. We need to link the two more closely together."

Chapter 29

"Wʜᴀᴛ ᴅᴏ ʏᴏᴜ ᴡᴀɴᴛ to drink, Lissoni?" Jake asked as Margot took a stool at a high bench table near the open fire at the hotel.

"Just a lite beer, thanks."

He left and weaved his way through the crowd towards the bar. She rested her chin on her hand and wondered what Jake could possibly want to talk about. He'd asked her to come for a drink, something he'd never done before. It was not from romantic interest, she was positive. There had been zero spark between them in all the time they had been at the Cooma Station together. In fact, truth be told, she'd always found him a bit of a nob. She didn't think it was an overture of friendship, either. They had not worked that closely before, a fact that the last couple of weeks in Jindabyne had made her sincerely thankful for. He was so … *overbearing.* Despite being the same grade, he'd assumed a superior attitude and often tried to tell her what to do.

The only thing she could assume, with the inspector's deadline looming, was that he wanted to discover how she was feeling about it. *Well, that'll be a quick conversation,* she murmured, still firm in her decision to stick with the inspector.

If she'll have me, she added. A sick feeling hung in the pit of her stomach at the thought of what it would mean if she was booted. The last few days, in particular, had reaffirmed her belief that the inspector was her means of moving forward with her career. The inspector was everything she aspired to, and Margot was determined to learn as much from her as possible *if* she got the chance.

Jake slopped a schooner in front of her and sat down opposite. Margot mopped up the puddle of beer with a cardboard coaster.

"Cheers!" Jake lifted his glass and downed a third in one long swallow.

"Cheers," Margot echoed and took a sip of her own. "What's up?" she added, eager to get this meeting over with.

"Just wanted to see whether you've decided what you're going to do." He looked at her keenly. "Are you thinking of sticking with it or chucking it?" Neither of them was under any illusion that Lissoni would not understand what he was referring to.

"Absolutely sticking with it, *if* the DI agrees."

Jake's eyebrows shot up. "Really?" He sounded completely shocked.

"I take it you're not?"

"I'm ... I'm still deciding." He frowned. "Ah ... *you* sound pretty certain, what's your thought?"

"The inspector is easily the best police officer I've ever worked with. She's brilliant, and she includes me in her thinking, asks for my opinion, and, in just the last week alone, I've learned so much. How can you *not* be thinking of staying?" she queried pointedly.

Jake sat back, stunned. He had assumed Lissoni would *not* want to continue with the inspector. She had always seemed to him to be a bit ... *lightweight*. Not that he had a specific problem with her. She was okay generally, but she didn't strike him as ... *competition*. Her decision to keep on with the inspector shook him. Farrow clearly had very high expectations of her staff and working for her was no walk in the park. She was a good detective, he'd give her that, especially after watching her in the last few days, but he struggled to connect with her.

He'd had a great relationship with his previous boss in Cooma, Inspector Franklin, easy-going and friendly. He felt valued and included in the team. But he knew a large part of the reason for that was Franklin's team was a boy's club; a testosterone fest, and he'd thrived under it. So deep down, he knew his success in the team had stemmed entirely from being male and not from any particular talent that he'd exhibited. And, if he was being totally honest with himself, he knew that his current struggle was not one he should be proud of. An easy life as one of the boys or advancing in the force through hard work.

"I can see you're contemplating going back to the Cooma Unit, Jake," declared Margot, barely hiding a sneer. She had worked under Inspector Franklin for three years and was well aware of why Jake would find that environment a lot more to his liking. He had been one of the boys, given the best jobs, invited to after-work drinks; in on the bets and sexist innuendoes that were rife in the department there. But it was clear from what had transpired in the last two weeks on the Webb case, that the level of policing under Franklin was sub-par. The initial investigation had been superficial, at best. In the short time she had been with DI Farrow, she could see how it all *should* have happened. She was not intimidated by the inspector's rather cool interactions with them. After all, anything was better than the macho environment she had endured at Cooma. And she felt that in time, *if* she earned the inspector's respect, she could establish a warm working relationship with her. A part of her hoped Jake would take the easy route and go back to Cooma.

"I haven't made up my mind yet," Jake muttered uncomfortably. He was still somewhat taken aback that Lissoni was so adamant about staying on.

"Well, sounds like you've got some thinking to do. My only worry now is whether I've done enough over the last week to show the DI that I'm worth her time and can convince her to keep me on next Friday," Margot declared, her chin thrust out.

Jake frowned. *His* prime motivation over the last week had been to show DI Farrow that she had misjudged him. He had assumed, right from the start, that the DI would want him on the team and that the decision to stay or go rested with him alone. But Lissoni's point about having done enough to convince the inspector she was worthy, shook him. He'd never taken the inspector's threat to dump him seriously; maybe he should have.

"I'm heading off," Margot stood abruptly, not wishing to extend the meeting now that they'd covered the issue.

"Okay, see you later." Jake nodded, barely looking up.

Lissoni walked to her car and sat inside but didn't turn on the engine. She really wanted to tell the DI about Jake's reaction last Friday night, sure that would be the final nail in his coffin. She didn't doubt the inspector would boot him if she knew.

Margot shook her head, remembering that night with a hot flush of shame … was it only seven days ago? The inspector had walked out after laying down her challenge, and barely two minutes after the door closed, Jake had erupted. 'Who the hell did she think she was? Telling *him* he had a fatal flaw! Geezus! How up herself was she to think she could pigeonhole him in just five days.' It went on and on. But Margot had been too submerged in her own humiliation to even acknowledge his fury. She'd just sat there … going over and over the scene in her mind, feeling sick, and shrinking further and further down in her seat. While Jake ranted over the DI's unfair and erroneous analysis of him, Margot knew that the inspector had pegged them both with deadly accuracy.

She had always been a pleaser, wanting to be liked. She wasn't sure when it started, but it had dogged her adolescence and early adulthood to the extent that everyone who knew her told her that joining the police force was a huge mistake and not for her. They all said she was too soft-hearted and wouldn't be able to project sufficient authority to be a copper. Work under DI Franklin had been an unwelcome revelation, with its macho, sexist vibe. Rather than galvanising her to stand up and assert herself, it had undermined her confidence still further. She realised her time there had only reinforced all those negative opinions, including her own. But she knew she had more in her … she knew she had to push herself out of her comfort zone to become the person she wanted to *be* rather than just accept the person she was. *This* was the time to step up. She had the perfect role model to emulate. *This* was her time.

She contemplated her earlier thought of talking to the inspector about Jake, but it made her feel mean and petty that she'd even considered it. Throwing Jake under the bus was not the person she wanted to be. But even as she dismissed the thought, an image of the inspector in full flight last Friday came to mind, and she was sure the DI had probably worked it all out anyway.

189

Chapter 30

ANNA WOKE WITH A start on Saturday morning, her breathing rapid and her heart racing. She took a deep breath and retraced the dream that had woken her. The images were still so vivid:

She had driven to a memorial service. The day was bright with brilliant blue skies and just the hint of a soft cool breeze; the lawns were a deep, lush green. She walked up the cobblestone pathway to the old sandstone church. Its ancient walls adorned with lichen and blackened with age. Its tall spire, topped with a cross, seemed like an arrow pointing to the heavens. She paused briefly on the threshold, letting her eyes adjust to the gloom inside. The pews were full, and the sound of soft weeping and snuffling greeted her. She walked slowly down the aisle towards the coffin mounted on its catafalque. Looking around to see who was there, she tried to work out whose service it was. She saw old friends, and then her mum and dad huddled together in the first pew, comforting each other. Dee and Riley were sitting next to them; Dee with her arm around him. They were both crying. Anna moved forward, hardly seeming to walk in the strange way of dreams but floating like a spectre. She reached the coffin; the lid was ajar, and she stared at the person nestled in white satin. Her own face stared back at her.

She shook her head disgustedly, her centimetre long hair rasping on the cotton covered pillow. *Well, it didn't need a psychologist to work that one out!* She knew the fear of dying was not what prompted the dream; it was the fear of leaving behind those she loved. Never to see them again. She was not religious, having been brought up agnostic, however, she recognised the value that faith in a hereafter could provide the dying. That assurance that you would not leave entirely; that you lived on in some altered state and would still see those you loved. It certainly had a lot of appeal. *Probably explained why a lot of people found religion when they became terminally ill*, she thought sarcastically. She sighed heavily, wishing momentarily, that she had that sort of faith to fall back on.

Stretching lazily, she chastised herself for being maudlin. Especially today. A small smile turned up the corners of her mouth. She and Cameron were going out. Her heart rate accelerated, and she couldn't deny the sudden burst of desire that erupted at her core and dampened her inner thighs. Wiggling her toes, she felt a mix of hedonistic excitement and simultaneous embarrassment at her enthusiasm, as if someone were judging her and finding it rather pathetic that a forty-plus woman would feel as giddy as a schoolgirl over a date.

She laughed at her reaction. *You are out of practice, my girl!* And anyway, there was no saying their evening out would end up in bed.

After all, my lack of breasts might put him off ...

Suddenly, for the first time, she regretted their absence. *Oh, for pity's sake, woman, get over yourself!* She flung back the bedclothes and stomped off to the bathroom.

"Where's he taking you?" Dee asked as they sat over the debris of a long, lazy breakfast.

"A Lebanese restaurant. His favourite." Anna felt the bubble of happiness that she had experienced earlier, well up.

"Ni-ice!" Dee smiled and then, with a quick check to see if Riley was in earshot, leant forward. "Packed your jammies?"

Anna flushed hotly and was then furious that she had.

"For goodness' sake, Dee!" she countered, but her embarrassment waned in light of Dee's delighted smile.

"Well, I have packed a lacy little something," Anna admitted with a grin, but then the doubt crept in, stealing her smile. "But I have to admit, I'm not sure it's a great idea."

Dee frowned. "Why not?"

"Well, I'm missing a few crucial components," Anna answered tartly.

"So? You've still got the most essential bit. And anyway, what's the big deal? He's seen you naked already. It's not like he's going to be shocked at your being boobless, is he?"

"It's not the same thing, is it?" Anna frowned into her coffee. "He looked at me as a doctor then. This is completely different. Now he's going to look at me like … a man."

Dee reached across the table and put her hand over her sister's. Her heart lurched, hearing her doubts. Anna had always been the strong one, her brave, fearless sister. She grasped the small, frail hand tightly.

"Love is always about taking a risk, Lina," Dee said gently. "No matter how self-assured you are; no matter how confident of the response; *truly* loving someone is about taking a leap of faith. Remember, he took the first step. He asked *you* for a drink. He told *you*, you were important to him. It's your turn now. If you want to be loved, you have to take the big step into the abyss and hope like hell the other person is there for you."

Anna nodded slowly. "I know. It's just … *hard*. I'm not that trusting."

"You're telling me!" Dee snorted, bringing a smile to Anna's face.

"And besides … so you don't have boobs. There are a lot of people out there who aren't perfect in their body. They may have lost a limb, or an eye … or be genuinely dead ugly—"

Anna grinned.

"—but people still love them. I think physical appeal is *one* part of the initial interaction between two people, but it isn't the only thing, and it certainly isn't what keeps them together. How many people mistake lust for love only to end up hating the person they're with? Even if they are gorgeous."

A thought of Samantha and Tyler Webb crossed Anna's mind.

"So, I'm fairly certain Cameron knows what he's getting into and is okay with it. Now, *you* have to trust *him* to treat you as you deserve to be treated." Dee squeezed her sister's hand. "And if he doesn't ... then you need to let him know that I will personally tear his balls off," she added succinctly.

Anna laughed and shook her head at her sister. "I love you."

"I love you too."

"This is divine," Anna sighed, scooping up another spoonful of fattoush. "I think I'm going to burst, but it's so good I can't stop."

"I'm so glad you like it," Cameron said, with a delighted smile that had hardly left his face the whole evening. "I love it. I must eat here at least once a week."

Anna cocked an eyebrow.

"No, not what you're thinking ... solo. Mostly takeaway. Hospital hours, you know."

"I know what you mean, police hours are a bit challenging as well."

"I imagine they are, especially as a detective. You're working the 'body in the lake' case, I presume?"

Anna nodded. "But year-old bodies are not so bad. It's the new deaths that mean the long, long hours."

"First twenty-four hours, isn't it? That's what they always say on those TV crime shows."

"Yeah. When a body has just been found, that's when you get a lot of forensic evidence, witnesses, CCTV footage, all sorts of things that help to build a picture of what happened. Fast forward a year, and basically, you have none of that and it's all about speaking to people and trying to work out even the most basic of facts: Who are they? How did they die? Why?"

"I can see that would make it a lot harder."

"Although in saying that, sometimes you can get information a year or more down the track that you wouldn't have been given in a day or so after the death," Anna admitted, but seeing Cameron's interested look, continued, "Witnesses are a lot more likely to say things about victims with the passage of time. People are generally reluctant to say negative things about a victim or admit to something that might put them in an awkward light just after an event. But leave it to marinate for a year and it seems less ... immediate or intimidating and therefore less threatening. Of course, it also might mean they forget or embellish the truth as well." She laughed.

Cameron smiled, enjoying the light in her eyes. "It's a tough job. But you seem to enjoy it."

"I enjoy the *hunt*," she admitted. "The challenge, the puzzle to be solved. But like any job, it has its frustrations, disappointments and ... unending bureaucracy."

Cameron chuckled quietly. "Absolutely. You want bureaucracy, come to a public hospital."

They smiled at each other. Anna wallowed briefly in the look of desire she saw in Cameron's eyes, before dropping her gaze.

"Would you like to see the dessert menu?" the waitress asked.

Anna looked up at Cameron and shook her head.

"No, thanks, just the bill," he said, his voice catching in his throat.

"Your place is lovely, Cam," Anna said, turning around as he put down her overnight bag.

It was a roomy apartment on the second floor. Its open-plan layout flowed onto a large balcony with views over Lake Burley-Griffin in the distance. She could just make out the jet of water shooting up and catching the strategically placed lights. Two small table lamps gave the room a soft glow.

He smiled. "Took me a while to find something I liked. I rented for ages. I hesitated buying something until I'd worked out my own style and preferences." He took her hand and led her to the large three-seater lounge.

"Really?"

"I suppose that sounds a bit strange. But when you get married at twenty, at uni studying to be a doctor, and then becoming a father at twenty-one ... working out what sort of décor appeals to you was not top of my priority list," he said with a shrug.

"No, I suppose not."

"And then it's not just your *own* style that counts either once you're married. Jules had some very definite ideas and I'm afraid I took the very male position of leaving her to it." He grinned.

Anna laughed. "Well, I think you did very well. A good idea to wait before buying to work out what you really wanted."

"Would you like a glass of red? I've got a very nice one from the Margaret River," Cam said, suddenly nervous.

"Yes please," she answered, her breathing becoming rather ragged at the thought of where this was leading.

Cameron stood and poured the glasses of wine. Anna, suddenly too nervous to sit still, stood and walked to the glass sliding doors that opened to the balcony. Thick velvety blackness stretched out before her, dotted with twinkling lights that yielded to the broad impenetrable darkness of the lake beyond.

"It's beautiful," Anna murmured, accepting the glass of wine he offered. She could smell its deep heady fragrance overlaid with a warm male scent that was his own.

He looked at her profile: perfect white skin showcased by the dark red halo of her head. Her ear, small and shell-like; the shadow beneath her cheekbone; her nose, straight but flaring gently at the tip. Her long lashes swept downward in acknowledgement of his scrutiny.

"You are beautiful, Anna," he said, the words catching in his throat.

She leaned toward him; they stared into each other's eyes. Her hand took Cameron's glass, and she placed them both on a small side table.

She turned back and put a hand up to cup his cheek.

His hands circled her and pulled her in. The kiss was long and deep, and Anna thought she might drown in the heat and desire that swept over her. His large hands caressed her back as the kiss deepened still further; they slowly descended to cup her bottom and lift her up and in towards him. She could feel his desire pressing into her belly.

Breathing heavily, Cameron pulled back so he could look into her eyes. "Is this okay with you? Tell me if not and we'll stop."

"No. I want you," she whispered.

Cameron leant down and picked her up in his arms. She pressed her face into his neck.

He carried her to the bedroom, dark, except for the moonlight streaming in from the window. He laid her down gently and stretched out next to her.

She ran a hand up his belly and across his chest, finding the buttons on his shirt and undoing them one by one.

His head turned towards her, and he watched her face and the emotions that skittered across it in the silvery light.

She spread his shirt and felt the rough texture of his hair, the nubs of his erect nipples, and the tense, solid muscles beneath. Leaning in, she kissed his mouth softly and he pulled her on top of him in one strong fold of his arm.

Anna kissed him deeply, hands cupping his face.

He massaged the cheeks of her bottom, spread wide across his hips, and his breath caught in his throat. Not able to wait any longer, he rolled them both over and, sitting up, tore off his shirt. His fingers went to undo his jeans, but Anna's hands stopped them.

Looking deep into his eyes, she undid the button and then slowly slid down the zip, feeling his desire bulge out against her hand. She slipped her hand underneath and cupped him, leaning in to kiss him hard on the mouth, cutting off his groan.

He drew back and gently pulled her hand away as his breathing became more ragged. He smiled, and Anna felt the world fade away, leaving only the two of them. Leaning on one arm, he stroked her face, then her neck and then, as softly as butterfly wings, deftly undid the buttons of her shirt, spreading it wide to reveal the soft silk of her camisole underneath. His hands brushed across her chest scars, sending a shiver through her entire being. His hand slid down the soft skin of her belly to the top of her jeans and, as she had, slowly undid the zipper. She lifted her bottom instinctively, as he sat to pull them off and the thin strip of lace that she had worn underneath.

He lay back, propped on one arm, his hand caressing her from face to thigh with long, feathery strokes. Anna arched her back as his touch became more intimate.

With a final groan of desire, Cameron rolled over, and, with his hand beneath the cheek of her bottom, slid inside her slippery heat.

They lay exhausted. Cameron spreadeagled and occupying eighty percent of the available bed, Anna curled into his side like a contented kitten.

His hand gently caressing her neck, he sighed heavily as if the air came from the soles of his feet.

"Oh ... my ... God!" he whispered into the silky wisps of her hair.

Anna grinned into his chest.

He heaved himself up on one arm to look down at her and shook his head. "I don't know what to say ... other than, when I can get my breath back, you're in trouble," he muttered throatily and flopped back down as she giggled delightedly.

Chapter 31

ANNA WOKE TO A tickle on her nose. She raised her arm slowly. It felt like it weighed a tonne. She managed to connect her hand to her cheek and realised her face lay pressed into a broad expanse of chest. A hair niggled at the tip of her nose. She smoothed it away and popped an eye open. Cameron was sleeping on his back, one arm flung over his head and the other planted like a large limpet on her hip, firmly anchoring her to his side. The low, rhythmic thump of his heart sounded clearly in her ear. Sunlight from the window caught the hairs on his chest, turning them a bright, ruddy brown. She idly circled his areolae—just a few millimetres from her mouth—with a barely-there touch and watched it pucker up in response.

Anna breathed deeply, smelling the warm male scent of him and the slight tang of their lovemaking. A huge smile broke out on her face. She twiddled her toes and, with a deep sigh of contentment, drifted back off to sleep.

Cameron handed her a mug of coffee. "When can I see you again?" They stood together on his balcony, enjoying the view over the lake and of each other.

Anna smiled up at him, put a hand on his chest and fiddled with a button. She couldn't seem to stop touching him. The feeling was obviously mutual as Cameron stroked her cheek.

"What about dinner mid-week?" she said, sounding hopeful.

Cameron grinned. "Perfect. But you can't drive up here every time. How would you feel about me staying down at your place?"

Anna looked out over the wind-ruffled lake to give herself a minute. If he came down, that would mean he would be sleeping with her ... *at Dee's* ... *with* Riley in the house.

"Too soon?" Cameron said, watching her face.

"I don't know." She wrinkled her nose. "Dee will have *no* problem with it. In fact, she'd be ecstatic, but ... I've never had anyone to stay at my place with Riley there. I'm not sure how he would feel about it. Can I let you know?"

"Sure. It's not a problem. I just don't want you to always be the one making the long drive." He didn't want any roadblocks in the way of them seeing each other.

The idea of Cameron staying over occupied her thoughts as Anna drove back down the highway. She didn't *think* Riley would have a problem with it. After all, he was fourteen now and aware of love, sex and relationships between consenting adults. *Just not that his mum was engaged in one,* said a small voice in her head. She'd have a talk to him, sound him out and see how he felt. Maybe he and Cameron should meet on neutral ground first and see if they liked each other. She shuddered at the thought that they might not and then gave herself a mental shake. There was no point in imagining the worst.

After another half hour recalling every delicious second of the evening before and the night that followed, Anna's thoughts turned to her case.

There seemed no doubt that Nathan Foley was involved with the Webbs in some sort of drug trafficking operation. But the link was tenuous at best. She hoped Jake would find some proof that Foley had been in Corryong, and prefer-ably, iron-clad proof that linked his presence there with Samantha Webb's trips. It was unfortunate that Fran Everington had not seen Foley near the Webbs' house. It looked like they had maintained separation for security reasons and communicated only via the burner phone. However, they must have met up initially to get the process worked out.

That might have happened in Corryong as well. She'd message Jake and ask him to show Samantha's and Tyler's photos around and see if he got a hit. It was a remote possibility. The setup of the operation would have been close to three years ago now, with Sam and Tyler both dead twelve months. Then, there was Monroe saying that the flood of drugs into Cooma had run for approximately two years before it dried up.

Anna doubted the Webbs would have entertained Foley at their offices. He was a distinctive-looking person, with his huge build, large bald head and deep-set, soulless black eyes. He would not have gone unnoticed. It was also unlikely, for the same reason, that they would have met at a pub or restaurant in Jindabyne. It was much more likely to be in Corryong, out of the way of anyone they knew, or ... possibly ... at the Webbs' home.

Ethan!

Anna breathed deeply as the child's face popped into her head. She needed to check if Ethan had ever seen Foley. She hated to drag him into it, but it had to be done. She could well imagine that neither of the Webbs would have considered Ethan a threat to their operation, and would not have bothered to hide a meeting with their associate from him, other than to tell him to go away and play. The more she thought about it, the more it seemed a likely scenario.

She had messaged Dee and Riley earlier to tell them she was heading back home but now she dialled Dee's number.

"Anna," Dee answered with a smile in her voice.

"Hiya Dee. On my way, but I think I might take a bit of a detour, so I'll be a bit later than planned."

"Okay, where are you off to?"

"I want to visit a family out near Dalgety and just ask a question. Shouldn't take too long."

"This about your case?"

"Yeah, probably end up being nothing, but since I'm driving anyway ..."

"You do realise that Dalgety is not a detour on the way to Mungunbah," Dee said facetiously. "It is, in fact, about twenty minutes past it."

"Yes, I do realise that, but it's bugging me, and I want to get an answer," Anna replied smartly. "So, all up, I expect to be about an hour later than planned. Can you let Riley know?"

"Sure, no problem. He's playing something on his Xbox with Madison; he probably won't even notice you're not here."

Anna knocked on the door again more firmly, but after several minutes had to conclude the Carter-Ellis' either weren't home or couldn't hear her. Working on the latter theory, she walked around the side of the house towards the stables. These were set back and at right angles to the house and adjacent to a large fenced-in paddock.

It was here she found the three of them. The old man was leading a horse by a head rein in a wide circle in the enclosure, a saddle on its back. The young mare seemed a bit twitchy. It kept pulling on the lead to glance around at the saddle as if wondering about the strange appendage adhered to her back. Anna could see her glossy brown coat shivering in irritation at the unfamiliar object.

Sally Carter-Ellis stood at the gate, watching her husband intently. Further around, Ethan had climbed up and was sitting on the top rung of the fence, totally engrossed.

Anna approached slowly and as silently as possible. She did not want to create a distraction, nor a reason for the horse to use her presence as a reason to lose its tenuous grip on its frustration and erupt in protest.

As she got close, she cleared her throat softly. The old lady turned, and her eyes widened at seeing Anna there. Ethan looked over and gave her a toothy smile.

Anna closed the remaining few metres and stood next to Sally to watch the proceedings.

"She's going really well," Sally whispered to Anna out of the side of her mouth, her eyes still on her husband.

After a further ten minutes, the old man looped the rein over the fence rail, pulled off the saddle and gave the horse a hard pat of appreciation.

"Hi, Inspector," he said, walking over. "Sorry to keep you waiting."

"Not at all. It was very interesting. I've not seen a horse being broken before."

Mark sighed. "It's a slow process of getting them used to the rein, the weight of the saddle and all the handling. But I love it," he added, grinning.

"Is she one of yours?"

"No, she belongs to our neighbour. I don't do as much breaking as I used to—just our own—but I'm doing this one as a favour."

"I'm sorry to barge in unannounced. I just had a very quick question ... *for Ethan*," Anna said, lowering her voice.

They turned as one. Ethan was still perched on the railings, feeding a carrot to the horse, well out of earshot.

"Ethan?" Sally turned to Anna; her brow furrowed.

Anna nodded. "I need to see if Ethan has ever seen Nathan Foley at his parent's place."

"*Nathan Foley?*" the old man repeated in a shocked tone.

"Yes," Anna responded, rather reluctantly. She hated having to be the bearer of bad news and dispelling the rosy picture people had of their daughter definitely fell into the category of bad news. But it was often a fact that victims of violent crime had some hidden agenda that did not cast them in a benevolent light. She knew that telling the Carter-Ellis' of their daughter's suspected drug trafficking with her old boyfriend was not liable to make either parent feel very friendly towards her.

"What's he got to do with anything?"

Anna licked her lips, and a small part of her brain registered that they were slightly swollen, probably from Cameron's bristly chin. She pulled her thoughts back sharply to the present.

"I believe that your daughter and her husband may have been involved in some dealings with Nathan Foley. We're still trying to get to the bottom of it."

"Dealings? You're not trying to say they were involved in something criminal?" the old man bit out. His wife put a hand on his arm and shot him a warning look with a glance toward Ethan.

"It's possible they were," Anna answered, not wanting to delude them. "There are some suspicious activities that we've unearthed and a lot of extra cash that is not accounted for."

The old man's eyes shot daggers at her, his mouth pinched, and he seemed to swell.

"Well, we always thought Tyler was trouble," Sally said softly.

Anna watched the old man's anger drain away as he processed his wife's words and accepted them, since anything else was just not possible in his mind. It had to be all Tyler's doing; Samantha could not possibly be at fault.

Anna recognised the deflection, and accepted it gladly, *for now*. She knew that he was going to have to face his daughter's criminality at some stage, but she was happy to defer it to another day.

"Well ... if anything criminal was happening, then it was definitely Tyler's fault, not our Sam's."

Anna heard the warning note in his tone. "As I said, we don't know the full story at this stage. But we do think Nathan Foley had something to do with Sam and Tyler."

"You don't think it was Foley that killed Samantha, do you?" Sally exclaimed suddenly.

"What are you talking about Sally?! Tyler did it!" Mark replied, looking at his wife as if she had lost her mind.

"Well, we don't know for sure, but it is a possibility we're considering,"

The old man's face blanched. "Foley?" he breathed out in a long sigh.

"As I said," Anna continued, "we're still trying to get to the bottom of it—"

"So, you need to ask Ethan whether he ever saw Foley at their house?" the old lady asked quickly.

"Yes, if you have no objections," Anna answered, grateful that Sally Carter-Ellis seemed intent on helping her. "Would you be comfortable with me showing Ethan a photo of Foley and asking him whether he has ever seen him, and if so, when and where?"

"Yes, of course! Don't we, Mark?" Sally glared at her husband, her eyes wide.

Mark looked wary, as if there might be a catch involved, but after several tense seconds, he nodded.

"Ethan!" his grandmother called.

"Yes, Gran." He jumped off the fence and ran over to them.

Anna smiled. "Hi, Ethan."

"Hi," he responded breathlessly, his squirrel-like teeth on show. *He would be a handsome man someday,* she thought ... *when he grew into his teeth.*

"Ethan, do you remember Inspector Farrow?" his gran murmured.

"Yes, you're investigating what happened to my dad."

Anna saw his grandfather flinch at the slight yearning in his grandson's voice.

"I have a question for you. Can you tell me if you have ever seen this man ... it would have been a few years ago." She held out her phone, on which Foley's mug shot was visible.

Ethan took the phone and then looked up. "Yeah ... I've seen him. But it wasn't years ago, it was on Friday."

Chapter 32

"Inspector?"

Anna dragged herself out of her reverie and turned. She had been staring blankly out of the kitchen window for some time, though the view was limited to the lights blazing from the stables.

"Yes, Margot?"

"Sally wants to know if she can put Ethan to bed now?"

"You've finished in his bedroom?"

Lissoni nodded. "Yes, we've checked everything in there. Nothing unaccounted for."

"Well then, yes, tell her she can put him to bed." Anna paused and then asked, "How is he, by the way?"

Lissoni smiled. "Oh, he's fine. He thinks the whole thing is fascinating. His gran, on the other hand ..."

"Hmm. I wish it could have been otherwise, but I can see only two reasons for Foley to have been lurking around: to search for something, or to kidnap Ethan and use him as a bargaining chip to threaten the Carter-Ellis' into telling him what he wants to know."

"But why would Sam or Tyler hide drugs here, though?"

"I agree. The premise is unlikely. But then why else is Foley here? And remember ... it's not what *we* think that counts ... it's what *Foley* thinks that matters. I think the chances of us finding anything are remote, at best, but I'm also hoping that Foley is paying attention and that if we find nothing after a thorough search then he'll move his attentions elsewhere and leave the Carter-Ellis' and Ethan alone."

"I see." Margot nodded, and though she had many more questions, she knew they would have to wait. "I'll go see Sally and tell her."

"Are there any more rooms left in the house that we need to search?"

"I think just the bathrooms—I'll do those now—that shouldn't take long," Lissoni turned and headed off.

A few minutes later, Donaldson and Mark Carter-Ellis came in through the back door.

"—pointless—" The old man stomped in and stopped short, seeing Anna standing there.

"Stables and barn are all cleared, Inspector," Jake reported, side-stepping the stationary old man to walk in. "Nothing that Mark didn't recognise, and everything searched."

"Good, thank you, Sergeant. How are SOCO going?"

"Just wrapping up at the stables now. They said they should be able to give you an update shortly. Having the family's exclusionary fingerprints and Foley's on file speeds things up."

Anna had called in both Donaldson and Lissoni, as well as the Scene of Crime Officers, shortly after Ethan's bombshell announcement.

Even now, four hours on, Anna was still reeling.

"Friday? You mean two days ago, Ethan?" she had said, an icy shiver running down her spine.

Ethan nodded.

"Where?" his grandfather whispered, his face grey. His grandmother, breathing heavily, gripped the fence with white knuckles as if to keep herself upright.

"I was waiting for you, Grandad ... you know, out front of the school," Ethan said, sounding a little cautious, as he picked up on the rising tension of the adults around him. He wasn't quite sure if he was in trouble. His eyes darted between the adults.

"And where was this man?" Anna asked with a gentle smile, tapping the phone screen.

Ethan turned to her gladly. She seemed not to be as upset, so he concentrated on her. "Well, he was leaning on the side of his car—"

"How did you know it was *his* car," the old man exclaimed.

"Mark! For goodness' sake! Just let Ethan tell it." Sally shot out.

Her husband clamped his mouth shut, his nostrils flaring with fretfulness.

Ethan stared at his toes in the uneasy silence that followed.

Anna bent down and looked into Ethan's face. "You're not in trouble, Ethan. Your gran and grandad are just worried about you."

Ethan looked up cautiously and caught his gran's eye. She forced a smile and nodded.

"So"—Anna gave him an encouraging smile—"you saw the guy leaning against his car. Can you tell me where his car was parked? Was it in front of the school, down the street, on the school side, or on the opposite side of the road?"

"He was across the road, like ... just the other side of the driveway," Ethan said with a small frown.

"The driveway into the school grounds, you mean?"

"Yeah." Ethan nodded vigorously.

"And then what happened?"

"Grandad pulled up, and I walked over and got in the car."

"I parked in the school pull-off zone," Mark added in a subdued tone. He reached over and gave Ethan's shoulder a squeeze. Ethan looked up and grinned, his grandad gave him a smile in return.

"And then?" Anna prompted.

"I saw the guy get in his car ... and then, when we drove off, he pulled in behind us." Ethan said. His grandad gasped.

"I saw him again when we turned off into our driveway," Ethan added to his gran's smothered exclamation of horror.

"What did he do? Did you see him drive away or ...?" Anna queried.

"No, he just pulled up and stopped."

"And you're *sure* it was this guy." Anna tapped on her phone screen again.

"Yeah, it was him." Ethan nodded. "I remembered him from ages ago."

Anna could feel her breath coming faster and took a second to recalibrate.

"You had seen him before, Ethan?"

He nodded. "At Mum and Dad's house."

"Do you remember what happened when he was at your house? Was the guy speaking to your mum or your dad?" Anna kept her tone light.

"He was having a fight with Mum." His eyes clouded over.

"Tell me about it."

"I wasn't supposed to come down. Mum told me to stay in my room." Ethan shot a cautious glance up at his grandad. The old man gave his shoulder another squeeze.

"I was really hungry, and it was getting late and ... so I snuck out and when I was on the stairs, I could hear yelling. But I just thought it was Mum and Dad, you know?" He looked up at Anna earnestly, and she nodded, sad that 'yelling' meant Mum and Dad to him. "So, I ... well I ... I know I shouldn't have ... but I ... I crept down to see who it was 'cause when I heard a bit more, I knew it wasn't Dad. On the last couple of steps, you can see right into the kitchen, you know?" Anna nodded again, not wanting to interrupt his flow.

"I could see him ... that guy." Ethan pointed at Anna's phone. "He and Mum were shouting at each other, but then ... they started smiling and talking real quiet-like. And then ... he ..." Ethan voice trailed off and his face flushed a bright red.

"Did he kiss your mum?" Anna said in a barely audible tone. She heard Mark's hiss of indignation.

Ethan nodded miserably.

Anna wondered how much more she could glean from Ethan without causing him and his grandparents any more pain.

"Ethan, do you recall any words that your mum or the guy used?"

His face suffused with a fresh flush of blood and Anna hastened to add, "Not swear words, Ethan, just any other words. Or did you hear what they were talking about?"

Ethan frowned in concentration, and Anna waited. "I think they were talking about ice cream and how it was going to make a lot of money."

"Ice cream?" Jake queried, late the following evening as Anna, Lissoni, and he caught up.

"I think what he heard was a conversation about ice, as in crystal meth. But as far as a little boy was concerned, it sounded like a discussion about ice cream," Anna said, thankful that Ethan was in better care now.

"So, with what you found out today, Jake, I think we can connect the dots at least as far as the drug trafficking operation is concerned."

Jake's trip to Corryong had yielded good results. In the end, it had been surprisingly easy. Foley, being a creature of habit and obviously confident that the reason for his visits would not be discovered, had stayed at the local pub on each of Sam's Special pick-up appointments. The manager of the hotel identified Foley immediately from his photograph, though he knew him under another name: Harry Upton.

Anna had since confirmed, through DI Monroe, that Harry Upton was a known alias of Nathan Foley. The hotelier also recognised Samantha Webb. She had, apparently, left an indelible impression.

"Nothing on Foley's whereabouts?" Jake asked. Anna had put it on the wire the previous night, to keep a lookout for Foley, after updating both the Chief and Monroe. Monroe, in particular, had been thrilled with her progress and again offered whatever resources she needed.

While Jake checked out Corryong, Anna and Lissoni had spent most of the day trying to get a trace on Foley in the Jindabyne area.

"No. Nothing so far." Anna got up, walked to the window and looked out over the lights of the town. Something had been nagging at her all day, but she just couldn't pin it down. There was something she was missing, she was sure of it. She sighed, hoping it would surface eventually.

Anna turned and leaned back against the filing cabinet. "Margot, did you get a chance to check with the Carter-Ellis' on how they were going?"

Lissoni nodded. "They're doing okay. A bit shocked and stressed still, but happy to have the police presence there."

Anna nodded. She thought it highly unlikely that Foley would make another run at the Carter-Ellis' property, but after his fingerprints had been confirmed at the barn and stables, she had immediately taken up Monroe's offer on their behalf and organised officers to be stationed at the house, just in case. Without being sure what Foley's motivation was at this stage, she preferred to err on the side of caution. Ethan and his grandparents had been through enough.

She briefly wondered how the old man was coping. He'd nearly collapsed after hearing Ethan recount the meeting between his mother and Foley in the kitchen. Anna sighed again. The higher you put someone on a pedestal, the further they had to fall. She knew that Sam's dad was now dealing with a most spectacular fall from grace: from outgoing, loving daughter, to adulterous, drug-dealing offspring.

"Okay, I think we need to call it a night. I'm beat and I'm sure you both are as well," Anna said, pushing off from her position against the filing cabinet.

"We'll continue looking for Foley tomorrow, unless we get lucky, and someone gets a line on him overnight."

"Hi, how's it going? How's your family faring?" Cameron's voice came through on her car's Bluetooth as he picked up her call. His deep voice was like a balm to her tired brain. They had spoken several times since she had left his apartment yesterday.

Was it only yesterday? It seemed so much longer than that. Their brief conversations were like islands of joy and peacefulness in the maelstrom that had erupted with those few words of Ethan's.

Anna knew Cameron was referring to the Carter-Ellis' when he said, 'your family'. She had filled him in as she stood in their kitchen the night before during a brief interlude of quiet, having swung the might of the police force into action.

"Still shocked and horrified to learn their daughter was involved in drug trafficking. I think the mum took it *reasonably* in her stride. I think she had a pretty clear idea of her daughter and the type of person she was, but the dad … well, *'blinkers on'* doesn't come close. He's absolutely devastated."

"That would be hard. Though I don't know which is worse. Sticking your head in the sand and believing that everything is rosy or acknowledging the problems up front. The former, at least, has the advantage of giving you some peace, for a time."

"True. But it's really only deferring the inevitable. I suppose I'm much more inclined to turn over the rock and see the scorpion underneath." She smiled.

"And if history is anything to go by … I'm the one who'll keep the rock where it is and avoid looking at it." Cameron laughed.

"A good balance then," she murmured softly.

"What are the chances of our date on Wednesday?"

Anna's heart skipped a beat at the small note of anxiety in his voice. "Well, at this point, pretty good, I think. Everyone is out looking for Foley, so other than that, it's business as usual."

"I don't suppose you've had any opportunity to speak to Riley about us yet?"

"No, I haven't. He was asleep when I got back last night. If I feel the moment is right, I might have a chat with him tonight." Anna tried to imagine her son's reaction. Every time she thought of it, she pictured him being pleased for her and happy to meet Cameron. But then, she felt that was more the result of her projecting what she wanted to happen, rather than an objective assessment.

"Okay, will you call me before you go to sleep?" His voice was like silk against her skin. She swallowed at the immediate reaction of her body.

"Yes," she whispered. "I will."

They rang off and Anna smiled. She could not ever remember being this ... excited and ... *invested* in someone before. God! She hoped Riley would be okay with it. *What will I do if he hates Cameron on sight?*

She shook her head, irritated with herself. The idea was barely worth thinking of. *But what if it happens?* her brain repeated, unable to leave it be.

For a brief moment she felt for Tyler Webb. Desperately wanting to extract himself from a painful and ugly marriage but unable to, because of the net Sam had woven with her drug connections that kept him captive. What recourse was there? Anna appreciated his need to reassure his girlfriend that he had a solution, but what possible action could be taken that would convince his wife to agree to a divorce? And without Sam's agreement and endorsement, there was no way Foley and his associates would trust Tyler. *She* was his link into the business. It was she who'd introduced him to Foley and sucked him down into the shady world of drug trafficking. They would not trust Tyler if Sam didn't. He risked being removed from the operation permanently if he left. So, what possible action could Tyler take to swing Sam's opinion in his favour? Clearly, Sam didn't believe Tyler would harm her. That video of her smirking at him as he threatened her with a knife was enough to confirm that. Now if the threat had come from *Foley*, Anna was sure Sam would have sat up and taken notice.

Anna sucked in a gasp as if she'd been punched in the stomach. A prickle of goosebumps rose along her arms and legs as adrenaline flooded her system. She pounded on the steering wheel. *God! How did I miss that?! It's so bloody obvious!*

Her brain raced. She pushed away a rising tide of irritation for not having made the connection sooner; she'd have time enough later to berate herself. Her breathing calmed as her thoughts moved on and she started to work through her next steps.

Chapter 33

ANNA SIPPED A CUP of tea and watched her son through the archway, absorbed in a program on the television in the next room. The dogs, never far from their favourite person, lay one on each side.

Dee sat opposite her and after several seconds of silence, cleared her throat loudly. "Earth to Anna, come in Anna."

Anna turned and smiled. "Sorry, just thinking about something."

"Work or Riley?"

Anna grimaced. "Cameron suggested he come down on Wednesday and we could go out. But as you know, it's a long drive so …"

Dee's eyebrows rose. "Er, so?"

"*So-o* … he'd need to stay *here*."

"Again … *so?*" Dee shrugged.

"Well, I'm worried about how Riley might take it … you know, his mum's boyfriend staying the night," Anna said, looking anxious.

Dee chuckled. "Oh, for goodness' sake, Lina." She shook her head. "He'll be fine with it. He's fourteen. He knows about the birds and bees. And besides," she added firmly, as Anna looked ready to interrupt. "He loves you. More than you can imagine. And he's not stupid. He knows Cameron must be someone special to you."

"Has he said something?"

"We've talked about it," Dee replied, but seeing her sister's eyes narrow, quickly added, "He was a little worried that this guy might hurt you. But I explained that all relationships come with that risk ... and sometimes, we just need to take a chance and hope we've chosen wisely. I told him I liked Cameron and, of course, he took that as gospel and now he's fine with it."

Anna shook her head at her sister's flippant comment. "But there's a difference between me going out with someone and having that someone over to stay," she insisted.

Dee's lips tightened. "Yes, there is. But there is a practical element to the process as well, Lina. The man lives in Canberra. It's a two-hour drive *one way* on country highway. It's just not safe to consider doing that on a regular basis. For you *or him*. You hit a roo at a hundred kay an hour and ..." Dee swallowed. An image of their parents flashed to mind. Not that their accident was the result of some poor innocent marsupial on the forage for food or romance; their parents had been killed by a drunk driver. But the result was still the same, with someone dead. In their case, two someones. And if Riley's sensibilities were the price for her sister not taking that risk—or Cameron, for that matter—then Dee was certain it was the right thing to do.

"Talk to him. I'm pretty sure he'll be fine," Dee said. "And if not, *I'll* talk to him and *then* he'll be fine."

Anna rolled her eyes and got up slowly. She walked into the lounge room and, nudging Spook aside, sat down next to Riley.

"Hey, Mum." He turned towards her. His blonde hair flopped over his forehead and his clear green eyes gazed back at her. Her heart squeezed.

Rubbing the dog's ears absently, Anna started, "Ah-h ... Riles ... you know I'm seeing Dr Childs ... er, Cameron?"

"Yeah, he sounds nice."

"Well ... you know he lives in Canberra?"

"Yeah, sure. Aunty Dee was a bit worried about you guys driving at night. You should stay over if you go out Mum, or maybe he can stay here ... it'd be heaps safer than driving late," Riley said in a matter-of-fact tone with one eye on the television.

Anna's mouth fell open. "So ... you'd be okay if Cameron stayed here?"

"Sure. I'd like to meet him."

Anna leant over and gave Riley a hug. He patted her back abstractly, his attention drawn back to the program on the screen.

Anna stood and turned back to the kitchen to see Dee smirking in the archway. She shook her head and Dee grinned.

Chapter 34

"Lissoni, you got any idea what's going on?" Jake called as he clicked the lock on his car and spotted her emerging from her own vehicle.

"None. I just got a text message last night. *'Please come in at seven. Farrow.'* I assume you got the same?"

"Yeah."

They walked in together and found the inspector in the meeting room sipping a takeaway coffee.

"Morning."

"Morning," they replied in chorus, and sat down at the table opposite her.

"Sorry to get you in early, but I thought we should get a strong start on the day. I have a theory on how Tyler's death might tie into the broader picture." Anna knew she had piqued their interest as they turned to her like bloodhounds on the scent.

"Really?" Margot said, eyes wide.

"You'll remember that Tyler promised Lucy Manning that he had a plan to extricate himself from his marriage?"

"But that was a load of bullshit. He was just spinning her a line," Jake said, and then wished he'd shut the hell up as the inspector's gaze turned in his direction.

"Well, that's what we thought at the time, wasn't it?" he mumbled, trying to soften his negativity, recognising he'd yet again reinforced the inspector's opinion of him.

Anna gave him a slightly exasperated look. "It *was* a possibility ... but why would he *bother* spinning her a tale? Lucy seemed to love him regardless, and she didn't mention that she had given him an ultimatum to get divorced or she'd break off the relationship. No, it was a loose end that needed tidying up.

"What I think may have occurred is that the day before Samantha's death, on the Wednesday, she had her usual rendezvous with Foley to pick up the drugs from Corryong. She brought them home, which we know from her car's location history. She left them there and went back to the office. According to the scheduling system, she had appointments in the afternoon. Now, we've deduced that Tyler is the delivery person from Jindabyne to Cooma or wherever. So, he leaves work at around lunchtime and comes home. But instead of picking up the bag of drugs and taking them to the drop-off, he waterproofs it in some way and hides it underwater in the old town." Anna stopped talking.

For the next several seconds there was stunned silence. The only sound was the rumble of distant conversations and general hubbub from the office outside.

Margot recovered first. "*That's* why he went for a dive. And then he had an accident and ... *died*."

"Jake?" Anna asked as Donaldson shook his head vehemently.

"But ... why would he bother doing *that?* Foley and his associates weren't just going to sit back and go 'Oh, shucks', over their missing drugs."

"No. Precisely," Anna said, looking at him expectantly, which only served to irritate him still further.

"Then what was the *point?*" He slapped a hand on the desk.

Anna gave a half smile. "He was blackmailing Sam into divorce." She sipped her cooling coffee. It had come to her in a flash in the car the previous night. *Sam* was the link to Foley and his band of merry men. *She* was the one Foley would come after if something went wrong. Knowing that, Tyler took the drugs and hid them where she couldn't find them, or retrieve them, even if she guessed where they were. Anna assumed his intention was to make her sweat, obtain her agreement to the divorce, and then retrieve the drugs, delivering them slightly later than planned.

"As Robert Burns wrote so eloquently, 'The best laid schemes o' mice an' men, gang aft agley'. Sadly, this plan went spectacularly 'agley'," Anna added, after she finished explaining her theory.

"But that's *crazy!*" Jake burst out. "Webb was always going to have to get the drugs or Foley would have killed them both."

"True. But the delay in delivery might have caused Sam some serious angst, enough to get Tyler what he wanted. Any sort of delay might have caused Foley to doubt their reliability and seek other distribution partners. Sam wouldn't have wanted to lose the goose that laid the golden egg now would she? You remember the phone calls. You said yourself, Jake, there were no calls answered on Tyler's phone after he left the office. There was no word from him *at all* after that point— he simply vanished into thin air until Stan fished him up from the deep. And then there were ... what? *Seventeen* missed calls from Sam to Tyler's phone between late afternoon on the Wednesday and early evening on the night she died, right? You don't think that sounds a little desperate?" Anna stared him down with raised eyebrows.

"Pull up those phone lists, Jake, and let's have another look." She watched him rise and walk out to get his laptop, looking like the proverbial deer in the headlights.

"So, at roughly 5 pm on the Wednesday, Samantha calls Tyler on her phone." Anna pointed out a few minutes later, as they sat looking at the screen.

"Let's have a look at the records from Ethan's phone."

Jake quickly pulled it up, so it appeared in parallel to Sam's phone record.

"There!" Anna tapped the screen. "An incoming call to Ethan's phone just a few minutes before the other call. That would be Foley calling Sam to see what the cause of the delay was. And this is the moment Samantha becomes aware the drugs haven't been delivered by Tyler."

"There are several more inbound calls from the burner phone throughout that evening. The last one was close to midnight," Jake said, his tone subdued, as the inspector's theory was rapidly becoming reality.

"I can imagine the calls were getting more and more threatening." Anna grimaced.

"It *was* Foley who killed her then," Margot said, picturing Samantha tied to the chair in the kitchen, bloodied and beaten, and her throat slashed open in what she imagined was a final fit of frustrated rage from Foley.

Anna nodded slowly. "Foley's associates would blame *him* for the non-delivery since he'd co-opted Samantha into the operation. No doubt he was in a towering fury at the position she'd put him in. It's a wonder *he's* still in the land of the living ... but he must have been more useful to them alive than dead."

"The drugs"—Margot sucked in a breath—"must be still down there then? At the bottom of the lake."

"I think they might be. Unless—" Anna started.

"Tyler had someone with him," Jake finished for her.

"And if there *was* someone else involved, it explains why they didn't report it. They could hardly say anything to the police in case the drugs surfaced at some point, which would implicate *them*. And also, *if* they reported it, then they'd have come to the attention of some, no doubt exceedingly angry drug dealers, who would have liked their property back."

"But ..." Jake stopped, thinking it through. "If Tyler had someone with him ... and then Tyler died ... maybe the other person grabbed the drugs for themselves? The drug dealers wouldn't have known about it. All that person would have had to do was stay under their radar."

Anna looked doubtful. "It's possible, Jake. But it would have been an almighty risk. A large amount of drugs go missing ... Foley and his mates would have been on high alert for even the slightest whisper about them. And if they'd discovered the theft, that person would have very quickly ended up like Sam."

Jake nodded slowly in agreement. "So, there's probably several hundred thousand dollars' worth of ice hidden somewhere in the old town, at the bottom of the lake."

"*That's* what Foley's in town looking for." Margot looked at Anna, wide-eyed. "That's why you thought he'd gone to the Carter-Ellis' to look for the drugs! Because now that Tyler has been found dead in Jindabyne, Foley's assumed the bag of drugs might be somewhere local, but he hasn't yet worked out they're in the lake." She rolled her eyes as everything fell into place.

Jake frowned. "But why would he assume the drugs are still around? He doesn't know that Tyler died that afternoon, he only knows he disappeared and then died sometime after the pickup."

"It's a good point, Jake. But again, I think Foley and his friends would have been on the lookout for even the slightest hint of that amount of ice in circulation in the Southern NSW community. Of course, Tyler may have been able to offload it in say ... Sydney, but that's a lot harder to do than you might think. The Sydney locals would have taken a dim view of someone treading on their turf. I doubt very much Tyler had the right contacts to make it happen without upsetting the applecart. So, my guess is that Foley's just hedging his bets. He wouldn't know for sure the drugs are still around, but if there is the slightest possibility that they are, then I think he'll be very keen to get his hands on them."

Anna turned to Margot. "I didn't think they'd be at the Carter-Ellis' property. I don't have a high opinion of Tyler, or Samantha for that matter, but it didn't make any sense for them to leave the drugs at her parent's place—"

"But that's clearly what Foley was thinking," Jake cut in. "His fingerprints were all over the stables and barn." His stomach gave a sour turn, thinking about what might have happened had Foley fronted little Ethan and his grandparents.

"Yes, I'm fairly certain that's what he was after. I think that family is very lucky indeed," Anna admitted quietly.

"That's why you had everyone attend with lights and sirens," Jake added in a stunned tone, the realisation hitting him abruptly. He'd thought it was gross overkill on her part to insist that everyone arrive lit up and screaming sirens on a Sunday afternoon. She'd even asked for every light to be turned on at the house, inside and out. Now he understood why. "You wanted him to know!"

Anna nodded. "Hopefully, between his own search of their outbuildings and the search we conducted of the house, he'll be assured that the drugs aren't there, and he'll leave them alone.

"But now that we've a clearer idea of what Tyler was up to in the lake, we have to assume that at some point, Foley might work it out too."

Chapter 35

Anna ended the call and, raising her voice slightly, reported, "Senior Sergeant Travers will be down at the lake at about one with the other divers. It'll be a little like looking for a needle in a haystack, but we have to try."

Jake stood up to peer over the partition. "Should we head out there?"

"No, they've got it. I want to pull in Dean Teasel for another chat, and I want you both there."

Jake walked around and stood next to her and Margot leant forward to listen in.

"Teasel is one of Tyler's best friends and a diver. He's also Sam's likely boyfriend and the probable triple zero caller. That puts him right in the frame. He must know a lot more than he's let on so far. So, I think we need to shake his tree a little. Let's pull up everything we have on him so far, get organised and then you can go drag him out of his hidey-hole and bring him in." Anna's eyes shone with anticipation.

"Mr Teasel," Anna began coolly, shutting the door of the interview room behind her.

"*What the hell?* Why did you have to drag me down here in the back of a police car? I was in the middle of an assessment! I had a client with me! It was totally unnecessary," he shouted, "and nothing short of harassment!"

Anna ignored him, walked to the table and took a seat. She noted his hair, smoothly slicked back at their last encounter, now quite dishevelled, as if he'd run his hands through it many times.

"Ah, well, you see, Mr Teasel, it's a matter of respect." Anna glared at him coldly. "I take a very dim view of being lied to, and so I didn't feel you had earned the privilege of an *invitation* to attend the station."

Teasel's face paled and he sat back. Anna could see his Adam's apple bob as he tried to swallow.

"Lie? I don't know what you're talking about." His eyes darted from her to the two sergeants sitting on either side of her.

Anna turned to Lissoni. "Sergeant, would you please start the recording and do the honours?"

Margot started the recording and introduced those present in a low tone. She hoped she sounded professional and matter-of-fact despite burning with excitement to watch the inspector in action.

"At our last discussion, you said that Tyler Webb was one of your best friends." Anna clasped her hands on the table.

"Yeah, he was," Dean answered warily.

"And was he aware you were having an affair with his wife?"

A ripple of colours crossed Teasel's face, first paling to a dead white and then flushing a deep red. A faint prickle of perspiration dotted his forehead. He opened his mouth and then shut it again. Anna waited.

"That's ... that's not true," Teasel stuttered out eventually.

Anna sighed heavily and shook her head. "Mr Teasel. Do you really want to do this?"

"Do what?"

"Continue to lie to me!"

"I'm *not* lying! I wasn't having an affair with Sam. I wouldn't do that to Tyler."

Anna tsked several times and then turned to Jake. "Read out one of the messages please, Sergeant."

Jake opened the file in front of him and, with an effort of will, suppressed the smile he felt rising. "My gorgeous, sexy girl—you drive me crazy with desire—I'm desperate to see you. I want to—"

"Stop!" Teasel yelled, shaking with rage and humiliation. He turned to Anna. "You have no right! They're my personal text messages!" He closed his eyes, breathing heavily. "You need a warrant! Did you bother to get one? If not, then you're in trouble," he sneered.

Anna let the silence draw out. Teasel shifted uneasily.

She leant forward. "Let me explain how it works. You write a text message," she said, in a tone that implied he was a bit slow. "That's your personal property and you *are* correct, I would need a warrant to obtain access to that. But then ... you pressed *send*. And your message winged its way through the ether and landed on Samantha Webb's phone. And as Samantha is a murder victim, everything about her, including her phone messages, is available to the police!"

Teasel swallowed and looked sick. A bead of sweat eked its way down his temple. He brushed it away with a forearm.

"Now, shall we circle back? Without the lies this time, if you please. When did your affair with Samantha Webb begin?"

"About two and a half years ago," he said to the table, looking like the stuffing had been pulled out of him.

"And when was the last time you saw her?"

Teasel tensed, and his eyes darted around the room. "Er ... I don't remember."

Anna sucked in a deep breath and let it out slowly. "This interview is going to go a lot quicker if you *just tell the truth*. You saw her the night she died, isn't that correct?"

Teasel's eyes opened wide with panic. "I didn't kill her!"

"I didn't say that you did. But you were there, weren't you?"

He nodded, swallowing painfully.

"Speak up, please," Margot said, with a nod to the control on the table for the recording.

"Yes! I was there! Okay?" Teasel cried. "But she was already dead," he added in a whisper.

"You called triple zero?"

"Yes."

"When was the last time you saw her alive?"

"The night before," Teasel replied in a monotone.

"Tell me about that visit."

His head dropped, shaking back and forth, seeking a way out. The seconds ticked by.

"Sammie was beside herself," he murmured finally. "She couldn't locate Tyler. He was supposed to have done something, and she was"— he shook his head, trying to find the words—"so angry and upset. She was in a screaming fury. I couldn't get much sense out of her."

"Did she ask you to call Tyler?"

He looked up and nodded. "She told me to ... she said he might answer *my* call. But he didn't, and she just went off her head again. Then her phone rang, and she screamed at me to get out ... so I did."

"Did you get any indication of what it was that Tyler was supposed to have done?"

He shrugged. "Deliver something, I think. I don't know—she was raving, and it was hard to follow what she was saying."

"Have you ever seen this man?"

Margot slid a photo of Foley across the table.

Teasel stiffened, then reached out to draw the photo closer. He shook his head. "No. Who's he?"

Anna's lips compressed briefly. Teasel would make a hopeless poker player.

"A very dangerous individual called Nathan Foley that Samantha and Tyler were involved with. We believe *he* may have been the one to kill Samantha."

"But Tyler killed her ... didn't he?" he said, in a confused tone that convinced no one.

Anna looked at him consideringly. *So, he's already twigged that Foley killed Sam. What else has he worked out?*

"You mentioned previously that you scuba dive, Mr Teasel," Anna added softly.

"What a pathetic little weasel ... Ha! he suits his name!" Margot laughed, returning from sending Dean Teasel on his way.

Anna, who was standing at the window looking out, turned and gave a wry smile in answer.

"Hmm, he is rather weaselly. But weaselly or not, he's far from stupid. He's already worked out that Foley killed Sam. That means he's probably well aware who and what Foley is ... *and* what he's after."

"Yeah, it was pretty obvious he recognised Foley," Jake agreed.

"And if he's worked that out, then he might have an idea that the drugs are at the bottom of the lake," Anna went on.

Jake frowned. "He might have retrieved them already."

Anna looked at him and nodded. "Yes, he may have beaten us to the punch. But I doubt after what happened to Tyler that he would attempt that on his own. So, if he *has* gone after the drugs, I would bet he's involved the other two 'best friends' in the venture. Which means we need to have a chat with Michael Bialy and Jonathan Russo.

"Let's do a quick check on both those men first, and then we'll be able to get one interview in this afternoon, I think," Anna said, checking her watch.

"If they've got the drugs already, then they're one step ahead of us." Jake's tone was low as he pictured the police divers at the lake.

"That's true, but I wonder ... have they underestimated Nathan Foley?"

Chapter 36

"Mr Bialy? Michael Bialy?" Margot called, as they approached a man with his back to them, standing in the warehouse where she, Jake, and the inspector had been directed.

He turned towards them with a frown, they could see he was on the phone. He said something into his mobile and ended the call as he walked to meet them. He looked to be in his early thirties, dressed in a company-logoed, collared T-shirt and khaki pants. Pallets of produce towered in every direction and the rank smell of fertiliser pervaded the air.

"Can I help you?" he said, looking them over, his eyes lingering on Margot.

"I'm Inspector Farrow and these are Sergeants Lissoni and Donaldson. We'd like to have a brief chat with you about Tyler and Samantha Webb." Anna noticed that he was not in the least surprised at this introduction, nor even willing to pretend he was. Clearly, Dean Teasel had been in touch.

"Yeah, sure," he beckoned them to follow. "Might be easier in my office."

A few minutes later they were seated around a coffee table in a long, somewhat utilitarian office. A large, slightly battered, wooden desk and several grey filing cabinets filled the far end. Large windows, along one wall, overlooked the work yard behind the building.

"What can I do for you?" His pale, rather cold blue eyes seemed at odds with his slightly hooked nose, olive skin, and black hair. He had very broad shoulders that strained his shirt as he leant forward.

"Do you recognise this man?" asked Anna. Margot slipped the photo towards him. He gave her a toothy smile as he picked it up. Margot barely blinked in reply.

Bialy glanced at the photo and then shook his head. "Never seen him before."

Anna paused for several heartbeats, but the question didn't come, confirming that Bialy was well aware of who he was, even if he hadn't clapped eyes on him.

"We believe this man was involved in a drug trafficking operation with Tyler and Samantha Webb." Anna watched him carefully.

His eyebrows rose lazily. "*Really?*"

"You don't sound at all surprised, Mr Bialy," Anna said with a tight smile.

"No, not surprised. Deano gave me a call and said you'd spoke to him about it." He smiled at Lissoni, looking smug. She didn't meet his eye.

"Had you any idea that Tyler and Samantha were involved in the drug trade before Mr Teasel mentioned it?" Anna continued.

"Absolutely ... *none*," he said slowly, with emphasis. The smug smile now little more than a slash across his face.

"Were you surprised to find that out?"

Bialy shrugged. "I was surprised that Tyler was involved. Not so surprised to learn Sam was though. Her whole life revolved around drama, strife, and a laser-focus on what she wanted. And what she wanted most of all was *money*."

"If you've spoken to Dean Teasel, you'll be aware that Tyler disappeared very near to the time of Samantha's death."

Bialy's fingers picked at the edge of Foley's photo. "Yeah, we assumed something happened to him around then. He'd never been out of touch more than a day or so before. So when we didn't hear anything after Sam's death, we suspected something had happened to him."

"I understand the four of you—you, Tyler, Teasel and another friend, Jonathan Russo—were very close."

"Yeah, best mates from kindergarten." He smiled, a genuine one this time.

"It seems strange then that Tyler would be engaged in something so ... *lucrative* ... and not involve you," Anna asked, her head cocked to the side.

Bialy's smile vanished. His eyes narrowed and his mouth twisted up. "You insinuating I'm involved in drug trafficking? You're wrong! I've never had anything to do with it."

"What about your arrest? For a drug-related assault, wasn't it? Good behaviour bond and mandatory drug rehabilitation. Ring a bell?"

Mick looked briefly taken aback and then resumed his scowl. "So? I had a bit of a problem when I was younger. I kicked it. That's got nothing to do with Webby and Sam."

He stood up abruptly. "Look, I'm busy, so if you haven't got anything more to ask then I'll get on with running my business."

Anna rose. "Thank you for your time, Mr Bialy."

Jake started the engine as Anna shut her door. "Anyone notice he seemed a mite peeved about Tyler not telling him he was in the drug trafficking business?" she asked.

"He did seem a little put out," Margot added from the backseat. Her skin still crawled from the way he'd looked at her.

"Do we think he's involved?" Jake asked, shooting a look over his shoulder and pulling out into traffic.

"I don't think he *was*," Anna said. "But my gut tells me Bialy would very much like to be. So, if we're correct in assuming that Teasel has worked out where the drugs are, my presumption is that Bialy is well and truly involved now."

At that moment, Anna's phone rang.

"Travers?" she answered, seeing the caller ID. "Anything?"

"No. Sorry. Not a cracker," he replied in a slightly muffled tone that Anna suspected was due to him towelling himself dry. "Now, if you wanted fence palings, concrete steps, wooden posts, trees, milk cans and about a thousand other household products, circa late fifties, I can help you with it. But bag or case of drugs ... nope. Nothing. At least around where we found the body. We searched a perimeter of about fifteen metres from where we found the body, but there are acres of stuff out there. We're assuming he died near to where he stashed it, but that might not be the case. We did focus more in the direction opposite to where he would have been coming out of the water, but nothing. Sorry. We'll take another look tomorrow. But we've burned our hours under for today."

"Ah, well thanks, Travers. It was always a long shot. But several hundred thousand dollars' worth of ice was worth a look. Let me know if you find anything tomorrow. Are you and the guys all sorted for accommodation?"

"Yeah, all good. Heading for a hot shower now and a beer." She heard the grin in his voice.

"Excellent, you deserve it. That water must be freezing." Anna shivered, imaging the feel of it.

"Oh, we're used to it. And to be honest, this is one of the more interesting dives, pretty unique in fact, so it's been a real treat. Better than looking for bodies in murky dams!"

They rang off. Anna sat quietly as Jake drove on. He and Margot had heard her end of it, so there was no need to explain further. That Traver's and his team had found nothing had been clear enough. *So, was it nothing because it was so well hidden? Or was it nothing because it had already been retrieved by Teasel and his mates? That was the question.*

The next morning, Anna pulled into the carpark to find Jake and Margot leaning on Jake's car, sipping coffees. They were huddled slightly against the rather brisk wind. The light drizzle that had accompanied her drive had fortunately stopped.

"Jake got you one too, Boss," Margot handed her a takeaway container.

Anna smiled. "Thank you, Jake."

He smiled back and noticed for the first time what a great smile she had. Probably because it was the first time he'd actually seen her smile at him. Normally, she surveyed him with an expression of slight exasperation or chagrin.

Anna wrapped her hands around the hot, waxed cardboard container, feeling the warmth penetrate her cold fingers.

"So, Jonathan Russo next, our third musketeer," she said, still smiling. As she caught a surprised look on Jake's face, she knew it was slightly out of character for her to smile so much. But she felt such a lightness of mood, such excitement in her belly, that it was hard to don her usual imperturbable professional mask.

She was seeing Cameron that evening. A fleeting note of warning from her internal barometer advised her that she was falling too hard and too fast. But while acknowledging it was right, she knew that she had no way of circumventing it. She pictured his face, his eyes—the colour of a summer storm cloud—his lips, warm and full and smiling down at her.

She glanced up to see both sergeants staring inquisitively at her and abruptly squashed any further musings on Cameron decisively. She took a gulp of hot coffee and forced it down, eyes watering and oesophagus and stomach aching with the burn. *Serves me right for daydreaming on the job.*

"Okay, let's go. Russo should be interesting," she coughed.

Jake pulled up in a spray of gravel in front of the property that Russo was working at that morning. Margot had spent some hours the day before trying to locate him. Apparently, he worked itinerantly, training difficult horses, according to those she had spoken to.

They walked up to the sprawling ranch-style house that would fit at least two of Dee's place in it with some left over, Anna reflected, as they approached the double-width front door.

The door swung open in answer to Lissoni's knock. The woman looked to be in her late forties, though Anna suspected she'd had a lot of cosmetic work done—her face had a slightly immobile, plastic-doll look about it—and therefore could have been a lot older.

"Yes?" the woman asked.

"Good morning, I'm Inspector Farrow and these are Sergeants Donaldson and Lissoni of the NSW police." Anna flipped open her ID. "Is Jonathan Russo working here today?"

"Is he in trouble?" she said, her voice sounding concerned, and a hand going to her throat, which Anna noticed in passing was less smooth than the face it held up.

"No, Mrs—"

"Bakersfield," Lissoni murmured in an undertone at her elbow.

"—Bakersfield. He's a friend of the man whom we found in the lake last week. You may have heard about it?" Anna gave her a mechanical smile. "We just need to talk to him and get some background information."

She could see the woman relax immediately. "Oh ... well, that's good to hear. I thought ... well, you know ... you never know, do you?"

"Is he here?"

"Oh yes, he is. He's out back with the groom and stable hands." She gave a dismissive wave of a well-manicured hand. "Come through the house"—she beckoned them in—"it's the quickest way."

She led them through a marbled-floor entryway and down into an enormous sunken living room with the largest lounge suite Anna had ever seen. It must have been able to seat a dozen people or more with ease. The room itself matched the furniture; it was cavernous with high exposed beam ceilings, a bar that any pub would be proud of, and a dining table to their left which sat thirty, if not more.

Anna thought of the cosy, comfortable kitchen at her sister's house, warm with the redolent smells of freshly baked bread and succulent meals, and the old wooden table with the scars and wounds of forty years of family dinners. She wouldn't trade any of it for this cold, pristine mausoleum.

They continued on through wide, concertinaed, sliding glass doors that bridged the lounge room to a vast wooden deck which overlooked the yard and beyond to the snow-capped peaks of the Australian Alps. The view was breathtaking, and the only thing Anna thought worth the money spent on this house that she had seen so far.

"He'll be over there." Mrs Bakersfield pointed to an enclosed yard off the stables in the distance.

The trio walked on, the sergeants matching their stride to Anna's. Eventually, they reached the high wooden fence enclosing the yard indicated.

Loud, angry voices heralded the arrival of two men from the adjacent stables.

"You need to speed it up," one voice said angrily. "You've been at it three weeks already!"

"You can't speed it up, you stupid bastard," another gravelly voice responded. "It's a bloody horse, not your *fucking* offspring. We need to give it time."

"We don't *have* time," the initial voice responded, frustration coating every word. "He wants him ready for the spring carnival."

"Well, he can shove—"

"Jonathan Russo!" Anna called loudly, cutting off the debate.

The two men turned and saw them standing at the fence.

"Yeah?"

"A word please," Anna stated with steel in her tone.

Russo shot a look at the other man, but he just shrugged and walked off into the barn, apparently happy to forego the debate.

Russo walked over to the fence, a scowl on his face. "Who the hell are you?"

"Inspector Farrow, and these are Sergeants Lissoni and Donaldson of the NSW police."

"Whaddaya want? I'm busy."

"So are we," Anna snapped back. She took stock of him. His dirty blonde hair was pulled back into a rough man-bun with wisps blowing around his face; his dark blue eyes shone with dislike, and he had an impressive five o'clock shadow. Anna wondered if the dislike was for them, the police, or whether he harboured the same dislike for humanity in general.

"We've been told you're a close friend of Tyler Webb—"

"Yeah, what of it?"

Anna breathed deeply. No wonder the four of them were best friends, no one else would have them. Tyler, the narcissistic loser, Teasel the weasel, Bialy the sleaze, and now Russo, the angry, 'the whole world is against me' tosser. She sighed, strongly doubting the trip here would be worth the effort.

"He and his wife, Samantha, were involved with this man. Do you know him?" Anna pointed to the photo that Jake was holding up.

"Nope. No idea." Russo smirked without glancing at the photo.

"Can you please *look* at the photo, Mr Russo? That usually makes it easier to recognise someone." Anna's every word dripped sarcasm.

Russo glanced at it and then repeated, "Nope. Don't know him. We done?"

"No, not yet," Anna growled, patience wearing thin.

"We believe that Samantha and Tyler Webb were trafficking drugs with the help of this man. Were you aware of their side business?"

"Nope," he said, looking bored.

"You don't seem surprised by that," Anna persisted.

"Old news. Heard it from the Teaser."

"You and your friends seem very close. It's strange that Tyler Webb would not have included you, or at least *told* you, of his ... *opportunity*," Anna said, watching Russo closely.

Only a brief tightening of his lips indicated that this had hit a nerve. "Yeah, well, he didn't," Russo barked.

"We believe that Tyler died very close in time to Samantha's murder."

Russo shrugged.

"In fact, we believe this man"—Anna waved a finger at the photo Jake still held up—"killed Samantha when one of their drug deals didn't go according to plan."

"So, did he kill Tyler as well?" Russo asked, showing a spark of interest for the first time.

"This man is very dangerous," Anna replied impatiently, ignoring the question. "It's obvious to me that you and your friends know quite a bit more about this matter than you're admitting to. But I need to warn you, you're playing with fire."

"Well, you can *fuck off,* dyke! We don't need your advice," he sneered, jabbing a finger in Anna's face.

Anna heard Margot gasp and felt Jake start forward, but she held up a restraining hand.

She slowly looked Russo up and down. "I can't charge you for being a rude, obnoxious bigot, Mr Russo, but I can make your life very uncomfortable, so I'd have a think about your attitude if I were you."

Anna spun on her heel and walked off, Margot beside her. Jake glared threateningly at Russo for several heartbeats, then turned and followed.

"Fucking arsehole!" Jake muttered angrily as he caught up with them.

Anna gave him a brief smile. "Don't let the turkeys get you down Jake, the world's full of them. I'm not after Russo's good opinion."

"Hmm," Jake grunted, still feeling the surge of adrenaline that he would have liked to expend punching the ugly bastard's face in.

"It's obvious that the remaining three mates are as thick as thieves," Anna said, as they walked back to the car. "But Bialy and Russo confirmed one thing for me. They obviously had no idea of Tyler's involvement in the drug trade. Much to their disgust, it seems, they're both still angry about it. Teasel, I'm not so sure of. I think he had a pretty good idea of what Sam and Tyler were up to. His saving grace was probably not wanting to get in on the action. And that was likely only a trade-off between having Sam or being part of the drug ring. He chose Sam."

Anna ended the call and, looking up at Margot and Jake's expectant faces, shook her head. "Travers and crew found nothing."

She pushed out of her chair and walked to her spot by the window. The chill wind and drizzle of the morning had dropped away, and the day looked deceptively sunny and bright, but she knew the air would have a chilly bite.

Still facing the window, she murmured, "So, it's either still there underwater somewhere or our three musketeers have already retrieved it."

"You think they might have had a better idea of where it was hidden?" Jake asked.

Anna turned. "You've seen those photos of the old town, dark green murk overlaying the decaying remains of old buildings and then silt covering it all like a thick grey blanket. They've dived there quite a lot, probably more than anyone else. But even so, I doubt they'd attempt it if they didn't have a good idea of where it might be in the first place."

"But you think they will," Jake persisted, detecting something in Anna's voice.

She nodded. "Yes—if they haven't already—I definitely think they will. Bialy and Russo are both angry they weren't invited into the operation. So, from a moral standpoint, or perhaps that should be a lack of, they wouldn't hesitate. They'd only see dollar signs. I think Teasel has met Foley in person and would therefore have a better feeling for the risk they'd be taking, but I also don't see him standing up to his mates.

"Have we *any* sightings of Foley in town?" Anna added in a frustrated tone.

Margot shook her head. "Nothing."

"*Bugger!* You'd think someone would remember his ugly mug ... Let's broaden the search area. Jake, see if your man in Corryong has caught sight of him lately. Let's check every possible accommodation in town and all the drinking holes. I might call in Monroe's offer of assistance and get some extra hands on the job. I don't think Foley will give up on locating his stash just yet."

Chapter 37

"He's here!" Riley yelled as a car drew up outside Dee's house.

Anna smiled and, with a last look in the mirror, walked to the front door. She had intended to wait there, not wanting to look too eager, but found herself walking out to the car. Cameron clicked the lock and, grinning from ear to ear, strode to meet her. Without pause, they swept into a tight embrace.

Cameron kissed the soft, downy hair on Anna's head before his head bent to her mouth, turned up to his kiss.

Their lips parted breathlessly, and they stood drinking in the sight of each other, unwilling to let go.

"You smell nice," Anna whispered, still slightly light-headed from that kiss.

Cameron grinned. "Not as good as you." He leaned in to smell her neck, which tickled and made Anna squirm.

"Okay, break it up you two," came Dee's voice from the doorway. "Come in before you freeze solid, and I have to chip you apart. I might accidentally chip something off in the process."

Anna groaned. But Cameron snorted a laugh and with his arm around Anna walked her towards the house.

Dee gave Cameron a quick hug. "Hi, Cam. Welcome to Casa Farrow."

"Good to see you again, Dee." He smiled and then his eyes were drawn to the young man standing a few metres away.

Cameron walked forward and held out his hand. "You must be Riley." He gripped Riley's rather hesitant hand in a firm shake.

Riley smiled and nodded.

"I hope you didn't mind me stealing your mum last Saturday night."

Riley smile widened to a grin. "No, she needs to get out more. It's good for her."

Anna's mouth dropped open, and Dee chuckled.

Anna swotted her arm and glared at her. "I can see you in those words, Daisy-belle," she muttered in an undertone.

Cameron laughed uproariously, and Riley and Dee joined him. Anna rolled her eyes, shaking her head. "This was *such* a bad idea. How did this turn into tales of Anna the Younger?" They sat around the table, the dregs of dinner scattered across its surface.

Dee patted her arm. "You're with family, my darling sister. That means you get teased, ridiculed, and embarrassed by those who really love you."

Anna smiled ruefully; it was her own fault after all. Dee had convinced her that it would be better to have dinner at home so Riley could get to know Cameron, and vice versa, instead of she and Cameron going out to a restaurant. It made sense, at the time, and she could see the advantages of it, but her sister was having way too much fun at her expense.

Still, she had to admit, seeing Riley laughing with Cameron made her heart sing. It was probably worth every embarrassing second so long as Dee's tales didn't put her beau off entirely.

Anna stood in her bedroom, dismayed. It was freezing, as the old house had no central heating. There was only the blazing wood burner that sat between the lounge and kitchen, making them toasty warm while they sat there, but the bedrooms and bathrooms had to fend for themselves.

"Sorry, it's a bit cold in here," she whispered as Cameron bumped in through the door and dumped his overnight bag, that he'd retrieved from the car, on the floor.

He grinned. "I don't care. We'll be warm." He waggled his eyebrows and pretended to smoke a cigar like Groucho Marx, making her giggle.

"I'll just go clean my teeth and be right back," he added, fishing in his bag.

She nodded, her breath coming faster, making it difficult to voice a reply. He looked so handsome in the lamplight. Quickly undressing, she left her silk camisole on as she had before, and shivering, dived under the covers. She shimmied around, trying to warm it up.

Cameron returned, dropped his toothbrush in his bag, and looked at her. She looked tiny in the big bed with the huge comforter pulled up under her chin. Her eyes looked enormous. He tried to swallow past the lump in his throat.

A quick shiver made him strip-off hurriedly and dive under the covers. He pulled her into a firm hug. "I just want to mention it's pretty cold in this room so ..." His eyes rolled, full of innuendo.

Anna laughed and burrowed into his side, basking in the warmth he seemed to exude despite his words. "Well, unless you've got something hidden in a pocket, I don't think the cold is going to be a problem," she answered with mock seriousness.

Cameron pulled her closer, breathing in her scent, and with one quick scoop of his arm rolled her on top of him. She put both hands on his chest and lifted her head so she could look into his face.

He swallowed. "I can't believe I'm so lucky." His hand slowly worked their way up her back, feeling the velvet-like skin and silky cloth of her camisole and coming to rest at the back of her head. He pulled her towards him, bridging the gap and sinking into a kiss that neither wanted to end.

His hands moved down and caressed her bottom.

She moaned, lost in the moment, the heat building between them.

He rolled them both over and then pulled back to look at her in the soft light. "You are so beautiful." He touched the thin silk strap of her camisole. "You don't have to wear this, you know. Not for me."

Anna reached up and stroked his face. "Then it's for me," she whispered. The sudden wetness in her eyes catching the light from the small lamp.

"That's okay then," Cameron murmured, brushing her cheek with a feather-like touch.

Anna's hand slid down his chest, and she looked deeply into his eyes, made a dark smoky grey in the dim light. Feeling the soft springy hair, she moved down across his firm stomach, until her hand closed over his rigid silkiness, making him groan deep in his throat.

Sometime later, they lay exhausted. Anna lay on her back with Cameron's arm and leg still across her. He nibbled tiredly at her shoulder. She smelt his warm maleness and a small bubble of pure happiness rose up and burst in her heart.

Anna sipped a coffee and watched Cameron over the rim of her mug. She couldn't stop looking at him. He was telling Riley some story and was doing all the actions and facial expressions associated with the tale. The punchline arrived and both males erupted in laughter.

Her phone buzzed. She looked down at the screen and frowned. Donaldson.

She stood up from the table and waved a hand at Dee and the two boys to indicate it was just work.

"Jake?"

"Body found, Boss."

"Teasel?"

"Foley."

"Foley?" she echoed loudly. "Are they sure?"

"Yep, apparently. Not much doubt, no mistaking that face."

Anna's mind kicked into high gear. "Where?"

"Creel Bay Road. I've called the pathologist already. And the scene's being closed off. I can head out there now," he added, a question in his tone.

"Okay, good. Thanks, Jake. Call Margot will you and give her the heads up and get her to come out too. I'll meet you there in about"—she looked at her watch and glanced up catching Cameron's eye—"forty-five minutes." She ended the call.

"Sorry, Cam, I need to go." She grimaced with apology.

"That's okay, I need to head too. I've got a patient at ten." They walked out to their cars together.

"Can I see you on the weekend?" Anna heard the slight pleading note in her voice and wondered at herself. She had *never* been like this before.

"Yes, please. I'll call you later, okay?" He then kissed her thoroughly. "Oh ... wow!" Cameron murmured as they pulled apart.

Anna nodded her agreement. "See you soon," she whispered and walked to her car. She stopped and turned back, exchanging a long glance with him. Then forcing herself to drop her gaze, she opened the car door and got in.

"Holy shit," she muttered, turning the ignition. *You have got it bad!*

Chapter 38

Anna pulled up next to Jake's vehicle, which she was pleased to see was parked well back from the boat ramp on the tarred surface. 'Boat ramp' was probably rating it a little highly. The road that wound steeply down from the Kosciusko Road, simply stopped at the lake edge, its last ten metres or so just gravel and dirt. Parking was limited to small clearings around the snow gums that dotted the foreshore.

Anna stepped out of her car, buttoned her jacket and pulled a beanie over her bare head. The air under the trees was damp and icy and a touch of mist hovered in pockets near the ground. She waited by the car and watched Jake stride up the track towards her.

"Jake," Anna called in salute.

"Boss," he answered, closing the gap between them.

Anna looked over his shoulder and caught sight of a white shoe poking out from behind a stunted black sallee just off the roadway, twenty metres or so below them.

"Good work on getting the area sealed off." The main turning onto Creel Bay Road was now blocked by police vehicles. "Who found him?"

"One of the National Park employees. He's in temp accommodation at Waste Point." Jake pointed over her shoulder in the direction of the staff cottages. These were out of sight several hundred metres away through the dense bushland. "The guy's a bit of an amateur photographer and he came to the ramp to get the morning mist over the lake. He got a bit more than he bargained for." He grinned.

"Where's he now?" Anna frowned, looking around, seeing neither car nor person.

"Ah, well … he needed to go drop his kid to school," Jake murmured. "I thought it would be okay. He said he'd come straight back."

Anna nodded. "Okay. No worries." Her lip quirked as she heard Jake's quiet sigh of relief. *Am I so scary?*

Looking around, she realised that she hadn't been to this area since she was a teenager. It was a secluded spot on a late autumn morning, and despite the National Parks Works Depot being within half a kilometre, the dense bushland rising up on either side of the road and the deep, chill silence under the trees made it seem as if she and Jake were the only two people on the planet.

A sudden rustling made them both turn sharply; they stood motionless as a small, rust-coloured wallaby emerged onto the roadway a few metres downhill from them. But within a few seconds, something—the sight of them perhaps or a whiff of death from near the lake edge—made it turn tail and bolt away.

The sound of a car driving down the road broke the silence that followed, and Lissoni's small sedan pulled in behind Jake's four-wheel drive.

"Morning," Margot said as she emerged from her car. She was bundled up against the frigid air so only her face showed, pale and wide-eyed, between beanie and scarf.

"Let's go take a look." Anna surveyed the steep, uneven roadway with a jaundiced eye.

"You want a hand, Boss?" Jake held out an arm rather tentatively.

Anna's first instinct was to reject the offer as unnecessary, but she quickly squashed it. Her days of refusing help were behind her; there was no point in risking a fall or twisting her ankle. She swallowed her pride. "Thanks, Jake."

Taking his arm, they walked slowly down the hill together. As they approached the end of the tarred surface, they slowed, looking for any evidence of footprints or tyre tracks.

"The National Parks guy, was he on foot?" Anna asked.

Jake nodded. "Yeah, he walked here. I took his shoe print before he left, it's in my car."

"Good," Anna nodded. That would help eliminate his prints from others they found. She dropped Jake's arm once they reached flatter ground and felt more able to manage on her own. Treading carefully, they closed the last few metres. The body was lying face up, the head slumped to the side and the arms thrown wide. At a quick glance, it looked as if he were sleeping. But the image quickly dissolved as sightless eyes stared unblinkingly at their ankles. The only movement was a hardy blowfly that suckled at the gory mess that was his neck.

Anna wrinkled her nose. "Someone made a good job of it."

"Monroe," Anna said, as he answered her call sometime later.

"Inspector Farrow," he countered brightly. "What's happening in Jindabyne this morning?"

"Well, we've located Foley."

"You're *shitting* me? Excellent. I'm on my way." The excitement was clear in his voice.

"We-ell, you might want to hold off on that. Our boy is deader than Julius Caesar."

"Aw-w shit," came the disappointed reply. "Oh, well, no great loss to society," he went on pragmatically. "But I would have liked to question him. How did he meet his maker?"

"Not sure of the ins and outs of it all yet, but it's definitely murder."

Monroe whistled appreciatively. "Impressive. He'd be a hard one to kill."

She nodded. "Well, they did a thorough job of it. Ever watch the Harry Potter movies?"

"Yep, sure," he said, sounding confused.

"Well, do you remember a ghost called Nearly Headless Nick?"

"Yeah," he said slowly and then, "ooh ... you're kidding me? That's definitive. I suppose if you're going to kill someone like Foley you want to make sure of it."

"Your crew get any hits on where he might be staying?"

Monroe had offered her bodies to try and track down Foley's location and they had the long and tedious job of calling every accommodation possibility in the Snowy Mountains region. No mean feat, considering tourism was the main income for the area.

"No, nothing that's panned out anyway."

"He was found at Creel Bay boat ramp. Could you maybe check accommodation options around Perisher Ski Resort and surrounds, you know ... Smiggin Holes or Guthega," Anna added, working on a hunch.

"He'd need National Park entrance access in any of those sites," Monroe said, thinking aloud.

"Yeah, I'll see what we can get in the way of traffic cameras at the National Park Entrance and see if we can get a vehicle ID. I'll keep you posted." She rang off.

"Anna!" called a voice behind her.

She turned to see Rodney Marchand, the pathologist, picking his way down the roadway, followed by several Scene of Crime Officers.

"Hello, Rodney, how are you?"

"Never better, thanks. Hear you've got a good one for me today."

Anna laughed and shook her head. "Only you would think this was 'a good one' Rodney."

"Well, I'm told he's a bad guy, so I have no compunction about finding the way he died of interest; he is not deserving of my pity, so I'm free to enjoy," he said with the spirit of a true scientist.

"Fair enough. Well, I think you might find this one of *great* interest then."

Rodney held out his arm and without a second thought Anna leant on it to walk the remaining few metres.

"Wow," he sighed, his interest piqued. "You are correct. Near decapitation is so rare!"

Anna shook her head wryly and let him cross the final metre alone. She had no wish to breathe in the thick metallic smell of blood again.

Rodney stared fixedly at the body without touching it. As his glance fell on Foley's outstretched hand, so did her own. She noticed two missing fingers, long since healed, that she had not registered previously.

Anna glanced around and saw the crime scene officers spreading out like the well-trained team they were. Some to take moulds of tyre and shoe prints, another photographing the site, others searching the surrounding area and conferring with Jake who had started that task, and another officer hovering near Dr Marchand. She seemed to be waiting to take soil samples and other evidence at the site of the body.

Anna walked in a slow circuit, out of range of the possibility of contaminating the site, and towards the lake edge. In the periphery of her vision, she noted Jake showing a Scene of Crime Officer his witness' boot print, but her focus was all on the lake. It stretched out before her in varying shades of blue—from the barest hint of silver to the deepest indigo—as the mist, sun, and surface breeze impacted its broad surface. She breathed deeply and smelt a faint whiff of eucalyptus overlaying the peaty smell of the wet shore.

Despite the presence of Foley's ghastly corpse and the murmur of Rodney's enthusiastic directions to a SOCO, Anna felt an overwhelming sense of peace, as she stood looking out across the lake. The tensions of the last year of anguish, surgery, treatments, desperation, and stress had gradually fallen away over the last three weeks. It had left her with a rare feeling of utmost calm.

Was it Cameron? She smiled to herself, feeling his arms, so large and warm, enveloping her as they finally slept last night.

She knew he was a big part of it, but she'd be lying if she attributed everything to Cameron. The feeling ... the healing of her soul had started when Riley and she had left Sydney for Jindabyne. There was something so cathartic, such a balm to a tired soul, in coming home. Seeing the familiar sights, and breathing the crisp, fresh air of her old home town.

She had thought her life in Sydney well organised and efficient, before her sickness, of course, when the world had turned on its head. And, if asked, she would have said she was content. That she had her work, and she had Riley, and all was good with the world. But now, in hindsight, she realised that her well-ordered life had been like two separate streams, winding around each other. And she, travelling along one or the other, switching between the two, mostly seamlessly, but occasionally clashing in a roil when home and work schedules butt heads. Now, her world was more of a weave, her life more unified and cohesive. Dee's presence filling in the holes neatly between her work and Riley, providing that safety net both for her and her son. And whereas she had pushed aside any thought of a relationship before as being too much of a stretch, too much disruption in her carefully balanced life, Cameron had just seemed to fit into the weave as if he were always meant to be there.

She breathed in deeply and smelt a faint hint of aftershave. "Jake," she murmured without turning around.

"Boss," he replied, wondering what she had been so absorbed in. He didn't think she'd even heard him approach.

"Dr Marchand's ready to transport the body. He wants to speak to you."

She nodded and walked back with him.

"Well, Anna," Rodney declared with satisfaction, pushing his glasses back up his nose with a gloved pinky. "He was killed here. No doubt. There's a large contusion on the back of his head, which is pre-mortem. I imagine it was meant to stun and then the coup de grâce was inflicted. The blade appears to be some form of a large, wide, and rather rusty blade, like a sword."

"*A sword?*" Anna repeated sceptically.

Rodney nodded. "But given we live in a farming community, I'd have to say it's more likely a scythe or something of that ilk."

"Okay ... well, that's more likely I think."

"Hmm," Rodney conceded with a smile, "but far less romantic."

She grinned and shook her head.

"I'll have a better idea when I get our friend back to the lab," Rodney added. "Now, I know your next question will be … when … *yes?* Well, I'd estimate that he died somewhere between 11.00 pm and 2.00 am last night."

"Great thanks, Rodney, that gives us something to work on."

"Well, better than that … *Marty?*" Rodney called to one of the crime scene officers crouched nearby, examining the dirt. The officer looked up, stood and walked over. Anna thought he might be late thirties, so a little younger than she was, with a strong kind face, though pitted with old acne scars.

"Marty, this is Inspector Farrow. She'll be most interested in your findings."

"Hi, Inspector. Looks like there's several shoe prints other than Foley's, the witness, you, and the sergeants that were in the vicinity in the last twenty-four hours," he said succinctly.

Anna looked surprised. "Mine?"

Marty grinned. "Yep. Easy as." He winked, patting the camera in his hand.

"Several others? You're sure?" she added eagerly.

Marty nodded. "It rained yesterday morning, which means these prints were all made in the last twenty-four hours. And the soil was still quite damp, so they're really quite clear impressions," he enthused. "They're all around the body and nearby. A couple of good tyre tracks as well. At least two cars. Looks like they pulled up, stood next to the car and then came the assault." He swung his arm around as he visualised it. "I'll try and map it out with what I have."

"You might want to get the divers in, Anna," Rodney added. "We haven't been able to find the weapon anywhere, so they've either taken it with them, or they've thrown it in the lake. My bet would be the lake."

"I've already given them a call, thanks, Rodney. I had the same thought. And thank you, Marty," she added, turning to him with a smile. He smiled and flushed in reply. He'd not noticed how attractive she was until that moment, but … *wow, that smile was really something!*

Chapter 39

ANNA DECIDED TO GO and speak to Inspector Krejci, her equivalent in charge of the uniformed squad. So far, she'd had no need to speak to him in person. He had provided personnel unquestioningly for securing the scene at the lake when they were raising Tyler Webb from the deep, and then again for the Carter-Ellis show. In both cases, Anna had just sent a quick thank you via email. But she felt it was time to beard the dragon and go see him face to face.

He'd been monosyllabic and dour at their first and only meeting, so she had fairly low expectations of this visit. But they were the same rank and the two most senior officers in Jindabyne, so they needed to forge some form of working relationship.

Anna knocked on the doorframe to Krejci's office and took a step inside. He looked up from a report he was reading.

"Inspector," he said evenly.

"Inspector," she replied in a similar tone, though she felt it came off as slightly tongue in cheek. "Thank you for supplying some people this morning. It was very helpful."

Krejci inclined his head. "So, you found your man."

"Hmm, yes, though somewhat deader than I would have liked."

She thought she detected a gleam in his eye, and could have sworn there was a slight upward quirk of his mouth.

"Still, no great loss," he added in the same deadpan tone.

"True, I don't think there'll be a lot of mourners at his funeral."

"What can I do for you?" he asked, his expression unchanged.

"Our friend was found at Creel Bay boat ramp. I wanted to see what traffic cameras we might have between town and there, and also from there to Perisher, including the Park Entrance."

Krejci nodded slowly, a few seconds passed. He leant sideways abruptly and looking around her and through the doorway called, "Lazenby!"

There was a scrape of a desk chair and then, "Yes Inspector," and a tall, well-built young man appeared behind Anna.

"Lazenby, you're reassigned to Inspector Farrow's team until she says otherwise."

"Yes, Inspector!"

Anna's eyebrows shot up.

"Thought you might need an extra pair of hands," Krejci added in the same monotone.

"That's very kind of you," Anna muttered, her tone full of surprise. "Much appreciated."

He nodded, then looked down and became engrossed in the report he had been reading. She was dismissed.

Anna nodded to herself, still slightly stunned at the sudden turn of events. She looked up at Lazenby, who was hovering eagerly at her elbow.

"Your first name's not George, is it?" she murmured as they walked away.

Anna thought she heard a quiet snort from the office behind her, but she kept walking.

"Margot, Jake, this is Constable Daniel Lazenby; he's joining our team for a while," Anna stated, walking up to where they were working.

Her colleagues looked up, stunned.

"*Krejci* gave you a constable?" Jake said incredulously.

Anna suppressed a desire to laugh out loud. Their faces reflected the shock she still felt. She would never have imagined Krejci would offer her help on an indefinite basis. Clearly, his inscrutable manner concealed a very thoughtful and professional man and, Anna suspected, someone with a good sense of humour if you dug deep enough.

"Hmm, yes, a bit unexpected, but very welcome." She turned to Lazenby with a smile. He was a collage of browns, dark curly brown hair, light brown eyes, and darkly tanned skin.

"Constable, you'll need a desk," she added, looking around. "I think we can fit one here." She indicated the spot next to her and opposite Jake. "Can you get one organised?"

"Sure. No problem." He wondered what he was getting into since he would be sitting right next to the inspector.

"Okay, I'll leave that to you, but for now let's have a quick review to catch up." Anna turned and walked into the meeting room. Jake and Margot followed and Lazenby trailed behind rather tentatively.

"Daniel?" Anna said with raised eyebrows as he hovered in the doorway. "You, too."

"Ah, Dan or Danny, if you don't mind, Inspector," he offered hesitantly, taking a seat.

"Sure. Okay, let's get on. Foley was killed where we found him. The dive team should be here in a couple of hours. They'll look for the weapon assuming that it was thrown into the lake. If it is, as Rodney—that's the pathologist," she said in an aside to Dan, "suspects, then it is a decent size, like a sword or the blade of a scythe, so hopefully, they might be able to find it.

"SOCO believe there were several people at the scene and at least two cars, which sounds like an arranged meeting," she went on. She turned to Lissoni. "Anyone notice or hear anything, Margot?"

Margot, who had traipsed house to house in the National Park accommodation area, nodded briefly. "The two holiday rental cottages closest to the ramp were vacant, as were the two old staff cottages on this side of the ridge. But I had a couple of people staying at Creel Lodge who heard cars arriving around midnight. But the National Parks staff tell me that's not that unusual—"

"No, it's a popular make-out spot," Anna interjected, noticing Dan's ears turn bright red. "Midnight? That works well with the timeline Rodney proposed. He mentioned Foley met his maker between 11:00 pm and 2:00 am. Nobody saw anything?"

Margot shook her head. "No, nothing from those I've spoken to. I have three more to contact. They're National Park staff and they left before we closed off the area."

"I've asked Monroe—Inspector Monroe, Drug Squad, Queanbeyan," Anna added in another rapid aside to Dan, "to have his team concentrate on checking accommodation in the Perisher Valley area."

"You mean to try and find where Foley was staying?" Jake said.

Anna nodded. "They've not found anything in Jindy itself, so far. And I think the choice of Creel Bay as a meeting point is an interesting one." She tapped a forefinger on her chin, before standing up and moving to the window as she normally did while thinking hard. There was something about the movement that always helped her focus.

"Are you thinking it was a half-way point? Between Perisher and Jindy? A meet-in-the-middle type of thing," Lissoni suggested.

"Exactly. Which is where you come in, Dan." Anna turned to him. "I need you to check every camera from Jindy to Perisher between 11.00 pm and 2.00 am. I want the registration number of every car going in or out of the area. Then, get some daytime footage over the last few days and see if you can identify Foley's ugly mug on the same route. He's managed to lie low while he's been in the area, so we can assume he's not driving his own car or using his own name at his accommodation. If we can get the registration of the car he's been driving, it might help locate where he's been staying."

Dan, head down, scribbled rapidly in his notebook.

"Pity Ethan couldn't give us more of a description of Foley's car," Margot sighed.

"Hmm, 'grey' doesn't really help much, but worth keeping in mind. It's the only real sighting we've had," Anna added.

Dan nodded, writing it down.

"Now there are three people I am most particularly interested in Dan—Dean Teasel, Michael Bialy, and Jonathan Russo. Get the make, model, and registrations of their vehicles. I want to know the instant you see one of their cars in the target zone last night." Anna turned to look out of the window again. The rather bright morning had disappeared under a swathe of heavy grey cloud. *We might get snow later,* Anna thought. *Thank goodness it had held off while they processed the scene.*

"You think they killed Foley," Jake said, but not as a question.

Anna turned and leant against the filing cabinet. She nodded slowly. "I do. So, I think our next stop is Teasel. He's definitely our weakest link."

Anna frowned. "He went out for lunch yesterday and didn't return?" she repeated after Margot finished telling her the results of her phone call.

"Yeah, that's what they said."

Anna stood immediately. "Let's get out to his place of residence. Dan!" she called, looking over at him. His flying fingers halted over his keyboard and his head jerked up. "Call or text me if you get any hits."

"Yes, Inspector." He nodded and resumed his focused assault on the laptop.

Ten minutes later, Margot pulled up to the kerb outside the block of units that Teasel lived in. It was a handsome block, the stucco painted a deep grey-blue, and each unit sported a wide balcony. Each set of four units was set back from the one below into the hillside, giving it the tiered look of a wedding cake.

Anna eyed the concrete steps that led to Teasel's unit darkly. She took a deep breath and, with a firm grip on the handrail, began to make her way up.

As they reached the first landing, they turned towards Teasel's unit. The front door was slightly ajar. The hairs on Anna's neck rose. Lissoni and Donaldson froze, picking up on her tension.

Anna indicated with a firm hand gesture that Lissoni walk along the balcony. Margot quietly edged along the wall to the large glass sliding doors that were closed. She stood to one side and darted several quick glances inside. Still silent, she looked back at the inspector and Jake, who were waiting at the front door, and shook her head.

Anna stepped up to the door and pushed it open with the toe of her boot. A waft of vomit hit her as the door swung wide. She stepped inside.

Teasel lay on his back, his head slightly tilted to the right. That had probably saved his life as the vomit had leaked out the side of his mouth onto the carpet and not choked him.

Anna closed the gap and, crouching down a little awkwardly, put two fingers to his neck. She sighed with relief as a faint, thready pulse bumped against her fingers.

"Ambulance, Jake," she called urgently, though he already had his phone in hand. "Tell them to put a rush on," she added, taking in the deathly white, clammy skin of Teasel's face and the slight blue tinge to his lips.

Anna looked around and spied a small prescription bottle on the coffee table nearby. Pushing herself upright and grimacing at the sluggish response of her legs, she walked over snapping on a pair of thin latex gloves from her pocket. She picked up the pill bottle. Oxycodone. It was empty. *Shit!* A glass sat next to it with a small amount of dark liquid inside. She sniffed cautiously. Rum. She sensed that his overdose was not accidental.

How did you descend so quickly to the level of despair that you felt killing yourself the only option? She had spoken to him only two days before and would never have guessed then that this would be the situation they would be in today. She shook her head. Suicides, or attempts thereof, always left her with a deep-seated feeling of confusion and bewilderment, even more so now that her own life was on such a tenuous hold. No matter that she had seen more than her share of victims over the years, it never got easier to deal with or commonplace with frequency. *Why did they do it? Was it a chemical imbalance? Or a combination of depression and a disturbance of the brain from drugs or alcohol that prevented them seeing a way forward?* She sighed heavily; she would never understand it.

The faint wail of an ambulance siren in the distance made her turn back to Jake, who was hovering over Teasel's body, anxiously watching each breath. She suddenly noticed Teasel's clothing.

"Jake, go to the hospital with the ambulance and take all of Teasel's clothes and boots into custody and get them immediately to the lab."

He frowned and then looked at the body in front of him. Teasel's blue linen shirt had a spray of dark spots in a V-shape at his throat. Something dark had also heavily splattered his jeans and boots.

"Looks like he didn't bother to change. There'll be a jacket somewhere," she muttered to herself, looking around. She spotted it behind the front door, where it had obviously been thrown.

"Margot, bag that, please. Jake, take that with you and give it to the lab too," Anna called over the deafening sound of the ambulance turning into the street. The siren died abruptly as it pulled up outside.

The next few minutes were chaotic with the arrival of the paramedics. Anna explained about the Oxycodone and rum. They both nodded grimly, too familiar with the situation to remark on it and too inured to the emotional trauma of it to react. They finished packaging up their patient for transport.

The scream of the siren grew fainter as it sped away and finally ceased to register to their hearing. The sudden silence was a catalyst for Anna and Margot to resume their activity as if the siren had held them in suspended animation, both wondering if that would be Teasel's final ride.

With the owner gone, other aspects of the unit came into focus. A smashed container of sugar on the kitchen floor; a stool drunkenly leaning on its partner at the kitchen bench; a large scrap of mud on the carpet near the door; and a coffee mug overturned, with the fluid long since ceasing to drip onto the kitchen floor but leaving a dirty brown splodge on the tiles.

"Definitely appears as if there was an altercation of some sort," Lissoni said.

"Hmm, and judging by the coffee, I'd say it happened a while ago. The office manager said that Teasel didn't come back from lunch yesterday," Anna said, knowing it was true but thinking aloud.

"Yeah, that's right. So, he came home for lunch … then, someone arrived while he was making a coffee and there's a scuffle," Margot surmised, looking around.

"I'd say that was correct. But then, if that *is* blood—and Foley's blood at that—on his shirt and pants, then he was definitely at Creel Bay last night."

"Then he came home and overdosed," Margot added in a whisper.

Anna's phone rang, breaking the silence that followed Margot's statement.

"Dan," Anna murmured, looking at the phone screen.

"Inspector, I found your guys!"

Anna smiled at his obvious enthusiasm. "Which ones?"

"Foley and Russo."

"Okay, give me the details." She felt the buzz of suddenly being on the scent.

"Right, so, Foley. I identified him, got his car rego, make, and model from the National Park entrance. Then, I found the *same* car coming *from* Perisher way *towards* Creel Bay on the traffic camera near the Surge Tank at 11.49 pm last night."

"Great work, Dan. And Russo?"

"Yeah … so Russo's car passed two traffic cameras last night. One just out of town heading west, and then again at the camera just up from the Thredbo River picnic area at 11.52 pm."

"Any indication of how many people were in Russo's car, or the identity of the driver?" The tension made Anna's voice low and urgent.

"No, sorry, Inspector, too dark. Just the car."

"What about Foley? Could you see if it was just him in the car?"

"No, sorry, I couldn't tell."

"No sighting of Teasel's, or Bialy's cars?"

"No, just Russo's." Dan's voice was now slightly anxious; three negatives in a row didn't sound too good.

"Brilliant, Dan. That's just what I need. Now, I want you to print off all the images, please. Then record the details of each image, that's time, date, and whose car it is. That's top priority. I'll need those for the search warrant. Also save copies of all the original videos, please. Then, I want you to look for both cars coming *from* the site and see if you can track them to a destination. Call me if you get an indication of where they went. Oh ... and call Inspector Monroe and tell him you found the car Foley was using, and that he was coming from Perisher way. He'll want a description of the car. Got all that?"

"Yes, Inspector," Dan said breathlessly.

"Great. We'll be back soon to get the warrants organised." Anna gave him the number to call for Monroe and rang off.

"He's going to be useful," she muttered to herself. "Margot, let's finish here and then go sort out Russo."

Chapter 40

"Boss, why did you ask Dan if Foley was on his own?" Margot asked when Anna finished filling her in on her call with Lazenby on the way back to the office. "Do you think he's working with someone else?" she asked, sounding anxious, wondering if she had missed something.

"I don't know for sure; he could have been ... but I was actually thinking of Teasel."

"Teasel?" Margot echoed in a shocked tone.

"Not as a partner," Anna assured her, "but as a hostage. Think about it. Why would Foley come to meet the dynamic trio? If *they* had the drugs, would they try selling them to the person from whom they were stolen in the first place? Doubtful! I'd think Foley would be a mite upset at that proposition. So, why else have a meet and greet? I think Foley had an idea that they had the drugs. It was obvious Teasel had seen him before. Therefore, we might assume that Foley was keeping a close eye on Teasel. He might have seen them diving and bringing up the booty."

"So, he kidnaps Teasel and offers to swap him for the drugs!" Margot declared as the penny dropped.

"But our mercenary little friends decide to have their cake and eat it too. They want their mate back and in one piece, but they want to keep their haul. So, they—"

"Kill Foley," Margot finished for her.

"Then it appears Teasel couldn't handle the whole situation and sought oblivion." Anna frowned, picturing his grey-white vomit-spattered face. "I imagine the brutality of Foley's murder was extremely difficult to witness whatever you thought of the man; it was a particularly savage and gory way to kill someone."

Three hours later, Lissoni pulled off to the side of the road just before the final turnoff onto the dirt track that led to Russo's property. They waited for their backup to arrive. After several minutes, two police cars and Jake's four-wheel drive pulled in behind them.

After a brief discussion on tactics at the roadside, they bumped their way down a rutted track for several minutes. Crossing two cattle grids, they finally crested a rise and a house and barn appeared in the distance. The small timbered house was dwarfed by the huge barn that loomed behind it. The boards on the house had not seen paint or varnish in perhaps thirty years and were a uniform grey in colour. Its corrugated iron roof was well rusted, and lichen etched circular patterns on its southern face. However, the enormous barn appeared as if it had been prepared for a photo shoot, it was so pristine. It was clear the priority for Russo was not the human living quarters.

A mud-splattered truck sat in front of the barn and Anna wore a satisfied smile as she recognised it from Dan's photos.

Lissoni and one of the police vehicles pulled up in front of the house and the other marked car, with Jake's truck hot on their tail, sped around the back.

After a brief pause to allow the others to get into position at the rear of the house, Anna thumped loudly on the wooden front door with the side of her fist.

"Russo!" she shouted and banged loudly again when there was no response. She nodded to the officers standing several metres behind her, and they started to spread out.

She decided to give it one last try, and with her fist poised to land a final strike, the door was yanked open. Russo stood there, his face dark with anger and his eyes blazing. His long hair, lank and greasy, hung about his face. He was dressed in dirty track suit pants and threadbare T-shirt.

"What the fuck?"

Anna, in the full blast of his breath, flinched with disgust. "Jonathan Russo. We have a search warrant for your house, clothing, and vehicle. Please step outside," she said loudly, holding up the paperwork.

A fleeting look of alarm crossed Russo's face before his eyes narrowed. *"Fuck that!* You can't just barge in here!"

Lissoni stepped forward next to Anna and the other officers edged up.

"Mr Russo!" Anna bit out. "I ... have ... a ... search ... warrant! That means I have the right to enter your premises and execute it."

"No way, *bitch!* You and your little dyke buddy aren't coming in here." He stepped back and threw the door shut.

Anna jerked her face back but left her booted foot in the doorway. The door slammed onto it and bounced back a few inches. She winced, but her attention was diverted from the pain in her foot to the violent scuffling and swearing coming from behind the door.

Upon hearing a heavy thump and a whoosh of air being rapidly expelled, Anna toed the door open to see Russo lying face down on the floor. Jake, with rather more force than was strictly necessary, was snapping a final handcuff in place. Both Jake and Russo were breathing heavily.

"Okay, Sergeant?" Anna cocked an eyebrow.

"Absolutely perfect thanks, Inspector." Jake grinned, standing up.

The two uniformed officers who had been behind him but unable to assist due to the small space in the hallway manhandled Russo onto his feet. They frog-marched him outside and pushed him into the backseat of one of the police vehicles.

"Well done, Jake." Anna cast an eye over him. "Any injuries?"

"Nah ... I get worse than that on the rugby field." He shrugged cheerfully.

Anna smiled at his bravado. Luckily, Jake had been prepared, having met the *delightful* Russo and his temper before, and they had all assumed he would not take their searching of his house or car lightly.

"Margot," Anna said, turning to her, "go make sure they don't take their eyes off Russo. He's a hairbreadth away from losing it on a good day ... and this is *not* a good day."

Lissoni grinned and walked off.

A van edged over the crest and eased its way down the slope towards them.

"Afternoon," Anna greeted the Scene of Crime Officers as they emerged from the van.

"Hi, Inspector," one of the officers said with a broad smile.

"Oh, hello, Marty," Anna said, recognising him as one of the crime scene officers who processed Foley's last stand.

"So, we think this is one of Foley's killers?" he said with a jerk of his head towards the house.

Anna nodded. "Yes. Just need to get enough to wrap it up. So, that's where *you* come in. Car and clothes are the priority. A *ginormous* bag of drugs would be a bonus," she added with a facetious smile.

Marty gave a brief snort of amusement and then divided his team into two groups, one heading for the car and the other for the house.

"Jake, can you take the house, please?" Anna asked. He nodded and turned eagerly inside.

Her phone rang.

"Inspector!" Dan said breathlessly. "I found Foley's car!"

"They found his car?" Dee queried later that night, handing Anna a glass of wine.

Anna gave a jaw-cracking yawn behind her hand and nodded. "Yeah, so we think they ambushed Foley. The doc said he had a skull fracture at the back of his head, and then one of them—my money's on Russo—delivered the killing stroke with a scythe blade, which they then tossed in the lake." She was still elated that the dive team had found the blade a few hours before.

"Inspector," came the deep, measured voice of Senior Sergeant Travers that afternoon. "You owe me a beer."

Anna's mouth fell open and her pulse increased rapidly. "You're shitting me! You found it?" Her voice ended in a squeak.

"Yes, we did," Travers said, his aloof professionalism falling away with the thrill of the find.

"Oh, my God!" Anna exclaimed, rarely so discomposed. "I thought it was such a long shot!"

"It was!" he agreed with a chuckle. "We found it on the last pass, twelve metres out, about ten o'clock from the boat ramp. Luckily, it stuck point down in the mud or we might never have seen it."

Anna shook her head. "I definitely owe you a beer!"

"Sure, one day soon. But I'll drop it to the lab on the way back home, so they'll get it tonight."

"Oh, that's even better, but are you sure you don't want to stay overnight in Jindy? I can get an officer to pick up the blade and take it to the lab," she said, aware she had impinged on his team's time enough over the last three weeks.

"No, all good." She could hear the smile in his voice. "I want to get home. Friday tomorrow and it's my kid's sports day. Don't want to miss it if I can help it."

"No, of course not. Well ... what can I say but thanks."

"A scythe blade!" Dee shuddered in horror, bringing Anna back to the moment.

"Hmm. Not pretty." She grimaced in memory. "I think the only person who was impressed was Rodney, the pathologist. You don't see too many scythe-blade near-decapitations apparently, and he was positively ecstatic!"

"Oow! … who'd do that job?" Dee shuddered. "So, then they drive away …" she said encouragingly, wanting Anna to continue.

Anna nodded and took a sip of wine, enjoying the slightly astringent bouquet of the red on the back of her tongue.

"Well, Dan—he's the new acquisition on the team, very capable and *very* eager—was able to track them to Cooma, and then along B52 towards the coast where they torched Foley's car in the bush, just outside Bega."

"Torched?"

"Yeah, not ideal, but they were in a hurry and didn't do a great job of it, which is fortunate for us," Anna said, hoping that it was true and that the partially burned-out car would offer up its treasure to the crime lab to which it had been removed.

"Why the hell would they go there? I mean, Bega for goodness' sake … it's easily a four-hour round trip from here!"

"Good question," Anna replied, stifling another yawn. "I presume they wanted to disassociate the car from Foley's body. The car is registered in another name, so we might not have linked the two given they were at such a distance."

"Wow! So they meet at midnight, kill the guy, then drive two hours to dump the car and then drive back to Jindy. They must have been getting home at dawn by that time." Dee's eyes shone with vicarious interest. "Why didn't they just throw the body in the lake?"

"Bodies float," Anna said bluntly. "Unless they took it offshore and weighted it down or anchored it in some way, it was going to be found anyway. You have to remember that very stressed people often don't make ood decisions. They rarely see all the permutations and options that, in other circumstances, they might have considered. Teasel's two friends would have been under enormous pressure and limited time … a bad combination. Good for police, but not so great for the bad guys. They knew the threat to Teasel's life was real, after all, they would have been fully aware that Foley was Samantha's murderer. I suppose it is one point in their favour that they went to rescue their mate. However, I think there was a lot of self-interest that weighed in on that decision. There were several hundred thousand dollars worth of ice at stake, too. I think it might have been fortunate that the drugs were in play, as I'm not *quite* sure that Teasel alone would have prompted such a definite response from his friends."

"What happens now?" Dee asked, knowing she should let Anna head to bed but unable to stop herself.

"Russo is in custody for obstruction," Anna stated with a grim smile. "He'll face court tomorrow morning. He refused to say anything, but I'm hoping we'll have some hard and fast evidence by then to charge him with murder. Teasel's still in intensive care. He's in a coma," she added with a frown.

Then, with another huge yawn, she stood up. "Got to get some sleep, Sis. See you in the morning," she said, giving her sister a quick hug.

Chapter 41

"G OT A FINGERPRINT MATCH to Bialy on Foley's car, Boss," Margot said as soon as Anna ended her call the next morning.

"Bialy?" Anna repeated, walking over to Margot's desk. Jake leant over the partition, eager to listen in.

Margot nodded. "His fingerprints were still in the system from his arrest eight years ago."

"Where were the fingerprints?"

"Steering wheel," Margot replied, her voice tight with tension.

"So, he was driving ... well, well, well," Anna said slowly. "I think we might go and have a chat with Mr Bialy then."

At that moment, both Anna's and Jake's phones rang. Anna walked away as she answered.

"Anna?"

"Rodney! Your team are working overtime. I just heard about the fingerprints on the steering wheel. You've made my day."

"Ah, well, I can add to your pleasure, then. We've got human blood on both the driver's side and passenger side footwells in"—Anna heard the rustle of paper down the line—"Russo's car. And human blood on the back seat as well. It looked like he made an attempt to clean up, but fortunately, not well enough. The blood on Teasel's clothing, and Russo's boots, is also human. We can't confirm it all belongs to Foley of course, at this stage, the DNA testing will take a few more days alas. But I do have something that will cheer you up … Bialy's fingerprints on the scythe blade."

Anna gasped and Rodney chuckled, happy to have shocked her.

"How? It was in the water! Can you do that?"

"Yessiree Bob," Rodney chortled. "Latest technology … and of course, it landed tip down in the mud and had been in fresh water for less than eighteen hours or thereabouts, which made all the difference," he conceded wryly.

"Rodney! Oh, my goodness! You are the man!" Anna could feel the blood tingling in her fingertips. "Thank you! And please thank your team as well."

As she ended the call, she turned to find Jake hovering at her elbow.

"Teasel's awake, Boss," he said, his tone filled with barely concealed excitement.

"Things just get better and better," Anna murmured with a smile. "Well, Rodney's just confirmed Bialy's fingerprints on the murder weapon. Margot, let's get started on an arrest warrant. Jake, can you head to the hospital and interview Teasel?" She watched the smile blossom on his face.

"Sure thing. I'll head out now."

"Great. Then head back here. We'll bring Bialy in. It would be good to have you both here for the interview." Anna grinned as she looked from Jake to Margot.

"Okay, we've confirmed he's at home. We'll pull up across the driveway. Stevens, you and Guthrie head around the back. Dinardo, we'll need you on the ram if he doesn't open up," Anna instructed, as the expanded team kitted up at the station before heading out.

"Questions?" She glanced around. There was a chorus of shaking heads. "No? Then let's get going."

Margot jerked the car to a sudden stop, blocking the driveway where Bialy's truck sat in front of the garage. The house was white stucco with a charcoal grey roof set at an angle like a cocked hat. It sat back on a small block, bracketed by Colorbond fencing and fronted with a rudimentary lawn. The house, like most others in the street, was brand new—all less than a year old—in a highly sought-after location, only ten minutes from the village centre. As with most new estates, it had a bald, rather sterile appearance, unrelieved by any greenery other than some pathetically small saplings planted enthusiastically by some of the neighbours.

Anna and Margot got out of their car, while Stevens and Guthrie ran lightly down opposite sides of the house to the backyard. Anna gave Margot a firm nod and they walked to the front door with the bulky presence of Dinardo bringing up the rear.

Out of the corner of her eye, Anna caught the twitch of curtain to the left of the front door as she crossed the last few steps. As her hand lifted to knock, the door jerked inward with a crash. She lurched backwards and stumbled, her body responding to the threat even before her mind registered the deafening crack of a gun.

Bialy stepped forward and grabbed Margot around the throat as he swung the rifle. It connected with Anna's head, catching her just above the temple. A burst of brilliant white light erupted in her brain and she dropped like a rock.

Anna registered the screaming engine and cracked an eye open. She gasped and rolled. The tyre—huge and black—knocked her arm a glancing blow as Bialy's truck passed at speed across the lawn where a split second ago her head had lain. It bounced down onto the road with the crunch of metal. The sound of its racing engine faded slowly as it sped away.

Anna sat up, wincing at the pain in her head and flexing her arm, testing the level of damage. It seemed only bruised, but her head felt like someone was trying to open it with a can opener. A blunt one. She looked over and saw Dinardo motionless on the ground. Her heart skipped a beat.

She crawled over to him as Guthrie burst out the front door and Stevens bolted from around the side of the house.

"*Oh, fuck,*" Anna muttered. The bullet had caught him high in the chest. His vest had taken most of the impact, but at such a short range, had not stopped the bullet entirely. His eyes looked into hers, blank with shock.

"It'll be okay. You'll be okay," she murmured, her hand pressed firmly against the welling blood.

It was hard to think past the god-awful pain in her head. She shook her head to try and clear it. But then a moment of clarity nearly stopped her heart. *Margot! Oh my God! He had Margot!* She grabbed Guthrie's hand as he knelt next to her and pushed it tightly over Dinardo's wound. She heard Stevens on the phone to the ambulance.

Pulling out her phone, she called the Chief. Thankfully, it was a short call, his attention laser focused on Margot. Anna felt marginally better that the full force of the police was now galvanising into action.

Her head started to swim sickeningly. She crawled away and vomited. Concussion, she registered briefly, dragging a sleeve across her mouth. She swallowed and forced her mushy brain to think. *Why the hell would he have done that? Why shoot first? Why try to run her over and take Margot?* A cold sweat broke out all over her body. *Margot. Oh, my God ... what if he killed her? No! I don't have time to think like that now. Later,* she viciously pushed aside the rising tide of panic. *Think!*

The wail of a siren in the distance pushed her to her feet. She swayed alarmingly, but after a few seconds, the ground stopped weaving, and she could take a few steps. She pulled out her phone again.

"Jake," she bit out; swallowing hard. "Where are you?"

"Nearly back at the office, Boss, I just heard—"

"Bialy shot Dinardo. He's taken Margot. We need to find out where he's gone. Get Dan looking at all the traffic cameras. Get Russo into an interview room. I'll be there soon," she ended loudly as the ambulance pulled up, siren screaming. The noise cut off mid-wail. The echo of it resounding in her splitting head. She turned, walked unsteadily to the edge of the house, and vomited again.

"Inspector," a voice said in her ear as she leaned drunkenly against the side of the house.

She swallowed and turned and saw a paramedic looking at her with a worried frown. "Let me look at you."

She shook her head and immediately regretted it. The pain swamped her. She swallowed hard. "Later."

"No, now," the paramedic declared firmly, taking her arm.

Feeling shaky and ill, she allowed him to lead her to the open doors at the back of an ambulance, casting a glance at the several other paramedics working on Dinardo.

"Is he going to be okay?"

"We think so," he answered briskly. "They're just stabilising him. He'll be flown to Canberra Hospital."

Anna suffered through a brief but comprehensive assessment.

"You need to go to hospital for some scans and observation," he said bluntly. "You most likely have concussion."

"I will. Just not now. I have a colleague in the hands of a maniac. That's my priority."

"If you collapse, Inspector, you won't be useful to anyone," he countered.

"I hear you," she conceded. "I'll go soon. I just need to get stuff organised."

He shook his head, recognising an immoveable force when he saw it.

"*Stevens,* I need a lift back to the station," Anna called.

In the bathroom, Anna splashed water on her face, taking a tentative sip to wash down a couple of painkillers and the taste of vomit. She hoped the tablets would stay down long enough to give her some relief.

Glancing in the mirror, she was too nauseous to even frown at the pale, greyish oval that was her face. Her eyes were deep, dark hollows of pain and panic. She took a deep breath. *Margot will be alright. She had to be.*

Anna squared her shoulders and walked out.

Chapter 42

"Nothing?" she murmured to Jake outside the interview room. He shook his head, looking nearly as sick as she felt. She nodded and, with a last deep shuddering breath, opened the door. The smell of sweat and unwashed clothes nearly sent her back out, but after a brief pause to convince her stomach to play nice, she walked in.

Russo and his lawyer were already seated at the table. Russo didn't look up from his contemplation of the floor as she sat down, but his legal eagle looked her over with interest. Malcolm McCluggage was fat ... very fat; his suit stretched to breaking point over a huge belly. His sausage-like fingers gripped together on the table in front of him.

Jake sat down next to her, and in a clipped tone, conducted the preliminaries for the recording.

"This is bullshit!" Russo spat out as soon as Jake concluded, his finger jabbing the air in front of Anna's face. "You bloody coppers assaulted me! I'm the victim here—"

Anna slapped the table hard, cutting Russo off mid-sentence.

"I am not here to discuss a charge of obstruction, Mr Russo. Matters have taken a rather more serious turn, and I suggest you listen *very* carefully." Anna's tone was low and menacing.

"Your car has been identified as being present at the site of the murder of Nathan Foley. Blood has been found in both the driver and passenger footwells of your car," she added, barely hiding the sneer she felt. "Your boots are covered in blood. Foley's car was located near Bega. An attempt was made to torch it, but fortunately, *for us,* it wasn't that successful. It's being processed as we speak."

Russo's face paled as she coldly recited the facts, and his prominent Adam's apple bobbed as he tried to swallow.

"It wasn't me—"

"On any other day," Anna cut him off, pushing fingers into her right eye in a vain attempt to prevent it bursting from her head, "I would be fascinated to listen to every last, *pathetic* attempt you might make to try and wiggle your way out of the situation, but not today. Aside from the evidence against you, we have strong evidence of the involvement of your ... *best mate*, Bialy," she continued, not bothering to hide the sneer this time. "On arrival at his home this morning, he shot a police officer in the chest, hit me in the head with a rifle, and tried to run me over before kidnapping my sergeant and taking off."

Anna's nostrils flared with anger and her eyes pinned Russo to his chair. His mouth open and shut several times, but no sound emerged.

"Bialy's options are limited. What I want from *you* is information as to where he might have run to."

For the first time since her outburst, she glanced at McCluggage who she hoped was a lot smarter than he looked. He swallowed and nodded briefly. "Let me talk to my client," he muttered, earning an astonished look from Russo.

"I'm not telling this bitch anything. She can go to—"

"Jonathan!" the lawyer snapped. "You are paying me to advise you. You appear to be in serious trouble. We *need* to have a discussion."

Russo sat back in his chair, scowling like a sulky teenager told to clean up his room.

Anna stood, and she and Jake walked to the door, where she paused. "You have ten minutes." She glared at the two of them, her mouth compressed into a thin white line.

As the door closed, she checked her phone. *No messages.*

"Jake, can you go find out if there is any news? Anything at all. I'm not sure Russo has the brains to see the opportunity in front of him. I'm hoping McCluggage can spell it out in words of one syllable for him, but I have my doubts," she sighed, hearing raised voices from behind the closed door.

"You okay, Anna?" Jake whispered, seeing her pale, sweaty face. She looked ready to pass out.

"I'll get sorted when we get Margot back." She swallowed the rising nausea both from the pain in her head and the thought of what Margot might be suffering at that very moment.

"We will," Jake nodded firmly, and then turned on his heel and sprinted away.

Bialy shoved Margot violently and without the aid of her hands to soften the fall—tied as they were behind her back—she hit the packed earth hard, winding her. She folded up into a ball, her mouth opening and closing like a fish out of water as she strained for air. Eventually, a wisp of oxygen slid into her tortured lungs, and with short gasps, she managed to slowly replenish her air supply. Keeping her movements minimal, she turned her head and looked back at Bialy.

He paced back and forth like a caged tiger, muttering to himself. He seemed, for the moment, completely absorbed in his own world, and Margot took the opportunity to assess her injuries.

She gingerly probed her split lip with her tongue. It felt grossly swollen and was very sore. An inventory of her teeth reassured her that none were missing, but unfortunately, several were loose, and a sharp edge told her that one was chipped. She could see out of one eye, but the other stayed stubbornly shut. She hoped it was nothing more than a solid black eye, and that there was no permanent damage to her sight. A deep, dull ache in the centre of her face told her that her nose was likely broken. She swallowed, trying to moisten her dry mouth that held the metallic tang of blood. Her hands felt like boxing gloves; swollen and numb from the tight restraints Bialy had immobilised her with while she lay stunned and incapacitated by his sudden and savage beating in the backseat of the car.

His initial assault, a quick but effective slam of her head against the side of his truck, had left her dizzy and disoriented. He had then thrown her into the back seat and driven off. But before she could recover, the vehicle jerked to a halt, and he had thrown open the door and beaten her senseless.

She regained consciousness only a few minutes before the car bumped violently to a stop and the door was yanked open again. Bialy grabbed her and half dragging her, half carrying her, they made their way across an open meadow and finally into the tree line. Bialy's fingers dug painfully into her arms, and though he muttered and swore the entire journey, none of it seemed directed at her. She kept silent.

Margot shivered as a bone-chilling cold seeped up from the ground. Her feet and pant legs were soaked from the boggy field they'd crossed. She looked over at him. Dressed only in a thin cotton shirt over a T-shirt, he must be freezing, but he showed no signs of feeling the cold. In fact, a sheen of sweat coated his face. His eyes darting here and there, and he was muttering constantly, running an agitated hand repeatedly through his thick black hair.

Had Margot no experience of the effects of crystal meth, she would be in no doubt that he was under the influence. As it was, she had seen first-hand what ice could do to people, and their families, and knew that Bialy was a ticking time bomb of anger and paranoia. She needed to stay calm and avoid any confrontation. In his state of psychosis, Bialy would be on a hair trigger and violently aggressive if he perceived her as a threat.

She slowly drew her knees up closer to her chest, trying to retain what warmth she could, and hoped the inspector would find her soon.

Chapter 43

"Anna!" Jake called as she emerged, pale and shaky from the bathroom and smelling faintly of vomit.

"Dan tracked them. He's in the National Park, somewhere between Sawpit Creek camping ground and Smiggins."

"*Shit!* That must be ... *what?* Ten kilometres, at least!"

"Closer to fifteen," Jake conceded.

"Still, he's narrowed the field down considerably," she muttered, making an effort to see the positive side.

She looked up to see Paul Krejci striding down the hall towards them. She hadn't previously appreciated how tall he was. His slightly hunched shoulders and thin build giving him the appearance of a large heron stalking towards her.

"Anna, I just wanted to let you know everyone is now redirected along Kosciuszko Road, including all the National Park personnel, until we locate the bastard. The chopper's arrived as well."

Anna nodded. "Thanks, Paul."

"Ah ... would you like me to sit in?" He gave a sharp incline of his head towards the closed door over Anna's shoulder. His usual poker face was etched with the stress they were all feeling at having one of their own kidnapped.

She hesitated. In other circumstances, she would have taken umbrage at such a suggestion, but she would not sit on her high horse while Margot was out there somewhere with a madman.

"I've walked all the trails in that area many, many times. Hopefully, if he offers up something, I can help pin it down a bit." He pulled several dog-eared maps from inside his jacket pocket.

Anna gave him a tired smile. "I'd welcome your involvement, Paul."

McCluggage straightened his jacket and cleared his throat.

Anna made a low sound of impatient irritation.

"My client has information he wishes to offer, in exchange for your commitment to put to the court, that he has been helpful and cooperative."

Anna looked at Russo and then back to McCluggage. Her eyes bore into him, her expression glacial. The silence lengthened. McCluggage dropped his gaze and cleared his throat uncomfortably.

"*Mr* McCluggage," she hissed, "if you think I will agree to telling the court that … *Mr* Russo, has been helpful and cooperative, when he has been anything but, and without him uttering a single word in support of that contention so far, then you are sadly mistaken." She bit off each word as if it were bitter in her mouth.

Anna swivelled her head to Russo and stared at him as if surveying something loathsome. "You are trying my patience, Russo. You do not hold the cards here. I do. If you tell me what I want to know, then, and *only* then, will I consider offering an opinion to the court on your behalf. However, it will need to be *solid gold* for me to do that."

Russo looked at his lawyer, who shrugged eloquently, silently agreeing with Anna's statement.

Russo muttered something beneath his breath, fortunately too low to be understood. He then said in a louder tone, "We used to go to a cave. It's off Rennix—"

"There are no caves along Rennix," Krejci interjected.

"Clear the spuds out of your ears mate, I said it was *off* Rennix," Russo derided loudly.

"You go about a kilometre along the Rennix track *after* you cross the second creek. Then you turn left, cross the bog, and walk into the trees. It's down over the hill about half a kay."

Krejci pulled out a map and spread it on the table, tracking the route with a blunt finger. He spun the map around and pointed to a spot.

Russo waited, knowing that for that split second, he held the power. Then, with a smirk, he leant forward, nodded, and pushed the map away.

"Anna, we've got everyone deployed to the area, you don't need to go. You should head to the hospital," Krejci said with a worried frown.

"She's my sergeant, Paul. She's *my* responsibility and I'll see it through."

He grimaced, and then turned to Jake. "Sergeant, make sure you look after the inspector," he snapped, then strode away.

"Let's go Jake."

"What happened with Teasel, Jake? I haven't even had a chance to ask you," Anna murmured in the car, desperate to find a distraction for the agonising pain in her head and waves of nausea that came with increasing frequency.

"Oh, right, yeah, well, they only gave me a few minutes. He kept zoning off, so it was all a bit disjointed. But from what I could piece together, Foley abducted him from his apartment, as you thought. Foley had been there before, he said, and it was clear Teasel was scared shitless of him. He, Teasel that is, said something about being kept in a bathroom, but that was all a bit fuzzy, and he couldn't describe where he was with any accuracy."

"Anyway, Foley came back some hours later, they got in the car and drove to Creel Bay boat ramp. It was dark; that's all he knew about the time. He said when they first got there, it was just Bialy that he saw. There was no sign of Russo. Foley held him around the neck. Foley and Bialy argued, and then Foley made some sort of grunting sound and dropped to the ground. Then Russo suddenly appeared with a tyre iron in his hand.

"Teasel got very agitated about then, and I was told by the nursing staff to bugger off. But as I was going, he was mumbling something about blood, 'so much blood' or something like that."

Anna knuckled her right eye and nodded. "Sounds like he was completely traumatised by the execution. So, Russo brought him down and from the fingerprint evidence, Bialy finished him off." She sat processing the information.

"Did you find out how they contacted Foley?"

Jake nodded. "I asked him. He said Foley had given him a phone ... but it was all a bit confused. He kept muttering something about Foley wanting to kill *Tyler*."

Anna frowned and shook her head.

"So, Bialy had the drugs?" Jake asked after several minutes.

Anna nodded briefly. "They found them in a dry bag in an old chest freezer in his garage."

"His behaviour suggests he's off his face on something."

"Hmm, the temptation must have been too much for him."

"I hope Margot's okay," Jake added in a barely audible mutter. Like everyone in the police force, dealing with drug-affected people was a staple of their work. He was only too aware how particularly vicious ice users were, being almost immune to their own pain and their paranoia being so well developed that they saw everyone as a threat.

Anna suddenly bent over in the passenger seat. A groan burst from her lips.

"Inspector, please let me take you to the hospital," Jake pleaded.

"I'll go when we have Margot back safe and sound." She straightened up slowly, her teeth clamped shut.

Chapter 44

Jake parked on the Kosciuszko Road, on the narrow verge opposite the Rennix walking track carpark, which was jammed to overflowing with police, National Parks and emergency vehicles.

Anna's phone rang, and after a brief one-sided conversation, she ended the call. "Bialy's car is there, on the far side of the carpark," she said, giving a quick chin thrust across the road. "They're working their way along the track now."

"So, it looks like Russo was telling the truth," Jake sighed with relief.

Anna opened the car door and eased herself out. The afternoon was rapidly waning, and the air temperature was dropping. She looked up at the clear, pale blue sky, now losing its brilliance as the sun headed towards the horizon. It would fall to near freezing overnight.

She wrapped her arms tightly around her body and breathed deeply. The air was so cold it made her teeth hurt.

Despite Jake's confidence, something didn't feel right. But she couldn't pin down the thought. There had to be close to fifty people closing in on Margot and Bialy now, so why did she feel as if it was all wrong?

"Inspector? Anna?"

She shook her head. "Something's not right, Jake. Can you feel it?"

Jake grimaced, looking at her. She was gazing off into the distance, where thick stands of stunted snow gums were darkening rapidly in the fading light. Her face, so white it almost glowed, and her eyes were deep black hollows.

He didn't feel whatever she was feeling, and he wondered if it was the concussion talking, but he was reluctant to voice his doubts.

"I know it sounds crazy," Anna said, echoing his thought. "But something isn't gelling. Something doesn't … *fit*. Something about today is nagging at me, but I can't seem to …" She growled irritably.

Jake rubbed his hands together to warm them. "Okay then. Let's run through what happened today and see if that helps you pin it down," he said, thinking about the day, that, in that moment, seemed to be well in excess of its usual twenty-four hours. "It must be after Margot was taken. We didn't know Bialy was off his head until that point. So, let's start there. He took off in the car with Margot—" he paused as Anna turned to him and nodded, her face full of concentrated hope.

"Then, you came back to the office," he prompted. His steaming breath briefly blurring his face with each exhalation.

"I spoke to the Chief … Krejci … Dan and … you," Anna said in a low voice, trying to get her brain to connect the dots, but it was like wading through thick sludge.

"Anything there? Anything ringing bells?"

Anna shook her head.

"Okay. Next, we interviewed Russo. We met his lawyer, McCluggage. You read them the riot act," Jake added with a smile in his voice.

"Hmm, yes, I probably should have been a little more in control there," Anna murmured.

Jake grinned and privately thought it was her finest hour. He had been so impressed with the cold steel in her tone as she spoke to Russo and McCluggage. He hoped one day to be able to emulate it.

"Then, Russo told us where the cave was …"

"A cave," Anna repeated, shaking her head. "There can't be any caves around here, surely! At least any cave big enough to hole up in. If there were caves here, they would have been found long before now. It would be known! This is a really popular area for walkers. The only caves I'm aware of are at least two hours away at Yarrangobilly, in the limestone there. It's all granite around here."

"Maybe he just meant a hollow or an overhang in the rocks—"

"And why the hell would Bialy hole up in a cave, anyway? Russo said it only had the one entrance. So, he's trapped in there!" She shook her head frustratedly.

"But Inspect—Anna, the guy's off his face on crystal meth. I don't think he will be thinking logically."

"Yes, that's true, Jake, but … Russo … isn't," Anna said slowly as the self-satisfied smirk on Russo's face sprang to mind.

"He's leading us on a wild goose chase," she cried suddenly. "That slimy, detestable, little prick!" She slammed her hand down on the car roof.

"But Bialy's car—" Jake started weakly.

"Oh, he's around here somewhere, just not in a bloody cave," Anna cut him off, her mind racing.

"He knew Bialy would head here," she murmured to herself. "But if you were intent on helping your mate … you would need to deflect all the searchers away from where he is … to give him a chance."

"But he can't get away. His car is there." Jake pointed across the road.

"And so is *everyone* looking for him," Anna said, turning deliberately to face the marshy fen on their side of the road. It separated them from a low rise of sub-alpine forest in the distance.

Jake followed her gaze and his mouth dropped open as he realised what she was saying. "*Oh shit!* No one is on this side. They're all searching the opposite side of the road along the Rennix track."

Anna's lips compressed into a thin line and nodded.

"I'll call Griggs," she said, referring to the search coordinator. "See if you can find any indication of where they might have left the road along the verge here, Jake. I'm sure Margot, if she was conscious, would have tried to leave a mark of some sort. I'll call Krejci too. Maybe there are some huts or natural structures Bialy could hole up in on this side."

Jake yanked down on his beanie and, crouching almost double, peered intently at the narrow strip of dirt and gravel that bordered their side of the road. Anna watched him as her phone dialled. His head swayed back and forth, and she had a brief flash of a bull elephant wagging its head in prelude to a charge.

"Farrow," a gruff voice said in her ear. "Nothing yet," he continued, anticipating her question.

"Griggs, I think we might have been thrown a furphy. I think we need to get some searchers on the opposite side of the road," she said abruptly.

A short silence ensued, and she held her breath.

"Makes sense, never heard of caves near here," Griggs answered. "I'll reallocate half the team to the opposite side. Any idea of what we're looking for?"

Anna breathed out in a rush. "Old disused hiking hut maybe, or an overhang—something young boys would have gravitated to—you know, a hidey-hole for an overnight camp maybe," she said with a frown, knowing that Bialy had headed here almost instinctively, and Russo had been equally sure of the location. Bialy's car, parked across the road, was a testament to the truth of that. This was somewhere they had both spent time; somewhere they felt safe; free to enjoy time together.

"I'll call you back if we get anything more positive." She rang off.

"Paul," Anna said as her second call picked up. "I think your initial thought was correct. I think Russo was spinning us a yarn. Bialy is definitely near Rennix—his car's here—but I'm thinking the whole cave thing was bullshit. Do you know of any place on the *opposite* side of the road from Rennix carpark? A hiker's hut maybe or ..."

"Ah ... give me a sec," Paul replied, and Anna was grateful that he needed no further discussion but had grasped the idea immediately.

"Let me call you right back," he said after a few seconds, and hung up without waiting for a response.

Chapter 45

"Anna!"

"You found something, Jake?"

"Here, I think," he called from his crouched position twenty metres in front of her.

Anna looked up; the colour was bleeding out of the day as the late autumn evening approached rapidly. The light breeze of a moment ago was swiftly picking up to a steady, frigid assault on her exposed face. She walked carefully towards Jake, feeling like her head was floating, like a gigantic balloon, several feet above her neck.

"Looks like a lot of scuff marks here and I'm pretty sure that's blood." He pointed out an arc of dark droplets.

She gave one brief nod. Shutting down any thought of what had led to that blood by the roadside.

"Let's go. The others are on their way. Krejci is checking on possible structures and will call back shortly. Turn your phone to vibrate."

"Anna, I think you should stay here. I'll go," Jake said, quickly changing the settings on his phone.

"No, I'm not losing you too"—her jaw clenched tightly—"you can help me." She grabbed his arm. "You have a torch?"

He nodded and pulled it from his jacket pocket, his mind churning. Her face had the sheen and colour of a dead fish's underbelly, and he already knew she was not that stable on her feet. But seeing her eyeballing him with those death ray eyes was enough for him to step out firmly.

The going was tough. The area around Rennix was a ten-thousand-year-old bog, and it was like walking on water-filled sponge. Each step they took sank into the soggy vegetation, and near-freezing water seeped in over the tops of their shoes. They slogged on, following a faint animal trail heading directly south. Jake, with an arm around Anna's back, and another under her elbow, guided her way.

I'm struggling … she must feel like hell on earth, Jake thought, pulling a foot out of the mud with a loud sucking sound. She occasionally grunted with effort or perhaps pain, over a particularly difficult stretch but made no other sound. He wondered at her stoicism. But Margot's face flashed into his mind, and he knew what drove them both—stumbling and sinking into the marsh—and the fading light making all depth perception disappear.

Finally, the ground firmed up as it rose gently, and its character changed from boggy meadow to alpine forest. Jake flicked on his torch as the small, twisted snow gums blocked the last remnants of daylight.

They laboured slowly through the trees, the light picking out the myriad colours of the bark on the snow gums, from pinks to creamy whites, pale greens to russet and deepest black.

Anna felt almost out-of-body; so light-headed it was like she was watching herself push on, with Jake's arms steadying her progress. The pain was constant now. The previous waves of blinding pain had merged into one unremitting continuum of agony. Her mind wanted to float away, and it was only with intense effort that she remained aware of her surroundings. Each step was an effort of will.

"Anna," Jake whispered hoarsely in her ear. "Your phone!"

"Oh! Yes," she muttered, not having registered it vibrating in her pocket, being so lost in pain and the effort of moving.

"Thank Christ I got you Anna," Paul cried with relief. "I've been calling and calling."

Anna gripped the phone hard and took a deep breath of freezing air, willing her mind to kick into gear. She leant into Jake so he could listen in. He pressed his ear to hers, cupping his hands in front of them to deflect the wind.

"Must have been in a telco black spot, Paul. What have you got?"

"We've been tracking you on GPS. You're close. There's an old miner's shack nearby. It's not marked on the usual tourist maps to avoid people seeking it out. It was built in the very early nineteen hundreds, before the park was created."

"Where?"

"It's only forty metres away from where you are. I thought you might walk right into it," he said, his voice tight with stress.

"What direction?"

"It's about two o'clock from the direction you were heading in which was directly south. So, you need to move sou'-sou'-west towards the creek. I've sent the coordinates to both your phones and to Griggs."

"Okay, wait a sec, we'll check."

Jake pulled back from her to look at his phone. He quickly zoomed in on the map that Krejci had sent. After a few seconds, he nodded.

"Got it," she said into the phone.

"Wait for backup, Anna. You two can't do this. Griggs' team is on the way."

"We'll just see if our hunch is right, Paul. He may not even be there."

"Okay, but if he is there, stay low and call me or Griggs. If you have no reception, send Jake back to this spot."

"Righto," Anna agreed and ended the call.

"Wind is in our faces, Jake, so Bialy shouldn't hear us approach, but we'll need to shield that torch." Jake looked around for a moment, then took off his glove. He bit a small hole in the leather at the end of one finger and jammed the small torch inside. A tiny beam of light was all that was left.

"Good thinking," Anna murmured, taking a tight grip on his arm and willing her reluctant feet forward.

They took each step carefully, Jake checking for loose branches, rocks, and hollows before moving forward. They started to descend slowly into a shallow gully where the burble of water in the nearby creek could be heard faintly over the gusting wind.

Anna's fingers suddenly dug into Jake's arm. He froze. A light had appeared to their left, barely five metres away. The thick scrub partially shielded them, but if that beam flashed in their direction, their pale oval faces would stand out clearly. She heard the faint click of Jake switching off his torch.

The light turned away, and they dropped to the ground.

Anna felt Jake ease up to her. "There's a boulder about a metre and a half to the right. It'll give us cover," he hissed in her ear. She nodded.

They belly crawled over and tucked in behind the boulder, which turned out to be an outcrop of several boulders. Further to the right of their safe nook, the trees gave way to a grassy meadow, and Anna realised that the old shed must be positioned only a few metres above the high-water mark of the spring flood of the creek.

She blinked, suddenly noticing that she could make out quite a bit more of her surroundings and looked up to see a quarter moon rising over the treetops.

Jake peered intently through a small gap in the boulders, and then, pulling back, waved her over so she could take a look. She edged into his position and peered through. Bialy paced, back and forth, in front of a small, rather dilapidated wooden hut; its door missing. The inside was pitch black and she could make out nothing inside. Anna strained her ears but there was no sound from within.

Bialy held a small spotlight and the rifle that he used on Dinardo. She lifted a hand to her head and felt the sizeable egg it had left there above her temple.

"Jake," Anna whispered into his ear. "Do you have reception?"

He looked at his phone and shook his head with a desperate frown.

"Can you make your way around to the right and get to the back of the hut?"

Jake's eyes widened. "I don't think we should try and take him by ourselves, Anna. We should wait for the others."

She made an irritated gesture and leant forward to his ear. "I don't give a tinker's damn about him! I want to find out if Margot is in there."

Jake nodded.

"Work your way around and see if you can see inside. Take your torch. If you can see her and you see a way to get her out, flash the torch twice. Give me a couple of minutes and then go for it. You'll know when. I'll keep Bialy on his toes."

"Shit, Anna, you can't do that! He'll kill you as quick as look at you," Jake rasped into her ear.

"I'll be okay," she replied huskily. "You just concentrate on Margot. If you can't see her in there, or can't get her out, just come back here and then you'll need to head out to intercept Griggs. He can't be more than ten minutes behind us now." They had to be close. Even though they were a couple of kilometres across the bog on the other side of the road to begin with, they would be travelling so much faster than she and Jake had.

Jake nodded, and Anna squeezed his hand and nodded back. "Be careful!" she mouthed.

He quickly slithered out of sight, swallowed up by the darkness. The sounds of his movement lost in the rattle of leaves and the whine of the icy wind through the trees.

Chapter 46

After he threw her inside the hut, Bialy left her alone. But just as dark started creeping in, so did he.

He propped his gun near the door and knelt down next to her. He dragged her roughly towards him, and shone the light slowly over her body. She shrank away. He stank of stale sweat and was breathing heavily. Her heart started racing. She knew what was coming and a rising tide of panic filled her.

Digging in her feet, she scuttled backwards, but he yanked her back and slapped her viciously. Blood began filling her mouth, and she gagged.

"Don't bloody move," he snarled, staring down at her with bloodshot eyes.

That was stupid. Stay still. Don't give him an excuse to hurt you. You'll be okay. You just need to stay alive until the inspector gets here. What does it matter if he rapes you? It's just sex. You've done it before. You just need to stay alive. Don't think about it. Just don't give him an excuse.

She knew she was expendable. He couldn't very well make his escape dragging her with him. She was here for one purpose. He'd shown his interest the day they interviewed him. Now she was going to pay for it. She forced herself to be still. She needed him to take his time. The longer he took, the longer she might stay alive.

"You look like shit!" he screamed, his eyes glaring wildly.

She lifted her chin. *You'll be okay. You'll be okay. They'll come find you. You'll be okay. They'll come. You just have to stay alive.*

"Don't look at me!" he shrieked, spraying her with spit. He hurled the light; it bounced off the wall and landed facing them. She would have preferred the dark.

She squeezed her eye shut and turned her head.

There was a grunt and then came the sound of cloth tearing.

It wasn't hers.

She started violently as something landed on her face. The smell of rank body odour almost made her retch. It seemed he'd torn his shirt off and thrown it over her head so he didn't have to look at her.

He ripped open her jacket and started clawing at her shirt and bra, laughing and muttering to himself.

She tried to block it out. *Stay still. They'll come! You'll be okay!*

Her breath came in short gasps. *God, please let them find me soon. Please!* She gritted her teeth, trying to keep silent as he squeezed her breasts brutally, his fingernails biting into her nipples. *You'll be okay!* His breathing was coming faster.

Suddenly, he froze, his hands still on her. And then he was off. Gone. She heard him snatch up the gun and torch and bolt outside, swearing and cursing.

She listened hard but couldn't make out anything over his yelling. *Was it the inspector? Please let it be someone here to help me. Please!*

Whatever or whoever it was, it had bought her a reprieve, and she was grateful for it. She felt herself shaking and knew it wasn't just from the cold.

Minutes passed, though it was hard for her to estimate how many. She could hear him ranting, though he seemed further away now. Deciding to take a chance, she caught hold of a mouthful of shirt and pulled it to the side, then bit it again and pulled. She stopped to listen each time, but Bialy still seemed wrapped up in his own world.

The shirt finally slithered off her face, and she sucked in a deep breath of cold, clean air.

It was fully dark now. She saw him stride past the door, silhouetted in the moonlight. His voice rising and falling as his internal argument raged on.

She waited until he passed the door again and then rolled over onto her side. She shivered violently and pulled her knees up to her chest. A small window caught her eye. She hadn't noticed it before. She looked back to the doorway and waited until he paced back in the opposite direction, lying as still as death while he passed.

Can I get out through there? She edged closer, keeping one eye on the door.

Chapter 47

ANNA PEERED THROUGH THE gap in the boulders. Bialy was gesturing violently, his torch light flashing wildly off the trees to her left. He was muttering loudly; the sound coming to her on the gusty breeze in snatches of words and phrases. He appeared to be arguing with someone, which meant he was hallucinating.

She edged around the boulder to her right and stared into the blackness next to the hut.

The seconds and then minutes dragged by. She pressed the heel of her hand into her right eye; reassured to find it still there but close to wishing it wasn't, the pain was so intense. It felt like it would burst from her skull at any moment.

Jake must have reached the side of the hut by now, she thought. *Maybe he's on his way back again. Damn it!*

But even as she finished the thought, a tiny light flashed and then again. Her heart suddenly ascended into her mouth. *He was there and he could get Margot!*

Anna took a deep breath and scuttled left to where she and Jake had first stopped. Then, she kept going until she judged she was opposite to where Jake must be on the other side of the shack. She knew Bialy was on tenterhooks. He was pacing like a panther and waving the gun at his imaginary opponent. It would not take much to set him off. She edged a little further into a small depression. It would have to do. She could see him through the low scrubby bush she hid behind. She felt around and found a good-sized rock, never far away in this land of glacial moraine. Gathering two more, she put them close to hand and unclipped her gun. Her last resort. With one eye unfocused, she doubted she could hit the side of a barn, but if it came to it, it was better than nothing.

Taking a firm grip on her first rock, she edged up onto her knees and threw it. It landed several metres in front of Bialy at the edge of the clearing. His reaction was everything she could have hoped for, and more.

He dropped the torch, firing wildly and screaming threats.

A bullet ricocheted off the ground near her arm, spraying her with dirt and leaves.

Maybe further away next time, she thought shakily.

Anna waited until his immediate reaction waned and then hurled another rock. He exploded into action again, firing and screaming incoherently. Anna pressed her face into the cold dirt, hoping that Jake was making good use of his time.

Bialy reloaded. She waited, and as he snapped in a new magazine, she lobbed her third missile into his field of fire. But this time, he didn't start firing. Instead, he started forward towards her, a malignant grin on his face. She swallowed, she'd made a mistake.

She felt like kicking herself. Once or twice, the noise could be considered someone positioning themselves, but three times smacked of trickery and Bialy had not fallen for it. Luckily, he was too far under the influence to work out it was a decoy to take his attention from what, she hoped, was happening behind him.

He marched forward into the scrub, his rifle barrel weaving left and right, seeking out his assailant. She edged her way further to the left. She had to get behind the hut. He was no more than a few metres away. Her ears strained to keep track of him as she crab-crawled from bush to bush.

The sound of a boot slipping on gravel from the far side of the clearing made her heart stutter. Bialy spun around. He raced forward, rifle raised.

Holy shit! Not that way! No! No! No!

Anna pulled out her gun and fired into the air. She couldn't risk firing directly at him, Jake and Margot were out there somewhere in front of him.

Bialy dropped to the ground, spun around, and fired. Dirt kicked up into her face. *God, he was good, even half off his face.* She had to move. *Now!* She lurched up and took off, floundering and crashing through the scrub.

He roared as he caught sight of her in the moonlight. "You're dead, arsehole!" he bellowed.

She ran on, bent double, trying to keep below the bushes. She knew she had only seconds. He was crashing through the bush, firing erratically, yelling obscenities and gaining on her.

Jake and Margot must be clear by now, she thought, collapsing behind a small, tortured eucalypt. She turned, raised her gun, took aim, and fired over and over.

He yelped with fright and then started laughing as the echo of her shots died.

"You missed me, ya *fucking* bastard! You're dead. You hear me? *You're dead!*" he roared.

Anna scrambled to her feet and ran. She could hear him thrashing through the undergrowth behind her. Branches slapped her face. Her feet tripped and stumbled. Fear pushed her to the limit.

The air woofed out of her as he crash-tackled her.

He flung her over and punched her viciously in the stomach. She grunted with the pain.

"*Fucking hell!* It's the dyke copper." He started laughing maniacally. "You are so DEAD!" he screamed into her face.

God! She'd dropped the *bloody* gun! Her hands cast about furiously in the dirt.

Bialy's hand closed on her throat and squeezed. Her eyes popped as she struggled for breath. Her chest heaved, desperate for oxygen. Her arms flailed. One clawed frantically at the fingers that dug into her neck, the other scrabbled wildly for the missing gun.

Lightning flashes signalled she was about to pass out. Her hand closed on a jagged rock. She swung with all her might. He screamed and reeled back, clutching his face. He fell sideways. Blood seeped between his fingers.

Anna dragged in a ragged breath. She rolled, hands pawing at the ground, searching for her gun. It had to be close. Her fingers touched the barrel.

Bialy reared. He yanked her back over. His rifle swung towards her. The black hole of its barrel staring at her like an evil eye. His mouth pulled back in a rictus, his face a mask of blood and his eye, bloodied jelly.

She swung her gun up and pulled the trigger in one movement.

God! No! She frantically pulled the trigger again and again.

It clicked against an empty chamber. *Oh my god!*

His face split into a slow grin. He looked into her eyes, the barrel an inch from her face.

The top of his head exploded.

Anna could hear shouts. Boots running. She lay there, Bialy slumped across her. He was heavy. She tried to push him off, but the struggle was insurmountable.

"She's here!" a voice yelled.

"Oh, shit!" another voice muttered.

The weight suddenly lifted off her, and Anna took a much-needed breath.

"We need help here!" someone bellowed.

She felt hands running over her body. She thought she should say she was fine, but it seemed too much of an effort.

A voice full of anxiety cried, "Inspector! Anna! *Oh, fuck!*" She thought she recognised it. She looked up. The night sky was a brilliant carpet of darkest indigo dotted with pinpricks of gold, edged with the black twisted fingers of snow gums.

"Mar-got?" Anna breathed out in a long sigh.

"She's okay, Anna. She's okay," Jake said, his voice sounding very far away.

"Good," she murmured, and with the last of the tension subsiding, she surrendered.

Chapter 48

THE NURSE GAVE THEM a smile as she tucked the inspector's hand back under the sheet.

"All good?" Jake asked.

The nurse nodded. "She's making good progress." She smoothed the sheets and wheeled the trolley from the room.

Jake leant forward, continuing the story from where he'd broken off. "I honestly thought she was gone when I got back there. She was so still. Covered in blood and gore from Bialy ..." He shook his head. "Talk about arriving in the nick of time. If Griggs' team had arrived a *second* later ... she'd be dead. Bialy literally had the gun at her head, finger on the trigger and then, whammo ... three shots ... and he was as dead as a doornail before the echo of the bullets stopped," he said in an excited whisper.

"Bullets?" Anna croaked; her throat was so dry she felt there was not enough spit on the planet to help her.

"Inspector!"

"Anna!"

Jake and Margot yelped together as they realised she was finally awake.

Anna cracked a gummy eye open. "Margot?" she mouthed.

"I'm here, Inspec—Anna." She grasped Anna's hand.

Anna moved her tongue around in hopes of gathering some moisture. "How are you?" she finally rasped out. "*Oh, shit!*" she added, her gaze finally focussing on the voice.

Margot put up a hand to her face and winced. "Yeah, I know, I look pretty bad. But the doctors tell me it will all resolve in a few weeks."

Had it not been for the voice, Anna doubted she would have known her. Her face was swollen beyond recognition and painted in a range of colours from dark purple, through shades of green and blue to faint touches of yellow at the edges.

"So ... no permanent damage?" Anna muttered, doubt obvious in her tone.

Margot chuckled. "No ... I know it looks like I should have, but the most I have is a chipped back tooth, which I'm booked in to get sorted in a couple of days."

Anna nodded. "Jake. You okay?" She turned to look at him.

He smiled. "Yes, Boss. All good."

"So ... what happened?" Her mind offered nothing but a confused maelstrom of images. Like a horror movie cut into random pieces.

"You remember us getting to the hut?" Jake asked, doubtful she would recall their painfully slow progress across the bog and into the trees.

Anna nodded.

"Well, after I left you, I crawled along the bank of the creek and then up to the back of the hut. I found a small open window and looked inside, but it was as pitch black, and I couldn't see a thing. I heard Bialy ranting on the other side of the hut so I took a punt and shone the torch inside and there was Margot lying on the ground. She looked up and was at the window in a heartbeat."

"I knew you would come. As soon as I saw the light at the window, I knew it had to be you guys," Margot declared, her voice choked with emotion.

"We waited a few seconds and then the shooting started. I nearly shit my pants, I can tell you," Jake said with a laugh. "But since the shooting was in the opposite direction, I knew we were probably safe. Marg threw herself out the window. Luckily, I caught her—since her hands were tied—and then we were away into the scrub down by the creek.

"The shooting stopped and we hit the dirt. Then it started up again, and we ran for it. Straight into Griggs' team!"

"We were lucky they didn't shoot us!" Margot grinned, though it had been a close call. Everyone was trigger-happy, with gunshots ringing out across the bush. "But Griggs had it. His team moved forward and then ... shots everywhere and lots of yelling," she added, swallowing hard. She had thought Bialy had killed the inspector. Her heart hammered in remembered panic.

"Griggs and his team?" Anna licked her lips to get the words out.

"All good. Only one minor injury ... a fractured wrist from a trip in the dark. Which, considering the situation, is *fricken* amazing! Griggs told me they thought they were walking into a firefight," Jake said, shaking his head.

"What about Dinardo? Is he okay?"

Jake nodded. "Yeah. Still in hospital but doing well. They said he'd be out in a day or two."

Anna sighed with relief.

"How do *you* feel ... Anna?"

"Better than you *look*, Margot." She grinned. In fact, her head, though feeling a lot like SpongeBob SquarePants, felt much better than it had in the last ...

"How long have I been here?"

"Two days, Boss," Jake answered. "You had surgery immediately after they brought you back Friday night. You apparently had a ... subdural—"

"Haematoma," Lissoni finished for him.

"Oh," Anna said. "Right. That makes sense."

"Does it?" a familiar voice said dryly.

"Cameron?"

"Yes, it's me." He walked over and sat on the edge of the bed.

"Hey, Cam," Jake nodded briefly, and he and Margot stood. "We'll head out now if you're okay here?"

Cameron smiled and picked up Anna's hand. "Yeah, mate, I'll take it from here."

"Cam," Anna murmured breathlessly as they emerged from a long, deep kiss.

"Your sergeants have been very worried about you." He stroked her cheek.

Anna looked up into his eyes. *How did anyone think grey was anything other than a warm colour?*

"Well ... I was supposed to tell them if they made the grade or not on Friday," she said, her tone slightly ironic.

"From what I hear—and the fact they have been beside your bed night and day since you landed here in hospital—they might have passed the test." Cameron smiled, eyebrows raised in query.

Anna looked startled. "Really? They've been here a lot?"

Cam nodded. "Margot got discharged on Saturday morning. They kept her in overnight for observation and some scans, but despite what she looks like, it's all relatively superficial, nothing permanent. She has a broken nose and some hairline fractures in her eye socket, but there's nothing to do for that other than painkillers and time. She'll be fine in a few weeks when the technicolour fades.

"Jake called Dee as soon as you and Margot were on your way to the hospital. And then Dee called me," he continued, his eyes clouding with the panic that had set in as he'd hung up the phone.

"You were both airlifted here to Canberra Hospital. Jake offered to drive Dee and Riley, but they were in the car and on the road before he'd practically hung up. I'm sure her drive to Canberra was pure hell. It was bad enough being here. But at least I could go down to emergency and speak to the team, and the surgeon who was scheduled to operate on you." He'd felt marginally better then. He was on his own turf in the medical world, and discussing the minutiae of her condition with a colleague provided something of a bulwark against his raging panic. But despite his intimate knowledge of what was going to transpire upon Anna's arrival, he was beside himself.

Anna grimaced, consumed with self-reproach. She hated that she had caused so much pain to those she loved. And looking at Cameron, she knew that despite it being only a few weeks, she loved him. His eyes told her he felt the same.

"I'm sorry," she whispered. "But I couldn't leave Margot out there ... alone ... *with him!*"

"I know," Cam nodded, stroking the light fuzzy down on her head. "I wish you were interested in knitting or macrame or something safe, but then you wouldn't be you ... would you?"

Anna smiled with tears in her eyes. *How had she gotten so lucky?* She caressed his cheek.

"Ahem," said a loud voice from the doorway.

Anna looked up. Dee and Riley stood there grinning.

Anna tried to sit up, but the two rushed her and she didn't have any choice but to lie back with their arms around her.

"Riles," Anna murmured, touching the rather bristly skin of her son's cheek.

"Are you okay, Mum?"

"Yes, Baby."

"*Mu-um!*" he whined, flushing with embarrassment.

"Sorry, but you will always be my baby, you know," she whispered at his red face. He grinned and nodded, reddening further.

"You didn't need to come; it's such a long drive!"

Dee's eyebrow shot up. "Drive? It's five minutes from here!"

"Dee and Riley are staying at my place," Cameron said.

"Oh, thank you, Cam," Anna murmured.

"Cameron is family now, Anna." Dee grinned at him. "And family is where they have to take you in."

Anna shook her head in mock disgust. "Oh my God! Robert Frost would be turning in his grave."

Dee laughed. "It's close enough."

"Jake is staying nearby at a mate's place and Margot went to her auntie's when she was discharged," Cameron added.

Anna's eyes popped open. "Everyone's here?"

Dee and Cameron nodded in unison.

"Like I said, your two sergeants have been here night and day," Cameron said, looking at her with raised eyebrows. "They were both *extremely* worried about you."

Anna read the subtext clearly: they are good people, and you need to recognise that. She nodded thoughtfully.

Later that night, after she convinced Dee, Riley, and Cameron to go and get some rest, she lay thinking about Friday.

It seemed weeks ago and yet it was only two days. She raised a hand and felt her tender head, covered now with only a small dressing. They had bored a hole in her skull and released the pressure that had accumulated from a bleed, the result of Mick Bialy's assault. Cameron told her she was lucky they had gotten her to the hospital when they had, as the pressure would have continued to build, and she might have died or become paralysed.

It all seemed like a nightmare now ... pushing herself each step of the way in that frigid bog, Jake's arms gripping her hard to prevent her falling. What hell had she put him through having to look after her? She shook her head. What should she have done? What *could* she have done differently? Gone to the hospital? Allowed others to look for Margot? But then, would they have found her in time? No! They were all looking where Russo had successfully misdirected them to ... the phantom cave. A good two or three kilometres from the miner's shack. How long would it have been before someone raised the question, doubted the source, and sent them back to the drawing board? What would have happened to Margot in the interim?

No. Despite the pain and anguish she had caused everyone by persisting, Margot being safe and well—relatively speaking—was worth it. *Did the end justify the means?* Her brain was too tired to ponder on it further. But one thing was crystal clear: whatever doubts she had about Jake and Margot had evaporated like smoke in the wind.

Chapter 49

"So, what about Teasel? What's happened to him?" Dee asked as she sipped on her wine, two days later. Riley had gone to bed, and it was just the two of them sitting in front of the red-glowing wood burner, toasting their toes.

Anna sighed and shook her head slowly. "Well, physically, he's made a remarkable recovery considering ... but emotionally, he's a mess. He seems incapable of seeing life without his friends to bolster him along. He just bleats on and on about how inseparable they were and how will he cope without them?" She shook her head again. "It's like he has nothing left, nothing to live for. He just doesn't seem to be able to function without his posse."

Dee tucked her feet under her, and leaning back into the sofa, nodded thoughtfully. "Yes, I'm sure he would be finding it hard to cope now. Two dead and the other one in jail. He's the last man standing. He's lost his entire support network."

"But they were horrible to each other! By Teasel's own admission, they treated him like dirt a lot of the time. They cheated on each other, abused each other; that's not friendship in my book," Anna snorted, shaking her head dismissively. "I'm really not sure what Teasel saw in any of them. I'm pretty sure he would have been much better off having not joined their little gang back in kindy."

Dee was quiet for a moment, staring into the fire. "It's maybe not so surprising that *you* think that, Lina. You're a bit different from the general population."

Anna gave a puzzled half smile. "What do you mean?"

"Most people need ... *people*. Friends. To feel fulfilled or ... validated, maybe. You don't. You never did. You're entirely comfortable just being you. You didn't fall apart at school because everyone thought you were strange and weird. It didn't eat away at you that we had no friends. You just got on with it."

Anna grasped her sister's hand, giving it a squeeze. "That was a long time ago, Dee," she whispered. "You were just having a difficult time of it. Those bitches at school—"

"No! No, this isn't a whinge about me. It *was* a bad period in my life … but my amazing older sister got me out of my hole … literally!" Dee grinned at her, thinking of the wombat burrow. "And she got me back into life by removing the obstacles and enabling me to find friends. And that changed my life. No, I'm just explaining that *I'm* the normal one!" She smiled and squeezed Anna's hand back.

"Well, Dad certainly agreed with you." Anna rolled her eyes. "I remember when I told him I was going to join the police force, he just shook his head and muttered something about getting the wrong baby at the hospital."

Dee chuckled. "Well, I might have believed that as well if you hadn't been the spitting image of Mum. But seriously, I'm not sure he really thought that through, because honestly Lina, out of the two of us, it was *you* who created your own path. You who went your own way, without parents or society pushing you one way or another. Which is exactly what they told us they wanted for us. Me … I've just followed in their footsteps. I'm still in their house for God's sake! I'm them … just younger and with less of a thing for lentils and tofu!"

Anna laughed.

"But what I'm saying," Dee continued, "is that you're entirely comfortable in your own skin. You don't need people. You choose people to bring into your inner circle, but you don't need other people's affirmation. It's a rare thing, especially in these days of social media, when the world seems to revolve around living in the public eye and desperately seeking other people's recognition or acceptance. So, of course, Teasel's situation is not one you can truly understand. Despite their rather toxic relationship, those four mates were all they had."

Anna stared into the fire. It was true. She had never sought friends or missed them overly much when they hadn't materialised. She had friends of course, a small cadre of true friends that she had made over the years. Perhaps they were the ones who had persisted enough to break into her inner circle. Or perhaps they were there only because she had recognised some trait in them that she valued, and she had *chosen* to let them in. She shook her head; she really had no idea.

"On another note," Dee said, interrupting Anna's ruminations. "It's your birthday on Saturday and people are coming over for a barbeque." She had been putting off telling Anna, as she knew what reaction she would get, but with it being only three days away, there was no sense in delaying. *Time to rip off the Band-Aid as they say.*

"Dee! No! Absolutely not!" Anna cried indignantly, justifying Dee's decision to leave it until the last minute to tell her.

"Good. I'm glad you're on board," Dee shot back sarcastically.

"Dee, seriously, I don't want anything. I appreciate the thought—"

"Too late, all organised," Dee said crisply, unfolding her legs and standing up. "I'm off to bed." And with that, she turned and walked away, leaving Anna gaping after her with a horrified expression.

Chapter 50

"You look gorgeous!" Cameron whispered in her ear.

Anna smiled up at him. He looked pretty gorgeous himself in jeans, white T-shirt, and tailored jacket, his eyes shining down on her.

She'd made an effort today—one she normally wouldn't have bothered with—and wore a dark green sweater that set off her eyes. She'd even added a light application of make-up to 'zhoosh' up her look.

"Shall we?" Cam offered her an arm.

Anna took a deep breath and nodded.

"Anna, could you come see my parents? They're very keen to meet you," Margot said, sidling up to the inspector as she was accepting a drink from Dee.

"Yes, of course." Anna nodded, a bit startled, not having expected Margot's *parents* to be at the party. But then she remembered that Dee said she knew them, and it made sense.

They walked towards a couple in their early sixties standing nearby. Anna recognised Margot's mother instantly; the resemblance was uncanny. *Strange to think you'd know what you would look like as an older person.* But Anna supposed that was not so unusual. Most people would see their older self in the face of their father or mother. Her own parents, dead in their late forties, seemed still young in her mind.

Margot's mother grasped Anna's hand as Margot finished the introductions.

"Inspector, how can we ever thank you?"

Anna, taken aback, shot a glance at Margot, who looked resolute and slightly embarrassed.

"Thank me?"

"For saving our Margot from that nutter!" Mr Lissoni said.

"Oh!" Anna murmured, and then with a brief smile added, "Well, you know that was a team effort. Jake—"

"Oh, yes, Jake, the dear man! We've already told him how grateful we are." Mrs Lissoni smiled, looking over Margot's shoulder at the man in question.

Jake, hearing his name, turned and joined them.

"We all played a part, Mrs Lissoni," Anna continued, a slight edge in her tone. "Jake did a fantastic job of not only finding where Bialy and Margot left the road, but he managed to get me across the bog, which was no mean feat, I can assure you, and then he helped Margot out of the old shack. But to be honest, I think the one who had the *most* to do with Margot being safe and unhurt ... or, at least, mostly unhurt," she added with a brief sympathetic smile at Margot's still very bruised face, "was Margot herself."

"Margot?" Mrs Lissoni echoed in a puzzled tone, looking from Anna to Margot and back as if there were some joke being played on her.

"Absolutely," Anna said firmly. "By comparison, Jake and I had the easy jobs. Margot spent six hours in the company of someone who was delusional, hallucinating, extremely volatile and violent. She survived that by being the professional she is. She never panicked, never lost her nerve ... do you have *any* idea how incredibly hard that would be to do? I do! And I'm so very proud of her. When Jake arrived at that window, she was ready to go, despite her awful injuries. The whole thing went like clockwork because of her bravery. You have a daughter to be proud of, and the police force has an excellent officer."

A stunned silence followed Anna's comments. She felt a large, warm hand on her shoulder and turned to find Cameron smiling down at her.

"Oh … well," Mrs Lissoni murmured, and then she flushed with pleasure and pride. "Oh, my goodness, I hadn't thought! … I mean, you're right! We are *very* proud of you, Margot." She took her daughter's hand, and Margot, shooting a look of incredulity at Anna, gave her mum a hug while her dad patted her shoulder, looking very pleased and a little teary.

"That was a nice thing to do," Cameron whispered a few minutes later as they made their escape from the Lissonis.

Anna shrugged. "It's true though. It's always harder to sit and wait than to do something."

"True. I think that's how doctors cope. Even if the situation is bad, there is always something to do, and that keeps you focused.

"I take it you had the *talk* with them both?" Cam said with a twinkle in his eye.

"Yes, I spoke to them a couple of days ago." Anna smiled. "They still have a lot to learn, but they've proved their mettle as far as I'm concerned. It was a baptism of fire for them both, but I meant what I said, I *am* proud of them. Had you asked me a couple of weeks ago whether they would have performed so well under the circumstances, I would have said a definite no. So, it just goes to show that sometimes you have to dig a little deeper to learn what a person is truly like. In hindsight, I shouldn't have given into my anger that night. Two weeks was not long enough … *well* … in most circumstances, it wouldn't have been enough to make that sort of call. But I'm very happy to keep them on the team and fortunately, they both wanted to stay with me as well."

"Why wouldn't they?" Cam murmured, leaning in to breathe in her scent and nibble her ear.

Anna squirmed delightedly as his kisses tickled.

Cam pulled back. "And what about your new recruit? I met him a few minutes ago. Dan, is it?"

"Ah, Dan. Yes, he's my new constable. Krejci told me I needed an extra body, and he felt Dan was a good fit, and Dan was very keen to stay on with us, apparently. I hope he doesn't think it's always this stimulating." She chuckled.

"He'll be in for a disappointment if he does. Two murders, an accidental death, one arrest, one death by police, a manhunt, and a drug haul! It's not your average few weeks."

"It's not been an average few weeks in more ways than one, has it?" Cam looked at her intently.

"No," Anna conceded with a shake of her head. "In some way, I feel like four weeks ago I walked off the edge of the planet and landed in a different dimension. The same me, just a different world."

"A good world?" Cam whispered.

"The best of all worlds." Anna looked deep into his eyes, feeling the heat between them build. *"Is this real?"*

"It is for me. You're worried because we've only known each other such a short time?"

Anna nodded.

"Why does that make it any less real? Time is not a measure of certainty. Nor is it a measure of how much you love a person. There are a lot of people who stay together for years that aren't very happy. I spent twenty years with the wrong person. It wasn't bad … but it wasn't this." He stroked her cheek with his thumb. "I would trade all of that for what I've had with you so far."

"It's just so … *unexpected*," Anna said, shaking her head. "I came back to my home town thinking to make sure Riley would be safe and cared for if something happened to me. But now, I'm the one safe and cared for. I have you and Dee, Riley is happy, work is meaningful. I feel like everything has fallen into place and yet a month ago I was … staring into the abyss … it's hard to explain. *How can I be grateful to cancer?"*

Cameron grinned. "Not many of my patients would say that. But some have. A diagnosis of cancer brings life into focus. Suddenly, everything is more immediate and raw. It's overwhelming and stressful and not everyone sees the opportunity to reach out to what's most important in their life and cherish it. Others do, and they reap the benefit, whatever the outcome of their cancer is. Your life turned a corner, and a new vista opened up … that's me, if you didn't get that," he added facetiously.

Anna chuckled. "You are a wonderful vista." She pulled his head down to her kiss.

Cameron handed her a glass of red wine and sat down next to her on the sofa. Placing his own glass on the small coffee table, he pulled her legs up onto his lap and started massaging her toes.

Anna groaned. She'd had a lovely afternoon but was happy that all of the guests had now departed, and she could relax. She could hear Dee and her friend, Brian, laughing in the kitchen as they got some snacks organised.

Riley sat on the floor in front of her, the dogs sprawled by his side, switching channels with the remote, trying to find something to watch. His blonde hair gleamed gold in the light from the blazing wood-burner. Anna reached out and smoothed down his cowlick. Riley looked back and took her hand.

"All right, Mum?"

"Perfect, Riles."

Note From the Author

The town of Jindabyne, NSW, Australia is used as the setting for this novel. The Kosciuszko National Park, Perisher, Thredbo, Rennix Walking Track, Tyrolean Village, East Jindabyne, Creel Bay boat ramp, and the old town at the bottom of the lake are all actual locations in this region.

However, Dee's house, Five Gates Farm, in Mungunbah, Mungunbah itself, Barker's Ridge, the police stations, and the houses of other characters are all a product of the author's imagination.